P9-ELD-698

The
KING
OF
TAKSIM
SQUARE

CALGARY PUBLIC LIBRARY

JUN - 2016

The
KING
OF
TAKSIM
SQUARE

EMRAH SERBES

Translated by Mark David Wyers

amazoncrossing

This is a work of fiction. Names, characters, organizations, places, events, and incidents are either products of the author's imagination or are used fictitiously.

Text copyright © 2014 Emrah Serbes

Translation copyright © 2015 Mark David Wyers

All rights reserved.

No part of this book may be reproduced, or stored in a retrieval system, or transmitted in any form or by any means, electronic, mechanical, photocopying, recording, or otherwise, without express written permission of the publisher.

Previously published as *Deliduman* by İletişim Yayıncılık in Turkey in 2014. Translated from Turkish by Mark Wyers. First published in English by AmazonCrossing in 2015.

Published by AmazonCrossing, Seattle

www.apub.com

Amazon, the Amazon logo, and AmazonCrossing are trademarks of Amazon.com, Inc., or its affiliates.

ISBN-13: 9781503951617

ISBN-10: 1503951618

Cover design by David Drummond

Printed in the United States of America

For Ceylan,
who said,
"On roads leading home
When darkness falls
When the cold turns frigid
When two people embrace."

Turkish Honorifics

Ağbi: Older brother, also used as an honorific for men.

Abla: Older sister, also used as an honorific for women.

Amca: Uncle, also used as an honorific for men who are older than the speaker.

Teyze: Aunt, also used as an honorific for women who are older than the speaker.

Bey: A respectful term of address used after a man's given name.

Hanım: A respectful term of address used after a woman's given name.

Hoca: A respectful term of address used to refer to a teacher or respected person.

GUIDE TO TURKISH PRONUNCIATION

Turkish letters that appear in the book and which may be unfamiliar are shown below, with a guide to their pronunciation.

c   as *j* in "just"

ç   as *ch* in "child"

ğ   silent letter that lengthens the preceding vowel

ı   as *u* in "put"

ö   similar to the "ur" in "burn"

ş   as *sh* in "ship"

ü   pronounced by saying "ee" as in "feet" with pursed lips

ONE

In the summer of 2013, a wave of social upheaval swept through the cities of Turkey, spreading like wildfire even to our small province of Kıyıdere. If you're wondering how it all got started, I'll have to skip over the tedium of the previous summer and tell you about my sister's beauty and some of her unique qualities. Why? Because if you don't know about them, you'll never understand how we overcame those painful years of feeling powerless and how we swung from pessimism to hope.

My younger sister, Çiğdem İyice, is nine years old. She's in third grade at Evliya Çelebi Primary School, where she is by far the top student. Unlike me, she has incredibly neat handwriting, so you don't have to be an expert on ancient scripts to understand what she writes. Also, she's quite sociable and isn't introverted and selfish like most students who are the best in their class. Everyone loves her—not just her friends, but every single living creature on the face of the earth. Let me give you an example: When she's out walking, cats and dogs stop to gaze up at her in adoration. I'll never forget the time we saw a turtle in the parking lot at Migros; even that forlorn creature poked its head out of its shell, nodding at her admiringly. She's quite tall for her age, and she's always pleasant and full of energy. At the same time, however, she's also calm, but not in a way that's unfitting for a child her age. It safeguards her youthful purity. She always walks proudly, but don't get me wrong, there's nothing stiff about the way she walks—her stride is elegant and noble. If you saw her approaching from a distance, you'd think to yourself, *Now there's a woman of breeding.* I say that on the presumption that nobility has nothing to do with age.

People who meet my sister are always charmed by her laughter and looks, not to mention her voice and even her silences. If you were to kiss her cheeks and forehead a million times, you'd still want more, so you could breathe in her scent one more time. When I look at her, I sometimes find it difficult to believe that we're actually siblings, and my eyes fill with tears. I know you think I'm exaggerating. Well, I am. There are so many numskulls in the world, and they don't understand a thing unless you exaggerate. I have to if you're going to fully grasp my sister's beauty and her particular qualities.

One of the most striking things about my sister is the fact that when she sits down in the living room, she spreads her legs 180 degrees, as if it were the most natural position in the world, and sits there looking you in the eye, completely at ease. What's more, she can juggle a ball with her feet 150 times. But the most amazing thing about her is how she does the moonwalk.

"Place one foot firmly on the floor," I told her last winter, "and then step back with your other foot. Slide your feet back in alternating steps, remembering to move your arms and hands so that it's all coordinated."

Because she's so talented, my sister immediately picked it up and began moonwalking on the parquet floors of our home, her movements seeming to defy the laws of physics. With the film *Moonwalker*, which we ordered from Idefix, and some videos on YouTube, we started adding some steps to her routine. Within a month, we developed it into a five-minute performance that left onlookers gasping in astonishment. But we didn't stop there; we went to Orhan, the tailor who hems our jeans, and ordered a white suit for Çiğdem, and then we spent two weeks wandering the shops trying to find a white tie, to no avail. In the end we had to order it online through GoingGoingGone. We ordered a blue shirt through Markafoni and went to every single shop in the KİPA shopping center looking for the boldest belt and buckle we could find. Then we put a black band on one of our grandpa's white hats and wound my sister's beautiful waist-length brown hair into a tight bun that fit neatly under the hat. At two o'clock in the afternoon on May 18, 2013, which happened to be a Saturday, we were waiting backstage at Uludağ University's auditorium, where Çiğdem was the twenty-first Michael Jackson in line to perform.

Seeing so many Michael Jacksons in one place is invariably going to get on your nerves, and that's precisely what happened to me. There were six Michael Jacksons who were going to perform after my sister. Of course none of them were great talents like Çiğdem; they were just there to get dressed up in a suit and hat. But still, when I saw them all, I chided myself for not having taught her something more original.

My uncle, who, by the way, is a complete bastard, taught me that foolishness of moonwalking, but I have no idea who taught it to him all those years ago. When I started doing the moonwalk, no one was interested in such things. It had its heyday back in the eighties and nineties. By the middle of the aughts, it had practically been forgotten, and that's when I got started. But then Michael Jackson died in 2009, and everything changed. There were the people who'd once said that he didn't have vitiligo but just wanted to change his skin color because he was ashamed of being black. And there were those who said that he loved children not because he had a child's soul but because he was a pervert. They all changed their tune: "Ah, our legend is dead! He's dead and gone!" Then, of course, the moonwalk became all the rage again. My sister heard about it from her classmates and wanted to learn it, too, so I taught her. Naturally, I had no idea this whole business would one day come to such a point. I'd thought, *Michael Jackson is a classic.*

No matter the place or the time, he'll never go out of style. It was as simple as that.

So there we were, together with my uncle because that's where all this really began, waiting for our turn in the elimination stage of a talent show, the name of which I'd rather not remember. Normally, even if I'd been paid hundreds of lira, I never would've watched a single episode of this damn show. There were so many Michael Jacksons the organizers decided to have them perform separately from the magicians, human calculators, glass eaters, brick breakers, jugglers, fire-eaters, and break-dancers. When I saw those talents from a distance, I began to have doubts about our decision to join the competition. I had a sudden desire to take my sister by the hand and rush away with her. Of course, I didn't let on to Çiğdem that I was nervous. But here's the thing: the reason we were there was because whoever saw my sister's performance, including neighbors, family, and friends, acted like they were astounded and said she should perform on TV. They swore on their souls and said, "You just have to take part in the competition, there's no two ways about it!" If she hadn't been prodded on by those morons, who have nothing better to do than idle away their lives in front of the television, I never would've allowed her to take part in such a pathetic event.

As we stood backstage, my sister said to me, "Çağlar"—even though I was her older brother, I never let her call me by the honorific "ağbi" and insisted that she call me by my first name—"I wonder if I should close my eyes before I perform like I always do, or if I should keep them open?"

"Why?"

"I feel like my vision is going blurry. I'm probably just nervous. But if I keep my eyes open and look at my feet, no one will even notice because when my hat is tilted forward it covers my eyes."

"Sweetie," I said, "I know that they won't be able to see your eyes. But you should never stray from your original plan. You keep your eyes closed so that you can concentrate and think about the fact that the

4

whole world is getting ready to watch you and that you're going to show all those insignificant people the most memorable thing they've ever seen. When you do open your eyes, you'll feel the spirit of MJ flowing through your heart."

"Yes, Çağlar, I suppose you're right," she said, trying to smile.

I could tell from her expression and the way she twitched her foot that she was nervous. Touching her gloved hand—we'd found a sequined leather glove for sale on sahibinden.com for eighty-four lira— I stroked her slender fingers, trying to give her courage. All great talents share something in common: after getting through the most daunting stages, they get hung up on trivial details, finding themselves on the verge of giving up. For example, when I was in the seventh grade, we had a classmate who was an absolute genius; he did so well at an interschool competition organized by the Scientific and Technological Research Council that the next year they sent him to America, as if he were too good for this country. But you know what? That nincompoop couldn't eat watermelon because he couldn't get the seeds out. The idiot! You go to the market, lug home a twenty-pound watermelon, cut it up, and serve him a slice, and that dolt can't take out the seeds. But still, he was a genius. Maybe now he's a professor in America and he's come up with a device for removing the seeds from watermelons; at his home in Alabama, he plunks the machine down on the dining room table and sits down to eat, pleased to no end, perhaps thinking about us, his friends from seventh grade. Don't judge, you never know!

As we stood there hand in hand, the Michael Jackson who had just performed walked backstage. He approached slowly, sat down on a chair, and put his hat in his lap. Drops of sweat were trickling from his temples down to his chin. There was an animal-like gleam in his eyes that baffled me; I was unable to take my eyes off him. It was one of those moments when even the most commonplace things seem to be full of meaning. The music coming from the stage rose and fell, at times giving way to ponderous silences. At such moments, an occasional peal of laughter could be heard coming from somewhere in the backstage darkness, but we had no idea who laughed or why. Sometimes a wave of excitement broke out, and a few stagehands wearing black T-shirts emblazoned with the program's logo would bustle backstage from one end to the other. I wondered what they were preparing for and why they were rushing around. Everyone watched them, but they never stopped to tell us what they were doing. The stress of waiting was getting to me. I noticed that my vision was going blurry, too, and everything around me seemed to waver in a haze. If I felt like that, who knows what my sister was going through or how her small, pure heart was pounding in her chest.

I knew that Çiğdem wouldn't be able to stand waiting much longer, so I hissed to my uncle, bastard that he is, "Go ask which MJ is on now and when it's going to be our turn." The idiot was bent down, trying to look busy by fiddling about with my sister's black-and-white shoes, which we'd special ordered from Fatih Shoemakers, polishing them with a cloth he'd mysteriously produced. In those days, I didn't know what a vile person he was. Sure, I knew that he had his share of faults, but I wasn't aware that he was a truly despicable bastard. The right situation just hadn't come about yet to reveal him in all his depravity.

"Sure, I'll go find out," he said and ambled away.

Now, even though I know it's going to make my blood boil, I can't go any further without sketching a portrait of my uncle. I know that describing him is going to be a complete waste of time, but what can I do? I've already gotten started and there's no point in turning back, so I may as well paint as objective a picture as possible. My bastard of an uncle is the mayor of our town, Kıyıdere. People there more or less like him. Of course, their respect for him is superficial, and if they knew what kind of person he really is, they'd squirm in embarrassment for having voted for him. But that's another issue. Anyway, there's something endearing about my uncle's soft mustache, as if it has just started growing in, and he always keeps a pair of sunglasses in the front pocket of his jacket. Since he was elected mayor, he wears three-piece suits, but his necktie is always crooked. Even though he ties it every morning, it looks like the one that's part of my school uniform, which I tie once when school starts and then wear it like that for the rest of the year. If you saw him out on the street, the last thing you'd think was that he was the mayor of a municipality. If people were voted into office based on their looks, he never would've had a chance of winning.

In any case, during the local elections of 2009, he applied to join the Giving Gramps Cancer Party, but they turned him down because they had their own candidates. So then he pulled together a posse of some more or less well-known dickhead morons from around the province and went to see the party representatives. "Think carefully about this," they said, "and have Altan run as your candidate. He's pals with everyone, both in town and in the villages, and he's got friends and family everywhere. He always says hi and bye, stops by for tea and soup, and he has notes and deeds as well as loans and debts. Not only that, he knows all about input and output, and he has had old and new loves that have fallen apart, too. If you don't have him run as your candidate, another party will take him on. Then what'll happen? You'll lose votes. God forbid! What if the You'll Vote for Us No Matter What Party wins the election?" But their words fell on deaf ears, and the other candidate apparently had stronger connections. So my uncle struck out on his own and started the Spurned Horses Party. During the election, there wasn't a single door in the province he didn't knock on, a single worker's guild he didn't visit and join for tea, a single child whose head he didn't pat, or a single cat or dog he didn't kneel down to pet. He went to every village, to every coffeehouse in every village, and to every house, barn, and cowshed. If you knew him, he reminded you about his candidacy, and if you didn't know him, he explained it all to you at length. "If you don't believe me," he'd say, "then go ask so and so, and ask so and so, too." In our town of Kıyıdere, he conned every living being, stooped to every kind of fawning and flattery, and drove everyone to such a point of exasperation that they pled for the election to end so that he would finally shut up. At dawn, the votes were tallied. Initially, objections were raised when the first count showed that he'd won by twenty votes; after the recount, he'd won by thirty-five.

If there are any disbelievers out there, you can check the 2009 local election results for the province of Kıyıdere on the website of the Supreme Electoral Council. No one at the main office of the Spurned Horses Party believed that they'd actually won, and they kept calling my uncle to ask, "Did we really win?" I'd answer his phone and say, "I swear, it's true." At the time, my uncle was busy with funeral arrangements. That morning, as the election results were being announced, my grandpa died. On the one hand, my uncle was overjoyed at winning, but he was also filled with grief. It was probably the most confusing day of his life, and quite likely instructive as well. Let's suppose that you're driving a Honda Civic and pass a Lamborghini Aventador. Your ego would burst with self-confidence, but then you might find your thoughts turning dark as you ponder the fleeting world and the fact that we're all rushing headlong toward death.

Anyway, after the election a group of blockheads who were tired of being shunted aside in the Spurned Horses Party decided to defect to the Giving Gramps Cancer Party, and they said to my uncle, "Come with us." "No," he replied, "I'd rather not." But in fact, he secretly wanted to join them. When the head of the district office of the Giving Gramps Cancer Party invited him, he put on the same airs. What he really wanted was a call from party headquarters. His pride was still stung by the fact that before the election they'd said to him, "Who the hell are you? Beat it!" So now he was sulking. A year passed without a call, and my uncle was frothing at the mouth. Then someone from the main office finally called him in to talk it over. In all my life, I've never seen anyone so happy and yet trying so hard to conceal their joy.

As if nothing out of the ordinary had happened, he said, "Çağlar, I'm going to Ankara tomorrow. They called me from the Giving Gramps Cancer Party headquarters. I wonder what their trouble is?"

At six the next morning, he headed off to Ankara, cocky as can be. That very same day, together with twenty-eight other defectors, a party badge was pinned on his lapel.

When I was a kid, my grandpa used to say to me, "Çağlar, you're a grown man now. In this fucked-up crock of a world, whatever you do, don't bring yourself to disgrace by running after women." My bastard of an uncle did just that. In this fucked-up crock of a world, he disgraced himself—by getting involved in politics. Before that, he really wasn't so bad. Just your average real estate agent, selling houses and plots of land that didn't belong to him. Whenever he closed a deal, he'd take me out on the town and buy me whatever I wanted. In those days, we couldn't have been happier. But then politics came along; it was the catalyst that brought out the disgrace in him. Everyone in the world—with the exception of my sister, of course—carries that seed of disgrace inside them, and it's a true sign of greatness if you can hold it at bay.

For example, if you're a greengrocer, you'll be brought to disgrace if you can't help but slip in a few rotten tomatoes when weighing them for a customer. I know because I've seen it. But at that point, you should take a deep breath and ask yourself: Why am I doing this? Would you find yourself lapsing into hopelessness if you didn't slip in those rotten tomatoes? Toss and turn at night, unable to sleep? Feel suffocated, as if you were choking to death? Become burnt out? Would it all be so completely meaningless? What if someone said to you, "You've suffered enough! Here's a return ticket and sixty-five hundred dollars in cash. Go to Singapore and screw every whore you want"? Would the pleasure you derive from slipping in those rotten tomatoes be taken down a single notch? I think not. If the earth was shaken to its core, if judgment day arrived, if aliens came and molested everyone in your family, would you still say, "Look, buddy, I'm going to keep slipping in those rotten tomatoes"? To a certain extent, people have direction in life, a goal, and if they don't have that, then at least they have a style, a stance, a way of doing things. So is your single aim in life palming off those damn rotten tomatoes? Suppose one day you've got grandkids and are savoring the fruits of retirement. Will the first thing that falls from your lips when you wax nostalgic about the past be those goddamn rotten tomatoes? You SOB! Ignominious ass! Take this text and hang it at the entrance of your shop. After that, turn your shop over to someone else and then fuck off! Find yourself another job. Anything! Work as a cashier. Work as a technician fixing anti-aircraft guns. Do whatever the fuck you want, but stop selling vegetables! Maybe if you start working as a cashier and find yourself thinking about whether or not to pocket a little money for yourself, you'll realize that the rotten tomatoes delivered you to such disgrace. If you start working as an anti-aircraft technician and find yourself thinking about making off with a few rounds of ammunition, yet again you'll see that it's those damn tomatoes that made you such a disgraceful bastard. That dumbass! What a dolt! My entire body trembles with rage. It was just too much! But still, let's try to forget about it all. That goddamn bastard! Slipping in two rotten tomatoes.

Anyway, if I remember right, I was talking about my uncle, who went to ask how much longer we'd have to wait. That idiot emerged lazily from the mysterious backstage darkness and said, "The twelfth impersonator just went on. So we'll have to wait a while longer." Thirty tense minutes passed. Our mouths went dry and cold sweat poured down our backs. Holding a black file to his chest, a stagehand wearing an earpiece approached and said, "The Michael Jacksons can all leave now."

People protested, saying, "What do you mean they can leave?" But the assistant merely replied, "The jury has seen enough Michael Jacksons. They don't want to see any more."

My uncle, who makes a habit of disappearing at the most critical moments, said, "Wait here. I'll go see what's really going on." With methodical steps, he disappeared into the darkness, yet again. The mothers and fathers of the Michael Jacksons surrounded the stagehand, pelting him with questions. The stagehand, pressing his index finger to his earpiece, said, "I'm just telling you what the jury told me. They've seen enough Michael Jacksons and don't want to see any more."

The stagehand was a short but powerfully built man, probably in his forties. He had the nose of a boxer and salt-and-pepper hair. His menacing glances, which didn't seem to target anyone in particular, were indifferent and authoritarian. I could tell that he was fed up. "Don't you understand what I told you?" he said, and then, emphasizing each word, repeated, "They. Have. Seen. Enough. Michael. Jacksons."

There was something in his voice that reduced us to nothing. We were mere cockroaches, and he was a boot. The blood rushed to my head, and I glowered at this man, my chest heaving. He had no concern for all the kids who had practiced for months and how their hearts would be broken. All he cared about was what he'd been told. We'd gone to such lengths to complete my sister's costume, traipsing from neighborhood shops to shopping malls and searching online for the things we couldn't find. We hurled ourselves into that chaos, a feat all its own. And then this brute comes along and says, "We've seen enough Michael Jacksons. You can go." What's that supposed to mean? Fine, say it with ice and steel in your voice. But what's the point of speaking so inhumanely?

Four or five of the younger Michael Jacksons broke down sobbing, and those who were slightly older stood there pouting, tears welling in their eyes. I looked at my sister; she was standing there, head bowed, toeing the ground with her black-and-white moonwalk shoes we'd ordered from Fatih Shoemakers. It was heartrending to see her in such sorrow. Taking her by the hand, I led her from the tumult of backstage into a hallway, where I sat her down on a bench. "You wait right here, pumpkin," I said. "You'll see, everything will be just fine." I winked at her and pinched her cheek, and then I went backstage and approached the stagehand.

My voice level and calm, I asked, "When you said there were 'enough' Michael Jacksons, how many do you mean?"

"I don't understand."

"A little while ago, you said that they'd seen enough Michael Jacksons. How many is that?"

"They've already seen a hundred Michael Jacksons."

"There aren't even a hundred of them here. There are twenty-seven, and the jury didn't even watch half of them. Even if they watched a hundred of them, I wouldn't care because they didn't watch my sister. She has more talent than a hundred people combined, and if she doesn't perform, I'll be more pissed off than a hundred people combined."

When I said that, the faces of those weeping Michael Jacksons were lit by hope. People started clamoring that I was right. Without ever taking my eyes from the stagehand, I shouted, "Just a second!" I looked him straight in the eye, wanting him to know that I'd be more than happy if he wanted to make this an issue between the two of us. I wanted to see how far he'd go, to see if he was as bound to this injustice as I was to my sister. If I myself had been so unfairly treated, I wouldn't have minded so much. But this was my sister, Çiğdem İyice, who goes to the Evliya Çelebi Primary School, so it was a sensitive issue.

"For two months, these kids have been practicing their hearts out for this shitty competition of yours. They trained so hard that they didn't even have time to eat ice cream," I said. That truly was the case for my sister. I have no reservations about making generalizations when large-scale injustices are committed.

The stagehand, not betraying the slightest sadness, and actually looking rather pleased, said, "There's nothing I can do."

"No? Well, how about a nice punch to the jaw then!"

At that moment, the laws of gravity broke loose and my feet were swept out from under me. Everything went dark; my mind flashed and time buckled. There was a sharp pain in my arm, and the world seemed to be pulling away. "What's going on?" a woman cried. "Keep calm, everything's under control," someone said. There was someone juggling pins, a kid spinning on his head, a dragon that took a sip of gasoline and spewed flames, a plaque of Ataturk's Address to the Youth and his concerned gaze. Where were we going? Stairs, floor tiles, and then I found myself in a small room with two security guards.

I was in a corner. One of them was opposite me, and the other was off to my right. Even though my vision was still blurry, I could tell that they were infuriated. In the other corner of the room, I could hear the crackle of a television, or perhaps it was a radio.

"What kind of goddamn funny business do you think you're up to?" one of them said.

As I gazed at him in bewilderment, the other one slapped me, sending my head thudding against the wall. I held my head in my hands, trying to pull my thoughts together. The one in front of me grabbed my shirt and shook me, shouting, "What the hell do you think you're doing?" I was pinned in the corner. Glancing around, I tried to find a way out, but I was trapped. For a moment, I couldn't breathe, and then I managed a deep sigh and looked at the man who had slapped me. He glared at me, brows furrowed. He had a thick nose and massive nostrils that seemed to have been created for the sole purpose of snorting in anger. The other one shook his fist in my face, saying again, "What kind of goddamn funny business do you think you're up to?"

"I'm not up to any funny business," I said.

Silence filled the room. They glowered at me, waiting for me to say something so that they could have at me again. The security guard in front of me raised his fist, and I hid my face behind my arms. "Now fuck off, so that I don't kill you here on the spot," he growled. The other one grabbed me by the neck and shoved me toward the door. As I opened it to leave, a feeling of relief welled up in me, and just before stepping out I turned and looked at the guards. The one who had slapped me said, "What the hell are you looking at?" and then he lunged forward and kicked me in the stomach. I tumbled down the steps onto the lobby's wooden floor. As I lay there, I saw him barreling toward me, but the other one held him back, saying, "Screw it, let him go." As I got to my feet, I looked around, thankful that no one had seen me get kicked down the stairs, and I walked away, trying to shake it off. When I reached the door of the auditorium, I stopped. My ear was ringing, my head was pounding, and I was in a daze, as if I'd been awoken from a deep slumber by the screech of a drill. I balled my hands into fists, trying to stop them from shaking. I thought, *If I don't go back and give those two idiots a piece of my mind, how will I be able to live with myself?* I decided to go back. Just then, I heard someone call out to me. Sometimes I hear a voice like that, calling out "Çağlar, Çağlar," but usually it's just my own inner voice.

Someone grabbed my arm, and I spun around in fear. It was my uncle.

"I kept calling you over. Why were you ignoring me?"

I couldn't find my voice.

"Where have you been?"

"Here."

"What happened?"

"Nothing, nothing at all."

"Come on, they're waiting for us."

"Who?"

"We've been looking all over for you. Let's go, there's no time for talk."

We entered a spacious room. A large-mouthed woman who was holding a walkie-talkie and wearing a black jacket approached us. "Altan Bey," she said to my uncle.

"You must be Afşar Hanım, the production manager for the competition," he said, shaking her hand.

"Yes."

"The head of Bursa province probably called you."

"He did. What seems to be the problem?"

My uncle smiled, pointing toward my sister as if she were the problem, and said, "Our little peanut here has been practicing for months. Why don't we have the jury watch her show?"

The woman looked my sister up and down before saying, "They've already seen enough Michael Jacksons."

"Well, that may be true," my uncle said. "But she's quite excited about it, and our regional representative just loves our little peanut here. Every time we get together, he says, 'Your niece is such a wonderful dancer.' If I'm not mistaken, he's a close friend of the producer here.

"I'm the mayor of Kıyıdere province," my uncle said, offering his card, like a swindler holding out his ace.

But who would care about Kıyıdere? If he had been the regional representative, it would've been better, but I know that he hadn't even seen my sister dance. It was a complete ruse.

The woman twirled my uncle's card for a few moments and then smiled. On the crown of his head, my uncle has a tuft of hair that always stands on end. That's what gives him a certain air of childlike innocence, despite all the dastardly things he's done. Women always find things like that adorable, and I've never met a woman who wasn't charmed by that tuft. But they don't know my uncle. They don't know how he drifts off to sleep at night with his mouth open, snoring away in the next room. So naturally they are caught defenseless, because they only see him during the day, when he's wearing a suit and sunglasses, with that tuft of hair poking up. Time and time again, I've thought of snipping it off so that people would see him for what he really is.

The woman stroked my sister's chin. Her fingernails were painted glossy red, and her hand made me think of a rooster's claw. "Okay," she said, "come along then."

My uncle smiled at the woman and winked flirtatiously. That's how he is, always bowing and scraping to the first woman who comes along, like a member of some pussy-worshipping cult. I burst out laughing. I couldn't help it. There we were, in the middle of that absurd tragic comedy, and it was all so ludicrous. That wink was the last straw. I doubled over, clutching my stomach. They turned and shot me confused glances, which sent me into another round of gut-wrenching laughter.

Two

Most people are utterly devoid of talent. That's the way it has to be. Otherwise, the concept would lose all meaning. Then there are those people whose abilities go unrecognized through sheer bad luck. We should hold such people in high regard—even if we don't know who they are—because they deserve our respect. On this point, a critical distinction must be made. The common characteristic of untalented people (we could refer to them as nontalents who are oblivious to this fact) is that they attribute their lack of success to one or two tiny details. For example, on our soccer team, Kıyıderespor, there was this guy I sat with on the substitute bench. For two years, I listened to him rant about how he never managed to score because he was always caught off side, and he said that the secret of Lionel Messi's success was that he knew how to toe the off-side line. On that rusty green bench, sitting with his elbows on his knees and his meaty fingers intertwined, he would go on about his small defects and the simple secrets of the great players, never taking his eyes from the field as he spoke, his socks pulled down and his shin guards unstrapped. He always parted his hair to the side, and he had dark brown eyes and a long face. No matter how he prattled on, I found myself captivated because he gave the impression that he really knew what he was talking about. Last year, I quit playing soccer, but he's still there on the substitute bench, probably pinning the blame for his inability to score off a header on bad timing and saying that the key to Cristiano Ronaldo's success is the fact that his timing is always spot on. He's tall and lanky, so naturally the others expected that he would score all the time. They didn't give a damn about timing, but they never said anything because his voice was so reassuring. Sometimes, I think of him, and when I do, I find myself unable to drive him from my thoughts as I wonder what he's doing and who he's ranting on to now. His name is Ethem Kudnuva. With a name like that, how could you ever forget him?

Standing backstage at a spot where I could see the jury and the performers, I thought about Kudnuva as I listened to the kid onstage playing guitar and singing. It was a great song, but he was hacking it to pieces. Still, despite all his efforts, he couldn't completely ruin it, because of the original greatness of the song.

I'd noticed him backstage as my sister and I were waiting. He was producing the most ridiculous sounds with his guitar, leaning in toward it, lightly slapping the strings with the palm of his hand, and humming along, eyes squinted. Across the room, we'd made eye contact a few times. Soon, he'd return backstage, claiming that he'd played a chord wrong or that there was something wrong with his guitar. He was probably even thinking up excuses before he went onstage. Someone should have told him that he wasn't born to play guitar and sing, and that he shouldn't try to explain away his failure. Of course, it would be better if someone who loved him told him this. People always love others—that's the last saving grace in the world.

However, I should point out that Stony Muzaffer, the Kıyıderespor coach, never liked me. One day after practice, he pulled me aside to the corner flag and put his blue-veined, bony hands on my shoulders. After giving them a squeeze with his trembling fingers, he said in a weary voice, "Çağlar, if your uncle wasn't mayor, I wouldn't even let you get near the soccer club building."

"I see, Hoca," I said, and then I cleared out my locker and left the Kıyıderespor Ragıp Baysal Soccer Complex. I even left behind my lock. I'd bought it two years before and put a sticker of the team's red-and-green logo on it. You see, I didn't take it because they might have thought I was stealing team property.

I'm trying to get at something here, but not as a self-righteous opportunist who leaps at the first chance to humiliate people who lack talent. No, I only speak based on my life experiences, and I only speak at night, so that at a certain point you'll feel as if you're speaking not with me but with the night itself. This is Çağlar İyice speaking, the patient voice of the everlasting night. He is seventeen years old and attends the Kıyıdere Kâtip Çelebi Anatolian Vocational School of Tourism and Hotel Management, but even at that lousy school, this blockhead has a hard time passing his classes. He doesn't have a single talent worth mentioning, and he will speak with you like the night itself, like the most authentic representative of reality, like the Marmara regional distributor of rescued words. Excuse him, because he has important things to say. Don't protest and say, "But everyone does." Indulge him. Please. Just for a few seconds.

So there I was, looking at the jury and the stage, with my sister beside me and my uncle standing behind us. There was a balding, serious-looking stagehand who was wearing a microphone headset standing nearby. I approached him and said, "I thought there were going to be some famous people on the jury." He looked at me blankly, as if he hadn't understood what I said. I couldn't be sure, but maybe he hadn't heard because of the headset he was wearing.

He finally said, "That's the preliminary round jury."

"So when are the stars going to come?"

Then the same scenario: his uncomprehending gaze, my tenseness as I wondered if he'd heard me or not, a long pause. "They'll come for the televised performances," he said in a bored tone of voice.

Even though my mind was swimming with questions, I decided to keep silent. Carrying on a dialogue with him was impossible; it would take years to get the answers I wanted.

My sister was next in line after the guitarist. She was fidgeting and breathing erratically, so I massaged her shoulders. That performance onstage was killing me. What should have been a four-minute song seemed to last for hours, and I found my thoughts drifting to the passing days, halfhearted enthusiasms, Kıyıderespor, and Stony Muzaffer. He'd had a blue mobility scooter that he rode everywhere, sometimes even up to the sidelines. Six months after I quit playing soccer, he died. He was quite old, as old as Luis Aragonés, so it didn't come as a surprise. My uncle and I went to the funeral to say our final farewells. I'd liked the old guy and knew he had been an honest man, but the fact that he didn't like me was a source of torment. After the service at the mosque, I went to the cemetery, but my uncle didn't go with me, as he had business to handle. Apparently, they were going to install a sprinkler system for the grass on the median of the main road in town. What could I care about sprinkler systems when people around us were being taken quietly by death? That day it was Stony Muzaffer, the next day it would be someone else, and then someone else the next. I had always felt like I was in a long line and my turn was drawing ever nearer at a snail's pace; but that day, the line suddenly began rushing along, and I found myself gasping for breath, as if I might die at any moment. Wearing a black cassock, an imam got out of the funeral coach and knelt beside the grave. Spreading his hands, he started praying, his voice filled with faith. Even though I couldn't understand the words, I could tell that his prayer was laden with sorrow. One by one, the members of the soccer team scooped three shovelfuls of dirt onto the body, which had been wrapped in a white shroud. When it was my turn, a chill ran down my spine and I froze. I handed the shovel to someone else. There was an honest man in that grave, a man who didn't like me. Maybe he didn't want me to put dirt on his grave; maybe he didn't even want me to be there. Or maybe it was the opposite, and if he could see his own funeral, the sight of me in mourning might have brought tears to his eyes. In the end, such questions don't have easy answers.

Carefully observe what's around you, and you'll see that there are hundreds of unanswered questions surrounding us all the time. In a midsized province like our own, there must be millions of questions roaming the empty streets, so just imagine what it's like in a big city. But it's so pointless that these questions get repeated over and over. Haven't enough questions been asked already? Hasn't everything been questioned and prodded enough? Wouldn't it be great if people would stop adding more questions to the billions and billions of them already swarming around us? Or if they'd say, "Damn it all, enough already!"

So in the name of humanity, I'm going to answer some of them, even if it's just a few.

Let me tell you what Stony Muzaffer would've said if he saw me at his funeral. "Çağlar," he'd say, "son, you know that I never liked you. When you left the team, I was so relieved. I would've preferred to pull ten players than have you play. But you know all this already. With my dying breath, I didn't think of you, nor did I think about the day when you so vaingloriously left the Ragıp Baysal Complex. I didn't say, 'Oh, what a proud young man.' No, I said to myself, 'It's a damn good thing he left that lock behind because I would've thought that he made off with club property.' You've got no knack for going to funerals. You got in line to take a turn at the shovel, but didn't you notice the surprised looks of your ex-teammates when you passed it along? The few times I let you play, they looked at you the same way, and I'd be tearing out my hair on the sidelines because you're a complete moron who is simply incapable of working the wings. When there was pressure on the middle of the field, you idiotically insisted on working the center. I explained it to you hundreds of times. I drew it on the board in the locker room again and again. At halftime during the match with Gölçükspor, I even threw a marker at your head so you'd remember. When I saw you make the same mistake again, I was so furious that I didn't pull you from the game because I couldn't bear the thought of even having to deal with you. At moments like those, I was overcome by an urge to hop on my scooter and mow you down right there on the field. That's why you should go home. Go home! Forget about me. At the very least, leave my soul in peace."

Finally, the guitarist finished his performance. A woman brought us to the side of the stage and told us to wait there, and then she approached the table where the preselection jury was sitting. She leaned over and said something to a man with long hair and a goatee sitting on the left side of the table. I surmised that they were talking about my sister, so I carefully observed his expression, fearing that he would say, "Another Michael Jackson? Enough already!" But instead, he nodded, and the two other jury members went along with it. I took their response as a positive sign. Even if they were just members of the pre-selection jury, they didn't seem to have any biases. The woman stepped away from the table and signaled to the tight-lipped stagehand, who turned to us and said, "It's your turn." The time had come.

Before she went onstage, my sister and I did our special handshake, which consists of a high-five, a fist bump, an arm wrestler's handgrip, and two blows to the chest to show that we performed the ritual in all sincerity. I know it might seem outdated, but my sister and I don't care about what's in or out of fashion. All that matters is the meaning of what we do, and we've been doing that for six years now—when I drop her off at school, when she comes home from school, before going to bed, after waking up, when we recall the name of someone we'd been trying to remember, in the morning on religious and national holidays, and sometimes for no reason at all. Some people watch us with envy, but we never do it with anyone else. It's something special between the two of us, and it'll always be that way.

My sister confidently strode to the center of the stage. Thinking of it now, if it had been me, I wouldn't have been able to walk like that. She'd cast off all her nervousness. Maybe she'd been waiting for someone to say, "It's your turn," so she could pull herself together. When she reached the center of the stage, she turned and bowed her head, pulling down her hat. "Billie Jean" started playing over the speakers, and during the first few moments of the song, she remained perfectly still. Then she raised the brim of her hat with her index finger and quickly turned her head to look at the jury. She gazed so intently into their eyes that even I felt a chill run through me. The spirit of MJ was there. The king of dance had returned!

First, she started with mechanical movements, and electricity seemed to flow in one arm and out the other. If you were there to see it, you would've thought that you were watching a robotic being that had circuits and cables instead of blood and veins. Then she struck a classic Michael Jackson pose and began slide-stepping, flowing across the stage with a grace that contrasted sharply with her robot routine. She added new variations to the dance with turns to the left and right. Her legs were moving incredibly fast, but her movements didn't seem rushed at all. It was as if she had been possessed by a monster that wanted to rush headlong at a hundred miles an hour, but she effort-lessly held it in check. As she was gracefully sliding along, she suddenly stopped and brought her fingers together under her chin and traced the four corners of a square with her head. Then she held her hands out to the side as if to say, "What can I do, there's just no end to the sorrows in the world," before brushing imaginary dust from her shoulder with the back of her hand. After a quick spin, she took off her hat and spun around three more times, coming to a sudden stop. Yet again, she shot the jury an intense stare, which meant, "You haven't seen anything yet. I'm just getting started."

Next came the moonwalk. First, she did a classic moonwalk, but the ease of her movements said, "This is a piece of cake." Then she started what could best be described as a sideways moonwalk. She placed one of her feet at a ninety-degree angle and the other at a forty-five-degree angle and then, by applying the principle of the classic moonwalk, began sliding sideways with alternate steps. Of course, this required much more mastery because it's hard to give the impression that you're sliding as you walk when you're moving sideways.

But these two styles of moonwalk weren't challenging enough for my sister, and she'd saved her best surprise for last. With one hand on her belt buckle, she swayed her hips back and forth, all the while making sure that her movements didn't look comical. MJ never danced for humor, he danced because it was his life, and that's how he offered up his soul to this soulless world. In typical Michael Jackson style, she strode toward the jury and fell to her knees, only to rise to her feet just as quickly. She then slid on her knees to the edge of the stage and then began the truly miraculous part of her routine: doing the moonwalk on her knees. I don't know how many people in Turkey can do this, but on YouTube we saw a group of performers from India doing it, and she spent eight whole days mastering it.

My sister was in perfect form that day. Honestly, I'd been worried that she'd lose her nerve, but she danced flawlessly. That's when I realized that she was born for the stage and that she felt more at ease there than anywhere else. For the finale, we had planned it so she would spin around six times like a whirling top and then freeze in place after tossing her hat to the jury. Then she would fall to her knees with her arms outspread and gaze upward. In that final moment, she would have no contact with the jury whatsoever; her only concern would be with Michael Jackson up above in the heavens, or perhaps with God, who knows. But some half-wit, probably astounded by the fact that he'd just seen Michael Jackson moonwalk on his knees and thinking it was the finale, shut off the music early. But as I said, my sister was in perfect form that day, and she didn't skip a beat as she pulled off the final move. She may not have done six full spins, and because the music suddenly was shut off she did pause for a moment, but in the end she held it all together. Her hat flew through the air. I watched it, as did my uncle, the jury, the stagehands, the competitors in line—in short, everyone there. It soared over the heads of the three jury members. A man standing beside one of the cameras reached out and caught the hat, grinning as if he'd succeeded in pulling off the greatest stunt ever.

Silence fell over the auditorium, five or six seconds of sheer silence. If there had been spectators, they would've begun cheering madly, and it seemed to me that even the empty seats were fidgeting with excitement. Everyone was holding their breath expectantly, and then the guy with the goatee sitting at the jury table wrote something down and said, "That was great. Next in line, please." The two other jury members nodded in approval.

"Next in line, please." What the hell was that supposed to mean? I couldn't believe my ears. They'd probably lost touch with reality, or maybe they were blind. I scrutinized the three jury members. *Maybe they're dead,* I thought, *under some kind of zombie spell.* If Michael Jackson himself showed up and did an imitation of himself, they would've watched with the same indifference. If Moses showed up and cleaved the stage in two and then led the tribes through it, they would've said, "Very nice, now let's watch the next breakdance routine."

That ass of an assistant who led my sister onto the stage started walking toward her, and I ran after him. I couldn't bear the thought of any of those people touching her, or even casting their shadows over her. I walked her offstage.

"How was I?" she asked.

Taking her face in my hands, I replied, "Sweetheart, that performance will go down in history! You were wonderful."

"So what now?" my uncle asked.

"We'll call you," replied Afşar Hanım, the production manager.

"When are you going to call?" I asked.

"Before the televised competition."

"Does that mean my sister is going to be on the show?"

"The jury will decide that. We'll know next week."

"Can we have the hat back? It belonged to our dead grandpa."

We walked out of the auditorium. One of the Michael Jacksons who had been kicked out was waiting there, hoping for a chance to go onstage, a tense expression on his face. The child's father pulled my uncle aside, trying to find out why my sister was allowed to perform. I'm not sure what he said, but my uncle managed to get away. All the while, the kid had his eyes locked on us. As we pulled away in my uncle's Honda Civic, I noticed that he was still glaring at us. Aside from my sister's performance, the most real thing I saw that day was the rage in that kid's eyes. Even after we'd driven away, I could still feel his angry stare burning into my back.

We set off down the two-lane road from Bursa to Kıyıdere. After all that excitement, I was exhausted. My uncle was rambling on, buoying my sister's hopes about performing on television. He was as sure as his own name that she'd be invited to perform on the show. No one could deny what they'd seen, and in any case, the head of Bursa province and the regional representative were on top of it. As we were leaving, Afşar Hanım had leaned in to say, "There's not a thing to worry about, it's all taken care of." My uncle kept droning on as he drove down that broad, straight road, the whir of the wheels a constant hum, and I was overcome by an odd sensation. We didn't seem to be moving forward. I opened the window and put my hand out, feeling the wind on my fingers. The car was filled with the roar of the wind, and from where I was sitting in the back I saw that my sister was looking at me in the rearview mirror. She always sits in the front, because that's where she likes to be.

THREE

It had been five days since the contest, but we hadn't heard anything yet. I had given them my number, and I sat there waiting, one eye on my iPhone and one eye on my sister. A couple of times, I asked my uncle if he knew anything, and he just said, "Don't worry, it's been handled." That's what one of the officials told him over the phone. They said they'd call when they scheduled the next round of the competition and that we should just continue working on her routine. We were trying to perfect the antigravity lean in the living room, but there was so much furniture there that we put the coffee table on the dining room table so we'd have more space. MJ liked to do that move where he'd stop in the middle of the dance, standing there with his hands curled into fists by his sides, and he'd tilt his body forward as if he were slowly falling, almost reaching a forty-five-degree angle, and then, as if it were the easiest thing in the world, he'd straighten back up. Of course, my sister could do that move, down to about a thirty-degree angle, and it was part of the routine we'd put together before the qualifiers. But she hadn't wanted to include it in her performance, saying, "I can't do a full forty-five degrees." I said it was fine, and better that way because the talent competition was going to take place in rounds, and it would be better if we had a move that we could set aside for the next stage.

There were some people who, out of sheer envy, made the claim that MJ wore trick shoes when he did the antigravity lean, something about a spike in the sole. I knew that it was an urban legend, but all the same I went to Fatih Shoemakers and asked the old man sitting at the counter if such a mechanism were possible. The old guy irritably scratched his white beard, which contrasted with the dark spots on his hands, and said, "Can't do it."

"I have no intention of asking you to do it," I said, "because I believe in my sister's natural abilities. I just wanted to know if it's possible."

He repeated, "Can't do it."

The strain of the years bore down upon him. Business was dead. No one came to get their shoes repaired anymore. He should have closed up shop long ago, but he insisted on holding out. He probably blamed the decline of business on twits like me. In the past, people would come to get their shoes resoled, but then I come along, asking, "Can you make a spike mechanism for shoes?" Questions like that probably drove him crazy. Such questions had brought about the demise of his trade, and who knows, maybe sooner or later they'd bring about the end of the world, too. I stood there in front of the shoelaces that were hung on the door of the shop, looking at that old guy as he stared at me, breathing heavily through his nose. His fury was so immense that it barely fit in that tiny shop. Feeling suffocated, I turned around and left. With the entirety of his soul, that old cobbler treated me with the utmost disdain, but I didn't take it personally. Perhaps he had dreams about shoes being thrown away and woke up in tears. I liked the old guy. After the holiday prayers at Bahçelievler Mosque, he would wait in the courtyard, looking around to see if there were any kids who would kiss his hand so that he'd give them a few holiday coins. Over the years, he'd given me quite a bit of spare change that way. He didn't remember me, but that's all right; I wasn't about to forget about it just because he didn't remember.

As my sister was working on that move, I'd stand in front of her, and at least eight or nine hundred times a day she'd wind up in my arms as I caught her before she fell to the ground. It takes two people to practice that move, and it's a test of trust as much as it is a dance routine. In the end, you have to give yourself over completely to the person in front of you. With every attempt, my sister was improving her angle, but it still wasn't enough.

No matter how often my uncle said that they'd call when the date was set for the performance, a sense of uncertainty hung in the air. Uncertainty can weaken desires. I thought I saw that happening in my sister's behavior, in the way she distractedly sat down and got up, in her wan smiles, in her silences. "Çağlar," she said the few times I asked her about it, "let's just keep on practicing."

She wanted so badly to be in the competition that she couldn't even let herself dream about it. That's how serious she was. Far from being an uncertain flight of the imagination, her desire was concrete, so close that she could reach out and touch it. Maybe it was the best of dreams—the first of its kind, a dream with zero mileage; and no reality could detract from its charm. Perhaps that's why she never talked about it. I began to wonder what my sister dreamed about at night. If someone you love doesn't tell you their secret desires, your only option is to peer into their dreams, because if you really want something, you dream about it. There's even an expression for that: "The stuff of dreams."

Take me, for example. Before I became the proud owner of an iPhone, I dreamed about it. The 4s had just come out. In my dream, I came home and there was an iPhone 4s box on the table. My father had bought it and said, "Give it to Çağlar." It was our home, but it was different; it was a wooden house and the windows were like the portholes of a ship. A rather irresponsible architect had designed that house, but it didn't strike me as strange at all, as though our house had always been that way. I took the iPhone out of the box, but I couldn't use it because I didn't know the four-number passcode. Every time I tried to enter it, a red light would flash and a message would pop up on the screen: "Wrong password, please try again." In the end, the screen said, "If you enter the wrong password, your phone will lock." Just then, my late grandpa showed up. At that time, my grandpa had already passed away, but I wasn't surprised when I saw him so I didn't say anything like, "Grandpa, you're alive!" Those odd things, like the weirdness of the house and seeing my grandpa, struck me as being perfectly natural. In any case, if a dream doesn't seem real, then what's the point? Of course, in the unfolding of the dream there's the excitement of being the owner of a new iPhone. My grandpa said, "Let's call your dad and find out what the password is." Then he took out his own phone, an old Alcatel that must've been made like a hundred years ago. He used it until the day he died. Pulling out the antenna before making a call when he was still alive, he'd say, "Çağlar, this thing is really a miracle. You can even talk on it when you're walking around." So anyway, in my dream, he used that phone to call my dad, and when my dad picked up, my grandpa shouted, "Sabahattin!" That's how he was. Normally, he spoke quietly, but whenever he talked on that phone, he shouted because he didn't believe that his voice would reach the other end of the line. "Sabahattin! You left a phone here for the kid, but he doesn't know the password." Of course, I couldn't hear what my dad was saying, but then my grandpa said, "Oh really, okay," and all the while my grandpa was looking at me intently, and at one point it even seemed like he was furrowing his white brows at me. I was thinking, *Why is Grandpa looking at me like that? Did my dad say something bad about me?* I kept wondering, *What did I do wrong?* That's the clearest part of the dream—that feeling as I wondered, *What did I do wrong?* My grandpa hung up the phone. "So?" I asked. "There's no password," he said. "What do you mean? The phone keeps asking for a password!" We just stood there, looking at each other. Then I woke up. I lay in bed looking at the ceiling, filled with a jumble of emotions. I wasn't sure if I should be pleased or upset. Those dreams are rare, the kind that start as dreams and turn into nightmares, and then at some ridiculous point they suddenly come to an end.

So that's how it was that morning; I was wondering about my sister's dreams as I prepared her breakfast. Why me? Because she won't eat breakfast unless I prepare it: a smiley face made of tomatoes, cucumbers, and carrots. The eyes are made from slices of cucumber, the mouth and nose tomatoes, and the hair slivers of carrot, and it's really realistic, too—just think of a woman with green eyes who dyed her hair orange and put on lipstick, whose nose has turned red from the cold. Yes, my sister loves how I prepare her breakfast. Trying to sound casual, I asked, "So, did you have pleasant dreams last night?" Her fork stopped in midair just as she was about to plunge it into a piece of fat-free cheese the size of a matchbox. Like all dancers, she ate healthily so she could stay in shape. She caught onto my scheme right away.

"Çağlar, why are you asking me that?"

"No reason," I replied, putting a glass of juice next to her plate—kiwi, orange, and pomegranate. I had just squeezed it myself. "I was just wondering."

After popping the piece of fat-free cheese into her mouth, she stabbed her fork into the left eye of the smiley face, looking at me suspiciously all the while. After eating the slice of cucumber, she smiled. Naturally, I smiled in response and that was the end of the issue.

That evening when my mom came home from her job at the registry office, my sister and I were still going over her routine in the living room. It was Thursday, May 23. My sister was standing there almost at a forty-degree angle, and although I was standing in front of her, I didn't have to hold her up. Our mom stopped in the doorway and flashed us a glance that said, "What have I done to deserve this?" before she stormed off. Indeed, what had she done to deserve this? Just what had she done to deserve having the coffee table moved from its original location? That coffee table was part and parcel of the immovable property of the house, and my mom held the deed.

So off she went in a huff and started unloading plates from the dishwasher, tossing them onto the shelf as if she were throwing them at our heads. It was heartbreaking, not to mention irritating. I mean, if she had just come in and yelled at us, shouting whatever was on her mind, or even actually thrown the plates at us, it wouldn't have been so bad. But each clattering plate was a psychological assault. That was fine for me, but my sister was only nine years old, and I couldn't stand the fact that she was being subjected to such treatment. Whenever my mom would go into the kitchen and start unloading the plates from the dishwasher, slamming them onto the cupboard shelves, I'd get the urge to pound on the walls. As absurd as it may sound, I'd also get a strange desire to grab a drill and start randomly drilling holes around the house. That's the sole reason why I was usually the one who unloaded the dishwasher. But that day I forgot because we were working on my sister's routine and she'd nearly gotten to a forty-degree lean. I told my sister, "Watch a little TV," and I headed toward the kitchen. I stood in the doorway and looked at my mom. She went on unloading the dishes, acting as if I wasn't there.

"What's wrong?" I asked.

She went on banging the dishes around for a while and then suddenly stopped, gazing sadly at a glass she was holding, and then sat down. Propping an elbow on the table, she covered half of her face with her right hand as if she'd just been dealt a stiff uppercut. A lock of hair curled down to her chin on the left side of her face. I saw that there were a few strands of gray.

"If you're upset about the coffee table, we'll put it back."

She pulled her hand from her face and gasped. "What happened to the coffee table?"

I realized that something else was bothering her so I sat down at the kitchen table. I picked up the glass she had put on the table, filled it with water from the pitcher, and set it in front of her. She looked at the glass but didn't touch it. "Çiğdem's teacher asked me to come to her school today, so I left work early."

"What did she say?"

"Çiğdem pushed Efekan down the stairs the other day."

"Which Efekan?"

"You know Adnan, the curtain maker? His son. Apparently Çiğdem pushed him down a flight of stairs and he hit his head. Now his forehead is all swollen. His mom went to the school and threatened to sue everyone."

"It's not true. The kid's a chronic liar. He's always picked on Çiğdem. Just last year, he scribbled all over that nice notebook she had."

"A substitute teacher saw it happen. She really did push him."

"If it happened two days ago, why did they wait until today to tell you?"

Irritably flicking back the strands of hair falling across her face, she said, "They didn't wait to tell us. They called your uncle that day. Do you know what he did? He said, 'Okay, I'll come right down.' But of course he didn't go. That's why they called me today. We sat in the principal's office and talked about it. Çiğdem's teacher is really young, so when Efekan's mother said that she was going to sue the school, she flew into a panic. For the last two days, Efekan's mother hasn't let him go to school."

"Is she really serious about this suing business?"

"How should I know? I called your uncle and told him how irresponsible he is and how he's caused us so much trouble. I asked him why he didn't even bother to tell me when he himself didn't go to the school. 'Go talk to Adnan and apologize,' I said, 'and don't come home until you have.' But he's still saying, 'What's the big deal?' That's what he said! 'What's the big deal?' I told him, 'Altan, I've had it up to here with you!' He said, 'Her teacher was crying; what am I supposed to do? What are they going to do, start an investigation? Send me into exile?

For years, I waited to get appointed, and now this happens. In any case, Çiğdem doesn't even do her homework!'"

"That's a lie!" I said. And it really was a lie. My sister does all of her homework. If something is bothering her and she's not in the mood, then I do it for her.

"Last week, she didn't do her math homework. Apparently she said, 'My uncle is the mayor so *I* don't have to do homework.' When her teachers tell her to go up to the blackboard, she refuses, saying, 'The district representative is my friend. So if I wanted, I could get you fired from this school.' She starts fights with all her friends and swears like a sailor. Her deskmate doesn't even want to sit with her. There were other teachers in the principal's office, and as that poor woman was explaining the situation, they started laughing. But at the same time, they were also appalled. I wanted to curl up and die on the spot."

My mom was about to cry. In fact, the tears had already started. I took a drink of water from the glass on the table.

"It's all your fault," she growled, shooting me a hostile look. "You and your uncle spoil her!"

"Don't yell at me. The next round of the talent competition is coming up. You don't want to bring down our morale before the show, do you?"

"As if we don't have enough problems already. Then you go off and get us tied up in this talent thing."

"Don't worry. I'll talk to her, okay?"

"What do you mean, 'I'll talk to her'? From now on, I won't have any more talk like that from you." She got up and yelled, "Çiğdem! Çiğdem! Get in here."

I held my mom back with one hand and stepped outside, shutting the kitchen door behind me. Çiğdem came running up. "Go to your room, sweetheart," I said. "Keep practicing. Stand in front of your bed when you practice, okay?" All the while, my mom was pushing against the door, demanding that I open it.

"Why's mom shouting?"

"It's nothing," I said. "She just had a rough day at work, and she's a little upset. I'll talk to her and come see you in a bit. Go on now."

My sister went to her room and closed the door. I slipped back into the kitchen and, leaning against the door, whispered, "Stop it! Don't ever do that again. Don't even think about raising your voice to my sister." I whispered so that Çiğdem wouldn't hear me. But my voice had a weird edge to it. My mom was looking at me with fear in her eyes. I was even a little afraid of myself, and I felt ashamed of what I'd done. Let me be frank here: I don't really like my mom much, but still, I didn't want things to go that far. My mom started crying quietly, looking at me with an expression of surprise and sorrow, as if she were trying to recognize me. She was probably thinking, *Is this really my son?* Every mother thinks that at one point or another.

Gently, I took my mom by the shoulders and sat her down. "I'll talk to her," I said. "I'm going to take care of this. Please, leave it to me."

But she wasn't listening to me. She wasn't even looking at me. She just sat there staring straight ahead as if something else was bothering her, as if she had a toothache. All the while, she went on crying.

"Are you okay?" I asked.

No reply.

"I'm sorry," I said.

Again, no reply. She was in another world. I didn't want to just leave her like that, but at the same time I had no desire to stay there. I felt terrible. For a moment, I considered pressing the blades of the hand mixer to my head and churning up my brain. The thought was absurd, of course, but also kind of funny.

"Okay then, I'm going," I said, but she still didn't say anything.

She opened her purse, took out a bottle of Xanax, and swallowed half a pill with a sip of water.

I sat down across from her and said, "How many have you taken?"

She looked at me for a second and then turned her gaze to the black countertop. We sat there, not looking at each other. There's no animosity between my mom and me, just a chasm. It's been like this for a long time now. We're like two cliffs, and there's a valley between us filled with anger, pain, and disappointment. As we sat there in that heavy silence, the hum of the refrigerator grew louder and louder. I propped my chin in my hand, looking at the refrigerator's red door. *Such a colorful life we have,* I thought, and waited there for like a million hours.

That night I couldn't sleep. I tried reading *Madame Bovary,* but I wasn't in the mood. I went on Facebook, but aside from T. C. Sinem Uzun, there weren't any decent chicks to chat with and I didn't want to bug her. So I decided to play *Hugo Troll Race,* but I didn't have the heart for that, either, and quit the game in the middle of the train tracks. I looked at the treadmill across from my sister's bed. There were five bound stacks of old unread municipal bulletins. In the end, I decided to go out on the balcony and take a few drags from my electronic cigarette. I looked at the paving stones glowing in the wan light of the streetlamp. I looked at the green dumpster at the edge of the street. I looked at the apartment building across the way, at the half-closed blinds, the dark windows, the rusty satellite dishes on the roof. I looked at the sky. I thought about the meaning of life in its purest state, so pure that it can't be boiled down to any other reality. I thought, *So if there is a God, what will he say to us strange people when the curtain comes down in the end? If I were God, I would say something really simple. Just one word.* I closed my eyes and listened to the night. *Heel, for example,* I thought. *That's what I would say. Or maybe something more complicated, something in the imperative, but what? I don't know right now. To empathize with God, you have to be some kind of prophet.* I went back inside and knelt down beside my sister's bed, watching her sleep so innocently, wondering what she could be dreaming about. Based on her facial expressions, I tried to guess what she might be doing in her dreams. It was nearly four o'clock.

At four in the morning, seagulls are the most evil creatures in the world. Why? Because for no reason at all, they start squawking their heads off as if someone had grabbed them by the neck. They do it for fun, just to piss people off. They never squawk at that decibel at, say, two in the afternoon. No, they patiently wait until four o'clock in the morning and then start screeching away so that you'll wake up and, in your slumberous state, think to yourself, *Someone probably just slit the throat of a two-year-old kid out there in the street!* I closed the balcony door and all the windows, but our room was still filled with the squawking of seagulls, and as the room filled with their squawks, my sister furrowed her brows in her sleep and her lips twitched. Her face was contorted with fear, and I wondered if she'd started having a nightmare because of the seagulls. I thought of waking her up but decided not to, as she was going to get up early anyway. In the end, I couldn't stand it and I kissed her hand, which was curled into a fist over the edge of the sheets. She opened her eyes.

"Çağlar, what's wrong?"

"It's nothing, sweetheart," I said. "Just the seagulls."

"Seagulls?"

"Didn't you hear them?"

"No. Why aren't you sleeping?"

"I couldn't sleep, but I'm going to go to bed now. You go back to sleep."

"Okay."

I got into bed and locked my hands behind my head on the pillow, looking up at the glowing stars. We had stuck small glow-in-the-dark star stickers on the ceiling, and when we turned off the nightlight, my sister and I would stretch out in bed and chat as if we were lying in a field watching the stars in the sky.

After a few minutes, my sister said, "Çağlar."

"Yes?"

"I can't sleep, either. Do you want to talk?"

"Let's talk, baby."

When my sister and I chat at night, we don't look at each other—we look up at the stars, and without being fake about it we try to talk about things that suit the atmosphere. That's the rule. I thought for a little while and then said, "My little MJ. On faraway roads, when darkness falls, when the cold settles in, when two people hug, of course I'm going to think of you."

My sister thought for a few minutes and said, "I'll think of you, too, Çağlar. Because we don't fight. Kings never fight."

I laughed. It was the truest thing I'd ever heard in my life. Look at it however you will, take any perspective you want, but it's true. You can be on the side of monarchism, constitutionalism, republicanism, or any style of governance not taught in schoolbooks, but it's still true. Kings never fight. You could say it as a critique or as praise. It makes no difference. It was a nine-year-old girl who said that—my sister. I thought a little bit more, thinking that anything I said after that would be fine, but I couldn't seem to come up with anything. It certainly wasn't easy.

"Çağlar," my sister said in the end, "Efekan loves me. He's madly in love with me."

It took all my strength to not turn to look at her. "Did he tell you that himself?"

"No. He told Mervenaz and Ecem. He said to them, 'I'm madly in love with Çiğdem.' Then they told me."

"Is that why you pushed him down the stairs?"

Instead of replying, she sighed, and a heavy silence filled the room. After a while she said, "I think I love Efekan."

I turned to her. She was lying there with her hands behind her head, a pleased smile on her face as she looked up at the stars. The seagulls were still screeching.

Four

I was trying to think about other terrible things, other disasters: earth-quakes, floods, erupting volcanoes, plane crashes, genocides, accidents at nuclear power plants, the sinking of oil tankers, the millions of people in the world who have cancer at this very moment, sexually abused children, people stabbed in the heart, people slowly bleeding to death, Alzheimer's patients who can't recognize their own sisters, people who get lost and never find their way home, the dead without graves. I thought, *If I think about those things, Efekan won't come to mind. There are so many other disasters in the world to count through before I get to that bastard Efekan.* But I just couldn't get him out of my mind. That punk, the son of Adnan the curtain maker, was madly in love with my sister, and to make matters worse there was a good chance that he was her first love. Look, I'm an open-minded person. I have accepted the fact that, politically speaking, I tend toward the conservative end of the spectrum. When I calmly evaluate a given situation, I'm quite open minded. Catch me on a good day, and you'll see that I'm even more open minded than most atheists. But my sister was just nine years old. She could have given me more time to prove just how open minded I am. Don't judge me so quickly, try to be fair and empathize. I mean, we're talking about my sister here, Çiğdem İyice. All night I waited by her side, and I swear to you that even as I write these words, my eyes are filling with tears!

The next day I couldn't stand it, and I said to Microbe Cengiz, who happens to be my best friend, "Microbe, I slept so little last night that it would've been better if I hadn't slept at all." He looked at me with his deep, sunken eyes. In all his life, he's never made a pointless comment. Instead of saying, "And then?" he just waits for you to go on talking. I went on. "Efekan told Mervenaz and Ecem that he's madly in love with my sister. Then they told her."

We were in cooking class. Not at school, but in the kitchen of the training hotel. Microbe and I were trying, for the fourth time, to make mayonnaise. I was whisking egg yolks with a high-speed blender, always in the same direction—that's the rule when making mayonnaise. Occasionally, Microbe was adding olive oil to the yolks. We were making mayonnaise for the fourth time because the chef who was teaching the class didn't like the color of our first batch, the consistency of our second, and the taste of our third. He was totally messing with us. That guy was an all-around expert in making people feel bad. We were trying to hurry up and whip up a perfect batch because we were the only ones making mayonnaise.

I don't know if you've ever taken a cooking class, but if you ever do, just remember that if the chef wants to humiliate you, he'll ask you to make mayonnaise. He'll ask everyone else to make something reasonable and then single out you and your best friend and say, "You two make mayonnaise." So everyone puts on their aprons, and for two hours they go about like master chefs slicing and dicing mushrooms, browning onions, grating cheese, and rushing to the oven whipping open the door as if the world's biggest problem were in there. The chef will peer gravely inside like it contained the black box of a plane that crashed, the ship's log of a sunken tanker, the shoes of people buried in the rubble after an earthquake, the identity cards of people washed out to sea in a tsunami, and even that brat Efekan himself, and after closing the oven door, he'll say, "I'll be with you kids in a bit," and then start working on a sauce at the counter next to yours. As everyone else is bustling about, you're the two guys in the back idiotically whisking egg yolks. It doesn't matter if your uncle is the mayor or if the district representative is your friend, even if it is just a matter of pretense. Once the chef has taken a disliking to you, there's nothing to be done. You could be the Son of God and he'd still force you to make mayonnaise. It's quite natural that he set his sights on Microbe and me. You know how it is, it's like when you see two cars parked end to end on an otherwise empty street, and you wonder why they're parked that way; it makes you want to separate them. That's how Microbe Cengiz and I were, two old cars parked bumper to bumper on an empty street.

Microbe was still looking at me as though a silent danger existed somewhere in between us. He's quite famous for his long looks. Those eyes fix on you like they're about to express something extremely critical, and then nothing happens. Then you can't be sure if he was looking at you as if there really was something important to say or nothing at all. Maybe there was, maybe there wasn't. I didn't know. In any case, in that shy voice of his so rarely heard, as if he's always afraid that someone might cut him off, he said to me, "Don't worry, boss. I already talked to Efekan."

"Microbe, you hardly even talk to me. When could you possibly have talked to Efekan?"

"Last year. After you told me that he'd scribbled on Çiğdem's notebook. 'Stay away,' I told him."

"You went up to Efekan and said 'Stay away from Çiğdem'?"

"No, I just said, 'Stay away.' He understood what I meant."

"Okay, but it's been a year since then."

"Don't worry," he said, winking as he added another splash of olive oil to the yolks.

He was holding the tin of olive oil with a napkin, maybe because he was afraid that his hand would get oily. His apron was an immaculate blazing white; there wasn't a single wrinkle or stain. It was cleaner than the apron of a chef who keeps as far away from the preparation of food as possible. Microbe is the cleanest, tidiest, most organized guy I've ever met. The reason he's known as Microbe is that years and years ago, what seems like centuries ago, when we were in eighth grade, some guys were passing around a cigarette in the school bathroom, and he stood there watching them for a while before saying, "You shouldn't do that, you'll catch a microbe." From that day on, he was known as Microbe, but he never seemed offended when people called him that. He struck a philosophical stance. When people tried to make fun of him by calling him "microbe," he'd just smile ever so slightly, and in the end no one could tease him because of his nickname. Everyone started casually calling him Microbe as if it were really his name, and no winds of animosity blew when you called him that. So there we were, that loon and me talking man to man as we tried to get the mayonnaise to the right consistency during our cooking class. You'll never know what it's like to sink to such lows.

"Gözde Hoca asked about you," Microbe said, adding a tablespoon of lemon juice to the egg yolks, which by that time had already soaked up half a cup of oil.

I kept right on whisking because if you want to get the right consistency, you have to keep up a vigorous whisk. Gözde was our literature teacher. She was a young woman, maybe twenty-four or twenty-five, with light green eyes and a cheerful personality. She was soothing to look at, although she was a little bucktoothed. When she smiled, she had this way of looking into your eyes that made her buckteeth seem like a virtue.

"Why did she ask about me?"

"She was wondering why you haven't been coming to class. I said that I didn't know."

"Good work, Microbe."

"She said that you should come to class."

After adding a little more lemon juice, we drizzled in the other half cup of olive oil and kept on whisking. I'd been holding the mixer for so long that my arm was starting to go numb. After we put in all of the oil, Microbe added a teaspoon of salt and vinegar, and of course I kept on whisking. I could tell by the way that the bowl was shaking that it had reached the right consistency. We'd added black pepper to our third batch of mayonnaise, which was the only one that the chef tasted, so I said to Microbe, "That guy's a real gourmet, so let's also add white pepper this time."

We put in a teaspoon each of black and white pepper. After stirring them in, I stopped whisking because that's what you have to do at that point. To get the mayonnaise just the right color, I added a tablespoon of warm water and stirred it for the last time. At last we were done! I tasted it, and it was pretty good.

"Try it," I said, handing Microbe a spoon. He tasted it, and then looked at me for a while. "Well, say something!" I said.

"Not bad."

"Not bad? That's all you have to say? A food engineer from Calve Industries couldn't make it this good."

I scooped the smooth, gleaming mayonnaise from the mixing bowl onto a plate. We'd nailed it this time. I could tell from Microbe's expression that he was thinking the same thing. We could now be proud of ourselves. If you study at the tourism school, you learn how to make really good mayonnaise. If you're wondering why it matters, just make some yourself. If you're so idiotic that you can't go to the store and buy some mayonnaise, for three times the price, you can make it at home. To get the right taste, color, and consistency, you'll go through a carton of eggs and a gallon of olive oil, but that's nothing to be upset about. Maybe you'll be married to a woman who is just as sentimental as you, and she'll fall in love with you as she watches you making mayonnaise.

"Just look," she'll say, "a man who makes everything himself. A man who thinks so profoundly about everything."

At the other end of the kitchen, the chef was tasting some chili-sauce chicken. We told him that the mayonnaise was ready to be tasted. Ten minutes later, he came over. He was one of those people who seem to feel a need to always look unhappy. First, he visually inspected the mayonnaise, and then he picked up the plate and sniffed it. Finally, he dabbed a spoon into the mayonnaise and tasted it. He moved the mayonnaise around in his mouth without swallowing, like he was tasting wine. He knew that it was different from the first three batches we made and that it was a lot better. At last, he swallowed it, and then he sniffed the mayonnaise again. I could tell by the gleam in his eyes that he was trying to find something wrong.

After a long while he said, "Did you add Dijon?"

I whispered, "Microbe, what's Dzone? Isn't that a website or something?"

"He said Dijon, not Dzone."

"Ah," I said. "No sir, we didn't use anything like that."

The chef squinted, gazing at nothing in particular, and rubbed his fingers together in a gesture that suggested money. "A good mayonnaise," he began, "should be just slightly more stringent, ever so slightly sharp. That's why you should add a dab of Dijon mustard." A smile reminiscent of a wall spread across his face, not the kind that brings people closer but the kind that drives them apart. He said "Do it again!" and walked away.

This guy was the head cook at the training hotel, so you couldn't ask, "Why didn't you tell us in the first place that we need to add some fucking Dijon mustard?" He wasn't very open to dialogue, you see, and you couldn't just sit down and talk it over with him. Your only option was to swear up a storm—while whispering, of course.

Chefs are among the cruelest people in the world. If you don't believe me, try working for a day in a hotel kitchen. Let's say you're supposed to be cutting tomatoes into squares, and you cut one that's a bit off on the ninety-degree corners. When you see the expression on the head chef's face, you'll know what I mean before he says a word. Last year, for example, in spite of all the social pressure I was subjected to, I read *The Brothers Karamazov* during the winter break. There was this know-it-all librarian who worked at the Safalı Yılmaz Public Library, and she said to me, "You won't be able to finish that over the winter break. Read *One Hundred Years of Solitude* instead."

"For the love of God, what's *One Hundred Years of Solitude*?" I said to her. "I've been alone for centuries! I'd much rather read Dostoyevsky at this point in my life."

To which she replied, "Çağlar, you won't be able to finish it."

I said, "We'll just see about that, Nermin Teyze!"

I did finish reading it, eager to find out whether it would be Dmitri or Ivan who would eventually wallop their father, Fyodor Pavlovich Karamazov. I was put off by his stepson Smerdyakov, who was working as his cook. Come to think of it, he pissed me off more than anyone else in the book. So after reading a thousand pages, it turned out that I was probably right—as I was separating the egg yolks for the fifth batch of mayonnaise, I got to thinking that Dostoyevsky really was a genius. He knew that cooks are bastards, and it wasn't for nothing that Smerdyakov was sent off to Moscow to study cooking.

As I fiddled with the egg yolks, thinking about the blatant vulgarity of Smerdyakov, suddenly an image of Gözde Hoca appeared in my mind. I just couldn't drive it from my thoughts. Even as I watched Microbe examine the cartons of eggs, the spices, the mixing bowls, and the jar of Dijon mustard he'd found, it seemed like Gözde Hoca was there as well. Of course, it was just an image in my mind, but that image was the true reality. Why had she told Microbe that I should attend her class? Usually, she'd wear sheer stockings and black miniskirts that hung a few inches above her knees, and she'd sit on a chair in front of the blackboard, one leg slung over the other as she read selections from classic writers, trying to get us to offer up commentary. If she was overtaken by the enchantment of the sentences while she read, her legs would spread open too far, and she'd decorously tug her skirt down over her legs. At times like that, I'd think about the misfortunes of life, about desires and absence. What I mean to say is that I'd ponder the greatness of literature, and I don't think that I was far off topic. If Gözde Hoca were my girlfriend, I'd like to sit across from her like that for a few hours each day, in silence. I'd be free to look at her all I wanted. I'd say, "You know, I'm a really lucky guy because I have a girlfriend who really turns me on." Of course, I wouldn't tell her that. If you say things like that to women, they generally leave you. You have to say things like, "You don't really turn me on"; "You should eat less, you're fat" even if she only weighs like a hundred pounds; "I need to be alone for a while, so give me some space"; "You're getting in the way of my ideals, and you have no such right"; or "I can't help it, I miss my mom." If you say things like that, women will fall in love with you. When there's nothing about you that's worthy of being loved, that's how you can experience impossible love.

I turned on the hand mixer and started whisking more egg yolks. The kitchen window, which had iron security bars, faced a yard behind the hotel. When seen from the outside, the sunlight streaming through the window spiraled through the steam billowing from the pots and pans on the stoves, lending an air of mysticism to the kitchen. But when you're inside, it's like the heart of hell. You have to find a middle ground to arrive at an objective judgment of the place.

I suddenly burst into laughter. When Microbe looked at me to see what was going on, I yelled, "I LOVE making mayonnaise!" What I really wanted was for the chef to hear me at the other end of the kitchen. Begüm Işıldar, student #341, heard me and looked up. She was opening an oven right then. She usually sat in the same row as Microbe and me at the front of the classroom and was just before my name on the roll call. Anyway, she looked at me instead of peering into the oven because I had become the most pressing problem in the world. Çağlar İyice, student #342, just loved making mayonnaise. I winked at Begüm and then burst out laughing again. Why? Because if someone, just for the sake of pissing me off, forces me to make mayonnaise for the fifth time when there's really no need other than breaking me down and taking revenge for whatever's oppressing him, I'll shout. That's what I do. I'll do my very best to look like I'm in a good mood, and after a while I really will feel better.

At the top of my voice, I said, "Hey there, buddy, would you mind handing me that jar of Dijon mustard? When I was a kid, my mother would put Dijon mustard on my bread in the morning. Those mornings would have a taste that was, how do I say, just a little stringent and sharp. Ever since then, if I don't have some Dijon mustard in the morning, nothing goes right. I recommend it."

"By all means, I'm going to try it, boss!" Microbe shouted.

FIVE

That day I was feeling pretty good, and I was able to keep up my high spirits until I got home. We left the training hotel, which is near the school, and as we passed the school I asked Microbe if he wanted to play basketball. Classes were over and the place was empty. We went in through the coal slot and got a ball from the gym, and then we headed out to the concrete rec area, where Microbe and I started playing a game of half-court. Making five batches of mayonnaise had put me in fine form. The chef hadn't even tasted our final batch. Apparently, some big wigs at the hotel had summoned him and he said, "Just leave it on the counter. I'll taste it when I get back."

As Microbe and I played basketball, I forgot about everything: the hand mixer, the egg yolks, the consistency of the mayonnaise, Gözde Hoca, the pathetic chef, Efekan. I almost even stopped thinking about my sister. We took off our ties and shirts, and threw ourselves into the game. It didn't matter who was winning. Toward the end, we didn't even bother to follow the rules. It was more like a fight than a basketball game, and whoever got the ball just rushed in for the shot. All that mattered was that we got that orange ball through the netless hoop, and we were having a hell of a good time. Eventually, we wore ourselves out and sat down, leaning up against some ridiculous palm trees that had been planted along the wall of the rec area the year before.

Even though we were completely out of breath, I turned to Microbe and said, "Let's do push-ups until it kills us." That's precisely what we did, eighty, maybe ninety, a million push-ups. Afterward, I lay on my back looking up at the clouds, my heart beating so hard it felt like it was going to leap up into my throat. Microbe took a blue towel out of his bag and started drying off his back and neck. He said that he was sweaty as hell and needed to go home and shower. I was ready to go, too.

Still feeling giddy, I got home only to find my sister sitting on a corner of the L-shaped couch in the middle of the living room looking crestfallen, gloomy, and wounded to her very core. She hugged me, as usual, but it was different. She didn't run up to throw her arms around me. We did our special greeting, but her heart wasn't in it. I noticed that my mom was sitting in a corner of the living room, and I glared at her as if she were the source of all the problems in the world. Anger welled up within me, and there was no way I could hide it. I'll never be able to tame that fury, and at that moment I didn't even want to. Was she the one who had upset my sister?

"We should talk," I said to my mom, my voice trembling.

We went into the bedroom I shared with my sister.

"What happened?" I asked.

"What do you mean?"

"Why is Çiğdem so upset?"

"She wasn't in the preview."

"What preview?"

"The preview for that competition. She wasn't in it."

"They've started airing the preview?"

"Yes."

"But they haven't even selected the competitors yet."

"How should I know?"

I went back into the living room. My sister was watching a dating show, some preposterous program I'd never seen her watch before, the name of which I'd rather not remember. A shriveled-up old guy was sitting on a tall chair on the stage trying to be charming. One of the women in the audience asked, "Why did you get divorced three years ago?" He had a house in Düzce, was retired, and was maybe like 130 years old. So why did he get divorced when he was 127? Great question. When they zoomed in on him for a close-up, I looked carefully at the guy. There were dark blotches on his face, and he had sagging cheeks. He didn't seem to know what to do with his trembling hands. He had lived out his life and been chewed up and spit out, and now he was heading straight for oblivion. "We didn't get along," he said in a squeaky voice that was barely audible. "Why didn't you get along?" Everyone in the audience was staring expectantly at the old man, waiting for his reply, their lips curled into sneers that seemed to say, "You can't fool us! We know what a bastard you are." Flustered, he tried to smile. It made him look all the more helpless. There was no end to it. I glanced at my sister, worried about how she might be feeling. She was sitting with her right arm slung across her stomach, cupping her cheek with her left hand.

"It'll be on in a minute," she said.

"What will?"

She didn't answer. But then the dating show cut to a commercial break, and the first one to come on was about the talent competition. It began with a member of the jury shouting, "Are you reeeeeeaaaaaady?" and then the audience rose to their feet shouting and clapping like mad. They were ready, they could feel it, and they lost their minds in the presence of all that talent. This was the happiest moment of their lives. A sexy girl wearing a miniskirt was just starting a sentimental song, and the camera panned to two women in the audience who were so moved by the music that they could barely hold back their tears. They actually started crying and were so swept away that they didn't even bother to wipe away the makeup streaming down their cheeks. Surely, they regretted that they'd been shouting like madwomen just a few minutes before, as they now saw that life is filled with sorrow and suffering. Then there was a guy breaking bricks with his elbows, and as if that wasn't enough, he started breaking them with his forehead. When he did the head routine, one of the stars on the jury put her hands on her cheeks, staring with openmouthed wonder, her eyes bulging from their sockets. Next was the young kid who had gone onstage before my sister at the university auditorium. In the middle of the song, he suddenly stopped playing, turned his guitar around, placed it to his ear, and hummed, and then started playing it like a *darbuka* drum. Those two women who were bawling just a few minutes before tied their scarves around their hips and started belly dancing. Life actually wasn't full of sorrow; okay, sometimes it is, but that didn't mean they couldn't belly dance. It seemed that they could accept the entirety of life with all its joy and suffering, and they were so wise as they danced. On top of all that, a guy who was as plump as a pig appeared onstage and started reeling off jokes about his own obesity. The audience was falling over themselves laughing, probably thinking, "Being fat is actually cool." As tears squirted from their eyes, I bet they were wishing they weighed four hundred pounds.

The program had it all: sadness, joy, awe. But then our worst fears came true when one of the Michael Jacksons appeared. When we had seen him backstage at the first round, I had guessed that he was about six years old. Now he had one hand on his belt buckle as he gyrated his hips. The audience ate it up, and when he started thrusting as if he were banging someone from behind, one of the men in the jury clapped and shouted, "You go, boy!" They didn't even include a decent moonwalk in the commercial. We were enjoying ourselves as well because we're sick in the head; Michael Jackson had given us all a sound screwing, but we didn't take offense because Michael was an alien. He had to get us pumped up, as that was the only way he could get the energy he needed to go back to space. He was homesick, you see, we knew what it was all about. What would you know!

If we were in a film, I would've grabbed the remote and turned off the TV. But we weren't in a film. Unfortunately, we were just living. I had no idea what to say to my sister. I looked at the Josephine chair in the corner of the living room, at the love seat across from it, at the two seats on either side of the love seat, at the armchair in the other corner of the room, at the beanbag in front of the armchair, at the hundreds of chairs around the dining table. The living room screamed at you to sit down, and that's exactly what we were doing. The dating show came back on, and we kept right on watching it. A woman called from the district of Ümraniye and asked the old guy, if he got married, would it be just he and his new wife living together, or would his children live there, too. When he finally found his tongue, he said that he had a two-story house and that he lived upstairs while his children lived downstairs. A member of the audience stood up and asked, "Okay, but are there separate entrances?" Those people asking questions had probably just been let out of the loony bin as if the doctors there had said, "We've all gone mad, so there's no sense in you staying here any longer."

I went into our bedroom and called my uncle, but he was on the line with someone else. I felt a need to bring some clarity to the situation. They'd said, "We'll call you before the televised performance." So why didn't they call? I decided that the best course of action was to directly call the production company, so I found the number on Google.

Someone picked up right away, not only on the first ring but on the first half of the first ring. Of course, when the phone is answered so fast it makes you hesitate, because you don't know what to say. Then again, even when the phone rings and rings and someone eventually picks up, I'm usually at a loss for words. The ideal time to answer the phone is just after the second ring—it's even better than a perfect opening break in billiards. For example, let's say that there's a girl you like. You call her, and she picks up after the second ring, and you come right out and say, "How about going to the movies tonight at Cinetime? *Fast Five* is playing. After that, we can go to the Palmiye Cafe Bar and grab a drink if you'd like." You don't have to say, "I really like you," or, like a hundred years ago, formally ask her out on a date, or, like a thousand years ago, get caught up in a devious game of unrequited love. If she picks up the phone after the second ring, you just wrap up your business. Even if it rings for a long time before she answers, the deal is done. But if it rings and rings and she never answers, then you better throw in the towel.

Anyways, I asked, "Is this Crapola Productions?" You see, I don't even want to remember the name of the company right now.

The voice of a woman nearing middle age, aggressive at the edges and a little high-pitched, confirmed that I'd called the right place. She seemed to have a stuffy nose. I explained the situation, saying that we'd been waiting for a call that never came, that we'd been told to expect a call before the televised performance, and that we were surprised when we saw the commercial for the show on TV. I spoke politely and saw no need to hide the disappointment in my voice.

"If you didn't get a call, that means your sister didn't make the cut."

"But you were going to let us know. You said that repeatedly."

Making it obvious that the conversation was getting on her nerves, the woman said, "We only call the people who make the cut. We can't call everyone." Her voice was reaching the point of exasperation, as if she alone were bearing the brunt of all the troubles of the world. It was impossible to get anywhere with her.

"There was that woman, the head of production, what was her name? Afşar Hanım. Is she there? I'd like to speak to her."

"She's not in."

"Okay," I said, "but don't you have a list? The least you could do is take another look at it."

"There is no list."

I took a deep breath and looked at the unpainted ash-gray garden wall of the apartment block across the way. Last year, they set up scaffolding, and we watched all spring as they painted the building. It looked great in the end, but no one ever thought to do the garden wall, too.

"Of course there's a list," I said. "Look, you work for a company. Surely there are a few people who aren't mentally challenged and had the bright idea of drawing up a list and said, 'Since we're putting together a show, let's figure out who we're inviting.' So find that list and read the names one by one until you're certain that Çiğdem İyice isn't on it."

"How dare you speak like that! Who do you think you are?"

"Look at the list!"

"No!"

You see, there are basically two types of people who answer phones at companies. The first type is polite, collected, and thick-skinned, and when the person on the other end of the line starts swearing, they just *click!* hang up the phone. The second kind is like the woman I talked to. They don't back away from a fight. If you swear, they start swearing, and if you shout, they start shouting even louder than you because they want their voice to ring through the whole building so that people will notice and see what they're suffering, and after hanging up they'll have a fake nervous breakdown and everyone will gather around, and even though they don't know who it was that called, that person will become their enemy; all the while, our employee will still be having a fit because no one understands her troubles, and so she'll go into the stairwell to have a cigarette; and then there's this guy who works at the same company, and she likes him, but last year gossip was going around that he's gay, which in fact isn't true; and that heterosexual man who is kind, handsome, and quickly rising in the company ranks will bring her a cup of coffee in the stairwell, where they will make plans to have dinner after work, after which they will go to a bar and go from there to our employee's home because repairs are being done at the guy's apartment, and there, in the glow of candlelight, their bodies will be united, but the next day at the office the man will act like nothing happened, and our employee will probably think, *It's better if the people at the company don't know about our relationship* and console herself by saying that it's not the time to bring things into the open; but at lunch she'll find out that the man has a girlfriend, and she'll say that it's good that he has a girlfriend; that is, if she's a good girlfriend, but they're about to get engaged, and our employee's heart breaks—*snip-snap*, she can even hear the sound of her heart breaking, the sound echoes in her ears for a long, long time, and she's afraid that if she starts to cry, she'll keep crying forever, but that's not her only fear, she's also afraid that if she starts to laugh she'll go shrieking mad, and while one part of her wants to quietly and composedly accept the situation another part of her wants to make a scene and so she's poised on a dangerous threshold, on the verge of a second nervous breakdown, a real one this time, and at that moment the phone rings so she snaps it up and it's me, Çağlar İyice, wondering what the situation is regarding his talented sister.

"I know why you won't look at the list," I said.

With that, she fell silent. For a while, I listened to that pregnant silence with my eyes closed, savoring every moment.

"It wouldn't take you thirty seconds to look at the list but you won't do it," I said. "Why? Because rather than taking thirty seconds to look at it, you'd rather argue with me for thirty minutes. Think about it for a second, and you'll understand what's going on here. Let me tell you, honey, we're all on the same side: you, me, my sister. We're worn out by impatience. We are those people who wait and wait for phone calls that never come. We're on the side of all those women who wait for a phone call the day after a wonderful night."

At that moment, I saw a cat turn the corner and start coming down the street with a pigeon in its mouth. It had sunk its teeth into the pigeon's neck, which was dripping blood, and the head of the bird swung ever so gently. It was the first time I'd ever seen anything like it. What was going on? Was this the wilds of Africa or what? The cat slipped under an Opel Corsa parked across from our apartment building. A couple of kids rushed up the street, asking each other, "Where is it? Where is it?" I said into the phone, "Hang on a second. Just so you know, I'm not done yet."

I opened the window and shouted down to the kids, "It's under the Opel."

When I picked up the phone, the line was dead. Maybe she hung up and started crying. I don't know. The kids leaned down by the car and flushed out the cat, and it ran off with the pigeon still in its mouth. When it leaped onto the unpainted wall of the apartment block next door, the cat dropped the pigeon and sat on top of the wall for a moment, looking down at the bird. When the kids came running up, the cat dashed away. One of the kids started poking the pigeon with a stick.

"Hey, what's going on?" I said.

"Çağlar Ağbi, it's nothing," one of the kids said. "We shot a bird and the cat ran off with it."

"You shot a bird? What the hell were you thinking? These aren't hunting grounds! Fuck off and go up to Hasanbaba if you're going to run around shooting things. I don't want to see you doing anything like that around here again!"

"Okay, Çağlar Ağbi. It was just for fun."

"What the hell, 'just for fun'? You don't shoot pigeons just for fun. If you're going to shoot something, shoot a damn seagull!"

Shouting at that pack of kids drained what little energy I had left. I leaned my elbow against the window frame made of fake plastic wood grain and rested my forehead in the palm of my hand. I was exhausted.

Sometimes around dusk, my late grandpa would get the urge for a drink, and with trembling hands he'd have a nip from a bottle on the balcony of our old apartment. In those days, he was still in the habit of saying, "Çağlar, I'm tired, boy. I'm tired of the spectacles of this splendorous world. I'm tired of the faces of all those generations of liars." I'd say, "Me, too, grandpa. I'm tired, too." When I said that, my grandpa would put his hands on his massive belly and chuckle, and then stroke my head. His eyes were a deep, soft blue. His eyebrows, just like his hair, were thick and gray. On evenings when I'm feeling tired, when the sun is going down and the shadows are growing longer and longer, when a bitterness wells up within me, when the person I call is on the phone with someone else, as usually happens, my grandpa comes to mind. I look out the window at the street below, half-lost in thought, and then I look some more, and then some more still; I look and look at the street until I see a dead pigeon.

Six

Fast and furious, I walked to the Kıyıdere mayor's office. As I was turning the corner, İrfan Amca, the owner of İlgi Stationery Shop, called out, "Çağlar, where are you running off to? Sit down, let's have a glass of tea." With a sharp wave, like I was trying to brush away a mad fly trying to get into my ear, I replied, "Another time, İrfan Amca, another time," and I kept on walking. I really liked that guy. On holidays, he never sent mass text messages. As I walked along thinking stuff like, *Was I rude to İrfan Amca? Was that unkind? Did he get the wrong idea?* my irritation with my uncle hit new peaks. I went straight up Yalı Street and into the municipal building, greeting a few relatives who, until recently, had done nothing but loaf around until my uncle gave them jobs. Now some of them were security guards and others were sitting at information desks trying to look serious as they did nothing at all. Leaping up the stairs two and three at a time, I went up to my uncle's office, but he wasn't there, which wasn't really a surprise because I'd never seen him in his office. I'm going to tell you something you may not believe, but even when he reads the Sunday paper he paces around the living room. Because he's always dashing about here and there, supposedly on the job 24/7, people think that he's hard at work. But the thing is, even if he weren't mayor, that twerp would still be rushing around. When he was a real estate agent, he was the same way. For example, when he pulled in a commission for a job and took me to Çınarcık, he'd park his old Renault Broadway at the entrance, and we'd walk all the way from the port to the pier. Blinded by the sun, we'd proceed along the colorless sidewalk that ran along the shore road, which was paved with tiny, sorrowful stones as if we were slaloming among the dusty trees. Because I was so small, I had a hard time keeping up with my uncle, and I practically had to run along beside him. Of course, he was thoughtless then as well, and he wouldn't notice that I couldn't keep up, but still we were happy. Those were innocent times, and we didn't feel a need to question everything. In any case, that's how I remember them.

Panting for breath, I said to my uncle's personal secretary—she was also a relative of mine, my grandpa's stepbrother's daughter—"Bilge Abla, where's my uncle?"

"At the creek," she said. "The pylons for the bridge arrived, so he went to take a look at the installation."

"Which bridge?"

"Don't you know?"

"No, I don't."

How would I know? I didn't know about anything that was going on in the world. I'd been assigned the task of examining all that happened and offering up an interpretation, but I hadn't even started living my own life yet. Bilge Abla muttered a few things about the bridge, but I didn't have the time to stay and listen. "I'll see it when I get there," I said as I left. I went down to the shoreline near the stream, and when I turned the corner by the post office, I saw my uncle in the distance. He was wearing an orange hard hat. "Hey," he shouted when he saw me. "Come on over." With his right arm, he hugged me around the shoulder, and then, putting me in a half headlock, he pretended he was punching me in the stomach. "You're the man," he said. "By the way, I was looking for you."

Breaking free, I pushed him in the chest. "Would you keep still for a second? What the fuck do you think you're doing? My sister's at home depressed as hell, and you're out here shooting the shit."

"That's why I was looking for you. I've taken care of it."

"Taken care of it! What the hell are you talking about? They're already airing the commercials, and my sister's not in them. I called the production company, and they wouldn't give me the time of day. You're getting my sister's hopes up for nothing and just making everything worse."

Just then, I noticed that a massive crane about fifteen steps away had started lowering a large steel frame across the creek. Workers under the frame were guiding it down with cables, and a guy with my uncle, probably the foreman, was talking to the crane operator by walkie-talkie. A group of about twenty curious onlookers had gathered on the other side of the creek. I knew some of them. They were Kıyıdere locals who liked to hang around watching construction work. Whenever they saw something going on, they stood there with their hands behind their backs, watching. It didn't even have to be construction. It could be some digging, landscaping, the installation of sprinklers on a median. It didn't matter, they'd just stand there and watch for hours. Even some small repairs would do. If you grabbed a hammer and started pounding a nail into the wall of your balcony, they'd stop and wouldn't budge an inch until you'd hammered that nail all the way in.

This time, it was the frame being lowered down by the crane, and they watched carefully, trying not to miss a single detail of the process. For them, it was a visual feast. When the frame got closer to the foundation, the workers, who were wearing thick gloves, started pulling the cables toward them, their faces turning red from the strain. Everything was covered in dust. Whenever the crane turned, it would beep like a dump truck's backing-up warning. *Beep-beep-beep-beep.*

"All day long, I've been working on this business about the program," my uncle shouted. "I know everything now."

"How do you know what's going on?"

"Your mom told me this afternoon that Çiğdem wasn't in the preview. So I called Afşar Hanım a few times, but she didn't get back to me."

"What, did you send her some messages on WhatsApp?"

"What?"

"Did you message her on WhatsApp or something?"

"Don't be ridiculous!"

"Then why didn't she notice when you called?"

"I don't know."

"I called the production company. They said there was nothing they could do."

"That's what they say to everyone. So I called Asshole Bey," he said. Right now, I'd rather not remember the name of this particular gentleman, who happens to be the district representative. My uncle went on. "I said, 'Asshole Bey, Mr. Representative, this is the situation, and they said that they'd call but then they went off and prepared the commercial without getting in touch with our little pumpkin, Çiğdem.' 'All right, Altan,' he said, 'I'm going to call them right now. Your niece is my niece. No one would dare hurt the feelings of our niece.' He called the channel directly and then called me back. He said, 'Don't worry, I've taken care of it.' They're going to call us in a few days. It's all under control."

"Are you sure?"

"Absolutely. I called Çiğdem and said, 'Don't get yourself down. Just keep on practicing.' The production company is a sham. It's the channel that's going to air the show, and they make the final decisions."

"How do you know? Maybe the channel doesn't want my sister on the show."

"Don't worry about that. We pull the strings with the channel."

"Who's 'we'?"

The steel frame was slowly getting closer and closer to the foundation. It was only about a meter away, and after a few failed attempts, it finally thudded into place. The workers removed the cables from the frame and gave the foreman a thumbs-up. The foreman spoke into the walkie-talkie: "All right, thanks everyone. Let's move on to the next job." Just behind the bridge was First Lieutenant Necati Karapınar Park, and lying on the grass were two huge white plastic half circles. The workers started lashing cables to them.

In case you don't know, a creek runs through the middle of Kıyıdere and empties into the sea. Out of habit, the old folks still call it Turd Creek, but years ago my grandpa figured out what the problem was and cleaned it up, so to be honest I've never seen it in its turdy state. Two bridges cross the creek. One is over by the post office, and it leads to the shore road, and the other one crosses over onto Fetih Street.

My uncle had taken off his hard hat and put his sunglasses on.

I asked him, "What good is this bridge going to do? There's already a bridge just fifty yards over there by the post office."

"This is a pedestrian bridge."

"People can walk across the other bridge, too."

"I'm going to open the shore road to cars."

I couldn't help but smile when he said that. I was going to give him a piece of my mind, but I held my tongue. If you're not familiar with Kıyıdere, let me explain. Imagine a town by the sea with a population of about a hundred, and the only place to walk around is the shore road. Now, let's have the weather warm up and ninety-nine of those hundred people walking up and down that narrow road in slow motion. They have no other entertainment. Let's say that their only purpose in life is slowly walking up and down that road, always in the same order, and that gives them a sense of contentment and peace. Let's say that by plodding serenely up and down that shore road they've come to understand the meaning of life, I mean, why we're really on this planet and a few other basic issues. Given this situation, naturally there's not enough room to swing a cat when the people crowd onto that road.

"You go ahead and open that road," I said, flashing him a gesture that said he'd be screwed if he did.

Laughing, he slapped the back of my head and said, "Don't worry, I'm not going to open it to everyone. It'll be a toll road. People will have to get a municipal tag to drive down it."

He was grinning at me like someone who is about to succeed in pulling off a major feat and who wanted me to join in the excitement. I saw my reflection in his sunglasses, and I looked anything but excited. I was fed up with uncertainty and the constant battering of my hopes. Time had become a toothache, and with every passing moment it throbbed, reminding me of its existence. If the situation seemed so dire to me, I couldn't imagine how my sister felt.

"Is my sister really going to be in the competition?"

"Yes."

"Swear on it."

"It's guaranteed."

Leaving my uncle to his whims, I started walking toward the post office. I'd gone to see him with the intention of starting a fight but left filled with hope. I had that blurred state of mind that occurs when you switch from one mentality to another. I propped my elbows on the railing of the bridge and started watching the cars going up and down Fetih Street. A blue public minibus was slowly approaching on the right side of the road, driving halfway on the shoulder. There was a sticker on the windshield that read "Butterfly Meadow State Housing Development." Standing on the side of the road, there was a plump elderly woman with sacks of groceries at her feet. She didn't even have to gesture for the minibus to stop. A middle-aged man emerged from the minibus and hauled up the sacks of groceries, and then he took the woman's hand to help her get on. The old woman, however, wasn't able to make it up to the first step. The driver set the emergency brake and got out, along with two other passengers. Holding the woman under the armpits, they tried to lift her up the step but couldn't manage. Finally, with the help of people pulling her up from the inside and others pushing from the outside, they got her onto the minibus. Before settling in behind the wheel, the driver noticed that something was wrong with the door. He slammed it with the palm of his hand and then stepped back to look at it. The passengers who had gotten off the minibus to help the old woman stood there with the driver, looking at the door. There was obviously something seriously wrong. They talked about something, and then the driver hit the door again. Apparently, that didn't solve the problem because one of the passengers hit the door again in the same spot. More discussions followed, and then two more passengers got off the minibus to inspect the door, which prompted further deliberations. In the end, the driver got back behind the wheel and the passengers all got back on board. The driver adjusted the rearview mirror, and after looking back over his shoulder to make sure that what he saw in the mirror coincided with the real world, he started the engine and shifted into first gear. The minibus slowly moved off along the shoulder of the road, never going faster than ten miles an hour.

I decided to go to Palmiye Cafe Bar to shrug off the weariness and stress of the day. I called our home phone to tell my sister that I'd be late and to ask her if she wanted me to bring her anything. She asked for some Haribo gummy bears. "Okay, sweetie," I said, and before hanging up I reminded her that I loved her more than anything else in the world. As I passed by Tadım Café, I saw Dr. İhsan and his wife eating ice cream. I went over to shake his hand.

"How are you, Doctor?"

"I'm doing well, Çağlar, how are you?"

"Couldn't be better."

"How is Çiğdem? She's still dancing, isn't she?"

"Yes she is, Doctor."

"Great. That's really great. She really must keep on dancing."

"Of course, Doctor. Dancing has become a lifestyle for her."

Bidding the doctor and his wife good day, I continued on my way. There was no one in the Palmiye Cafe Bar when I walked in, so I went into the kitchen. Erol was standing at the sink washing dishes. He didn't see me at first, so I stood there waiting for him to notice me. After turning off the tap, he dried his hands and looked up.

"Hi, Çağlar," he said. "It's good to see you."

"How's it going?"

"The usual. How about you?"

"Give me a big draft beer."

"You want a Bomonti? We've got that now."

"I don't go for that trendy stuff! Screw that diet crap. Give me a draft beer, and keep them coming." As I left the kitchen, I muttered, "What's the world coming to?"

"What are you so worked up about?"

"Erol, that's all British foolishness," I said. "Malt beer is a British fad. We should go back to the German school of beer."

The Palmiye Cafe Bar was a nice place with a sea view. I decided to sit at a partly secluded table facing the shore road. The year before, Efes had given the cafe some tables and chairs as part of a promotional deal, and they were cordoned off from the sidewalk by a blue fence. The wind blowing in from the sea was heavy with the bitter scent of seaweed. Chinese lanterns were hung above the tables. In the blue glow of dusk, they cast a yellow light, and those colors whisked away your fatigue.

Erol was limping toward my table, his right hand dangling by his thigh, a beer and coaster in his other hand. It was a small miracle that he didn't spill the beer with that gait. First he put the coaster on the table, and as he was setting down the beer he said, "That uncle of yours is quite a man. He's putting a bridge up over the creek."

I sipped the froth off the top of the beer as if biting into it and said, "In our family, my uncle is the most mediocre man of his generation. He's just power-hungry; that's why he's where he is now. If anyone else in our family from his generation had political ambitions, they would've become deputy prime minister. They wouldn't have fooled around with being mayor. One of my relatives brought down the government of Albania."

"Who?"

"My grandpa's stepbrother. But forget about that and bring me a double order of fries."

"You got it."

"Actually, make that a triple."

"What the hell do you mean, a triple?"

"A portion for three, you fool."

Even though he wouldn't join me in this feast of fries, I decided to invite Microbe over. It would be good to have him around. I sent him a text: I'm at Palmiye. Burn rubber. You see, I'm not a nihilist—I don't like drinking alone.

Taking a big gulp of beer, I looked around at the dusty bar, the empty tables, the deep blue of the water. A small fishing boat was puttering out to sea. I felt odd. A sense of relief and a strange feeling of melancholy had fallen over me. In the center of my chest I could feel it, but it didn't make any sense. While it seemed like everything was going to be okay, I knew that unsettling feeling of sadness would keep me in its grips. The heaviness I felt in my chest wasn't going anywhere. It was as if I had fallen in love with someone who didn't exist. I grabbed my beer and got up, heading toward the kitchen. Propping an elbow on the old restaurant refrigerator, which must've been like 150 years old, I looked at the sooty ceiling and the stove and ventilation hood blackened over the years with dirty oil. Erol was tossing the potatoes he'd peeled into a plastic bowl filled with water. Knife in hand, he turned to me and said with a smile, "What's Cengiz up to?"

"He'll be coming here in a little bit." I took a sip of beer. "So Erol," I said, "last year there were some wooden chairs here. What happened to them?"

"Wooden chairs? What made you think about that?"

"Nothing, just asking."

"A lumberman from Taşköprü probably took them."

"What's a lumberman going to do with chairs?"

"Chop them up and sell them to a baker who has a wood-burning stove."

I opened the refrigerator and looked inside. There were white platters of cheese, fried eggplant, spiced chopped tomatoes, yogurt with dill, and other things I didn't recognize, all covered with plastic wrap. I closed the refrigerator door. With the back of his knife, Erol was scraping wedges of potato into a pot on the stove, and the sound of sizzling filled the kitchen. With the back of my finger, I wiped away the condensation that had formed on my glass.

"Did he sell the chairs?"

"What?"

"Did the lumberman sell the chairs to a bakery?"

"Çağlar, how would I know?"

"If only we'd eaten the bread that was made by burning those chairs."

"Çağlar, you're really a piece of work!"

I stepped outside and breathed in the evening air, sucking it in deep as if something had been burnt but left behind a pleasant scent. The devil was saying, "Fall in love with someone unfaithful in that sweet air and then cross your arms and stand aside, watching with a grin as your life goes to shit."

"At least those Chinese lanterns are still here," I said.

"We're going to take them down," Erol said from inside. "Bomonti is going to give us an illuminated sign."

I went back to my corner in the kitchen and took a long pull from my beer, my nose deep in the glass. I looked at Erol, trying to appear serious. He was taking the fries out of the pot with a pair of tongs.

"Ketchup, mayonnaise?" he asked.

"Ketchup."

I went back to my table. In the meantime, Namık Ağbi from Advantage Real Estate had shown up and sat at one of the tables facing the sea. When he saw me, he said, "Hey, Çağlar. I didn't know you were here."

"You didn't see me."

"That's how it goes. So, I heard that your uncle is going to open up the shore road to traffic."

"It's too early to say. They're still in the planning stage."

"What happened with the fifth plot?"

That business with the fifth plot was another matter altogether. It's been going on for a year now. Ever since our town of Kıyıdere was founded, in the early days of the Neolithic era, it had been known as a holiday retreat. But then, of course, when the sea became as filthy as dishwater, people stopped coming for vacation. The holiday villages built in the town's heyday started falling into disrepair. After the earthquake, they really went to ruin. With a few exceptions, they're all ghost towns, and now they're just rented out on the cheap to people who come to work on the road or do other odd jobs. After tourism dried up, some people started saying that the best thing to do would be to build a thermal spa resort. You see, there are hot springs here and there around Kıyıdere. So some people approached my uncle and said, "Find a bit of public land where we can build a hotel. Let's use those connections in Ankara and get the ball rolling." So my uncle went poking around and found a plot of land on Samanlık Road, which the directorate of agriculture had somehow forgotten about. Five plots of public property, to be precise. The guys in Ankara wrapped up the deal, and a construction company stepped in, signing on for a forty-nine-year contract. Everything was in order, so-and-so financiers were committed and all ready to go. The only thing left to do was lay the foundations. Then Baba Sadi Hoca showed up at the mayor's office one day and said to my uncle, "You prick! I'm going to kill you and then fuck your damn dead corpse!"

To which my uncle replied, "Now calm down, Sadi Hoca, and put down the gun. Look, my nephew is here. We don't want any accidents to happen. So tell me, what's going on? Why are you so upset?"

"You slimy prick, whose land are you planning to use to build a hotel?"

So my uncle called my mom, and she looked into the land registry records and found out that four of the plots belonged to the directorate of agriculture, but the fifth one was owned by Baba Sadi Hoca, who inherited the land from his grandfather. The deed was old and didn't appear in the new registry system. Baba Sadi Hoca was our science teacher at a tutoring school we went to before taking the high school entrance exam. Back in the day, he had also been my uncle's teacher, but he retired and started working at the tutoring school. I'll never forget the day when a pretty big earthquake happened. We were all petrified, but this old guy, this pure-hearted lunatic, just got irritated and started shouting, "Who the hell is shaking the desks?"

"That business should be wrapped up any day now," I said.

Namık Ağbi from the Advantage Real Estate office looked at me, his tiny eyes rolling around in their sockets like the balls of a tilt board. "Seems that Sadi Hoca is saying he won't sell the land."

"That's what he was saying, but my uncle convinced him to sell it."

"He'd been going on that he wanted ten percent of the profits, but big companies like that never pay out profits. They increased their offer, but when they saw that he wasn't backing down they threatened him. That's what I heard through the grapevine."

"Who threatened him?"

"Dickhead Bey's men."

Dickhead Bey, whose name I'd rather not remember, is the owner of Fucknut Construction and the son-in-law of Asshole Bey, our regional representative. We live in a fucked-up screwy country. But if you say that, people will say, "Çağlar İyice, what a disgrace, please don't talk like that about our country. Our image has been tarnished, and they won't even give us the Olympics."

"My uncle wouldn't let a thing like that happen," I said. That's really what I thought, at least back then, because in those days I didn't know what a bastard my uncle is. But still, while he might try to get his paws on public land, he respects private property. That's why one day he gave me a long earful when I swiped my friend's 0.7 Rotring pencil during my primary school days. But it wasn't just that he chided me; he was so upset that his entire world was shaken. That stayed with me in the form of an odd feeling, as if I had committed the gravest of crimes. Never again did I swipe anyone's pen, and after that day I was even embarrassed about asking my classmates for pencil lead.

One of the reasons that I stood up for my uncle that night was because I knew Namık Ağbi of Advantage Real Estate was even more of a slimy lout than my uncle. For years he plastered over the cracks of buildings damaged in earthquakes, paid off engineers and inspectors to get clean structural certificates, sold the buildings cheap, and made off with fat commissions. But when the guys in Ankara said they were going to tear down every single building that supposedly isn't earthquake-proof and then go through the state housing authority to use their own contractors for the new buildings, his game was up. In general, bad people are the first to catch on to the evils committed by others. When they don't have the opportunity to commit their own evils, they weigh in with the heaviest judgments when other people do. I can't speak ill of others with people like Namık Ağbi of Advantage Real Estate. But if Erol asked, I'd bad-mouth my uncle to no end. Erol's a straightforward guy, he leads a plain life, thinks simple thoughts, doesn't gossip. You see, out of principle I don't speak ill about a bad person with another bad person.

Erol came out with my order and I sat down at my table, cutting off the conversation with Mr. Advantage Real Estate so I could focus on my fries. Just then, Microbe showed up, and we settled in with our electronic cigarettes and moved on to an evaluation of the day.

At one point, I looked up and saw T. C. Sinem Uzun approaching the Palmiye Cafe Bar from the shore road. When she was about fifteen yards away, she saw us and smiled. If beauty were defined in purely physical terms, I'd say she's an easy ten, a bombshell even. But in terms of personality, she'd score a clean zero. She'd taken a picture using CamWow with an ugly friend of hers and put it up as her profile picture on Facebook. But just to make it clear that she wasn't the ugly girl, she put a selfie she'd taken in her mirror on her wall, which showed plenty of cleavage. I'll let you imagine the rest.

"How are you, Çağlar?" she asked.

"I'm great," I said. After a pause, I added, "Why do you ask?"

"So," she said, "we're not going to ask each other how we are anymore? I was just asking, that's all."

"If you were just asking, then here you go: I'm great!"

"Did I say something? Why are you so upset?"

"I'm not upset," I said. "What gives you that idea?"

Smiling in an attempt to defuse the tension in the air, she turned to Microbe and asked, "Hi, Cengiz, how are you?"

But instead of answering, he just looked at me with a dumbfounded expression as though giving me power of attorney to speak on his behalf, eager to see how I'd reply. I think that Microbe was quite charming as he sat there like that, but then again I'm his best friend so I may not be able to give the most objective opinion.

"Hey, Sinem! Sinem, how are you?" shouted Advantage Real Estate's Namık Ağbi.

"I'm good, Namık Amca, how are you?"

"I'm fine. Why haven't you been coming around to study with Beril?"

"We have study time at the tutoring school."

"Still, nothing beats studying at home. Come on over sometime."

"Sure, Namık Amca, I'll come by." As she turned back to me, a puff of exasperation escaped from between the red-rouged lips of her small mouth. "So Çağlar, I heard that your sister's going to be on the talent show."

"Yes."

"But I didn't see her in the commercial."

"You will soon enough. Sit down, I'll buy you a beer."

"Thanks, but I'm going to the old Bankers' Clubhouse." Then, after a pregnant pause, she added, "My friends are waiting for me."

Rather than ask who those friends might be, I took a drag on my electronic cigarette and exhaled a puff of steam into the air.

"They serve you beer here?" she asked.

"We were the ones who issued the owner a liquor license. We got one from the mayor's office, and Microbe and I nailed it to the wall ourselves."

"That explains why you haven't been going to the old Bankers' Clubhouse."

"I haven't set foot in that place in six months," I said. "I'll never go there again."

"Nice shirt," she said.

"Thanks," I said.

My uncle had this black denim shirt that was like fifteen or twenty years old. I cut off the sleeves, thinking I'd wear it when the weather warmed up. Of course, I was careful to make sure there were some dangling threads because it wouldn't mean anything if you couldn't tell that the sleeves had been cut off. I thought that it would look pretty good worn over a T-shirt. The first person I showed it to was Microbe. He'd told me it was a bit flashy. I trust his taste.

Without bothering to say "See you," T. C. Sinem Uzun started walking back down the shore road. I watched as she walked away and noticed that she was wearing jeans that were so tight that, forget about however she managed to get them on, at the end of the night when it came time to take them off, she'd have to hook a rope to the cuffs and have a friend pull them off with a tow truck. As I turned around, I saw that Advantage Real Estate's Namık Amca was also watching T. C. Sinem Uzun as she walked away. When he realized I'd caught him in the act, he looked away, the sly weasel.

When Microbe and I met each other's eyes, we smiled heavyheartedly and clinked our beer glasses. Then we sat in silence, listening to the regular pounding of waves against the shore. I balled my hand into a fist and sighed deeply.

"Boss, don't go there," Microbe said.

SEVEN

My ex-girlfriend looked like Trinity in *The Matrix*. Soften the severe lines of Trinity's features a little, make her femininity a little more childish, imagine that her straight black hair is actually wavy brown, make her eyes dark brown instead of blue, and picture her as the kind of person who wouldn't pick up a gun to save her life. That's her. Okay, she doesn't really look like Trinity in the end, but it's a useful starting point. It's like when you give someone directions—you have to start at the most basic point. For example, if I had to describe my sister to you, I'd start by comparing her to Uma Thurman in *Kill Bill*, especially her expression as she's about to draw her samurai sword from the scabbard on her back.

Last summer when I ran out of money, I started working at the old Bankers' Clubhouse because of certain idealistic desires prompted by some family issues we were having at the time. That's where I met my ex-girlfriend. The old Bankers' Clubhouse had fittingly been called the Bankers' Clubhouse in the past, but the bankers moved on and the name changed. The name of the new place was the Meltem Cafe Bar, but everyone referred to it as the old Bankers' Clubhouse. There were two sections in the clubhouse. The side that faced the shore road was more like a coffeehouse. There were four types of people who went there. The first were the ones who tirelessly played rummy all day long, and the second were the ones who watched them play and took sides as the games proceeded. The third type of people were the kind that would try to get others' attention by suddenly slapping the table as hands were being dealt. Then there were the ones who didn't do anything; they didn't join card games, watch TV, read newspapers, order tea, or speak to anyone unless asked a question. For hours, they would sit doing absolutely nothing, not even smoking cigarettes. The more I looked at them, the more bored I got. I'd get to thinking. *Çağlar, have you ever wondered how these people got this power of doing absolutely nothing? How can they live as if there were no world out there, as if they don't have a single need in the world?* I wouldn't answer myself, but a discomforting silence would well up within me.

The old Bankers' Clubhouse also had a rear garden. In the evenings on the weekends Anıl, the nephew of our boss, would sit down with his guitar under the acacia trees, which we'd strung up with lights and speakers, and play music. After each song he'd carefully shuffle through the notes on his music stand and then start playing again. He wasn't too bad, actually. He'd attended a few classical guitar classes, so he mostly played classical pieces. Obviously, he was aware of his limited skills, but he did his best, and he had developed his own particular style. I respected that. No one, however, appreciated his efforts. People would insist that he sing popular songs, and he would grudgingly comply.

It was on one of those nights that I'd noticed my ex-girlfriend. She was sitting with T. C. Sinem Uzun and two chumps from the science school who were talking loudly and breaking out in laughter as if trying to prove how much fun they were having. They'd discovered a "crazy" TV show and over the course of three days watched the first two seasons. The show was so damn good that if you were watching anything else, you were a complete knob. Anyway, from the bits and pieces I picked up, that was the kind of banal conversation going on at their table.

As I said, this was the first time I'd really noticed my ex-girlfriend. She was sitting there watching those chumps loudly prattling on as if she had other troubles in a faraway place. Even from a distance, I was entranced by her eyes, which pulled in and reflected all the lights around her. It occurred to me that we knew each other when we were kids. She didn't remember me, but that was okay. The story of how we first met was a bit unfortunate. But what can you do? Sometimes it happens that way, one day you fall in love with someone you've known for a long time. Let me tell you, my friend, those kinds of things happen all the time. Anyway, there were a few acacia and pine trees in the garden, which cast an impression of a calm, quiet place far from the world's troubles, as if an agreement had been drawn up saying that after doomsday the handful of people still alive would gather there. Everything was purer there, a little more enchanting.

Who knows how the idea occurred to them, but at one point they asked Anıl to play a song. Anıl's repertoire, especially when it came to requests, was lamentable. Taking a sip from a glass of cherry juice, he said, "I can play it, but I don't know all the words." Because he didn't drink alcohol, we would set a glass of iced cherry juice on a side table so that people would think he was drinking a vodka-cherry. That twit T. C. Sinem Uzun started insisting that my ex-girlfriend sing, and then the others in the group started pressuring her. When my ex-girlfriend finally gave in and took to the stage, I was busy getting drinks because the people sitting at tables four and five, which we'd pushed together, had ordered eight shots of Jägermeister.

I don't want to tell you the name of the song right now, but imagine a slow version of your favorite regional pop song, something at least fifteen or twenty years old that has held up over time. My ex-girlfriend started singing in a hoarse voice, not giving much hope to the people listening, as though at any moment she might forget the words, sing off key, or run off the stage in tears. But as the song progressed, matters improved. It was more like she was carrying the song rather than just singing it. Bowed under its weight, she took a deep breath and went on singing, as if it were the one and only thing binding her to life. Despite that she wasn't trying to be the star of the stage and not once did she get ahead of the song, but if she did, it was because the song couldn't be sung any other way.

Her voice was tense, somewhat childish, and a bit unsteady during the high notes. Still, it was a voice that didn't shy from becoming emotional when the time was right and smiled at you even during the song's most bitter moments. She sang of the puddles that gather by the sidewalk after a heavy rain, wet park benches, street dogs shaking their coats dry in the middle of the street, the moist darkness of apartment ventilation shafts, and plants sprouting in abandoned telephone booths. Her voice tapped into all the troubles that have befallen us, and that's why her voice unexpectedly broke your heart. But even as it broke your heart, there was something in her voice that consoled you. She sang the song in such a way that it became a challenge rising up, a traffic accident, an ambulance howling in the night. As I lost myself in the depths of the music, a strange feeling came over me, as if that very moment had come crashing down, piling past moments ahead and driving them away, itself driven away by future moments. I felt that perhaps everything would be forgiven.

When the song drew to a close, I was so stunned that it didn't even occur to me to applaud. I drank down two of the Jägermeisters that I'd poured, despite my principles about drinking on the job and the fact that I think it tastes like crap.

The chumps from the science school immediately started clapping like baboons. Not because they were impressed by my ex-girlfriend, who after my sister is the greatest talent I've ever seen, but because that's what they'd planned on doing anyways. Showered with applause, my ex-girlfriend squinted out of a slight sense of embarrassment and smiled ever so slightly. It was obvious that she had no need for admiration. That's a quality of virtuosos, a matter of temperament. You're born with it, and it can't be imitated.

I turned to Microbe and said, "Hey, what's that girl been drinking?" Naturally, Microbe was working there, too. He'd started working as a waiter three days after me so that we could jointly endure the sufferings of ideals that had left us penniless. Without even checking the bill he said, "Lemon sparkling water." "Are you sure?" I asked. You have to be a saint to be able to pull off miracles like that while sober. Microbe didn't reply. When Microbe doesn't reply, that means the first thing he said was true. If he doesn't say anything at first, then it's okay to press him for more information. But he had been taking care of that table so he knew better than me what they'd ordered.

The cafe was licensed to stay open until one o'clock in the morning, but because the owner had friends at the police station they could stay open until two or three on the weekends without any problems. Microbe and I were of the opinion that after each and every working day we deserved a long vacation. You see, we were the two waiters who took care of the customers in the garden, and the tables were always packed.

A few years earlier the chairs in the garden had been stolen, so at the end of the night we had to chain them all together and lock them up. After turning off the lights, we grabbed two bottles of Efes Pilsner and sat down on the stairs facing the garden. It had been a pleasant summer night and the scent of pine hung in the air. The garden of the old Bankers' Clubhouse is one of the few places in Kıyıdere where you feel that you can really stop and take a breath. Maybe it's the only place like that. The wind was starting to blow, making the leaves on the intertwined branches of the acacia trees rustle, giving the impression that it was raining.

"Çisem," Microbe said.

Two hours earlier, I'd declared to Microbe that I might have been in love with this singing girl. I'd asked him to learn her name. I took a long pull on my beer; it was so cold it made my teeth ache. As I sat there looking at the chairs bound tightly together with the chain, I felt like I was bound together with Çisem in the same way, even though I had forgotten her name after all those years.

But enough of that, I don't want to talk about my ex-girlfriend right now. In any case, this is the story of my sister. If I hadn't been part of one of the major peripheral roles, and in that way if certain events during those stormy days hadn't directly affected my sister, I wouldn't have bothered even mentioning my ex-girlfriend. And maybe I'll go over this in the future and decide that my ex-girlfriend really doesn't have much to do with this story, and then copy those parts into a different file, which I'll name "Class Notes 3, Front Desk Management" so that no one will be tempted to read it. But if you're reading this now, it means that I didn't take my ex-girlfriend out of the story. It means that some memories are still sizzling inside me like water dribbled onto a searing-hot pan. If I don't write about those memories, it means that I feel like those sizzles of pain tormenting me now will continue to do so for the rest of my life. It means that I hope God won't afflict anyone else with such pain! Hallelujah!

On Saturday, May 25, the day after we met up at the Palmiye Cafe Bar, Microbe took Efekan out to the jetty and called me to let me know what was going on. At the time, my sister and I were taking an afternoon break from working on her routine, eating a flourless, fat-free, sugar-free diet cake I had specially made for her. It tasted more or less like a brick, as you can guess. As I left, I said, "Microbe's dad isn't feeling well. I'm going to go check on him." The long concrete walkway on the jetty was baking in the afternoon sun, and as I drew near I saw that two photographers had set up a tripod on the dark mossy stones at the end of the jetty. They were using what appeared to be an antique camera, fiddling with the viewfinder settings, probably trying to take pictures of the islands of Istanbul that appeared closer on that cloudless day.

It stank out there on the jetty. Three months earlier, the transformer at the sewage plant had broken down, and as they waited for the new parts to arrive from overseas, sewage was being dumped straight into the sea. Seagulls were flying low over the water, eyeing the swirling, foaming filth to see if there was any crap to eat. I could see Microbe and Efekan sitting between the two warning lights at the end of the jetty. I headed toward them. Without even glancing at Efekan, I greeted Microbe, shaking his hand and kissing him on both cheeks, and then I sat down on a boulder opposite Efekan. I stretched out my left leg and placed my hand on my thigh, and started working at my teeth with a toothpick.

Efekan was a chicken-legged twit with braces and light brown hair parted to the side. That day he was wearing a Ben 10 Swampfire T-shirt. The thin shadow of a utility pole stretched out between us. Maintaining my air of seriousness, I sat there looking at him intently, making my gaze as menacing as possible. But rather than animosity, I wanted him to feel that I was approaching the situation like a cop who wanted to understand the inner workings of what was going on. I was looking at Efekan with the same amount of friendliness as a cop eyeing a suspect. I waited for him to say the first word: a confession, an apology, an expression of fear, anything. But he just sat there silently, his eyes darting around as he looked at me, Microbe, the sea, the photographers, and the seagulls. Finally, he bowed his head like a criminal who understands that he's been caught.

"Efekan, you're like a brother to me," I said. "Don't ever forget that."

"Okay, Çağlar Ağbi."

"Now tell me," I said, "did you ask Mervenaz and Ecem to deliver a message? Did you say that you're madly in love with Çiğdem?"

"No! I didn't do anything like that," he said, his voice trembling. At first, I couldn't tell if his fear gave him away or if he thought he was about to get screwed over because of a misunderstanding. I could see the fear in his expression, but at that moment I was actually afraid of *him*. I was afraid that Efekan was going to take my place at the center of my sister's life.

I stood up and, placing my hand on his shoulder, smiled at him in a fatherly way. At the same time, however, I started squeezing harder and harder, and I said, "Efekan, you're like a brother to me. Brothers never lie to each other."

"Çağlar Ağbi, I swear to God I didn't say anything."

Microbe suddenly slapped Efekan on the ear and said, "Enough of your damn lies!"

As his eyes filled with tears, Efekan turned to Microbe and said, "Cengiz Ağbi, I swear to you I didn't do anything!"

"Shut the hell up," Microbe snarled. "You say one thing, but your eyes say another, you sneak! You want me to throw you into the sea? Huh? Is that what you want?"

Efekan started to cry, and between sobs he was gasping for breath. I could tell that he wanted to say something.

"Stop it, Microbe," I said, pulling Efekan toward me. "Efekan is like a brother to me."

But Microbe knelt down in front of Efekan, grabbed him by the chin, and stared intently into his eyes. Microbe had a knack for being able to instantly grasp the inner workings of a situation. He was firm, merciless, and wise. My best friend. He got up and motioned for me to follow him. We stopped between the green and red lights, which start flashing when night falls.

"Don't worry," Microbe said. "I'm not going to throw him into the sea. I'm just going to grab him by the ankles and dangle him over the water a little. The little twerp won't talk otherwise."

I glanced at Efekan. He was watching us with tears in his eyes. My sister probably was in love with him, which meant that I loved him as well because now he was part of my sister's life. I was caught up in a maelstrom of emotion. My love for my sister had quelled my anger, but in all that tumult my sense of compassion had been shunted aside. Microbe was standing there as still as a statue, his face fixed, immobile.

"Thanks, Microbe, but there's no need for that."

At that moment Efekan bolted and we ran after him. Microbe caught up with him in the middle of the jetty. With a strength that still baffles me, Efekan squirmed out of his T-shirt and slipped from Microbe's grasp. As Microbe stood there staring in disbelief at the Ben 10 T-shirt, I raced after Efekan, finally catching him in front of those amateur photographers.

One of them shouted, "Get out of the way! We can't get a bearing with you standing there."

"What bearing?" I asked.

"Move it!"

"Look, I'm not just a run-of-the-mill citizen here. I'm the nephew of Altan Baysal, the mayor of Kıyıdere. Now tell me what this 'bearing' business is about," I said, handing him my card.

ÇAĞLAR İYICE

KIYIDERE MUNICIPALITY
OFFICE OF PUBLIC RELATIONS
SPECIALIST STAFF MEMBER
E-MAIL: GECENINSABIRLISESI@GMAIL.COM

"In that case, don't you know what's going on?" he asked, twirling my card.

"What do you mean?"

"They're going to build a marina here. That's why we're surveying."

Efekan looked like he was about to say something, but I covered his mouth and started marching him by the shoulders back to the end of the jetty. Microbe was walking toward us, irritably swinging Efekan's T-shirt, and when we drew near he tied the shirt around his head.

"Çağlar Ağbi, please don't throw me into the sea," he said. "I don't know how to swim very well. I'll drown."

"Tell me the truth then," I said.

He started crying again.

"Efekan, stop crying and just tell me the truth. I'm not going to hurt you. I just want to know what's going on, that's all. Right now I'm filled with a desire to know the truth. We're living through days when we have more need of the truth than bread, water, or *Grand Theft Auto*. Now tell me the truth."

"Çağlar Ağbi, I didn't do it."

"Efekan, when you lie there is a pure place in your heart, in your mind. You can feel it. Now, it might not speak to you directly, telling you to do this or that, but it's there, you can feel it," I said, grabbing him by the shoulders and giving him a good shake. "Can you feel it now? Let that honest part of you talk."

"Çağlar Ağbi, I didn't do anything."

"Efekan, do you think you're the smartest guy in the world? Do you think that now that Steve Jobs is dead you took his place? Is that what you think? That all your conniving is going to stay in your inner world for eternity? Efekan, do you think you're me?"

"Çağlar Ağbi, I haven't done anything wrong."

"Then why did Çiğdem push you down the stairs? If you didn't tell her that you're madly in love with her, then why did she push you?"

"I don't know."

"Why would a girl who wouldn't hurt a fly push you down the stairs? Roll that around in your mind."

"I don't know."

"Try to know."

"I don't know, Çağlar Ağbi, I really don't know."

I gave him back his T-shirt. He held onto it and looked at me, tears still streaming from his eyes. After a little while, he got the bright idea of actually putting it on.

"When did you get braces?"

"Last summer."

"Do they set off metal detectors?"

He didn't answer.

"Okay, go on then. Get going," I said.

He stood there, sadly looking at the ground.

"Efekan, go. Leave."

He came to his senses and took off running, tripping occasionally as he dashed down the jetty. He snuck a few glances back in our direction. There was something sneaky about the way he ran off, as if he had just stolen someone's wallet and was trying to hightail it out of there. The surveyors waved him to the side of the walkway, but he didn't notice and kept right on going.

"What do you think?" I said.

"There's something fishy going on," Microbe said.

"What is it?"

"I don't know."

"That's about as much as I know."

EIGHT

In the afternoon on Sunday, May 26, I walked the length of the shoreline, which at that hour was desolate and covered in rotting seaweed.
There was so much seaweed in the water that you couldn't tell where the
sea ended and land began. No one ever swam there, but I'm sure everyone who walked past thought, *Isn't the sea for swimming?* Inevitably,
you'd find yourself thinking, *If only I were in there with all that seaweed.*
Clusters of flies buzzed around the heaps of blackening seaweed on the
shore, and occasionally down on the rocky end of the shoreline a few
crows would fly down, but after scratching around once or twice, they'd
fly off. My uncle had asked me to meet him near Acacia Beach. I could
tell by the tone of his voice that trouble was stirring, yet again. Little
by little, I increased my pace. The stench was even worse than overflow-
ing sewers. As I walked along, I kept getting the urge to vomit, but I
fought it back and kept going. I thought, *If I were to go up to the shore
road and zip along like this, speeding along as if I were a natural part of
that isolated world up there, people would stop and stare, wondering what
had sped up my rhythm, what had shattered my harmony.* I couldn't let
that happen, so I stuck to the shoreline. There was also the chance that
I might run across one of my friends. Naturally, they'd want to stand

around and chat, and I didn't want to run the risk of hurting their feelings because I'd have to just speed past with a wave of my hand. To this day, Çağlar İyice has never hurt anyone's feelings, except for the people who deserved it.

In the distance, I saw Oaf Tufan Ağbi in his standard-issue neon-orange overalls, raking up the seaweed into piles. He worked slowly, but it wasn't out of laziness; rather, his composure was the result of self-confidence and the fact that he knew his job so well. When you handed him a rake, you could be sure that not a single strand of seaweed would be left on the beach when he was done. Parked nearby, there was a backhoe and a dump truck that belonged to a private company, the name of which I can't recall now.

My uncle was leaning against one of the odd palm trees they'd planted the previous year in a row along the sidewalk. The tree cast only a sliver of shadow, but still he stood there, his sunglasses pulled low on his nose, legs crossed, right hand in his pocket, his right shoulder slumped slightly lower than his left. His gaze shifted back and forth between the piles of seaweed being raked up and a place out over the sea in the direction of Pendik on the opposite shore in the distance. When he saw me, he turned slightly, as if he were unsure of what to say. But I knew. I knew it from the very beginning, and he knew that I knew.

"They're saying that they'll have her perform on another program."

"Which program?"

"A dance competition. Only dancers will participate. They're going to have her perform on that show. In September."

I couldn't let myself get angry because I knew that if I did, I wouldn't be able to keep it under control. My uncle was looking at me, his eyes betraying a slight sense of guilt. That was the thing about him that fooled everyone. There was always an air of guilt hanging over him, and when you grow so accustomed to it, you don't even notice when he really screws things up. You say, "That's just how he is. Last time he looked guilty like that, but he took care of business for us." And even as you're going on like that, he's already fucked you over good. There are people like that who just don't give a damn, and in any case I wasn't there in the capacity of expert psychologist. There was nothing I could do but stare at my uncle in silence and try not to have a nervous breakdown.

"I tried, but it didn't pan out. What can I do?" he stammered. "The shooting for the first round is over. Asshole Bey talked to the manager of the channel and the producer, too, and he asked if she could join the second round. They said it would cause problems for the show's stages of elimination. They said, 'How could we have someone join the second round when they didn't pass the first one?' The same company is going to start a dance competition in September. They'll just put her on that one."

"Enough already. Just shut up."

When Oaf Tufan Ağbi and the other workers wearing neon-orange overalls started pounding the piles of seaweed with the backs of their rakes to pack them down, a backhoe operator started the engine and drove toward the beach. There was a dog lying on the beach scratching its ear, but when the engine roared to life, the dog pricked up its ears and watched the backhoe trace an arc in the sand as it approached.

The seaweed stank to high heaven, and I could even smell it from where we were standing. Some people who were passing by covered their noses. My uncle and I couldn't cover our noses because we were representatives of the municipality. Our job was to think that things would proceed at least somewhat smoothly as we watched how the seaweed was cleaned up. That meant thinking that the seaside would start to smell pleasant again, that only the shadows of boats and fish would flit over the surface of the sea, that one day we would listen to the sound of stones skipping over the glassy surface of the water, and, just like in the old days, the sea would be so clear that we could count the pebbles lying on the bottom. The municipality was hard at work, and it would continue to be until the past was brought back to life, until we no longer needed to be nostalgic for bygone times. I took my electronic cigarette out of the pocket of my black shirt. The nicotine even tasted a little bit like seaweed. I think it was psychological, but what isn't psychological in life?

"Give me a puff of that," my uncle said.

I held out my electronic cigarette. Normally, I don't let anyone touch it out of principle. You see, electronic cigarettes are something personal. The reason I don't share it has nothing to do with being selfish, but people usually don't understand. When they ask for a drag, I say, "Sure, and you give me your toothbrush so I can brush my teeth."

After taking a few puffs, he handed it back to me and said, "It's no big deal, we'll just go in September."

"We're not going anywhere in September. With some things, you have to do them at the right time or not at all. I know my sister, and she's not going to go anywhere when September rolls around. If you weren't sure, why did you keep building up her hopes?"

"Why would I give her hope if I didn't have good reason? They told me that if they couldn't bring her on as Michael Jackson, they could have her perform as a comedian."

I put my electronic cigarette into my shirt pocket and squinted at my uncle. I waited for him to go on but he didn't. "Comedian? What the hell are you talking about?"

"Well, you know."

"What do I know? Did you agree to have her join the competition as a comedian?"

"No. It's just that they said she could have performed as a comedian, worst-case scenario."

"My sister isn't a comedian," I shouted, punching the palm tree beside me. "My sister didn't come into this world to make people laugh. No, she's here to send a message to petty assholes like you. She was going to deliver that message by dancing. What kind of jerk would go off and make a deal like that?"

"What, now I'm the guilty one? Why are you mad at me? And stop hitting the palm tree. It was imported from Italy."

"Screw your palm trees! Are they more important than my sister?" I said, looking at the tree. "Why the hell did you buy these from Italy? Don't we have trees in this country?"

My uncle put me in a headlock, cutting off my breath. "You ass," he said. "What did I tell you in the beginning? It's your fault that we're not going to the competition!"

"Why?"

He let me go and tried to loosen his tie, but in his irritation he just twisted up the knot, which irritated him even more, and he started struggling with the tie as if it were a snake wrapped around his neck. In the end, he got it off and threw it on the ground. After trying to kick it a few times, he settled with stomping on it.

"You shouldn't litter," I said.

"Of course I wanted her to be in the competition. I wanted Çiğdem to compete on TV. I love that girl like my own daughter. She's everything to me. But it's your fault that she didn't get on."

"Why is it my fault?"

"Why? In the beginning, I was going to make some phone calls. 'Absolutely not,' you said. It was you who said, 'My sister doesn't need anyone's help. If I even hear any gossip about you pulling strings, I'll pull her from the competition.'"

"Do you think she needs you to pull strings for her? Have you ever seen her dance? No, of course not. The only person you see in the world is yourself. If Michael Jackson rose from the grave, you would have your own people dance rather than put him on stage to moonwalk."

"You prick, I'm going to tear you a new—"

"Shut the hell up. Don't cut me off when I'm talking! You've got no shame, going off like that and offering to have her take part as a comedian."

"Who's offering anything? Me? If they don't want a fat Michael Jackson, why is that my fault?"

Just a little ways off, the backhoe, the bucket of which was loaded with seaweed, was approaching the dump truck. The dirty white dog lying on the sand watching the backhoe turned and looked at us, cocking its head. I took my electronic cigarette out of my pocket and twirled it between my fingers as I scrutinized my uncle's face. As I took a drag, the seaweed fell with a thud into the back of the truck. I exhaled a plume of steam, and the backhoe started backing up.

"Fat?" I asked. "What's fat about my sister?"

"Your sister barely fits into the armchair."

"She did six spins in the competition."

"She didn't even do two."

"You're lying. Everyone's a little fat," I said, pinching my stomach between my thumb and forefinger. "Look, I'm fat, too!"

"Your sister weighs more than you."

"No, we're the same weight. She's still growing."

"You're incapable of looking at your sister objectively."

"Why should I look at her objectively? She's *my* sister."

"But she's not other people's sister."

That last sentence struck me like a hammer. A strange silence fell between us, so thick you could reach out and touch it. As happens with silences that follow silences, we were stuck in a period of time that had no clear boundaries, crushed under the weight of an indescribable feeling. With every passing moment, more weight was added to the burden on our backs. My uncle was startled to see that a crowd of people had started gathering around us. Just about everyone knows my uncle, and I'm no stranger in Kıyıdere, either.

With a cold glance targeting no one in particular, he shouted, "What are you looking at? Don't you have things to do?"

That was the first time I saw him shout at his constituents. I'm sure they felt hurt, angry, and resentful. If elections were held that day, they would've buried him. My uncle glanced back at the seven or eight votes that he'd just lost and stormed off.

As I watched him walk away, I could feel the poison of those words he'd just said spreading throughout my entire body. None of the scorpions and rattlesnakes I'd known in my life had ever poisoned me like this. Maybe that was the poison of reality, the kind that seeps the fastest into your blood, the most dangerous kind. An odd quietude settled over me, leaving me feeling numb. I couldn't pull my eyes away from his back.

"Are you happy now?" I finally managed to shout. "My sister is as fat as a cow! Are you happy now?"

My uncle turned around and punched the trunk of a palm tree, yelling, "You dumbass! Did I say anything like that? You know damn well I didn't."

"Don't you ever forget that my sister was dancing to give her soul to this soulless world."

My uncle madly scratched his head with both hands and said, "What the hell are you talking about? What soul, what world? She was dancing because Dr. İhsan told her to. She was dancing because he said that putting her on a diet wouldn't be enough and that she needed exercise. She was dancing to lose weight. But just like everything else, you blew it out of proportion, and now look at this crap we're dealing with. You're the one who convinced her that she's a dancer."

With those last words, he punched a small green trash can that was affixed to a utility pole. It flew off and started rolling down the sidewalk toward me. He stormed off in the opposite direction. There was a sticker on the trash can that read "Kıyıdere 2012."

"So what," I called out to him. "At least I got her to take up dancing. I gave her a compass in life, I helped her come up with a goal, an aim, a style, an attitude, a position, an agenda. I didn't try to turn her into a comedian. Unlike you, I didn't want them to laugh at an MJ who is as fat as a cow."

My uncle turned around, and at first it seemed like he was going to unload on me, but he changed his mind and knocked his fist against the side of his head. In a rage, he started punching the little green trash cans hung on the utility poles as he walked away, sending them flying.

"You ass, stop hitting the trash cans! You son of a bitch, do you know how much garbage tax these people have paid?"

My uncle turned around and started running straight at me. "Get your ass over here."

"I'm right here," I said, holding out my hands.

His hands were in fists, he was clenching his teeth, and he was wearing a rather silly expression of anger. Coolly, I said with a smile, "Bring it on."

I spread my legs and leaned forward, and when he closed in I drove my fist into his stomach. From where he was slumped over, he managed to sneak in a good left hook that caught me on the side of the head. Then he got me in the jaw with a right hook, and I felt my teeth shift in my mouth. We were living in a world that was full of utility poles, islands, clouds that slyly intermingle, planes that rise up leaving white trails in the sky, and glances laden with tension. We were living in a world filled with pain, and most of that pain had no logical explanation. We were living as if we were tumbling into an empty expanse surrounded by slippery slopes. We had been wrenched from our true essence. Just as I was about to hit the ground, Oaf Tufan Ağbi grabbed me by the collar and pulled me up. I had no idea where I was.

When I came to my senses, I snapped, "My sister is as fat as a cow," and spit a mouthful of blood in my uncle's direction. "Are you happy now, you ass? Are you happy now, you son of a bitch?"

"What the hell are you saying? You're the one who called your sister a cow!"

Oaf Tufan Ağbi grabbed my uncle by the collar and held him away from me. "Calm down," he said. For some reason, those words had a strange effect on us, perhaps because no matter what Oaf Tufan Ağbi said there was a tremulous undertone of gratitude in his voice. He held onto us until we stopped trying to get at each other. In the end, he relaxed a little, and when he saw that we had settled down he let us go. Without looking back, my uncle walked off. A few officials who always trailed after my uncle kissing his ass had heard us fighting and had come to see what was happening. They shot me dark glances as they followed him.

Oaf Tufan Ağbi went to the corner market and came back with two boxes of fruit juice. With a wink and a tentative smile, he punched me in the shoulder and gave me one. As he started drinking, I looked at the box he'd handed me: 100 percent mixed fruit. I wiped the blood from my mouth with the collar of my black denim shirt. I pulled the straw from its plastic wrapper and plunged it into the box and drank half of the juice in one gulp. With my second gulp, I felt the box shrink in my hand. Unfolding the corners of the box, I blew it back up, tossed it on the ground, and stomped on it. It didn't pop.

"I've probably lost my mind," I said quietly.

"Çağlar, do you think so?" Oaf Tufan Ağbi asked, calmly studying me, as if trying to understand if I really had gone nuts. He took off his neon-orange hat and scratched his head, looking at me all the while. A few strands of sweaty hair clung to the side of his neck. The hat had left an impression on his forehead.

"Yes," I said. "I've lost it."

"Why?"

"I don't know, Oaf Tufan Ağbi. This turned out so badly. To be honest, I wasn't expecting it to go this far. If I was going to go mad, I should have at least become a happy lunatic."

I leaned back against the rough bark of the palm tree, crossed my arms, and looked at the sea. For some reason, I couldn't calm down. My heart was beating faster and faster, my temples were throbbing, and my chin was quivering. Probably thinking that it was best if I spent some time alone, Oaf Tufan Ağbi picked up my empty juice box and my uncle's dusty necktie and walked off. He tucked the tie into his pocket and tossed the empty box into the back of the dump truck, which was full of rotting seaweed. I went on looking at the sea. Out beyond the white line of breakers there was a tanker. I couldn't tell if it was moving really slowly or just sitting still. It was probably moving, but with such agonizing slowness that you'd only believe it if an experienced seaman told you so. I wouldn't want to be on a tanker like that; the slowness would drive you nuts. The letters *MSC* were written on the side of the tanker, and it was full of shipping containers, stacked at least three high. Toward the front of the tanker there was a huge tower, probably where the captain or some other expert would sit and handle the wheel. A faint trail of smoke rose from the smokestack, which was in the rear. The smoke was the color of clouds, and it rose up, disappearing into the clouds. This was all happening far out at sea. After a while, I stopped looking at the tanker because I couldn't take it anymore.

I went down to the beach and picked up one of the rakes stuck into the sand near the yellow backhoe. I held it up and spun it around a few times, and then put it over my shoulder like a rifle and started walking toward Oaf Tufan Ağbi's team of men and the seaweed, which stunk even worse than those dreams of ours that have been fucked over and cast aside. I worked with so much enthusiasm that it seemed I might lose myself. I couldn't get enough of raking that seaweed stuck to the sand. It was as if that seaweed had eliminated my sister from the competition and called my sister fat. It was as if that seaweed had driven me from my ex-girlfriend and was always breaking our hearts. I raked and raked, pushing it into piles.

Dripping sweat, I managed to push together four big piles. My back, arms, and legs—actually every part of my body—had gone numb. And I was probably suffering from heat stroke because the seaweed started to look yellow. When I packed together the fourth bale of seaweed with the back of my rake and called over the backhoe, Oaf Tufan Ağbi only glanced at me and said that I was doing it all wrong. He knew that what I really wanted was to die as I went after the seaweed. He respected that.

Oaf Tufan Ağbi is one of the most steadfast people I know. Always smiling, he looks at the world around him through the purest of eyes. His lips, which are usually slightly parted, are somewhat blubbery, and his teeth are yellower than a toilet bowl. But that's just a matter of hygiene and has nothing to do with the goodness of his heart. He's the son of Papa Reçko, my grandpa's stepbrother who brought down the government of Albania. Whenever there's a nasty job that needs to be done, Oaf Tufan Ağbi is put to the task. For example, if scratching rats are heard at one of our relative's homes, they clear out the place and give Oaf Tufan Ağbi the key. After my uncle became mayor, he started passing out jobs to all of our lazy relatives. The worst jobs were handed out as contract positions, and Oaf Tufan Ağbi was handed a rake and given the duty of dealing with the seaweed problem. Last year, he was hired on as the supervisor of the sewage plant. Well, they said he was the "supervisor" of the plant, but in fact he was more like a full-time janitor, caretaker, and watchman.

Two hours later, I threw down the rake and lay down, blinking as I looked up at the sun. Oaf Tufan Ağbi was still working away at his slow, confident pace, and the other workers were continuing on in the same way. I was thinking that if only I was in a crappy fairy tale that took place in some uncertain time, I could say that there was surely a lesson to be learned from all this.

That night, as my uncle and I walked through the door of our home, we acted like nothing had happened between us. We were joking around, laughing and playfully punching each other as if we were the happiest people in the world. Why? Because we were both lying sneaks and we were going to trick my sister. My uncle had come up with a plan that was ingeniously idiotic. It took him thirty-four minutes to explain it on the phone.

When we came in, my sister was standing opposite my mother practicing her antigravity leaning routine. I couldn't believe my eyes. She was standing there at a forty-five-degree angle, and when she saw us she straightened back up as if it were the easiest thing in the world. Just like MJ. Even my mom was smiling.

The night before, when we'd been full of fresh hope, my uncle had joined us as my sister practiced her routine. At first, my mom stood there in the doorway of the living room with her usual haggard, cold expression. But when she saw the three of us leaning forward like that, she couldn't help but laugh. We all started laughing, and suddenly we felt like we were truly together. We were a family. It had been a long, long time since we'd felt that way. Rarely do we laugh together in our family because usually something that makes one person laugh makes another cry.

"We've got some good news for you," my uncle said. "Çağlar, why don't you tell her?"

"No, you tell her. After all, you're the one who put it together."

"Okay, next week at the festival KIYFORC is sponsoring"— KIYFORC is the Kıyıdere Folklore Research Club—"you're going to perform onstage as the last act. You're even going to be after the skits about Mustafa Kemal Ataturk."

When she heard those words, my sister's lips trembled. Tears welled up in her big bright blue eyes and soon her cheeks were wet with tears. She understood everything. When a smart kid like that gets eliminated from a competition, it breaks your heart all the more. The event we mentioned was the Sixteenth International Turkic Tribes Festival. If my sister had fallen for it, we were going to tell her that in addition to Kıyıdere TV, there were going to be major TV channels there; that was the second act of our lying scheme, as if the big channels had been covering it for the last fifteen years and weren't about to miss the sixteenth year. Leaning down in front of my sister, my uncle gently lifted her chin and started telling her about the dance competition that was going to be held in September. My mom even expressed her support for the idea. I, however, remained silent. But my sister, still in tears, wasn't listening to them. I knew that she would go on crying.

My sister's fits of crying are quite interesting. She goes into a trance, and she can cry like that for eight or nine hours. You really start to worry. She cries but doesn't complain. I'm not talking about whining or getting riled up so you cry even more, I mean the weeping of the monster you carry within, the kind of crying that's your last recourse before losing your mind. In fact, when you cry like that, you do lose your mind.

I said to my uncle, "Get out of the way." I took my sister's hands and started slowly kissing her tears. We sat down together on the love seat. If she were crying out of a fit of rage, she wouldn't have held my hand like that; her hands wouldn't have fluttered. She was weeping out of desperation. It was an attempt to cling to life.

Last year, the son of the solar panel distributor publically made fun of my sister's so-called obesity, and she cried nonstop for three days. That time, Microbe actually threw the kid off the jetty into the sea, and I had to swim out and get him. Later, the boy's father cornered me in front of the taxi stand near the pier, and even though I hadn't done anything wrong he beat me, or perhaps I should say that he couldn't get his fill of beating me. He was a mountain of a man with a handle-bar mustache and beefy neck. Each and every time I'd get back up, my mouth and nose a bloody mess, and slip away from the taxi drivers trying to hold me back so that I could go after him again. Spitting a chunk of tooth in his face, I said, "Who do you think you are, you son of a bitch! You sell two solar panels and then go off thinking that you're the nuclear-power-plant mafia! They're going to put in a hydro plant up in Teşvikiye, and after that electricity is going to be cheaper than water. Within a year, you're going to go bankrupt, so stick those panels right up your ass!" Then I added, "Are you the prick who taught that bastard kid of yours to call my sister fatso without bothering to look at your own fat ass? If I don't make you and your whole damn family pay for the tears my sister cried, then my name's not Çağlar İyice!" Even though he had five of his buddies with him, he couldn't get enough of beating me, and I couldn't get enough of telling him off. I didn't get in a single punch, which still pisses me off. The same night, Oaf Tufan Ağbi went over and beat the guy up, but he had a friend who's the chief of police, and the chief, along with eight or nine other cops, tried to beat up Oaf Tufan Ağbi. When my uncle heard about this, he had a fit and he left me there at the emergency room where I was being held for observation. People started gathering in front of the county governor's office, and he flew into a rage and shouted at them, "What the hell is going on here!" as people were gathering in front of his office. A battle was imminent, but then my mom let out such a shriek that everyone regretted what they'd done.

That all happened in the past, and it's not very important, but as we sat on the love seat holding hands, my sister said, "I told all my friends about it. They were going to watch me on TV."

When we sat down to dinner, she wouldn't eat anything. On her plate was one slice of rye bread, a skinless chicken breast, and a salad, along with half a serving of Paşaköy yogurt and a bowl of vegetable soup. I had the same meal in front of me. When I saw her like that, I felt miserable. I didn't eat anything, either, except for a spoonful of soup. For those of you who don't know about my sister's eating habits before she started trying to lose weight, let me just say that she was such a protein addict that she'd put a fried egg on top of a steak. She wasn't picky at all and would eat whatever was on her plate. She'd eat salad, watermelon, honeydew melon, and dessert, and, if it were possible, she would have eaten her plate and the tablecloth and then devoured your surprise and silent laughter. So when a kid who likes eating so much refuses to touch her food, what difference does anything make? Does it matter or not if someone makes us feel wretched yet again? If we get shot in the heart one more time? If we fight back against the blows raining down on us? Tell me, motherfucking preselection jury, what difference would it have made if you hadn't eliminated my sister from the first round? Would my beautiful, talented sister have been such a burden for you?

NINE

Our lives were enveloped in sorrow. But it wasn't the kind of transitory contractual sorrow that leaves behind a bitter taste. It seeped into all we ate and drank, all our words and silences, all our thoughts and actions, everything we couldn't even think about or do because of that disappointment. The days seemed to drag on forever, and when evening slowly settled in, we felt like a wire that was being pulled just a little tauter, like a time bomb that had been set for as long as all the hours in a century and was counting down, second by second. On those interminable days and gloomy nights, we knew that we'd slipped into some timeless zone and that even if there were two of us, we were infinitely lonely. Two fish that were washed ashore would know that feeling. Well, most of the time.

My sister was still crying, and her weeping reminded me of the forest fire that had broken out in Teşvikiye the year before. Sometimes it slowed down and sped up, but just as you were about to say, "It's out," with a single spark it flared up again. It was Tuesday, May 28, and my sister was curled up in a corner of the love seat staring at the blank screen of the television, her whole body wracked by sobs. I was lying on the floor at her feet with one elbow propped on the rug.

I looked into the pupils of her eyes, which were glistening with tears, and said, "Baby, I just don't know what to say," getting up and pulling over the beanbag so I could sit in front of her and wait for her to look at me. When our eyes finally met, I whispered, "Light of my life! You may not be going on a TV show, but that doesn't change the fact that you're a wonderful dancer."

"Why wouldn't it change that?"

"It's enough that you dance so well. Even if no one saw you dance, it would be enough. All that matters is that we know."

"Çağlar, why should just the two of us know? If I had gone on TV, everyone would've known. That would've been better."

"Everyone would've seen you, yes. But would they really have understood how talented you are?"

"Why wouldn't they, Çağlar?"

I took her hands and placed them on my shoulders. "Look," I said. "That's just not how it works. Let's think on this in more detail. What about Karl Marx?"

"Who's that?"

"Or those groups of like fifty or sixty people who get together to protest things and get beat up by the cops?"

"You mean like Aunt Ayla?"

"No. Think more radically."

"Orhan the tailor."

"No. Think a little more leftist."

"How?"

"You know, the police squirt stuff in their eyes, they cry, everyone gets upset and posts things on Twitter, pandemonium breaks out, your time line goes haywire, and people stop reading your tweets. Times like that."

"You mean like when the woman in the red dress got pepper sprayed by the police today at the park?"

"Exactly. Karl Marx is their leader."

"So?"

"He said, 'Religion is the opium of the people.' He was an atheist. But if he lived today, I'm sure that he would've said, 'TV is the opium of the people.'"

"What's opium?"

"It's like hash."

"Hash?"

"Like weed."

"Weed?"

"You know that guy Ercan Mehmet Erdem? He wrote the song 'The Judge.' The police are always arresting him for one thing or another. There isn't much weed left on the market anymore, and people say that he smoked it all single-handedly. Anyway, forget about it."

"Does it taste good?"

"No! You get dizzy and everything looks blurry. TV is like that, too. People see you, but you look blurry to them. They really don't see you at all. That's why TV is so central for those idiotic famesters. You're lucky. You're dealing with this sticky dilemma now. All big stars have to face up to it at some point. You see, they have to make a decision: virtue or fame. How many people do you think would choose virtue? But the ones who do are leading the world. They have a vision that's even broader than a high-definition TV."

My sister was listening to me with mournful intensity. After wiping her nose with the back of her hand, she said, "That may be true, but it would've been better if I'd been on TV."

Then she continued crying silently. Perhaps the false solace that my uncle had been parading around for the past few days had made us blind to the true value of consolation. Who could blame her? Even I realized that as I was trying to console my sister I actually wanted to console myself. I also wanted her to be in the competition, and I also believed that she was going to teach those lazy psychos whose sole passion is watching TV a lesson they'd never forget. I imagined it like this:

A lazy ass sees my sister on TV and gets up and says, "Suzan"—that's what he'd say if that was his wife's name—"Suzan, if a nine-year-old girl can pull that off, I've been living for nothing all these years! The earth has gone around the sun thirty-nine times since the day my umbilical cord was cut, and I haven't contributed a single thing to the world. What a shame, what a crying shame!"

That afternoon, my uncle came home with a dog on a leash, hoping to placate my sister. It was a scrawny, yellowish mutt with pointy moist-looking ears. Actually, I couldn't tell if it was yellow or just dirty. It was panting, drooling from its pink tongue, and its eyes gleamed with ravenous hunger. When my mom saw the dog, she put her hand to her forehead and, feeling her way along with her other hand, went into the kitchen and shouted, "Altan, get that dog out of here! Get it out of here right now!"

My uncle said, "What's the problem? It's just a dog. We can keep it on the kitchen balcony." He held the dog by the scruff of the neck, trying to show it to my sister. "Let's name it."

But my sister wasn't interested. She glanced cursorily at the dog and then crossed her arms, fixing her eyes on a painting on the opposite wall. My mom had painted it when she took an oil-painting class at the community center. Boats tied up to a pier, a calm sea, a few seagulls: everything about it—the color harmony, composition, perspective—was just as it should be. It was more like a lesson in landscape painting than a landscape painting itself.

I had climbed onto a chair that I put on top of the table and stood there with my head bowed so I wouldn't bump it against the ceiling. You see, I'm afraid of dogs. During the local elections in 2009, when my uncle was campaigning for the Spurned Horses Party, I joined him on some of his tours so that he wouldn't feel like too much of a loser. In Çınarcık, just up from the old Castle Disco, there's a place called Twin's Farm. Their products are really fresh, you should go and see for yourself; they have farm-fresh eggs, goat cheese, and fresh milk, and they do retail sales as well. There was a sign on the gate painted in red that read "Warning: Killer Dog."

Right after I said, "I'll give the dog a little dried meat from one of the gift bags we've been handing out," the killer ran up and bit my kneecap. Oblivious to the meat I tossed down, it just latched onto my knee without a growl of warning or anything.

My uncle's attempt to please my sister had failed, so he turned the poor animal out. My mom and I watched from the balcony as he walked to the street and unhooked the dog's leash. "Go on," he said. The dog took a few steps and stopped, turning back to look at my uncle in confusion. Clearly, the dog was a little upset about this turn of events. Pointing to the end of the street, my uncle said, "Get going." After looking at my uncle for a little while longer, the dog started walking away, head hung low but taking proud, measured steps.

My mother took a bottle of lemon-scented *kolonya* from the fridge, and as she was rubbing it into her wrists, she called out from the balcony, "Altan, why did you let the dog go like that? Where's it going to go?"

"To the municipal shelter. It knows the way."

As I watched the dog walk away, I don't know if it was because of my profound irritation with my uncle or because I sensed in the dog's confident, proud steps an approach to life that said, "There's a solution to all problems," but I had an idea that I should've had long before: we would use social media. When that happens—I mean, when we get an idea that we should've already come up with—instead of feeling stupid, which would be the proper thing to do, we tend to think of ourselves as geniuses. It's an interesting psychological twist, but this isn't the time to dwell on it. I ran into the living room and said to my sister, who at the moment was counting the tassels of the rug with a forlorn, distant expression, "We're not going to give up, sweetie. We're going to make a video and put it on YouTube. We're not going to get up from the computer until a hundred million people have watched it and we've made you a global star."

Immediately, she stopped crying and the crisp light of hope glimmered in her eyes. A feeling of hope flooded me as well. We hugged, and I breathed in the scent of her hair, trying to hold onto it as long as I could. Just as we have a tendency to be overtaken by hopelessness at any moment, we carry within us a tendency to be overtaken by hope as well.

The previous year, my uncle had a three-story villa built in Butterfly Meadow, which he had furnished but never stayed in, not even for a single day. I decided that we would shoot the video in that garage. As my sister was doing her final preparations upstairs, I put our '94 Renault Broadway into neutral, and with Microbe pushing from behind we got it out of the garage. Since he's more talented than me in the visual arts, he was going to be the film's art director. You can follow his work on Instagram; his username is altinelkadraj_96. His black-and-white photos are particularly good.

Striking a contemplative pose, Microbe was leaning on the flaking hood of the milk-white Renault with his right hand and holding his chin in his left, scrutinizing the façade of the villa. With the intensity of people who rarely ask questions, he asked, "Why doesn't Altan Ağbi live here?"

"He's terrified of being alone," I said, pulling the emergency brake as if I were putting a period at the end of a sentence before getting out of the car. "As if it's not enough that he's always hounding after people all the time, he leaves his bedroom door open even when he's sleeping so that we all can hear him snoring and watch him drool."

"So why doesn't he get married?"

"Because he's never gotten a good beating. Microbe, you know me. I'm against the institution of the family because in the end there's so much unhappiness. And I'm against unhappiness because it doesn't do any damn good. But if the issue is about my uncle getting married and becoming unhappy, I'm not against it because the bastard deserves that bitter end more than anyone else. I waited a long time for him to get married so he would get out of our hair."

"There was that woman named Nilüfer who worked at the cultural affairs office. What happened to her?"

"He chased after her for months, bowing and scraping to her, and in the end the sneak managed to seduce her. They would meet up, drink tea, eat together. When her family said that it was time to put a name to their relationship, my uncle fucked off. We sat him down to talk about it and said, 'Look, you ass, she's a family girl, and you've gone off and shamed us.' He got all riled up, but we calmed him down. 'Sit yourself down and chill out,' we said. 'Did we say that you have to marry Nilüfer? You could marry Ayşe, or Fatma, or Merve, it doesn't matter. But you're at that age now when you need to get married. Think about it. You've gotten into politics, and being a bachelor is against the nature of that business. They won't let you in.' But we couldn't get him to listen to reason. He stalled for time, saying, 'First I should finish building the villa.' Well, he finished it, and it's been standing here for a year. What's the point of owning a home if you haven't got it in you to get married? In the end, all you've got is a worthless land title and property taxes."

Microbe kicked the front tire of the car twice with the toe of his shoe and said, "Hmm." Then he leaned over and looked carefully at the tire. He then went on to subject all the car's tires to the same treatment. Following after him, I inspected them as well. "They're all worn out," he said. "Bald."

I rubbed the toe of my shoe against one of the tires. "Not yet," I said. "They've still got some life in them."

He placed his hand on the right front tire and, after giving it two solid punches, gave it a squeeze and a slap. Looking at me with an expression that betrayed the hopelessness of the situation, he said, "You need to get new tires."

I sighed patiently and didn't insist. After all, at home he had every single Pirelli calendar that had come out since they started making them in 1994. Still, I was pretty irritated. That Broadway had been handed down by my grandpa, so in my eyes it was perfect. I kept it perfectly clean and wouldn't let anyone speak ill of it. In the end, however, Microbe was my best friend.

After deciding to use social media, we were getting ready to start shooting in a few short hours. In deep concentration, my sister was standing in the middle of the garage, head tilted forward as she held the brim of her hat, waiting for Microbe to say, "Action." He stood at the ready with his iPhone in video mode, waiting for the light of the setting sun to come streaming through the rectangular windows of the garage. As he said, "It'll create a more epic atmosphere." In the meantime, I was jumping up and down to kick up some dust to add to the effect. A lot of MJ's videos start that way, with an enchanting space filled with glowing specks of dust.

"Microbe," I said, speaking gently so that I wouldn't break my sister's concentration, "since we have the time, wouldn't it be better if we move the camping equipment out of the garage?"

Behind the space where my sister was going to dance there were two tents, three sleeping bags, three rolled-up mats, three camping packs, and three mountain bikes, one of them a children's bike. But Microbe said that it would be better to keep the dusty camping equipment in the background because it would lend a more gothic atmosphere and remind young people that it wasn't too late to go after their dust-covered dreams. At first the idea struck me as somewhat illogical, but I decided that since he was going into such a detailed explanation he must be right. He was the art director, so I had no choice but to respect his decisions.

When the sun started shining through the small windows of the garage, the effect was even better than we'd hoped. I pressed the "Play" button on the iPod, and "They Don't Care about Us" started playing over the speakers we'd set up. I'm not going to go into a long explanation about how my sister danced, but suffice it to say that she was on fire. She did the antigravity lean as well. She pulled out all the stops. As is apparent from our choice of song, the choreography was more aggressive and intense than before, as is usually the case when you realize that you're using your last chance. It's like gamblers who start betting bigger and bigger when they realize they've started losing. If you're interested in that subject, you might try reading Captain Dostoyevsky's "The Gambler"—unfortunately, you see, I can't explain everything to you, because I just don't have the time.

We saved the video on the computer and did the final editing on Movie Maker. With the peace of mind of those who know they've pulled off a particularly good job, we popped open two cans of Efes and munched on roasted chickpeas. Sitting on one of the rolled-up sleeping bags, I said, "Great work, the clip is perfect! We watched it a hundred times and there's not a single slip."

Microbe twisted his mouth to the side and winked. I don't know if that expression was supposed to be a sign of humility or pride. As I looked at the camping equipment, a strange feeling of nostalgia crept over me. I sighed and asked Microbe if we were going to head off into the wild this summer. He raised his head from the computer and looked at me, and I noticed that his eyes were bloodshot from having looked at the screen for so long. He took a large gulp of beer from the side of his mouth and chased it down with half a handful of chickpeas. As Microbe sat there looking at me, his jaws slowly working, I decided to do an overview of my life. I examined each and every one of the seventeen years that I'd been in this world as he sat there chewing.

Çağlar İyice, I said to myself, *you've had some good days and some bad days, old boy, and you've had friends and enemies, too, of course. There are people who like you and, unfortunately, people who dislike you, but that's just the way it has to be, because otherwise being liked would mean nothing, absolutely nothing at all. So hold on a second, my man, just hang on a second, just think of all that's to come. You don't know what days and nights await you; you have no idea what you'll experience and miss out on;*

and what you'll say and what you won't say is a big, big secret. Who knows, maybe you have a superpower that you're not even aware of, and one day by chance you'll discover it, and suddenly you'll find that you're someone like Spiderman, but for now let's see Microbe Cengiz eat those chickpeas, let's see that dear friend munch and munch away, and maybe in a little while he'll explain to you the meaning of life.

Microbe mumbled something at that point.

"What?" I asked.

"Sure, we'll go."

"It's my sister that I'm worried about," I said. "I'm not sure if she's in the right state of mind. Last year, she said she'd come, but this summer things have changed. Her world now is all about the bright lights. I can understand that. I mean, who wouldn't want to meet her? Especially a kid of her caliber."

"Well, boss, we've burned the bridges for our internship in the name of this cause." Then he added with a gentle but decisive air, "If we said we'd go, then we're going to go."

For those of you who may not be aware of the situation, let me give you a summary. The summer before, we'd had some big dreams. Microbe Cengiz and I were going to go into the heart of the wild, far from all those selfish, arrogant people out there thirsting for praise. Naturally, my sister was going to go with us. There are weasels, wolves, and bears out there, but so long as they didn't mess with my sister, there wouldn't be any problems and we'd live in harmony with nature. We weren't going to go into the wilderness just to wander around. No, we were going to be on a genuine search for identity. We'd explore the boundaries of what we can do and come to understand at which point our quota of freedom became filled. You may ask why. But how should I know? "Let's become free, and after that we can think about what we're going to do with that freedom," we said. Maybe we wouldn't have done anything at all. That feeling would've been enough for us. We usually think that freedom is doing whatever you feel like doing, but above all else it is a feeling. That feeling comes before action. It's that feeling that makes people act or not act.

It was that feeling that prompted us to drop our mandatory internship at the training hotel, even though we were well aware that we'd fail the year if we did. My mother reacted violently to our decision. She interpreted our desire to go into the wild as a desire to lose ourselves, perhaps as the result of various personal inclinations. Since my sister was part of the plan, the clash between my mother and me flared up even more. As I mentioned before, it reached such a point that the clash was transformed into a chasm. That's why I severed all economic ties with my family and started working at the old Bankers' Clubhouse. My goal was to buy enough camping gear so we could move into the wild as soon as possible. But by the time I had saved up enough money, the summer of 2012 was over and school had started again. That's around the time when Microbe and I decided to drop out of school. Neither of us saw a future for ourselves in tourism. Since we wouldn't be able to register for a different department at the university anyway, the best plan seemed to be to finish high school through correspondence courses. As we set out down this path, our aim was to simplify our lives to the greatest extent possible. If we were to go on getting stuck worrying about that nonsense of careerism, what would be the point of being in the wild? All that would've happened is that our discontent would've been moved from one place to another. For us, living in the wild would have been the curriculum. Idleness leads to decay. That's a fundamental law of physics. If it's not, they should take the trouble to make it one.

When our families realized that our ideas were maturing and our decisiveness was becoming all the more entrenched, they offered up a new agreement. According to their terms, the following summer they would let us, my sister included, go up to the Erikli Highlands. That's the closest wilderness to Kıyıdere. In return, they wanted us to continue with school. Microbe and I sat down and pored over the agreement, and in the end we decided to go along with it so that my sister's education wouldn't suffer.

I got up from my perch on the sleeping bag and said, "I'm not going anywhere without my sister. You know that. I don't want freedom without my sister."

"Don't worry," Microbe said. "It's all in the cards."

I wasn't sure what he meant by that.

"The video's finished," he said. "When Çiğdem gets so famous that she can't go out in public, she'll want to join us."

Without taking my eyes from Microbe, I took a swig of beer, ate a few chickpeas, and thought about what he said. Maybe he was right. I popped a few more chickpeas in my mouth. Famous people always want to go into the wild. Well, maybe none of them have actually done it, but that doesn't matter. Trusting in my sister's solid character, I knew she'd come along with us. So I decided to let her get famous, and then once she was fed up with the lies of that world of pomp and splendor, she'd come to me and say, "Çağlar, I forgive everyone who broke my heart. Come on, let's go into the wild."

That night we uploaded the video, which we titled "Nine-Year-Old Girl Does Extraordinary Moonwalk and More." To keep it circulating, we added links to the YouTube page on Facebook and Twitter and sent out a mass message to all the people on our friend lists and in our e-mail contacts. That night 124 people watched the video. By the next day, that figure had crept up to 216. I tried not to let my sister know that the situation wasn't looking very promising. Still, I sat there at the computer, chin in hand, waiting for happiness to be uploaded, filled with a sense of hope that astounded even me. But it didn't. Our Internet connection was really slow and our buffer was filled with sorrow. I was thinking that Microbe and I should go to Colombia and get into the palm oil business, and once we'd solved our financial issues we'd send for my sister. Perhaps the best thing to do was to try our luck in other walks of life.

But during that period of waiting, fortune smiled upon us. I want to tell you something that you should never forget; make a note on one of those sticky pieces of paper, the name of which I can't remember right now because I'm filled with so much joy, and stick it on the refrigerator, smacking it with the palm of your hand so that it sticks real good. Here's the deal: fortune will smile upon you, too, one day. By the way, I just remembered what they're called: Post-its.

Here's what happened. A Twitter phenomenon with tons of followers watched my sister's video and was so amazed that he tweeted, "Chubby girl goes wild doing the moonwalk," and included the link to the video. Our video spread across Facebook as his followers reposted it, people started threads when they saw the post, others saw the threads and started forums, and others read the forums and posted it back on Facebook. Suddenly, our video had gone viral. The number of views rose from 216 to 12,000 within an hour. The next hour, it was up to 23,000. An hour later, it rose to 38,000. With each passing hour, we were getting 10,000 more views. We were ecstatic! On paper, we did rough calculations. At that rate, my sister would be world famous in a week or two. There's probably a mathematical term for numbers that steadily increase, and we probably could have drawn up an equation to calculate precisely when my sister was going to become famous, but that would have meant calling Kepçe, our math teacher, and we weren't too keen on that idea. I've never liked the guy.

The 979 comments made about our video were generally good. Most of them were along the lines of "You said she's nine years old, but that girl could join the state wrestling team!" But I didn't pay them much attention, and I didn't let my sister read the comments. "Big talents," I told her, "shouldn't waste time with critiques because they are so talented that they are their own worst critics. If they have any flaws, they know about them long before anyone else notices." My sister said, "I agree, Çağlar." Since she was getting ready to be world famous, she decided to improve her foreign-language skills. So she started watching the movies I'd downloaded from Torrent, making sure they had English subtitles.

When we had nearly fifty thousand views, Yıldız Abla, the daughter of the owner of the old Photo Star, called. She was the general production manager of Kıyıdere TV. "Çağlar," she said, "I just saw Çiğdem's video on the Healthy Life Forum."

"Really, what was the topic?"

"'Obesity Is Not Your Fate.' Look, I wanted to ask you something. People were saying that she's going to be in the talent competition, but from what I've heard that's not going to work out. Would you like to have her join our weekend show?"

"Thank you, Yıldız Abla," I said, "but we've decided to stick to social media. We've closed the book on TV appearances."

At first, she didn't believe me. Then perhaps thinking that I'd change my mind if she went into more detail, she started telling me about the program. Holding the phone away from my ear, I thought about Kepçe, that math teacher of ours, wondering if maybe he wasn't so bad after all and I'd been a bit hasty in my judgment of him. Still, I knew it would be hard to ask him for anything, so I decided against it. I glanced at my sister, who was leaning toward the computer screen, her face lit by its glow. She shouted, "What the fuck is going on here, huh?" Speaking into the phone, I said, "No thank you, Yıldız Abla," whereupon my sister said to the computer screen, "Hey. Take it easy, man!"

What happened next, my friend, changed everything. Yet again, our luck ran out. Protests broke out in Istanbul, and our progress, which had been racing ahead at a rate of a hundred miles per hour, crumpled like a butterfly slamming into a brick wall. We were stuck at seventy-nine thousand views. In the following hours, we got something like fifteen or twenty views, nothing more. Hoping to stave off another round of sorrow, I told my sister, "YouTube is having some technical problems. They'll get it sorted out soon." But as the hours went by, the plausibility of my explanation fell into tatters. In the end, my sister slammed her fist against my external hard drive and hissed, "Çağlar, what's going on with the Internet! Tell me the truth."

"A group of radicals who usually get punched around by the police just became unpunchable, sweetie," I said. "And that pissed off the cops. Those are my first observations."

"Çağlar, what's it to us? For the love of God! With all my being, I was sad. I'm tired of being sad. I don't want to cry anymore. Why aren't they watching our video?"

"Now people are only watching the videos of the protests. Those are the only clips getting shared now. That's what happens during times like these. But don't worry. It's starting to get dark. The police will put down the protests in an hour or two. After that, social media will go back to normal."

However, nothing turned out like I expected. On the night of May 31, they took the resistance a step too far. For years, all those people who'd quietly minded their own business rose up in revolt just as my sister was about to become famous. So naturally, we were consumed by the feeling that people weren't rising up against the government but against my sister. They hadn't just taken over the streets but social media as well. Our video had been forgotten, as if those 79,356 viewers had vanished. I tried to get in touch with the people who had commented on the video, but in all that tumult our voices were lost.

With each passing hour, my sister's face fell deeper into shadow, and in the end she slipped into a mood that was darker and grimmer than any I'd ever seen. That night, the night of the uprising, she said to me, "Çağlar, what did I do to deserve this?"

"Nothing, baby, nothing at all."

She narrowed her eyes and smiled maniacally. "Do you know what I want right now?"

"What do you want, sweetie?"

"To eat six scoops of ice cream and then do myself in."

TEN

At night in the months of September and October, when hungry wild boars would come down from the dark, craggy mountains to the cornfields on the plain, passing along the most inaccessible paths that led through narrow passes never trod by humankind, my grandpa would grab his fifty-year-old shotgun, and I'd put my canteen in my backpack, and we'd set off to Hasanbaba. My grandpa had a friend there, an old military buddy who had once participated in joint military exercises with my grandpa in the Istranca Mountains years and years ago. I would sit on the flat roof of the village house pounding on a steel drum to keep the boars away from the cornfields. My grandpa and his friend would wait on the winding paths leading up into the mountains. If they sensed a shadow moving down toward the fields, they would fire off a blank, the sound of which would ring out over the entire plain. Despite all our efforts, however, in the morning we'd see that the boars had eaten part of the crop. On those mornings, my grandpa would always say, "Çağlar my boy, when you come up against the greatest misfortune and see that all your efforts are in vain, you have to just go on living." I'd agree with him, not even knowing what "misfortune" meant. While I didn't understand all the words he used, his weary expression and the undulations in the tone of his voice told me exactly what he was saying. If I was still mystified, I also could tell by the lengthening ash of the Maltepe cigarette he held between his yellowed fingers. He exposed me to real-life experiences, and they have nothing in common with meaningless conversation. Real-life experiences are acquired during long, sleepless nights, and during the day they don't do me a damn lick of good.

Anyway, so what was I saying? Ah yes, my sister. Realizing that all her efforts had been in vain, and faced yet again with a wave of fresh disappointment, she threw herself on the bed and pulled the covers up over her eyes. It was May 31, the night before that fateful June 1. When I tried to stroke her fingers, which were curled around the edge of the sheet, she pushed my hand away.

"Don't worry, baby," I said. "These protests will come to an end. Think about it. Doesn't everything come to an end?"

Yanking the sheet down below her chin, she stared at me with eyes bloodshot from sleeplessness and tears, and said, "Screw every single one of those protesters."

Placing my index finger over her lips, I said, "Please, sweetie. Swearing doesn't suit you at all. Plus, children aren't supposed to swear. The new constitution says so."

"Screw it, Çağlar. I'm unhappy."

She disappeared beneath the covers again, pulling her knees up to her stomach as if she wanted to disappear. I sat by her side until morning, twirling one of her unworn tennis shoes that had been sitting on top of the municipal bulletins on the treadmill. I knew that she wasn't sleeping, but there was nothing I could do. There are some situations that leave you completely helpless. For example, if I had gone to Istanbul that morning and said, "Now look, everyone, let's just drop this protest business, I'm begging you. It's not because I like those pricks who are in charge, and don't think that it matters any less than what you're fighting for. But believe me, we have a really important message to deliver to the world," who would listen to me? Was it the right time? You say it wasn't? Well, sorry.

Before you condemn my sister, who was so miserable that she was ready to swear at those hundreds of thousands of people taking to the streets, I suggest that you think over one thing before you haul her off to your discriminating court for judgment: When the protests broke out, why didn't any of you, from the most average of citizens to the most sophisticated state leaders, stop to think about how it might affect my sister? She was just nine years old; in the morning, she'd put her notepads and books into her light-green backpack and set off to school, sleepy eyed and a little distracted, walking along with who knows what thoughts rolling through her mind toward Evliya Çelebi Primary School, where she'd sit down in class 3-A and listen intently to her teacher along with her best friends Mervenaz and Ecem. She liked her other friends as well, and everyone liked her, too. Of course, as her older brother, I love her very much. All of these are extenuating circumstances.

Toward noon, I made breakfast for my sister. I made her a heart-shaped grilled cheese sandwich buttered inside and out, eggs with pastrami, and sizzling hot sausage, and then I put jam and honey on the tray as well, along with black olives with oregano sprinkled on top. As the tea was steeping, I dashed off to the Yağmur Bakery and bought an assortment of pastries and breadsticks, which I put on the tray along with the jar of Nutella, which my mom had hidden away. I even added a packet of Haribo Fantastic Mix. My goal was to prepare a breakfast she couldn't refuse. I knew she wouldn't give a damn about her diet. For months, she'd been starving herself. But why, for God's sake? So that the son of the solar panel distributor wouldn't call her "fatso"? So that a preliminary jury consisting of three retired zombies could reject her? So that, just as she was about to become famous, everyone could rush out onto the streets and say, "Now's not the time, step aside because we're going to save the country"?

I took the tray to her bedside. She was still lying there with the covers pulled up over her eyes. Before I could utter a word, she smelled the food and murmured, "Çağlar, I don't want to eat."

"Come on, sweetie, just take a look at what's here."

She didn't budge.

"Just take one look."

Slowly, she pulled down the sheet. Her initial expression of curiosity quickly turned into a ravenous stare. Everything that had been forbidden for months was on that tray.

"No, I don't want to eat."

"So, you're rejecting life."

"Çağlar, are you trying to hurt my feelings?"

"Why would you say a thing like that?"

"In two months, I've only lost two pounds. If I eat that breakfast, I'll gain five pounds, I know it. Everyone goes around eating whatever they want and nothing happens. But everything I eat sticks to me."

"Forget about the diet for now. During days of oppression, dieting is fine, but when there's a rebellion, anything goes. You need calories during such times. It's the law of history. This morning, a crowd of people marched across the Bosphorus Bridge just to have breakfast in Beşiktaş."

"But I didn't cross the bridge. Let them eat it."

"It doesn't matter. You have a right to eat, too."

"Okay, Çağlar, you're right. Give me the tray!"

As my sister was eating breakfast, Microbe sent me a request for a video call on Tango. I stepped out of the room and accepted it.

"Do you have the phone number of anyone at the Channel That Delivers More News than the Sports News Channel?" he asked, standing on top of his family's house.

"Why?"

"I called Goof International and said, 'I've got a video that I think is going to interest you,' but they turned me down. I called some other channels, but the line's always busy."

My sister called for me. She wanted some more olive oil. So I told Microbe to hold on for a second.

"And red pepper paste!"

"Why?"

"To spread on the bread."

"In that case, we've got Dijon mustard, too. It was an award from the training hotel."

"Be quick about it!"

"What's going on?" Microbe asked.

"My sister went off her diet."

"Good for her. Why don't you ask your uncle if he has the number of anyone at the channel? Maybe we can get them to air the video."

"All right. I'll get back to you."

When I went back into our room, I saw that she'd already finished off half the food on the tray. She didn't look happy as she greedily ate. I stepped out and called my uncle. "What the hell are you up to?" I asked.

"I'm at the office."

"Scared out of your ass?"

"Don't be frigging ridiculous!"

"Then why are you sitting at your office, dummy? What gave you that bright idea?"

"Çağlar, talk to me like that again, and I'll break your damn nose!"

"My sister's having a crisis and went off her diet. Get your ass home and bring the campaign gift bags with you."

"What the hell have you done? Goddamn it, are you trying to kill her? Take away whatever she hasn't eaten yet. Don't let her eat any more."

"Ha! That's funny coming from you. You've eaten the whole city, and you're still not full."

"Çağlar, I'm warning you, don't let her break her diet. This is serious. You know what Dr. İhsan said."

"Then come home."

"I'll come in the afternoon. I have a meeting now."

"With another political party?"

"Screw off!"

"Where were you last night?"

"There was a meeting at the provincial office."

"I just don't get it! You and your party have driven the whole damn country to revolt and you still dick around with pointless meetings," I said, able to hear my uncle getting anxious. "Whatever you do, don't hang up! I've got one more thing to say. Do you have the number of the Channel That Delivers More News than the Sports News Channel?"

"No."

"What do you mean? They had you on live TV for the opening of the sewage plant."

"I wasn't the only one. There were opening ceremonies for forty-eight plants. So no, I don't have the number," he said. "And don't let your sister eat!"

"Whatever, just hang up and stop wasting my time."

I Googled the number and called. The line was busy. I noticed that the number ended in oo, so I decided to call from o1 to 99 to see if I could get through. Sure enough, someone picked up when I dialed 17 as the last two numbers. "Hello," I said, but got no reply. I heard a sob. "Hello," I said, "is anyone there?" Again silence, and then another sob followed by a slight moan. It was as if someone was silently struggling in the throes of death. I pressed my ear to the phone, and in the end I concluded that there was a woman crying on the other end of the line.

"I think you're crying," I said gently. "What's the problem? Please don't be shy, talk to me. I'm a specialist in public relations."

A young woman's voice asked, "What did I do wrong?"

"You didn't do anything wrong, darling. Believe me, nothing. So please don't cry. I'm not the kind of inconsiderate guy who goes off on the first person who answers the phone when they call because they're pissed off about something the company did. So tell me, is the manager around? Can you patch me through to the manager? Or the guy who loves planes, or the bald guy who does the noon news, or the blond Lolita from the evening news, or the old guy who does the weather? Just connect me to someone."

"I can't."

"But don't you see? We're on the same side here."

Another round of sobs. "I can't," she said. "I'm sorry."

"Don't be sorry, sweetie. Whatever you do, don't be upset. It's not your fault, so don't be sad. Çağlar İyice is always by your side. You can add me on Facebook. Whenever something's bothering you, send me a message. Tell me all about your problems. Tell me about all the troubles in your life. Tell me about your dreams, about the false pleasures into which you've been driven, about your true desires. Write to me when you can no longer bear the turmoil swirling around you. Write to me the moment before you take off your shoe with a sexy flick of your wrist, with the intention of throwing it at the news editor. Write to me with wild abandon. Just let it all pour out; there's no need to put anything in order. I'll sort it out."

"Mmm," she said, and hung up.

Fifteen minutes later, my mom showed up, but she couldn't get in because I'd latched the door chain. I went out into the hallway and called out, "Who's there?" as if I didn't know.

"It's me," she said.

"What do you want? Don't you have work to do at the office? Isn't anyone filing a claim for property today?"

"Çağlar, open the door this second!" She started pushing and pulling at the door, making an annoying racket. "Your uncle called and said that Çiğdem went off her diet. What's she eating?"

"She's having breakfast, just like everyone does."

"Open the door!"

"Don't open it," my sister shouted.

"I'm not going to open the door," I said. "We're hungry. We want to have breakfast in peace. To hell with you all. The whole country's burning, and you're still counting every bite we eat."

My mom stopped trying to force open the door. After waiting a little while, I tiptoed toward it and peered through the gap. She was sitting on the stairs in the dark beside the water meter with its red valve. Her right hand was covering her eyes and she was silently crying, like a child who has come home only to find that there's no one there. I unhooked the chain and opened the door.

"What did I ever do to you?" she asked. "What did I ever do but love you? Why do you act this way with me? Why do you make your sister see me as her enemy? Aren't people supposed to love their mothers? What did I do to deserve this?"

"Come in," I said. "Those are difficult questions. Let's talk inside."

She came in and hung her purse on the coat rack. A strange calm had settled over her, and she was moving with the slow deliberateness of the elderly. She kept looking at me, as if she had come home to see me, not my sister.

"So?"

"What do you mean, 'so'?"

She was waiting for me to answer the questions she'd just asked. But it's so hard to talk about things like that. It's even harder to silence them. Immediately, you know when someone tries to silence them; even the most skilled liar can't pull it off. All you can do is foolishly smile, which is sheer agony for the other person, and you tear yourself to pieces as well. Everything collapses between the two of you. All is smashed to smithereens, reduced to a horse with a broken leg, never to be set right again, and there is no longing for the past or expectations of the future, or a moment that can be lived in the present. There's nothing left at all.

Who was the sharp-witted moron who divided time into past, present, and future anyway? In that present, everything happened long before and came to an end; all that is lived is over, all that can't and won't ever be lived is over. It all comes to an end in that present, all that cannot be lived. Is that pessimistic? Is that despairing? Damn it all! My mom was asking me why I didn't love her. What's pessimistic about that, what's so despairing about it? This is my life, this is your life, this is that place where we all find ourselves cornered at one point or another, the first big regret, the mistake that never can be made right, that wound that will never heal, a horse that can't get to its feet, a drowned fish. Do you want me to explain it all, instance by instance, and add an appendix of precedents, like at the end of law books? Tell me, friend, what about all that understanding? Where is your sense of understanding now?

My sister emerged from our room holding a jar of jam and shouted, "As if you're so beautiful, Mom! You're not! If you were beautiful, Dad wouldn't have left you!" She then flung the jar of jam at a still-life painting on the wall, and the daisies that my mom had painted in the eleventh session of the oil-painting class she attended at the community center were splattered with strawberries. I took a long look at the painting and understood yet again that my belief in my sister's artistic talent was certainly not for nothing. That mediocre still life was suddenly transformed into a modern work of art. As my mom and I stood there looking at the dripping daisies, my sister rushed past us into the bathroom and locked the door, announcing that she would not leave until the protests were over.

My mom stumbled into her bedroom, and I was left standing in the hallway. I knew that my sister would keep her word, but to be honest I wasn't very worried about it because I was sure that the police would take control of the situation in an hour or two. On the night of May 31, things had gotten a little out of hand, but I thought that everything would return to normal. Then we'd shoot a new video and try our luck again. There was also the possibility that our old video would be rediscovered and we'd leave our stamp on the summer in its very first week.

Microbe called the next day and said, "Well, boss, the protesters laid into the police and gave them a one-two combo. They've taken over Taksim Square."

I looked at a few pictures posted on Facebook and held my head in my hands. "Aw hell," I said. "We're screwed!"

My sister called out from the bathroom, "What happened?"

"Nothing."

"Are the protests over?"

"Almost. You can come out now."

"I'm not coming out until they're completely over."

"Great."

I was in shock, complete and utter shock. I raided my uncle's stash under his foldout sofa and poured myself a double Jack Daniel's. After adding two ice cubes to the crystal tumbler, I swirled it around. Normally, I wasn't the kind of guy to drink whiskey in the middle of the day, but nothing made sense in this country anymore. In the beginning, I didn't realize that the leftists who got the protests started were so daring. I'd thought that they'd just cry and run away after a few squirts of tear gas. What had happened to them? If they were such superheroes, how come no one ever bothered to tell us? I'm not saying that in praise of leftists. Çağlar İyice never praises anyone, and even in the most emotional of moments, he's careful to maintain an objective stance. But why should I? Sometimes even I feel like I'm not my father's son. Ooh! Jesus Christ!

I approached my mom's bedroom and watched her in the wardrobe mirror. Most likely, she'd taken some antidepressants because she'd fallen into a deep sleep. She had tossed her skirt and jacket onto the floor and lain down on the bed, not even bothering to get under the covers. I can't remember what they're called because I'm not interested in stuff like that, but she wasn't wearing anything on her legs. I noticed that her breasts weren't saggy and that her thighs were still quite firm, and there was a tiny mole on the back of her upper thigh, a cute, tiny black mole that made you want to kiss it, and it had a twin on her left ankle. For a while, I looked at the red marks left behind by her bra, and then I knelt by her bed, observing her small face. My mom has a cute, small face that makes her look younger than she really is. I should point out here that if any of you think that I'm describing my mom like this to turn you on, you've got the wrong idea, and I'll fuck you up good if you're getting horny. I'm trying to explain something completely different here. My mom was a beautiful woman in terms of the criteria of beauty in this day and age, and she was still attractive. That's what I'm trying to say, but she was very unhappy. If she were happy, she would've been even more beautiful. Don't we all become a little more attractive when we're happy?

From the bathroom, my sister called out, "Çağlar, what's the situation now?"

Drinking down the rest of the whiskey, I savored the burn as it coursed down my throat, and then I pulled a blanket over my mom. "I'm going to be honest with you," I said. "We've lost Taksim."

"What do you mean?"

"At 3:40 p.m., Taksim Square was taken over by the protestors."

"That's impossible. I don't believe you!"

"I can't believe it, either. They started by protesting against the cutting down of the trees in Gezi Park, and now they've got control of the entire square. There's not a single cop there."

"The nerve!"

My sister came out of the bathroom and asked to see my phone. She looked at a few videos and scanned through some pictures. She saw the massive crowd in Taksim Square. She saw the expressions of victory on people's faces, which spelled their defeat. She saw the expressions of joy on their faces, which spelled their sorrow, and the sense of freedom that strangled them. Her face flushed bright red and she handed back my phone. She was so angry that she couldn't even cry. Dashing into the kitchen, she pulled the bread knife from the wooden cutlery block. I threw myself in front of the door to our mom's room and spread my arms out, thinking that she was going to attack her, but instead my sister went into our bedroom. She opened the wardrobe and took out the white coat that Orhan the tailor had made for us and started hacking at it on the bed. I ran up and grabbed the jacket, holding it above my head so she couldn't get to it, but she came up to me with the knife, and for a moment I felt like a matador in the arena.

"Stop it," I said. "You're going to do more dancing in that jacket. It's not over yet."

"It's over, Çağlar. It's all over!"

She went back to the wardrobe and started slicing away at the blue shirt, the hat, and the moonwalk shoes. Grabbing her by the wrist, I wrenched the knife away and held it up over my head. When she realized that she'd never get the knife back, she started tearing at her hair.

"You are just going through a crisis, which all great talents go through."

"What do they want from me?" she screamed. "What's their problem? So what about the trees; they get cut down every day! As if today were the only day that some trees were going to get cut down. Why are they doing this? Why?"

"If you want to know, I'll explain it all to you. But first you have to calm down. Sit down. Do you want me to tell you who started all this business?"

She sat on the corner of the bed. Trying not to cry, she was biting the inside of her lower lip, making dimples appear in her plump cheeks. "Okay, so who started it?"

"Who else! Those atheist architects who just hang around all the time, living the bachelor's life. Dad and his friends."

My sister looked at a picture frame on her bedside table. It was a picture of our father. She'd taken the picture last year as he gazed into the distance at a restaurant by the sea.

"Dad wouldn't do that," she said.

"He did. They did. Why do you think Dad hasn't come to see you in the past two weeks? Because he's been stirring up these protests. They've been working on the plan for a year now. I know about every step they've made along the way. I didn't want to tell you because I thought you might get upset. But if you want, I can call and give them a piece of my mind."

"Are you going to call Dad?"

"Let's not do this personally, but through official channels."

After turning on the speaker on my iPhone, I called the number of the Istanbul branch of the Chamber of Architects. It rang and rang, but finally a woman answered. Women always answer the phone when you call places like that.

"Chamber of Architects, Istanbul branch. How can I help you?"

Her voice was cheerful, flirtatious even, and confident. And why not? She was young, beautiful, and she'd taken over Taksim Square. What else could you want from life?

"Can I speak with Sabahattin İyice?"

"Who's calling?"

"Çağlar İyice."

"Just a moment." Half a million seconds later, she picked up the phone again and said, "He's not in his office. Would you like to leave a message?"

I glanced at my sister, who was gnawing on her lower lip out of curiosity and anger. "Yes. Please write this down."

"Go ahead."

I thought for a little while, but nothing came to mind. "Goddamn it!"

"I'm sorry?"

"No, don't write that. Sorry. Just a second. Okay, write this: 'First of all . . .' No, don't write that. Write: 'To whom it may concern,' so that it's more formal. Yes, that's it. Write: 'To whom it may concern. You are utterly disloyal, ignorant of what really matters in life. What the hell do you want?' No, don't write that. Write: 'What's your point with all this? Tender feelings are involved.' Yes write that: 'Tender feelings. Those tender feelings that we all have! Goddamn you! My sister's only nine years old! Didn't anyone ever stop to think of her? Damn you, isn't anyone thinking about her?' No wait, don't write that, write something else. Write: 'There's a girl here. A girl who never gives up in the face of any and all misfortune. Her name is Çiğdem İyice. Don't you ever forget why this girl who never gives up in the face of any and all misfortune isn't giving up! She wants you to put an immediate end to these protests.' Did you write it all down?"

There was a moment of silence and then the woman said, "Okay. I'll have Sabahattin Ağbi give you a call."

"What? What did you say?"

"I'll tell Sabahattin Ağbi to call you."

"Screw your Sabahattin Ağbi! Who gives a shit about Sabahattin Ağbi? I'm making an official statement here. This is an official statement to the Chamber of Architects. This is an ultimatum! Sabahattin Ağbi. Take your 'ağbi' and shove it up your ass!"

"What are you saying?"

"I'm saying you have no right to talk down to me like that! If we wanted to talk to your Sabahattin Ağbi, we would've called him ourselves. This is an official statement. You're going to take down what I said and give a copy of that memo to all the managers at the Chamber of Architects. You're going to give that memo to every single one of them, including Sabahattin Ağbi. That motherfucking Sabahattin Ağbi is going to get the damn memo, too!"

Next we heard a click and then the drone of the dead line. I sat listening to the sound for a little while. Unable to take my eyes from the phone, I glared at it as if it were a dark door that had just slammed shut in my face. There was a roaring in my ears, and I found myself gasping for breath. "Sabahattin *Ağbi*!" I shouted. "Screw your ağbi! Since when the hell is he Sabahattin Ağbi?"

A wave of heat surged through me, and I pulled off my T-shirt and punched the wall. Tears of frustration welled up in my eyes. My hands were shaking, and I balled them into fists to stop the trembling.

"Çağlar," my sister said. "Calm down. Please."

"I am calm," I said.

But I wasn't.

ELEVEN

That night, we went to Tadım and sat down under the acacia trees at a table facing the sea. It's a nice place and has every kind of ice cream you could imagine, from chocolate chip to mastic and honeydew melon. If you have the time, you should check it out sometime. They stay open till fall every year. When the waiter came to take our order, I asked my sister what she wanted, but she didn't answer. So I said to the waiter, who was standing there pad and pen in hand, "We'll have a mixed bowl. Six scoops of everything, with a double topping of chocolate and nuts."

I had an urge to say, "We're really unhappy," but I held my tongue. That's what sociology demands, the silence of emotions. We ate in silence, just like how after my grandpa died we ate our commemorative halva in silence as we mourned him. At the time, my sister was only five years old, but even at that age she understood the gravity of the situation. That's when I first noticed that her personality was evolving into a multifaceted and complex state of being. We drank two glasses of water after finishing our ice cream and paid the bill, and when we got the change we started walking home down Fetih Street with weak, mournful steps, as if there were nothing left for us to do in life but wait for death.

As we got close to home, we heard a banging sound echoing down the streets, so we stopped and looked around. Three or four housewives had stepped out onto their balconies and were banging spoons against cooking pots. When others heard them, they also went out onto their balconies and joined them in making that racket. Some clapped their hands, some waved flags, and some brought out more pots and pans. Within just a minute or two, more people were banging away at cooking pots on their balconies or turning the lights in their apartments on and off. One particularly talented driver had turned on his emergency flashers and was driving slowly down the street, beeping the horn with one hand and flashing a victory sign out the window with his other hand, prompting a new round of applause from the balconies. After that, others driving down the street started blaring their horns, too, and suddenly Fetih Street was transformed into a dissonant symphony. An old guy walking down the street seemed to have sensed the dissonance, and he started waving his hands as if he were conducting an orchestra, a nonchalant smile on his lips as he set off in search of some kind of order. I saw our seventh-grade national history teacher dancing on a balcony above Fidanlar Market; she was a chatty one and an easy grader, so it didn't strike me as odd. A guy leaned out of the window of his apartment, raising a glass of *rakı*, shouting, "Government resign! Government resign!" Everyone on the street turned and looked at him. "What are you looking at?" he yelled. An old man nearby muttered, "God save us all." The wife of the man shouting from the window said, "Seyfi, get back inside." He turned and looked at his wife, and then he looked at the people outside looking at him. At that moment, we were all looking at each other as if trying to understand what we should be looking at.

I held my sister's hand so she wouldn't be afraid.

"Çağlar, what's going on?" she asked.

"The protests have spread to Kıyıdere," I said. "That's my first observation."

With rapid steps, we continued on our way home. At the corner of our street, I saw the dirty yellow dog that my uncle had brought home. It fixed its eyes on us, looking at us with an expression that was both threatening and hurt, and barked. Giving the dog a wide berth, we scampered up to our apartment. People had started banging pots and pans on our street, too, and it seemed as if the racket would never come to an end. As the sound got louder and louder, my sister started biting her fingernails, and then she pressed her hands over her ears. Realizing that there was nothing to be done, she went after the small pillows on the sofa, trying to tear them apart with her teeth. I couldn't get her to calm down. As soon as I took one pillow away from her, she snatched up another one and started gnawing away. We seemed to have a limitless supply of pillows and cushions in our living room.

I stepped out onto our balcony and raised my hand as if calling for calm. I saw Ayla Teyze on her balcony across the way, banging away on a pot. I called out, "Ayla Teyze, hold on a second! Why are you banging on that pot?"

She held her hand up to her chin and said, "We've had it up to here!"

"With what?"

"For years, we've been silent. Enough already! Get yourself a pot, too!"

"Ayla Teyze, why should I bang on a pot? I've been speaking my mind all these years. If I want to say something, I say it."

"So, what have you been saying then? What are you standing up for as you sit there at home?"

She was trying to give me a lesson in opposition by banging on a pot, but I couldn't take her seriously and contented myself by flashing her a dirty look. For me, taking a stance of opposition was a way of life, a manner of existence. During times when I've needed to stand up for something but remained silent, I've always been overcome by the feeling that I haven't really been silent but simply ceased to exist.

Cutting off the conversation with Ayla Teyze, I focused on what was happening on the street. People were banging away on pots and pans with all their might, and it gave me the impression that I was watching a high-speed film, with sound, of course. When I saw all that enthusiasm, I turned to our neighbor and changed my tune, offering some advice about the right way to go about things. "Aren't you following what's happening on Twitter? There's going to be a protest of solidarity tonight in Kıyıdere down by the pier. You should bang your pot there. It'll be more effective."

"We're protesting here, not on Twitter!"

"Did I say there was a damn protest on Twitter? I'm just saying that the time and place has been posted there."

Swinging a rolling pin, my sister ran out onto the balcony and screamed at the people banging pots, "I'm going to complain about all of you to our representative Asshole Bey!"

It was a struggle, but I managed to get my sister back inside. Just as I was closing the balcony door, I heard one of our neighbors across the way say, "What a shame, they've even turned their kids into religious nuts."

When I heard that, my blood boiled. Spreading my arms apart, I roared, "What? We're religious? For the love of God, what's religious about us?"

If they were thinking that we were religious because my uncle had switched to the conservative Giving Gramps Cancer Party, they should've known that when I was younger I'd say that I was going to evening prayers at the mosque but in fact sneak off to play pool. When he found out what I was up to, my late grandpa cracked a pool cue over my head. But I didn't say anything about that, and I didn't give a damn what they thought about my uncle. Placing one hand on my sister's shoulder, I said, "We're not religious. My sister and I are agnostic!"

"Agnoswhat?"

"Go back inside, you ignorant fool! Arguing with you is a waste of time."

Just as I was about to go back inside, my mother came rushing out onto the balcony in a panic, a stunned look on her face, as if she'd just surfaced from the depths of the ocean. "Çağlar, what's going on? Çağlar, Çağlar, Çağlar, tell me what's going on?"

"Nothing," I said. "Calm down."

She listened to the sound of the banging pots for a few seconds and started shouting, "They're going to kill us! They're going to kill us!"

Grabbing her firmly by the shoulders, I said, "Don't be ridiculous."

"But they have guns."

"They don't have guns, they're just pots and pans. Calm down."

"They're banging at the door. I just know it, they're coming for us."

"No one's at the door. That's just your medication. So settle down and come inside."

I pulled her in and sat her down at the kitchen table. My sister was standing in the kitchen doorway looking at us. I said, "Sweetie, go sit down in the living room." I didn't want her to see our mom like that. She had put on my blue sweatpants, but she was wearing them backward. Her hair was a mess, and she didn't look like she had just woken up but rather like she hadn't slept for days. I tried to get her to drink a glass of water, and I rubbed some kolonya onto her wrists and forehead. Her eyes were wide with fear.

"They're going to kill us," she moaned.

"Why would they kill us? We're not such important people."

"Why were the neighbors yelling at you?"

"They think we're religious nuts. It was just a little misunderstanding, a little argument."

She leaped up and cried, "They're banging on the door!"

"There's no one at the door. The sound is coming from outside."

Opening the balcony door a little, I said, "See? It's just the people out on their balconies."

But when she heard the roar of banging pots, her eyes filled with horror. I closed the door and tried to think of another way to calm her down.

"They're banging at the door of the apartment building. They're trying to get in," my mother said.

"No one's banging on the door."

"Yes, they are."

"Okay then, let's go take a look."

"No way. Not me."

"Come on!"

Taking hold of her elbow, I pulled her up to show her that there was no one at the door. But she wouldn't leave the kitchen. A strange strength had come over her, and I couldn't get her to budge. She was holding onto each side of the doorjamb, her feet planted firmly on the ground. As I struggled to get her out of the kitchen, the collar of her T-shirt ripped. In the end, I leaned down and grabbed her by the waist, and pushing with all my strength managed to break her grip. We tumbled to the floor, and she landed on top of me. Immediately, she tried to scramble back to the kitchen, but I caught hold of her arm and she fell down beside me.

"Look at the front door of the apartment building," I shouted.

I tried to get her to turn her head to look, but she scratched my face. Those five fingernails tore into my cheek like a cat lashing out with its claws. Taking advantage of my shock, she scampered back into the kitchen.

Pressing my hand to my cheek, I snapped, "Would you please come here and look at the door?"

My mom had sat down on the floor in front of the kitchen counter and pulled her knees up to her chest, holding her hands in front of her face like a boxer putting up his guard. For a moment, I considered taking down the front door of the apartment building and bringing it up to show her. I approached my mom, and she stared at me with wide eyes.

"Don't get near me!" she screamed. "Don't you dare get near me!"

But she wasn't just looking at me with fear. I realized that she didn't even realize who I was. I'm not saying that she was looking at me with an expression of *trying* to understand who I was. She simply didn't recognize me. I'd never seen her look at me like that before.

"Mom, what's going on? What's happened to you?"

"Who are you?"

"It's me. It's me, goddamn it! Me!"

For a moment, I thought that she really had lost her mind. That thought drove me to such despair that I punched the kitchen cabinet.

My sister came rushing up and held my arm. "Çağlar, stop it!"

"Sweetness, go watch some TV. Please just turn on the TV, okay?"

I went into my mom's bedroom, grabbed her purse from the nightstand, and brought it into the kitchen. After emptying it on the table, I separated the bottles of Xanax and Prozac from the rest of the junk that spilled out. I picked up one of the bottles and shook it in front of her face.

"Are you taking these pills so that you won't recognize me anymore? Is that it? So that you won't know who I am? Great! In that case, I'd like to have a few of these myself."

As I was opening the bottle, my sister grabbed me and said, "Çağlar, please, please, please don't!"

The bottle flew from my grip, and little blue pills scattered on the ground. My sister started picking them up and stuffing them into her pockets. At that point I noticed that my phone was ringing. It was Microbe.

"What are you up to?" he asked.

"Going insane."

"That's too bad. Come down to the pier."

"Microbe, don't tell me that you're joining the protest, too."

"No. Mervenaz and Ecem are here. There have been some developments in the Efekan situation."

TWELVE

My heart was pounding. When I left the apartment building, that dirty yellow dog started following me, glaring menacingly with its head cocked to the left. As I walked down Fetih Street, I stopped a few times and looked back, and each time it would stop behind me. The dog didn't pay attention to anyone else. I was its sole target. I had visions of it waiting for me to turn down a dark alleyway so it could leap up and attack me. When I passed by the labor union's local office, I heard a minibus approaching from behind, and I turned to wave it down, but it went roaring past down the middle of the road. "Slow down," I shouted, running after it. The dog chased me. Eventually, I stopped to catch my breath beneath a streetlight. The dog was just a few steps away, ears pricked up, breathing heavily through its nose. I could see rows of pointy teeth in its half-opened mouth. In desperation, I looked down the street, but the blue minibus was long gone.

I continued walking, slowly at first. Occasionally, I glanced back over my shoulder, and then I quickened my steps. At the end of the street, I turned toward Liberation Square. When I saw Constable Hakkı on the stairs of old Atacan Pub, I breathed a sigh of relief. I ran up and shook his hand, and asked, "How are you, Constable?" I had one eye on the dog, which was looking up at me, but it couldn't bring itself to come up the stairs because I was standing there with a cop.

"I'm fine, Çağlar," he said, without turning to look at me. "How are you?"

"I'm getting by."

Constable Hakkı was wearing a black suit and holding his walkie-talkie up to his ear as he stonily looked out over the square and the crowd of people that had gathered there. Because he was balding, his forehead appeared broader, and he stood there trying to look serious, but there was something distracted about his expression, as if he were perhaps a little sad about something or had suffered an injustice. I'd seen him like that two years before when a double murder he was investigating had drawn the attention of the national press. His bodyguard and driver, a massive man, was standing beside him now, and he appeared to be even more agitated than the constable. Wherever the constable looked, the bodyguard would turn and look in the same direction. I also started watching the crowd in the square. It was the biggest one I'd seen since the Republic Day celebrations of October 29 the year before, which had included a free public concert and fireworks show.

Because there was no podium or stage, it seemed like the people didn't really know where they should be looking. Some of them were looking at the statue of Ataturk, which had been moved last year, and others were looking at the rusty ferry in the town square. Most of the people were holding flags and posters of Ataturk. There was a group of twenty-five or thirty people from the organization Rights for the Little Fish near the ferry. Three months earlier, they had formed a human chain around the AKSA factory after a fire broke out, claiming that there had been a chemical leak. They tend to chew your ear off, but I like them; they've got a hot-tempered approach to life. They even managed to talk me into signing up for a subscription to their magazine. It still comes every month, wrapped in green plastic, but because I've been delving into the literary giants these days I haven't had time to read the issues. But one day I will.

Glancing up at the clouds passing in front of the moon, I stood there listening to the roar of the crowd. My mind was filled with question marks that night. After the protests broke out in Istanbul, they spread to the other big cities and even reached our little town of Kıyıdere. Millions of people were gathering in squares around the country. That's all well and good, but what were those people going to do? Bring down the government? Start a revolution? Hang people like my uncle? If so, what would my uncle's last wish be? What would become of our relations with the EU? Would we still be granted the right to travel without visas? Above all, I wondered what developments Mervenaz and Ecem were going to reveal to me concerning Efekan.

I called Microbe and told him that I was in front of the old Atacan Pub. Then I saw a team of riot police approaching from the right. There were about twenty-five of them. I had only seen them before at Kıyıderespor matches and when the We Call Everything Something Else Party made press statements. Constable Hakkı signaled for the head of the riot police to stop, and he started walking toward them, his driver/bodyguard following behind him. The dog trotted up the steps when they left and approached me from the left, so I headed down the steps on the right, but it trailed along behind me as I approached the crowd. Just as I was thinking about pushing my way into the crowd as a way of shaking off the dog, someone grabbed my arm. I whipped around. I breathed a sigh of relief when I saw that it was Microbe.

"What happened?" he asked. "You're as white as a sheet."

I pointed out the dog. Furrowing his brows, Microbe walked up to the mutt until he was practically on top of it and then snapped his head to the side in a gesture that said "Beat it." That poor dog tucked its tail between its legs and scampered off. If it were possible to change the world without uttering a single word, I'm sure that Microbe would be the one to do it.

"Where are Mervenaz and Ecem?" I asked.

"Follow me."

We started walking toward the old Ataturk statue. Mervenaz and Ecem had come to the protest with their mothers. They were waving Turkish flags, chanting the slogan, "Turkey is secular and that's how it will stay! Turkey is secular and that's how it will stay!" When they saw us, they started shouting even louder. It was like being at those soccer matches attended only by women and children when the teams are being punished for something and men aren't allowed to attend.

"Girls, can we talk?"

They went on chanting as if they hadn't heard me.

"Girls," I said. "I promise you that Turkey is going to stay secular and you'll go on tanning on the beach. So let's go somewhere and talk about this Efekan business."

"We already explained it," they said, "to Cengiz Ağbi."

"That may be the case, but tell me about it, too. Did Efekan ask you to tell Çiğdem that he is madly in love with her?"

"No," Mervenaz said.

Ecem also confirmed the denial. They tended to either repeat what the other said or complete each other's sentences, and the latter made them seem like affable twins.

"Çiğdem told us that she was madly in love with Efekan," they said. "She wanted us to tell him."

"Did you tell him?"

"No."

"Why not?"

"We didn't want to bother Efekan. Last year, she fell in love with him, and that time we did tell him. Efekan said that he didn't like her. So Çiğdem drew a heart on his notebook. When Efekan erased it during third period, she went and scribbled all over his notebooks."

"But Efekan scribbled all over her notebook."

"She did it first."

"Girls, aren't you Çiğdem's best friends? Whose side are you on here?"

"We don't talk to Çiğdem anymore."

"Why not?"

"She said something really terrible when we didn't tell Efekan that she loved him."

"What did she say?"

"We can't. It's too terrible."

"Whisper it in my ear."

Simultaneously, Mervenaz said it into my left ear and Ecem said it into my right ear. I'm not going to write here what my sister said. She's a well-behaved girl, but of course in those times she was under a lot of stress. She had a broken heart, and she was alone. Suffice it to say that at the age of nine she was carrying a spiritual burden that would be difficult to bear for someone her age.

"What was the deal with her pushing him down the stairs?"

"We didn't see it happen. But apparently he wasn't paying attention to her so she went up to him and said something really bad about his nose or ears or something and then pushed him down the stairs. Çağlar Ağbi, are you teaching her how to say all those bad words?"

"Of course not, don't be ridiculous. It's the older kids at school."

Waving their flags, Mervenaz and Ecem went back to their mothers. People of all ages were passing by. Some of them were carrying flags and some of them were carrying posters, and still others were carrying handwritten statements and some had nothing at all, but they were all driven by some emotional compulsion, something like anger, or disappointment, or, I don't know, maybe curiosity. Everyone was shouting, and they looked angry, but there was something strangely joyful about them as well, and when they took a break from chanting slogans they got into animated discussions. They all had their own opinions, but in the end their voices were united when they started chanting,

"Government resign! Government resign!" I bowed my head, holding my forehead in the palm of my hand.

"What's wrong?" Microbe asked.

"I'm tired."

"Let's go then, if you want."

"Microbe, what's going to come of this?"

"We'll talk to Çiğdem."

"That's not what I mean."

I gestured to the crowd of people around us. I stood among them, but I didn't feel that I belonged there, as if I'd been sent there as a Colombian observer and was surrounded by people speaking a language I didn't understand.

"The people are upset," Microbe said. "They're fed up."

"Yes, but why?"

"I don't know. Maybe they're tired of always feeling the same thing. Maybe they're tired of seeing the same faces and dealing with the same problems. They want something new, something different."

As we walked toward the seaside to get a breath of air away from the crowd, I saw Yavuz Amca, the president of the You'll Vote for Us No Matter What Party's central district office. He waved at me and called out, "Hey, Çağlar, so you're here, too?"

"Wherever Kıyıdere is, that's where you'll find me, President Yavuz."

"Good for you," he said, slapping me on the shoulder. There were fine blue veins on that eggplant nose of his, and I could smell rakı on his breath, but it would be more true to say that he was spiritually drunk. "It's a beautiful night."

"Yes it is. Now, if you could give us a minute."

"Hang on," he said, grabbing my arm.

He narrowed his eyes like he had something really important to say, but then he smiled, and I got the feeling that he'd decided against it. Trying to present the blankest expression possible, I looked back at him. He could say whatever he wanted, but I wasn't about to encourage him.

After a long pause he said, "What's going to happen with the road at our complex?"

"The raw asphalt's ready. We're waiting for the Ministry of Transport to deliver the gravel."

"It's been a year now."

"President Yavuz, it's a complicated business. You see, my uncle didn't mention this to the management at your complex, but the main road was torn up by all the dump trucks during the construction, and now it's full of potholes. For months, we've been working on patching them up. So think about the position we're in. How can we start working on the side roads when we're still busy with the main streets?"

"You could have at least laid down some crushed rock."

"Why do that when the raw asphalt is ready?"

"Your uncle said that same thing, but it seems like you're giving us the runaround."

I felt completely sapped. I turned and looked to Microbe for support. His gaze was fixed on President Yavuz, his eyes flashing anger, but the president hadn't noticed the silent curses being hurled at him.

"President Yavuz, why would we give you the runaround? Far from it," I said. "For years, I've been working for the municipality, and I've never let anyone in my family get involved in partisanship, including my uncle. We provide services to everyone equally. There's no discrimination whatsoever. We even have an Alevi employed as a contract worker at the industrial works office. Papa Reçko called from Tirana and said that guy was a friend of a friend, an acquaintance of sorts, and so we drew up the contract. We didn't care that he was Alevi. Next year, we might hire him on permanently."

"That is, if you guys are still in office," he said, slapping me on the shoulder and grinning.

Microbe took me by the arm and signaled with a tilt of his head that we should get going. We walked off, not bothering to respond to President Yavuz. Just then, I saw a few guys I was on bad terms with because of an issue that had come up about a referendum. They were members of the youth wing of the You'll Vote for Us No Matter What Party. They spotted me and shouted, "Government resign! Government resign!"

Microbe said, "Come on, let's go."

"Hang on," I said, before calling out to these guys. "What's that got to do with me?"

When I said that, they started shouting even louder. President Yavuz stepped between us, spreading his arms, and said, "Çağlar's got nothing to do with the government."

But in all that commotion, he couldn't make himself heard. Others in the crowd turned to see what the guys from the youth wing were looking at, and more and more people in the square, not just the members of the You'll Vote for Us No Matter What Party, started shouting at me, "Government resign! Government resign!" I nodded, a sad smile on my lips.

Microbe made a move to go after some of the guys who were shouting at me, but I held him back and said, "Don't bother. Let them shout."

I stood there watching them, and a weight bore down on my chest. As I listened to them shout "Government resign!" at me because I happened to be the mayor's nephew and there was no one else at whom they could direct their anger, I thought that if it had been possible, I would have resigned from being myself. What were they going on about? What right did they have to attack my character, personality, and standing with their verbal punches, blows, and slaps? I felt doubly snubbed, doubly wounded. That night, I wanted to talk to all these people one by one, and, if necessary, beat them until they came to their senses. A long while has passed since then, and I'm no longer in that frame of mind. Now, I want to understand all those people I wanted to beat that night. I don't just want to understand their thoughts and feelings, but the purest points in their hearts and the deepest, most secret corners of their souls. Then I'd say, "All my brothers and sisters out there, do you really want to know what kind of a person Çağlar İyice is?"

Now that I'm thinking about it, one of the reasons that night left such a deep impression on me is that right after all that shouting I saw my ex-girlfriend. Microbe and President Yavuz had taken me by the arms and were leading me away from the crowd of people accosting me. We saw T. C. Sinem Uzun near the ferry waving to us so we headed in her direction. My ex-girlfriend was there as well. After we broke up, we'd run into each other once during a snowstorm. I was losing a snowball fight with the kids from our street, and using pine trees as shields, I was retreating toward Yağmur Bakery, firing off tactical shots along the way. When I turned around, I found myself face to face with her in front of the bakery's windows, which were steamed up by all the hot bread inside. On this night, she had tied a Turkish flag around her neck, and in the middle of the flag there was a picture of Ataturk wearing a calpac. She was standing there with her new boyfriend. Something snapped inside me when I saw him, like pieces breaking away from a satellite launched into space. If you have any feelings at all, no matter how much they've faded, chance encounters like this always stir them back to life. If I tried to explain it all to you now, it would take till morning, so I won't go into it. But it will be enough to say that yes, we had some wonderful days together at the old Bankers' Clubhouse, at the old Atacan Pub, at the old Ergun Wedding Hall, on old Şefika Street.

Quite at ease, she asked, "How are you, Çağlar?"

Unable to control the trembling in my voice, I replied, "I'm good, Çisem. How are you?"

Her new boyfriend was also quite unruffled. After we shook hands, he didn't even bother to turn and look at me. I wondered if it was just me who was uncomfortable with the situation and at a loss for words. In those days, I had given up on chasing after her, and I wasn't making the slightest effort to try to get back together with her. But there wasn't a single day that I didn't think about her, and not a single hour passed in which she didn't cross my mind. And she knew it. Everyone knew it. Even the seagulls knew it. That's why they screeched in the early hours of the morning, without anyone asking their opinions on the matter, just to be assholes and say, "We know, we know!"

After that brief chat, they went back to chanting slogans. As she shouted, T. C. Sinem Uzun raised her hands in the air as if she were dancing at a nightclub. As for my ex-girlfriend, she was rather regal. With an expression that was pure, calm, and full of love, she joined in with the chorus of the crowd. If I had been Mustafa Kemal Ataturk, I would have drafted her as a soldier on the spot and appointed T. C. Sinem Uzun to the back lines so that she wouldn't walk around distracting my army.

Microbe and I left them there and walked toward the ferry. I reached out and touched its rusty hull, watching my ex-girlfriend out of the corner of my eye. Inevitably, my thoughts turned to that bastard of an uncle of mine. Sometimes, I really pity the guy and find myself filled with compassion for him, thinking, *Did anyone ever love that prick when he was a kid? Didn't anyone stroke his head, whisper words of love into his ear, buy him a teddy bear, take him by the hand for trips to the seaside on the weekend, or teach him how to make sandcastles?* Probably not. Maybe that's why as soon as he became mayor, the first thing he did was have a ferry that had been junked by Istanbul City Lines brought to Kıyıdere and set up in the town square. Ferries ply the seas and people walk town squares, so how is it that he didn't think of the fact that sooner or later a scrupulous inspector might show up and ask, "Where did you get the authority to spend the people's tax money on such ridiculous things?"

After he got the ferry, he decided to turn it into a hotel. He added a third floor, but it looked like shit so he had the extra floor removed, and then he had the bright idea of turning the ferry into a restaurant, but that project was shelved, too. As it stands now, on the side of the ferry facing the pier there's a sign that says, "No Trespassing," and on the port side there's a placard that reads, "Thank You, Mayor Altan Baysal, for Your Support for Kıyıderespor."

I stood there leaning with my hand on the ferry, unable to take my eyes off my ex-girlfriend. My only consolation was that in all that chaos she couldn't see me. Only Microbe noticed that I was looking at her.

Microbe said, "Maybe we should get going."

"Hang on a second," I said. "Let's just stay a little bit longer."

I had fallen in love with my ex-girlfriend the summer before, but it wasn't until winter that I gathered enough courage to make a move. In the meantime, I had been plunged into the dark wiles of unrequited love. In those days, she was coming around to the old Bankers' Clubhouse almost every day. In the fall, she was hanging around at the old Atacan Pub and old Port Cafe. We more or less moved in the same circles, and while I can't say that we had any mutual friends, we did have mutual interests. We had a wonderful friendship, the kind that can go in any direction. But still, I was uneasy. There's something about her that awoke in me a feeling of shyness, and at the time I felt that if I went any further with her, I'd be committing the gravest of crimes. Of course, when you wait so long, passion pulls you in with all its violence. One evening, unable to bear it any longer, I snatched up my iPhone and on the second ring she answered. We went to see *Fast Five* at Özdilek Cinetime, and afterward we had drinks at the Palmiye Cafe Bar.

Nearly a month later, I said to her, "You really appeal to me."

"Çağlar, that's not how I see you," she replied. "I tried, but it didn't work out. I just don't see you that way."

When I asked, "If you don't see me that way, then who was the guy you kissed on old Şefika Street?" she didn't answer. That question stuck in my mind. Later the same night I called and asked, "Were you thinking of someone else when we kissed on old Şefika Street?"

"That was a mistake," she said.

That's how she brought that topic to a conclusion. We make a lot of mistakes in our lives. Old Şefika Street, for example, no longer exists.

Sometimes I walk around there, and from about twenty yards away I look up at the place where we kissed. An underpass is being built there. It's going to connect to the Crossroads Overpass, and from there to the İzmit-Istanbul highway.

So that's how it was. My ex-girlfriend said that she didn't see me that way. But my question about our kiss stuck in my mind, and I never got a satisfactory answer. So naturally, I started thinking, "How *does* she see me then?" I downloaded a mirror program for free from the App Store and sat there looking at my face, trying to understand how someone who isn't seen that way actually looks. I looked and looked until my battery died. Afterward, I felt a need to go for a few beers at a place where no one knew me. So I went to a beer hall in Karamürsel. I sat down at the middle of the bar, where everyone could see me, and ordered a draft beer. But that night the people in the bar just sat there watching a popular TV show. Even the cat sitting at the entrance of the beer hall was watching it. I knew that my ex-girlfriend watched the show, too, as did my sister, my mom, and my uncle if he was at home. All the housewives watched it, all the unemployed people, all the workers, the youth, the elderly, the night owls and alcoholics, the street cats and street dogs. Even the spirits of the dead watched this show. And since God himself is closer to us than our own hearts, even he was watching it that night. There was a magical air about the show that charmed everyone, binding them together and making them all equal. For a moment, I wished that I were in the show. I wished that there were a small role for Çağlar İyice. It would be enough if I appeared in just a single scene, and it wouldn't matter if I said anything or not. While I was watching the show, I charged my phone, and during the commercial break I called Çisem.

"Did we really break up?" I asked.

"Yes, we broke up."

"Was it because of the people in the garden at the old Ministry of Agriculture building? Because of the Brit?"

"I don't understand."

"I told you about it."

"Çağlar, what does that have to do with anything?"

"It's got everything to do with everything."

"It's been years since that happened. I don't even really remember what happened. So what possible connection could there be?"

"So we really broke up then?"

"Yes."

Her voice had the calm air of someone who had firmly made up her mind.

"Okay then," I said, hanging up and ordering another beer. I looked at the guy selling sandwiches just outside the bar. Perhaps hoping that someone would come out to buy a sandwich during the commercial break, he stood up behind the countertop of his cart, rubbing his hands together in the cold night. I scrolled through my contacts list, thinking that it might be nice to talk to someone, but I didn't want to talk to anyone who knew me. So in the end I called 171, Turkey's tobacco quit line. When a woman picked up the phone, I said, "My girlfriend and I broke up. I think that it's like trying to quit smoking. That's how it feels."

"Look, don't waste our time."

"Why not?"

"It's a crime."

"A crime? What's criminal about it? Isn't there a single intelligent person left in this country? Has everyone gone crazy and I'm the only person who doesn't know it?"

"I can see your phone number in the system. It is unlawful to misuse public services."

"Fine then, I'm hanging up. Are you going to feel good when I hang up? Are you going to feel the pleasure of having prevented a crime from being committed? Are you going to be able to sleep peacefully when you put your head on your pillow tonight? Will I ever come into your thoughts again? Is it so easy to give up on me? Is it so easy to forget me for all time?"

"Yes."

I hung up and stepped out of the bar.

The chubby bartender called out, "Hey, where do you think you're going?"

"Across the street to buy cigarettes."

"But you haven't paid your tab."

"I'll be right back. I'm just going to buy cigarettes."

"How do I know you're going to come back?"

"Because I'm just going to buy cigarettes, that's why. I've never stiffed anyone for a tab."

"Fifteen lira."

"Okay."

I paid my tab and walked to the liquor store across the street.

"Can I have a pack of cigarettes?"

"What kind?"

"Hmm . . . Maltepe. Maltepe's good."

"I only have one hundreds."

"Even better."

I went back to the beer hall and sat down. I lit a cigarette, holding the smoke in my mouth for a few seconds before inhaling it.

"You can't smoke here," the bartender said. "It's against the law."

When he said that, I felt a few circuits blow in my brain, setting it abuzz.

"Smoking's against the law, too? Goddamn it! What the hell *isn't* illegal in this country? Please give me a list of the things that aren't against the law."

"You can smoke at one of the tables near the back door. But you can't smoke at the bar. They've been sending inspectors around these days."

"What am I supposed to do with the ashes?"

"Use the peanut bowl."

I sat down at one of the tables in the rear and texted my ex-girl-friend: Do you think that one day maybe you will see me that way? After waiting half an hour for her to answer, I texted her again: This is quite cruel. And then: How about friendship? But no, that's not enough. I sent another text: Screw it, I don't love you anymore. Immediately followed by: I'm sorry. And then: Friendship is enough. Nothing was working. I wrote: Çisem, I'm ready to give you everything, but what about you, are you ready to receive all that? I downed my beer and wrote: Even if I were just a droplet of water that dripped onto your head from an air conditioner as you walked down the street, you should answer me. For the grand finale, I wrote: If you condemn someone to nothingness, inevitably they will want to be your everything. Certain that she would answer that last message, I sat back and waited. I wasn't expecting any words of comfort or understanding. Any sort of reply would do, even just a symbol, an expletive, it didn't matter so long as she answered. It had boiled down to a struggle between my iPhone and me. A sweet feeling of determination welled up within me, saying that at any minute my phone would beep. And indeed it did beep. But I didn't look at the message right away. I ordered another beer, savoring the fact that a message had finally arrived. After a big gulp of beer, I read the message: It's now cheaper than ever to text. Send 500 messages per week for just 5 lira. If you want to take advantage of our SMS deal, type YES and send it to 2222. Don't miss this offer! Text your loved ones to your heart's content.

Naturally, I was a little melancholic in the days right after the breakup, but it was a productive melancholy that had the potential to be transformed into another kind of energy. She may have said, "I don't see you that way," but I was waiting for the day when she would. We'd kissed on old Şefika Street. What's left of old Şefika Street knows it. Microbe knows it. Microbe and I were waiting together. I tried to get him to start smoking. "I started," he'd said, and he would carry around a pack of Marlboro Lights. When he was with me, he'd smoke one or two, but I knew that he hadn't really started and that secretly he wasn't smoking. One day, he showed up with an electronic cigarette and said, "I'm going to smoke this from now on." "Give me a puff," I said, and I also went electronic.

As Microbe and I puffed away at our electronic cigarettes, we looked at the crows perching on rooftop satellite dishes, at the seaweed tossed ashore by the waves, at the dogs sleeping in the middle of the sidewalk, and at the cats napping on top of cars, all the while waiting, waiting, waiting. Then we'd listen to the roar of jets in the distance. Sometimes, I felt that I'd lost my intensity and was slipping away into emptiness. My state of mind was heavy and oppressive, but my body felt like it was becoming lighter day by day. Microbe stayed by my side, and I pulled him into that inner world of mine as well. As a good friend who stuck with me through thick and thin, Microbe Cengiz knew that I'd dragged him into that world and he went along willingly. If it hadn't been for him, I might have surrendered to the feeling that I was adrift, even utterly lost.

It was during those dark days that T. C. Sinem Uzun told me that my ex-girlfriend had started dating some chump from the science school, which was right next to the tourism school. Every day I waited there when school got out, and I watched him carefully, trying to figure out why she didn't see me that way. And that, in short, is how I hit rock bottom.

People don't go to pieces when they're abandoned; no, that happens when they no longer have any hope that they'll be reunited with the person they love. At that point, life is transformed into a massive tangle of tedium. It's like you missed the last ferry and you're stuck on an island, and as the sun slowly sets they tell you that there won't ever be another ferry and that this isn't a joke but cold, hard reality. That was my situation. That winter, one person had left me, but it felt like 250 people had abandoned me.

Now, an old man approached us from the square and placed his hand on my shoulder. He was well dressed and smooth shaven, and he had a button with Ataturk's picture on it pinned to his lapel. Gesturing to the crowd, he asked me, "Son, why aren't you protesting?"

"We're not Ataturk's soldiers."

"Then whose soldiers are you?"

"Microbe, whose soldiers are we?"

"Boss, we're the soldiers of sleepless nights."

Thirteen

It was Sunday, June 2, and my sister and I were sitting in the garden of the İDO Cafe near the ferry terminal, drinking tea and eating chocolate-covered cream puffs. The sea was glimmering in the sunlight. Just past the pier there was a white-haired guy trying to catch fish. He was sitting on a low stool, leaning back against a utility pole. He had placed the handle of his fishing pole into a bucket that had been filled with concrete with a hole in the middle. I'd never seen anyone use such a technique. After she finished her cream puffs, my sister said, "Çağlar," but she never finished her sentence. I could tell that she wanted to say something but was unsure of herself.

I pressed my finger against her tiny nose and said, "What is it, baby doll?"

"Why did Mom and Dad separate?"

I trailed my spoon around on my plate, trying to think of an answer, and in the end said, "I don't know. These days, people break up so fast."

"I asked Mom, and she said that they weren't getting along. But I think there should be a more serious reason than that."

"You're right. There should be ontological reasons for people breaking up."

"What do you mean?"

"Like when something makes one person happy but makes some-one else unhappy."

"Why did that happen to them?"

"Who knows?"

A waiter came with a tray and started clearing the plates and glasses from our table.

"Do you want some more cream puffs?" I asked my sister.

"Yes but no."

"Come again?"

"I want some but I won't eat them."

I placed my hands on the table and started twirling my thumbs. "Since we're talking about that, there's something I want to say to you. But don't take it as a criticism, okay?"

"Okay."

"It would probably be best if you don't bring up the issue of beauty with Mom these days. She's going through a rough time."

"I know, but yesterday I was really sad and upset. That's why I said that. But I made sure I didn't say anything about her cellulite."

"Mom doesn't have cellulite."

"Have you looked carefully? I wouldn't be so sure if I were you."

There were a lot of things we didn't talk about with our mom, espe-cially things like that, because we didn't want her to lose her temper. When she found out that our dad had gone on holiday to Prague with his new girlfriend, she smashed all the porcelain plates in her dowry chest. That was the only time I broached the issue.

"Look," I said, "what you should do is get yourself a boyfriend and go to Amsterdam with him."

She replied, "Don't you dare talk to me that way."

"Fine," I said. "While Dad's out screwing around, you break all the plates in the house. Perfect. We'll be a lot happier that way."

If my mom had a boyfriend and he occasionally stayed at our place, if he was nervous around us, and if we acted cold when he tried to get close to us and then lost his nerve, that would have been a thousand times better than the situation we were in now. Or would it? It might. Maybe. I mean, I'm not sure. After talking to my mom, I went out onto the balcony, my mind swirling with questions. The television was on in the apartment across the way. I could see the right half of the huge screen, and I stood there looking at it. A man was talking to someone on the screen, but I couldn't see who it was. He pulled out a gun and fired a shot. But what did he shoot? Or who did he shoot? Then the scene changed. Even at times when I felt that I understood everything, doubts would creep into my mind. As I watched the neighbor's TV and thought about my mom's nonexistent boyfriend, I felt like I was about to cry. It was as if the schmuck were sitting in the living room. He didn't have any problems with me. He actually thought I was a good kid. After he and my mom made love, they'd talk about me, saying, "That Çağlar is a smart kid. I like the rascal. I'm glad you brought him into this world." For a full week, I couldn't get that imaginary boyfriend out of my head. In my mind's eye, I could see him kissing my mom's neck and shoulders, and then he would unhook her bra and start kissing her breasts, planting a kiss on each and every one of her moles, and then he would screw her doggy-style in front of the mirror. I would shout, "My God, what the hell are you guys doing!" I started going through her purse and checking her phone because I had suspicions about a few of her coworkers. Without any proof at all, I accused her of having an affair. The more I accused her, the angrier I got at my father, and in the end I found myself transformed into the most irritable person around. "Goddamn it!" I screamed one night. "Just look at what you've done to me. Take a good look at what you've done to Çağlar İyice!"

A ferry was approaching, churning the sea into white foam as it maneuvered to dock, and then the dockhands lashed it off. My sister and I walked toward the exit ramp, and as we stood there a little ways away, I puffed on my electronic cigarette. I classified the passengers as they got off the boat: young and old, with baggage and without baggage, those who immediately lit cigarettes and those who didn't, people looking for taxis and those who weren't, those looking around in a daze and those who were focused, those who had people waiting for them and those who didn't, Japanese tourists and those from the rest of the world, and couples and solitary travelers and groups. Everyone got off the ferry, with the exception of our father.

"Maybe we should call Dad?" my sister said. "I hope he didn't fall and crack open his head on the boat."

I called my mom and said, "Give him a call and find out why he didn't come."

My sister said, "Çağlar, why don't you call him?"

"We talked about this already, baby. Let's not start that argument again."

"I want my own cell phone. Maybe he got hurt and he's still on the boat."

"Don't worry, I promise you that he didn't fall down on the ferry. Mom is going to call us in a minute."

"You're cruel."

"I'm cruel?"

A hollow opened up in my chest, and then it filled with pain like the stabbing of a knife. I felt like I had just drunk a glass of searing-hot oil.

Tugging at the collar of my shirt, I called out to the attendant who had opened the exit ramp gate a few minutes earlier. "Excuse me! By any chance, are there any passengers who fell down and got hurt and are still on the ferry?"

"No."

"See?" I said to my sister.

"He just didn't see him."

I took my sister's hand, and we started walking toward the ferry.

"Hey, where are you going?" the attendant said.

"We're just going to take a look around the ferry."

"You can't go on the boat, it's forbidden."

I held out my card and said, "Kıyıdere municipal public relations officer."

"Doesn't matter," he said, not even looking at my card. "It's forbidden."

"Look, I'm the nephew of the jackass who had that big old junked ferry brought all the way from Istanbul and put in our town square. Don't think that I'm the nephew of just any mayor. We paid for a damn ferry that can't float. Maybe we'll be put on trial for that one day. But today we've got our rights so we're just going to have a little look around the boat because otherwise my sister isn't going to be able to relax."

At that moment, my mom called. "He said that some important business came up and he didn't have a chance to call. He said that he's really sorry."

"What could he have to do on a Sunday?"

"He has to give a talk."

"What talk?"

"I don't know."

"What do you mean you don't know? Didn't you ask?"

"Çağlar, don't yell at me! It's something about what's going on in Taksim. There's a protest or something, and he's going to give a talk there. How would I know? This isn't my fault, you know!"

"Okay. It's not your fault. Explain to Çiğdem that it's not your fault. She thinks he fell down on the ferry."

I handed the phone to my sister. She stood there looking at the ground as she listened to our mom explain what happened. In the meantime, the attendant was looking at me.

"It's a family matter," I said.

After my sister finished talking to my mom, we walked in the direction of the man who was fishing. His fishing pole jiggled and he got up from his stool. After checking the pole, he started reeling in the line. A black plastic bag draped in seaweed emerged from the water.

I felt my phone vibrating in my pocket. At first I ignored it, but after a few rings I couldn't stand it anymore and I pulled it out to see who was calling. It was my dad. I rejected his call.

"Was that Dad?" my sister asked.

"Yes."

"Then why did you hang up?"

"He ties up my mind enough as it is. There's no need for him to tie up my phone, too."

"Maybe he wanted to talk to me."

"If he wanted to talk to you, he'd be here right now. He wants to talk to the people occupying Taksim Square."

My phone started vibrating again.

"Look, he's calling again," I said, showing her the phone. "If you want to talk to him, go right ahead. If you want to talk to the person who has put us in this situation, be my guest. If you want to talk to that atheist agitator who left Mom and got himself a fresh young girlfriend, who hasn't come to see you for weeks and, if that weren't enough, is starting rebellions all over the country, then here you go. I won't get in your way."

I handed her the phone and added, "But if you talk to him, don't bother ever talking to me again."

Pouting, she looked at the phone for a while. "I guess you're right. He hasn't come to see me in three weeks. He doesn't care about me, and he always has those architect meetings that are more important than me."

"It's a bachelor meeting. They're trying to decide who to seduce next."

"That's not true. It's about us."

"What do you mean, 'us'?"

"That's what he said to me. He said, 'It's about your future.'"

"Such demagoguery! He should fix all his past wrongs before even thinking about trying to fix our future."

"I guess you're right. He didn't come for a week, and then that became two weeks, and now that he hasn't been here for three weeks my future really has become my past."

"You're quite the philosopher."

"I'm not going to talk to Dad ever again."

"Let's not take things that far. After all, biologically speaking, he is still your father. So don't burn all your bridges, just put a little distance there."

We walked to Lieutenant Necati Karapınar Park and sat down on a bench behind a row of swings that were swaying slightly in the breeze. At the center of the park, there was a massive decorative cannon and standing beside the cannon was a woman pushing a green cart selling cups of corn.

"Do you want some corn?" I asked.

"No." My sister's eyes were fixed on the empty swings. "Do you remember when I was in first grade and I got stuck on a swing?"

"We had a lot of fun that day."

"I didn't have any fun at all. I only laughed because everyone else was laughing," she said, still staring at the swings. "Çağlar, why am I fat?"

Turning to my sister, I pinched my stomach and said, "Look, I'm fat, too. What's the big deal? If justice is going to be brought into this world, the fat people who have been teased all their lives are going to make it happen."

"No. You're not fat. Even though you like light beer you drink normal beer, and you drink it with a bunch of fries. You're trying to get fat, but you can't pull it off. You're not fat, Mom's not fat, Dad's not fat. Am I some kind of alien?"

"Don't be ridiculous. Grandpa was fat. You know Oaf Tufan Ağbi and Bilge Abla. And what about Papa Reçko? He's fat. You carry the structural characteristics of the superior side of our family. The hardiest side of our family, both physically and in terms of character. They're hardy folks in every single way. They took down the government of Albania."

"How about if we get some corn?"

"Ketchup and mayonnaise?"

"And mustard if she has it."

"You got it."

Just as I started walking toward the cart, my sister called out, "Çağlar!"

I stopped and turned around.

"Do you really love me?"

I walked back to her and held her cheeks in my hands. "Sweetie, of course I love you. What kind of question is that?"

"You're probably the only person who loves me," she said. "I fell in love with Efekan because he has braces. But he doesn't even love me."

FOURTEEN

That night, Microbe and I sat in the pilothouse of the ferry in the square and watched the solidarity protest. We sipped our beer, trying to come up with solutions for the injustice my sister had suffered. We thought about shooting another video, but we weren't sure if we'd be able to come up with something sufficiently interesting for all those eyes that have had their fill of such clips. In the end, we didn't come up with anything, but we sure had a lot to drink. There were fewer people at the protest than the day before, but there was still quite a crowd. My gaze lingered on my ex-girlfriend. When someone set off a couple of fireworks, she applauded with the rest of the crowd. After taking her boyfriend's hand, she stood on tiptoe and kissed his cheek, and then leaned her head against his shoulder. Just then, I pulled the cord of the ferry's horn and my ex-girlfriend raised her head from her new boyfriend's shoulder. Everyone in the square turned to look at the ferry, and they started clapping because they thought someone from the protest had snuck inside. Buoyed by the applause, I sounded the horn again and again. The people in the square went wild, and my ex-girlfriend started jumping up and down out of excitement, and she gave her new boyfriend a long, joyful kiss on the lips. I stopped blowing the horn. The crowd starting shouting, "Again! Again! Again! Again!" but I ignored them. "This has gone far enough," I said to Microbe. "Let's grab something to eat at the old Life Pharmacy." A month earlier, the pharmacy on the corner of the square, which had been there for sixty years, closed down, and a fast-food place called Taksim Döner opened in its place, as if it were in Taksim Square, not Kıyıdere Square. We locked up the pilothouse and got down from the ferry. To avoid making eye contact with my ex-girlfriend, I walked behind the banners of the Up Yours We Planted a Tree on Your Birthday Foundation. I didn't want to run into her again. My fear was that the anger she inspired in me would be transformed into a permanent grudge, so I preferred to let it melt into sorrow.

As we were leaving the square, someone called out, "Çağlar! Hey, Çağlar!" and when I turned around, I saw Özer Ağbi. He was from Kaytazdere and had a modified red '98 Polo with tinted windows and a rear spoiler. There was a sticker under the spoiler that read, "My mistakes are my style." The sight of him soothed my searing anger like a glass of cool water. When we approached him, he asked, "What the hell are these idiots doing?"

"Özer Ağbi, they're protesting to support what's going on in Taksim."

Putting his cigarette in the corner of his mouth, he leaned out the window and started applauding the people in the square, shouting, "Bravo, bravo!" When he realized that no one could hear him, he blew the Polo's horn and shouted some more. I wasn't sure if he was supporting the protesters or protesting them. Finally, a few people noticed him and applauded in response. Özer Ağbi yelled, "Talk about the economy a little, the economy!" He flapped his hand at them, and shouted a few more times, "Talk about the economy. The economy!" The veins in his neck were standing out and his face was bright red.

At one point a middle-aged guy turned and said, "What are you talking about?"

Özer Ağbi flapped his hand at the guy and said, "The real issue here is what are *you* talking about? Just now, as I was crossing Istanbul Street, I saw that Butcher Ömer's place had been replaced with a Garanti Bank ATM. What the hell did you do to Butcher Ömer? His shop had been there for forty years."

"What, is it our fault that he went out of business?"

"Of course it's your fault. You're the ones who buy your meat at the new KIPA supermarket," Özer Ağbi said, making like he was going to get out of his car.

I stepped between them and told them both to settle down. Two years earlier, Özer Ağbi had stabbed the owner of the old Castle Disco and spent four months in jail, after which he was released on parole. People had said they would never let him out, but I think someone stepped in and smoothed things over.

"Çağlar, my man, do you want to go to Çınarcık? There's going to be a DJ at Castle; we could hang out there a bit."

"Really?"

"Get in."

"What about Microbe?"

"He should come, too."

I sat up front and Microbe climbed into the back. Özer Ağbi took one last look at the people gathered in the square and revved his car's engine, slipping it into first and disengaging the emergency brake. After peeling out for a bit, he popped it into second with the palm of his hand. We headed up Samanlık Road, and he tried to pass a pickup truck on the left, but the driver wouldn't let him by so he whipped past on the shoulder. As I watched the rocks thrown up by the wheels, I listened to the roar of the glass-pack exhaust pipes. That '98 Polo really was a work of art. We turned onto the road to Çınarcık, passing some construction. They worked at night so traffic wouldn't get backed up. Just as I was about to call my sister so she wouldn't get worried, Özer Ağbi pointed to the bulldozers and said, "Çağlar, you guys may have taken over the municipality, but you haven't done shit for the roads!"

"Özer Ağbi, I'm not connected to the municipality."

"Like hell," he said, scratching his scarred eyebrow. "From the pants on your ass to the iPhone you're holding, whatever you've got it's from the municipality. The other day, your uncle came to Kaytazdere and walked past Ricoy's Internet Cafe. I was sitting back in the garden, and when I saw him I said, 'Hey, get the hell over here.' He just stood there on the sidewalk looking at me with a couple of ass-lickers standing behind him. The elections are coming up, so they're trying to dig up whatever votes they can get. So I said, 'Hey, get your ass over here. Don't just stand there looking at me like an idiot.' He came over and sat down. 'Özer,' he said, 'don't talk to me like that in front of people.' So I said, 'Screw off, you son of a bitch. You think we don't know who you are? You're Altan, that twit from Kıyıdere High School who thinks he's a big man now.' You remember Papa Sadi, right? I swear that Papa Sadi gave him a flying kick back in the days when Papa Sadi was Papa Sadi. Your grandpa came to the school. There's a real man for you, a real solid character. He did a lot for Kıyıdere. So he said to Papa Sadi, 'Who the hell do you think you are beating up my son? That's my job.' Papa Sadi said, 'Ragıp Bey, step over here and talk with me for a minute.' They talked for a bit, and when your uncle got home, he got another beating. Do you know what the bastard did? You know Nuran, the daughter of the Aygaz seller? Your uncle grabbed her ass during PE!"

"What a prick," I said.

"The prick of pricks," Özer Ağbi said. "He kept saying it was an accident, trying to play all innocent."

As we veered onto the Koruköy turnoff, I saw the sign for the old Castle Disco. The name had been changed to Club Castle. Under the fiber-optic lights, people were joyously dancing, hands held up over their heads. Özer Ağbi pulled up to the Dostel Liquor Shop, held out a fifty-lira note, and said to me, "Get your ass in there and buy six cans of Efes and a few cans of cola."

"I've got money," I said.

"Screw your money," he said, slapping my head and stuffing the fifty lira into my shirt pocket.

I came back to the car with the beer and cola, and as I was handing him the change he said, "Let's smoke a joint in Koruköy before we go to the club." He parked the car at an overlook, turned off the headlights, and started sorting out the seeds. "You going to smoke some, too?" he asked.

"If you pack a lot of weed into that firecracker, I might."

After rolling a joint as big as a rolled-up bedsheet, he stuck it in the corner of his mouth and turned off the interior light. His eyes, which were fixed on the darkness outside, shone like two steel points each time he took a drag. He passed me the joint, and I took it between my thumb and forefinger. Tilting my head to the right a little, I closed my eyes and took a good long pull, breathing the smoke deep into my lungs and holding it there, and then I breathed out. After a few seconds, I said, "Now that's a good joint. It goes straight to your head."

I offered the joint to Microbe, but he waved it away, so I passed it back to Özer Ağbi, who peered into the rearview mirror and said, "Cengiz, were you hitting the bong at home or what, man?"

"No, I quit."

I said to Özer Ağbi, "Do you want your cola now?"

"No, not yet."

I opened two cans of Efes and handed one to Microbe. With a deep breath, I took in the clean summer air and looked at the islands. Whenever I see the islands faintly twinkling in the distance, a feeling of melancholy comes over me.

"Stony Muzaffer died," Özer Ağbi said. "When I found out, the funeral was already over. He was a good man. God rest his soul."

"May he rest in peace."

"May God give him eternal rest," Microbe added. "He was a good man."

Squeezing the back of my neck, Özer Ağbi said, "Çağlar, do you remember the Kaytazdere match? You were hopeless, man. You couldn't get the ball within a mile of the goal."

"Yeah, I remember. The opportunities just didn't pan out."

"What opportunities? Cengiz was dribbling right past everyone and lining you up for perfect shots."

"The matches just aren't the same anymore."

"What the hell are you talking about? Stony Muzaffer turned bright red that day. He was tearing at his hair and at one point started clutching his chest. We thought he was going to die. Hell, man, you're probably the one who killed him."

I felt like my neck was in the grip of an iron claw. Leaning my head out the window, I took a deep breath. At first I relaxed a little, but then I started feeling even worse. That iron claw just wouldn't let go. My heart started pounding. I got out of the car and undid the buttons of my shirt.

"Çağlar, what the hell's wrong?"

"Nothing."

"What's going on with your eyes? Are you tripping or what? This isn't that crappy synthetic stuff, you know. My dealer always gets me good shit."

"No, that's not it."

"What is it then?"

"Just don't say that."

"Say what?"

"You said that it was my fault that Stony Muzaffer died. I really liked the old guy. Why did you say that?"

"Man, I was just kidding," Özer Ağbi said, getting out of the car. "Just look at the things you're getting hung up on. Did you take that seriously? Fuck it, man, I'm sorry then. Get a hold of yourself."

"It's okay. I'm all right."

He hugged me and said, "Man, that's just the way things happen. It was his turn, next it'll be ours. Who the hell are you to think that he died because of you?"

"He was really old," Microbe said. "Mentally, he was having trouble getting the team ready for games."

We got back into the car.

Özer Ağbi said, "You killed my high," and he started rolling another joint. He took a few hits, looked at me, and said, "Are you all right, man? Should I let you have another hit?"

I took my electronic cigarette out of my pocket and said, "I'm good. I'm going to stick with this for a while."

"Does that electronic stuff get you high?"

"Sure. When you take a few hits, you feel like a robot."

Slapping the back of my neck he said, "Man, that's how I like you. I like how you take the piss out of everything."

I opened two more beers and handed one to Microbe.

"So how did all this protest shit get started?"

Rubbing my face, I sighed and said, "Things just reached the tipping point."

"What's going on with you, Çağlar? You're on your uncle's side, aren't you?"

"Özer Ağbi, when have I ever been on my uncle's side? My mission for the municipality is something different altogether."

"Good for you, man. That's what I've always liked about you. You've got character. You took over the municipality, but you're still against your uncle."

I couldn't say anything in reply. Özer Ağbi pointed to the bottle of cola down by my feet, and I handed it to him. He opened it with his teeth and asked, "So, Cengiz, what's your take on the situation?"

"There are some pressing issues."

"What pressing issues?"

"Problems that need to be solved immediately and solved in a perfect way."

"Whose side are you on?"

"We're on our side."

"Who is this 'we'?"

"We'll see."

"In any case, I'm going back to Istanbul."

"Why?" I asked.

Özer Ağbi fixed his eyes on me. His right eyebrow, the one with the scar, looked like it was higher than the left. "I was the one who opened Gezi Park to the people. Didn't you know?"

"No."

"Didn't anyone tell you?"

"No, we haven't heard anything."

"That's just fucking unbelievable."

Silence fell over the car. Özer Ağbi took a long pull on the joint and then rubbed his nose with his thumb and forefinger, sucking in some snot. "Unbelievable," he said. "You really didn't hear about it?"

"No, what happened?"

"Never mind, I don't want to talk your ears off."

I looked at Microbe, but he had nothing to say, so I said, "I'm curious. I've been following what's going on from the very first day. I guess I missed this part. So tell us, what happened?"

Özer Ağbi took another long drag from the joint and turned off the radio. "The other day, İsmail—you know who I mean, the İsmail from Altınova, the guy who does LED signs? Well, he said, 'Ağbi, I've got to take some stuff to Istanbul, why don't you come along?' So we hopped in his Caddy and off we went. We dropped off the stuff in Dudullu and he said, 'Let's cross over to the other side of the city. I have to pick up some stuff in Eminönü.' So we went there and picked it up and then parked the car at the parking lot in Karaköy and sat down at a restaurant under Galata Bridge and ordered a big bottle of rakı. We poured out some doubles, and I tossed in some ice on the second round, and then İbo—you know, the guy from Gölcük who does digitally printed signs—he called and said that his aunt died, rest her soul, so he had gone to Maltepe on the other side of Istanbul. So İbo drove over in his Kangoo and I told him to park it at the parking lot in Sirkeci and join us. We ordered another big bottle, and it started getting dark. The people fishing on the bridge were casting their lines up above and motorcycles were whizzing past, and I was feeling good. I noticed that İsmail and İbo were thinking something, but they weren't spilling the beans. So I said, 'Out with it, what's the deal?' 'Ağbi,' they said, 'you know Turan Ağbi from Club Karizma in Aksaray? Why don't we drop in for a visit and have a beer or two to chase down this rakı?' 'For one,' I said, 'you cannot chase rakı with beer. Secondly,' I said, 'İsmail, you told me that we were just going to drop some stuff off. I'm not here to chase down girls.' Then I turned to İbo and said, 'When the hell are you going to grow up and be a man, you graphic fucking designer. You went to the funeral and did a good deed, and now you're all about going off and fornicating. What's the deal with that?' 'No, ağbi, it's not like that at all,' they said. 'We're not interested in hooking up with anyone; we just want to have a chat. We'll just have a drink and leave. If we don't stop in to see Turan Ağbi, it'll be rude because he's expecting us.' So I said, 'Fine let's get going then,' and we went to Club Karizma to see Turan Ağbi and his friends. Those nitwits İsmail and İbo ordered beer and I had a double Jack. You shouldn't chase rakı with weaker liquor, and anyone who does shouldn't be drinking it in the first place. Anyway, Turan was rubbing his hands and fidgeting, and he just wouldn't leave our table. He sent three Uzbek girls to our table and one of them sat next to me. When they sat down, we asked them what they wanted to drink because it's rude if you don't, and I ordered a Jack for the one closest to me. She was pretty, just twenty years old, and she'd come to Istanbul from Tashkent two months earlier. She said that her mom was sick and that she was trying to save up money. She finished her drink and said, 'Do you want to go to a hotel?' and I asked, 'How much?' and she said four hundred per hour or six hundred for the night. 'Look,' I said, 'for one, I'm known in my circles as a social democrat, and paying for such things goes against my principles. Second, you've just come to Istanbul so let me give you a few words of advice. There are more jackals in Istanbul than in the rest of Turkey combined, and you'll come to a bad end if you get tangled up with them. You're young, beautiful, and you have a nice body, but for the love of God find yourself another line of work.' I gave her my card and said, 'I'll be your ağbi from now on. Call me anytime you get in trouble and feel free to visit me in Kaytazdere,' and then I took her number and sent her packing. Just then, İsmail leaned in and said, 'Ağbi, we're going to take these ladies to a hotel. It'll be rude if we don't because we already made a deal.' 'What deal?' I asked, and they said, 'Seven hundred and fifty lira,' and I said, 'You idiots, you could screw all of Uzbekistan for seven hundred and fifty lira. I've got no pity for you guys as your ağbi. Do whatever the hell you want.' Anyway, they left and I knocked back another Jack and walked outside and saw that it was morning and the skies were gray. Hang on. Çağlar, what the hell was I telling you about?"

"Gezi Park."

"Right, so I walked outside and decided to go to Taksim to have soup or tea or something. I hopped into a cab, and as we drove up to Taksim I saw a bunch of young people crying in front of Gezi Park. I said to one of them, 'Stop crying now and tell me what's going on here.' 'Ağbi,' they said, 'the police came and beat us up and burned our tents and threw us out of the park.' 'Who the hell did that to you? Show me!' They said, 'Come on, ağbi, we'll show you,' and we walked to a place where some cops were standing on the side of the park facing the monument. 'Officers,' I said, 'this morning you roughed up these kids here. What's the deal?' Some police captain with stars on his shoulders shouted, 'Who the hell are you?' and I said, 'I'm from Kaytazdere so don't even think of talking to me like that again! This is how we roll.

So who the hell do you think you are? I'll tell you what, I'll shove your way of doing things up your ass!' When I said that, the captain gave the order, 'Take them down,' and that's when they started shooting tear gas everywhere, *pop-pop-pop*. Everyone scattered, but I caught one of the tear gas canisters in midair as it zipped past. It was smoking like a smokestack, and one of the kids said, 'Don't hold it like that, you need gloves.' I said, 'I'll hold this damn thing however I want!' and I went back to the police captain and said, 'Get the hell over here! You think you're high and mighty giving orders, but if I don't shove this canister up your ass, I'm not Özer of Kaytazdere! And I started chasing down that cop with the tear gas canister until I cornered him in an alley off İstiklal Street. But at that moment the canister sputtered out, and I was so furious and I threw it at him, and I slapped him hard a few times, and my hand was still red hot. I dragged him to the front of the park and gave him a few more slaps there. Then I said, 'Now clear out of here and fuck off! I don't want to see another cop in Taksim ever again. If these kids set up tents, leave them the hell alone.' So the police left and people came and set up camp in Gezi Park. Then these two protesters came up to me with bandanas tied over their noses and mouths. 'Ağbi,' they said, 'why did you chase away the police? We were going to fight with them some more.' 'Show me your faces,' I said, and when they did I slapped them both and sent them packing. I said to the others, 'Those guys are agitators, don't let them hang around here.' After that, everything was all calm and peaceful, and I found myself surrounded by guys and girls. They were all playing guitars and singing, and they thanked me and stuff and said, 'The press is here, they want to interview you,' but I told them that I wasn't into that kind of thing. Then this girl came up to me, she was wearing these really short shorts, and she said, 'Özer Ağbi, I think I'm in love with you.' I told her, 'Get out of here. For one thing, I didn't come here for entertainments of the heart, and for another thing, you look like jailbait to me,' so I took her number and sent her off. Around that time, Cemal Sürreya, that pain-in-the-ass parliamentarian, showed up. He thanked me for opening up the park and stuff. I said, 'You look like a good guy, not like the other terrorist Kurds in your party, but leave me alone or I'll send you packing. I know that you've been going to İmralı Island to talk to that terrorist Abdullah Öcalan and now you're all thanks and gratitude. When the going gets tough, your leader doesn't come up here from İmralı. No, it's Özer who comes up here from Kaytazdere to pull your asses together. I'm fed up with all this.' Then I asked him, 'Cemal Bey, is it my fault that people know me as a social democrat?' And he said, 'But my dear Özer, you're being a bit rough on me. I got teargassed, too.' And I said, 'In Kaytazdere, we catch these tear gas canisters with our bare hands.' I showed him my hands, which were bright red, and said, 'Look.' He said, 'Oh wow,' and I sent him off, too. Then I said to everyone, 'Look, I'm going back to Kaytazdere, so put yourselves in the hands of God.' They all started crying, saying, 'Please, Özer Ağbi, don't go.' I told them that I had business to take care of and that theirs aren't the only problems in the country. 'We've got problems in Kaytazdere, too,' I said, 'and I have to handle them, too. Whenever I come to Istanbul, I get a splitting headache from all your traffic, and there's no end to the fights and noise, harassment and druggies, thieves and corruption. It drives me up the wall.' 'But if you go,' they said, 'who's going to protect us?' I said, 'Don't worry, I called the Hazard Crew and told them to bring a tough team of guys to look over you. But I've got things to do now, so I'm off. If you get into hot water, call me and I'll be here in a flash.' So that's about it. I didn't mean to, but I just got pulled into it all."

Then there was a long silence. It was as if the first person to speak was going to lose their chance at winning the New Year's jackpot. Özer Ağbi relit his joint and fell into a fit of coughing. "So what do you think?" he asked between coughs. "What should I do? Should I go to Istanbul?"

"Ağbi, I think you should go. They probably need you."

"I'm going to go, Çağlar, but they just don't know the value of what I've done for them. This isn't the first or the second time. Who knows how many times this has happened? Everyone is out to show off. Our acts of silent heroism are all forgotten. Kaytazdere has been forgotten, Taşköprü, Altınova, Değirmendere, Gölcük. They've all been forgotten. What's torn down is torn down, and whatever's left has slipped from memory. Anyway, I shouldn't talk your ears off. Let me take a little nap for a few minutes, and then we'll go to Castle."

Özer Ağbi reclined his seat and closed his eyes. I grabbed our third round of beers, and after I checked to make sure the emergency brake was set, we got out of the car. Microbe and I silently walked toward the edge of the cliff, stopping just a few steps away, and sipped our beer.

"It's strange," I said. "If we take one more step, we'll be dead."

"That's true."

"Sometimes I don't get it. I just can't wrap my mind around the fact that death is so easy. If someone wants to die, that's the end of it. You can just open the window and jump out, or tie a rope around a hook in the ceiling. Easier yet, just go into the kitchen and turn on the gas. Or here, you could take a step and that would be the end of you."

As I stood there looking down at the dark boulders below, my knees started to tremble and my feet went numb. It was as if a power I couldn't control was going to drive me to take that step. I took a few steps back and sat down on a large stone. Microbe sat down beside me and said, "Özer Ağbi is right. Sometimes it's all so overwhelming."

"True."

"But I think he was exaggerating a bit. I mean, that girl wearing shorts falling in love with him and stuff."

I looked at Microbe and smiled. He didn't say that out of naïveté. There was something pure about him that didn't believe that people needed to lie. But he was smart. When he was just five years old, he taught himself how to read. We started first grade together, sitting side by side, but a week later they moved him up to second grade, which he didn't manage to pass, so the following year we were in the same class again. He wasn't twice the student of everyone else, but one and a half times their better. That's how he always was, one and a half times what other people are, but never enough to be two. Maybe that's why he was silent most of the time.

We waited fifteen minutes and then went to wake up Özer Ağbi, but he wouldn't wake up. Pushing my hand away, he muttered something and turned his head the other way. A few minutes later I tried again to wake him up but again had no success. I leaned over and spoke into his ear, "Özer Ağbi, we're going to leave." Again he muttered something incomprehensible. "Ağbi, we're leaving. Thanks for everything." Microbe and I walked along the lane bordering the olive grove until we reached the main road. Fifteen minutes later, we got on a passing Koruköy–Kıyıdere minibus, which we took to the old navy yard. With our arms slung over each other's shoulders we stumbled in the direction of our homes. By that point, I was pretty tanked. We shook hands and kissed each other on the cheek in front of my apartment building and I made my way up to our flat.

As I stretched out in bed, I closed my eyes, but immediately opened them again. Everything around me was spinning. I tried to focus on one of the stars on the ceiling. It looked like there were two stars instead of one, but it was better than closing my eyes. I broke out in a cold sweat and threw off the sheets. The window was open, and I thought about opening the balcony door. As I gripped the side of the bed in an attempt to get up, I realized that I'd feel even worse if I tried to get out of bed so I decided to stay put. But at that moment, I felt pressure building up in my stomach, and then my throat filled up and a bitter taste flooded my mouth. Scrambling out of bed, I stumbled to the bathroom. I looked at my face in the mirror and felt a sense of relief as I stood there waiting to see myself turn into a green monster. Then I knelt down in front of the toilet, heaving but unable to vomit, so I thought back to the stench of seaweed on the seashore and finally managed to puke. That was an interesting discovery; just thinking about that stench made it fill my nostrils. It occurred to me that perhaps this was my superpower. I tried to recall the scent of my ex-girlfriend, but it was an exercise in futility. I suppose it wasn't the right environment. Maybe if I had been watching a film at the Özdilek Cinetime theater, or drinking beer at the Palmiye Cafe Bar, or walking around on old Şefika Street, it would have worked. When I flushed the toilet and got up, I saw that my mom was standing in the bathroom doorway.

"Have you been drinking?" she asked.

"Yes."

"Why?"

"For natural reasons. I drink and you take antidepressants. In this world, we're all trying to numb ourselves one way or another. So let's not judge each other. Please, let's not go there."

"You're possessed by the devil."

"Bravo. That's the answer I've been looking for all this time."

I walked past her, heading to the kitchen to take an aspirin. But when I got there, I forgot why I was there. I felt better after puking and the world was no longer spinning, but my eyes felt like they were on fire. There was a photograph on the refrigerator held in place by a magnet. It had been taken two years before on my sister's birthday. My sister was in the middle, blowing out the candles on her cake. My uncle and I were on her left, and my mom was on her right. Microbe had taken the picture with his iPhone, and we got a printout of it at Engin Color. I tore the picture into four parts, each one containing a different member of our family, and stuck them on the four corners of the refrigerator with magnets. Then I went back into my room. After looking around for a while, I stood on my bed and started taking down the stars. In the middle of the ceiling was a smiley-face moon, which I decided to leave up. I lay down in bed and stared at the ceiling, and found myself silently crying. Looking up at that dark, starless ceiling stirred my emotions.

That night, I dreamed of my father. We were at a soccer game, and my father was playing. Whoever won would advance to the finals. My father was sweating like mad as he ran up and down the field, and I was afraid that something was going to happen to him, that he might get sick. My dad's team was losing and the dream kept skipping ahead so I didn't really see what was happening in the game, but I knew they were losing. After the match, my father was pissed off because they lost. He had taken off his sweaty jersey and put on a leather jacket, and he was standing there holding a small oval aquarium that was full of fish. He drank some of the water in the aquarium, but when he realized what it was he spit out the water. Our match was next. Ethem Kudnuva shouted, "Çağlar, come on!" and I ran onto the field. The game started but I couldn't run. I thought, *Why can't I move?* Then I noticed that one of the players on the other team was holding me and wouldn't let go. Clearly, that was against the rules, but when I tried to call out to the referee I couldn't speak. I looked at the bench, but Stony Muzaffer wasn't there. I scanned the crowd, trying to find my father, but he wasn't there, either. Then the dream skipped ahead. We won the game and were going to play the team that had beaten my father's team. But the setting had changed, and we were on the beach. It was going to be a beach game. I kept looking for my father on the beach, but I couldn't find him. Then I woke up.

My sister was standing beside me. She had put a damp washcloth on my forehead. "Çağlar," she said, "are you all right?"

"Sure, baby," I said. "What's going on?"

"It's nothing, just the seagulls."

"Seagulls?"

"Didn't you hear them?"

"No."

"Why did you take down the stars?"

"I don't know. I really don't know. I'm sorry."

"It's okay Çağlar, we'll put up new ones."

Emrah Serbes

"Why aren't you sleeping?"

"I was sleeping, but I woke up when you started talking in your sleep."

"What did I say?"

"I couldn't understand. Some jumbled stuff."

"Go back to bed, you have to get up early in the morning."

"Do you want to chat a little?"

"I'm drunk, baby. I'm tired and I had a really crappy dream."

She glanced at the door to make sure it was closed and whispered, "Just listen then. Just listen. I have a plan. Do you remember when you asked me what I would do if I had to choose between virtue and fame?"

"Yes."

"I came up with a plan that has both."

"What's your plan?"

"We'll go to Istanbul and join the protesters. That's the virtuous part. I'm going to dance in front of one of the riot control trucks, and you'll shoot the video. We'll upload the video on YouTube with the title 'Ten-year-old Girl Moonwalks in Front of Riot Truck.' That's where the fame comes in. What do you think? Is it a good idea?"

I placed my hand on my sister's cheek.

"I thought about it all night," she said. "Please say that it's a good idea. You told me that I didn't need to read the comments that people had posted about my video, but I decided to read them. They watched our old video because I'm fat. No one even paid attention to how I was dancing. So I thought that if I dance in front of a riot truck, they won't notice that I'm fat."

I kissed her on the cheek.

"Please tell me it's a good idea."

"It's a wonderful idea, sweetie. But before you start dancing you have to push up the brim of your hat and give the police a long, cold stare."

"I will."

"If you get hosed by the water cannon and get soaking wet, you have to keep smiling. You have to always keep the psychological upper hand."

"I will."

"When you start dancing, you'll have to shout, 'You can't hit Michael Jackson with your tear gas.'"

"I've got this."

FIFTEEN

When you wake up in the morning with a hangover, there's that shadowy period of time in which you remember bits and pieces of the previous night but don't get the whole picture. There's no problem so long as you don't try to assemble your thoughts before your brain screws its neurons together. Those rather unpleasant memories will continue to roam in the peaceful, shadowy darkness, drifting aimlessly and selfishly in the tranquility of your mind. They're not clear enough to remember, and they're not fuzzy enough to forget. Just like the world. That's how it is. Those unpleasant, half-forgotten memories are just like the world. Nearly everyone needs that kind of shadowy mental darkness. The reason that alcoholics start drinking in the morning is not so much because of a desire for liquor, but because they long for that shadowy tranquility.

It was June 3, 2013, a Monday. With my hands clasped above my head, I was lying facedown in bed as if I were relaxing on a pool raft. I'd given myself the order to get out of bed a few times, but the opposition within me held out. In the end, I got up and sat on the edge of the bed, holding my head in my hands. A ferry blew its horn, and I recalled that everyone in the square had applauded me and that we'd left Özer Ağbi in Korüköy by himself. I felt like my mind was still lazing on the pillow, and I wanted to go back to bed, but I forced myself to get up. Drawing back the curtains, I peered out the open window.

It was a sunny day, and half of the street was in the shadow of the apartment building. On the shadowy side of the street, a rather old woman was expertly perched on a dumpster, rummaging through the garbage with a hook. She had a two-wheeled cart with a large sack, like the ones used by scrap collectors. I watched as she pulled a half-deflated blue ball from the garbage. She handed the ball to a boy who was sitting in the cart and then went on digging through the dumpster. The boy's hands were so small that the ball slipped from his grasp into the sack, and he started digging around trying to find it. For some reason, that reminded me of the argument I had with my mother in front of the bathroom, and then I remembered seeing my ex-girlfriend with her new boyfriend in the square. Then I remembered puking the previous night.

At that moment, my sister came into the room and said, "Çağlar, I'm ready. Come on, let's go! We don't have much time. We have to leave before Mom gets home."

She was wearing her Michael Jackson outfit, and I noticed that she'd safety pinned together the tears in her white jacket. She held out a white face mask and said, "I got this from the pharmacy for you. It wouldn't be right if I wore a mask. I'll just rub some Vicks under my nose. That'll be better."

Holding the jar of Vicks between her thumb and index finger, she held it out toward me, a cute, mischievous grin on her face. I looked back at the old woman, who was still rummaging through the dumpster. The way she was balanced on the rim made me think she might fall in, but she just went on digging around in the depths of the garbage with her hook. She was a real pro. I'd watched lots of people dig through garbage, but that was the first time I saw anyone do it with such vigor. She turned the profession of scrap collecting into a veritable art. Indeed, we truly were living in a country that promised hope, and there were so many hardworking people, young and old alike.

A pain shot through my chest. I looked at my sister, and then up at the starless ceiling. At the other end of the street, a city worker started a jackhammer and began pounding away at the asphalt. I rubbed my temples with my thumbs, and then turned to Çiğdem. "Sweetie, we can't go to Istanbul today."

"Why not?"

"Because the city will give you a really bad headache."

"No, it won't."

"Yes, it will. Grandpa had a friend who used to be in the national boxing league. Whenever we went to his shop in Bostancı, he'd look at the cars whizzing past and say, 'Selami, this damn place is giving me a splitting headache.'"

"This damn apartment is giving me a splitting headache."

"Sweetness, don't swear."

"If you get ready to go, I won't."

She was trying to put the jar of Vicks in the front pocket of her backpack, but it was so big that it didn't fit. I walked over to her said, "Let me take care of that." I opened the zipper and checked to see what she'd packed. When I saw my uncle's old slingshot and a pouch of steel balls, I shot my sister an astonished glance but didn't say anything. I slipped the jar of Vicks in behind the pouch and closed the zipper. There's no such thing as a small backpack, just poor packing. I got up and walked out of the room.

"Çağlar, where are you going?"

"To the bathroom."

After I finished peeing, I flushed the toilet, but I went on holding my thing for a while. I do that sometimes, hold onto it and talk to it. "Look, son," I say, "I'm the one who makes the decisions around here. If you respect that, we'll get along just fine." Sometimes he protests, "But wait just a second . . ." and I snap back, "Shut the hell up, or you'll get a beating you'll never forget!" "Ağbi, I'm sorry, I didn't mean anything." "It's okay," I reply, "I know that you went through a rough time with

T. C. Sinem Uzun and were pretty torn up. But what the hell was that business with Gözde Hoca! I mean, really? Gözde Hoca? What the hell is up with that?" That day, I didn't talk to my thing; it wasn't the time or the place, so we just gazed blankly at each other. I washed my hands and my face, and cleaned my ears with a cotton swab. I opened the container of the stuff my mother rubs under her armpits (I can't remember the name of it now) and breathed in the scent. Just then, my sister knocked twice on the door.

"I'm coming," I said.

"Çağlar, hurry up."

I closed the toilet lid and sat down, and as I sat there with my face between my hands, I stared down at the designs on the floor tiles, trying to discover a symmetrical pattern. There were small squares of different colors on each tile, and none of them were alike. I made complex mathematic calculations, trying to find the trigonometric connections between them. I knew there just had to be one because there was no way that the tiles could have been just randomly laid. At the very least, there had to be an emotional connection between them. But it would take a committee made up of a tile master, a mathematics professor, and someone wracked by sorrow to figure it out. My sister began pounding on the door. I opened it and said, "As always, I'm going to be frank with you. We can't go to Istanbul."

"Why?"

"Because the police in Istanbul are really irritable today. Even though the new constitution doesn't say they can, they're firing tear gas canisters at people's heads. People are losing their eyes and going blind."

"Great! Maybe I'll get blinded, too. If I were blind, everyone would cry for me. No one would ever say that I'm fat."

"They're shooting water cannons at everything. At cats, at dogs, even at laundry drying on balconies and people in wheelchairs. Damn it all, they're even hosing down Japanese tourists. They're filling all the riot control trucks with water and blasting people in the face."

"It's hot today, so that won't be a problem."

"Sweetie, I love you more than anything, but as your older brother, I just can't take that risk."

"Çağlar, to be a king, you have to take risks. MJ became the King of Pop because he took risks. Now, Çiğdem İyice is going to take a risk. There's no choice—we have to go."

My sister was staring at me like this was her last chance, her eyes filled with both hope and sorrow as if all her future happiness depended on whether or not her desire would be fulfilled. I knew she felt that with all her being. People only fall into mistakes like that once in their lives, twice at most. Stroking her hair, I said, "One day, your time will come for taking risks. Don't worry, one day we'll go. When you get a little older."

"When I grow up, we won't go because we'll just be hanging out with people like us."

"Okay, we won't wait that long. We'll go next year. Maybe there'll be more protests."

"There won't be."

"Sweetie, I'm sorry but we can't go. They'll recognize us on the ferry. Because of our uncle, some of our relatives got jobs at the ticket counter. They'll know that we're running off and won't sell us a ticket."

"We can go from Topçular."

"Even if we go from there, they won't let you go to Istanbul."

"Why not?"

I went into the kitchen and my sister stormed in behind me. Opening the blinds, I stood and looked at the bars of light shining on the countertop. Moving my index finger up and down, I tried, and failed, to find a fifth dimension among the beams of light.

"Why won't they let me go to Istanbul?"

"They don't let kids into Istanbul anymore."

"You're lying."

"I swear to God. In Istanbul, all the kids either stay at home or sell bottles of water along the roads. I can't even go to Istanbul. This is beyond me."

"Why?"

Sitting down, I placed my elbows on the kitchen table, sighing deeply as I cupped my chin in my hands. I started thinking. I do that a lot. "Now think, son," I tell myself. "Put a little thought into it." In Istanbul, there are twenty million people, two million cars, and even more seagulls. In Istanbul, you look for seagulls inside seagulls, you look for cars inside cars, you look for people inside people, trying to find something that calls out to you, something that has a soul. But you find nothing.

"It's no place to be," I said.

"Dad lives in Istanbul."

"No, he lives on Burgaz Island. That doesn't count as Istanbul because there aren't any cars there. You know what Dad's like, he's always chasing after pleasure. So even though he can't stand being stuck in traffic, he still insists on living in Istanbul. Because he doesn't really know anything and only uses his brains to escape from the realities of life; he thinks he's smarter than everyone else."

"You promised me last night."

I got up from the table and opened the refrigerator. I took out a bottle of water and a box of cookies. After drinking a glass of water, I popped a cookie into my mouth and slowly began chewing.

"You don't love me," she said. "Last night, you tore up our picture."

"What picture?"

That's when I saw the torn-up photograph on the refrigerator. I was so stunned that I forgot about the cookie I was chewing. I leaped up and pushed together the pieces, holding them in place with a magnet that read "Happy Kıyıdere."

"That was just the alcohol," I said. "It was out of my control. No more drinking for me. From now on, instead of beer I'll be drinking cold Nescafe."

"You said that six months ago, and then you started drinking again."

"Stress drove me to it." I suddenly realized something and slapped my forehead. "Aren't you supposed to be at school?"

"I got permission from Resul Amca to go to the stationery store during our first break, and I came home."

"What kind of school does a thing like that? Do they always let kids just walk out? Isn't your teacher going to notice that you aren't in your second class?"

My sister picked up her hat from the table, examined the inside of it, and then put it on. Tapping her chin twice with her thumb, she said, "That jerk can't mess with me. When there's a class I don't like, I just play in the schoolyard. But if Resul Amca doesn't see me there, he might call Mom. That's why we need to leave right now."

"Peanut, we can't go."

She put her fists on her hips and stomped her right foot a few times, shouting, "Why, why, why? Last night you promised we would go. You said, 'You've really thought this through.' You said, 'We've got the psychological upper hand.' So, was it all just blather? Or are you a coward?"

"Sweetie, what would I do if a tear gas canister were to get anywhere near your pretty head? I don't mind if they shoot them at me—I'll take it in the chest and send it right back at them. I'm just afraid for you."

"Don't be afraid for me!"

"How can I not when I love you so much?"

"Are we going or what?"

"No, we're not."

"Bastard-shithead-moron-ass-fag!"

I clamped my hand over her mouth, and she bit my fingers. Her face was livid. With the tip of her shoe she kicked me in the shin, and I howled in pain.

"It's always your fault!" she shouted.

"What's my fault?"

"That I'm in this situation. Our uncle was going to make all the calls beforehand, but then you said that if he made the calls, you wouldn't help me practice. You said that you'd make me quit dancing and take up swimming instead. You said that if you had any doubts about it, you'd make me drop out of the competition."

"Did our uncle tell you that?"

She took off her hat and sobbed. "No, I heard it when he was talking to Mom. I was asleep. I was crying in my sleep, listening to them talk. As I slept there crying, I hoped for a miracle. I always listened to them when they talked."

"Would you have wanted to win by cheating?"

"Çağlar, I didn't care about winning. If I'd been on television, Dad would've watched me perform. Dad would've loved me. I would've moved to Istanbul to be with him. If just that once someone had pulled some strings for me. When we took a field trip to Ataturk's grave, no one wanted to sit next to me on the bus. But did I say anything to them? No. Here, everyone makes fun of me when I go outside. Do I say anything? No. In Istanbul they don't laugh at fat people or turn around to stare at them because it's so crowded. No one notices you there."

I tried to hug her, but she pushed me away.

"I wish I were dead. I wish I'd killed myself the day I got stuck in the swing. I wish I'd killed myself instead of listening to you. You're not my brother anymore! I'm all alone in this world. If you say a single word to me, I'll stab myself. I swear on everything that I'll stab myself!"

With that, she stormed into our room and slammed the door so hard that its glass pane shattered. I got the broom and swept the shards into a dustpan, then used the vacuum cleaner to pick up the slivers.

SIXTEEN

Whenever I feel like a worthless piece of crap, I go to the municipal sewage treatment plant, as if I could purify my shitty life there. I walk around the waste vats and pools, looking at the machinery and equipment that make it all work, and I say to myself, "Çağlar, my boy, the tasty slices of the cake of life have been passed out to others. All that's left for you is loneliness, pain, and crap. Get used to it. Get used to it so you won't get any more upset than you already are."

That afternoon, I was walking around the treatment plant with a cloth mask over my mouth and nose. When I had tried to talk to my sister, she plunged the needle of a compass into her arm. I couldn't get that image out of my mind. I took the compass from her and stuck it into my own arm. "Goddamn it!" I said. "That really hurts. How could you do that to yourself?" Microbe said, "Go outside and get some fresh air, boss. I'll talk to Çiğdem." I patted Microbe on the shoulder and went out, stepping into the elevator. I stood there in the elevator with my face up to the mirror, nearly touching it with my nose. It started fogging up as I looked into my pupils, searching for something, a hidden spirit perhaps, a wounded monster, a deranged seagull, a rabid dog, a bloody slave, anything. Something had to be there. I went on staring into my eyes until the elevator reached the ground floor. I rode back upstairs and quietly said to Microbe, "I can't get that compass out of my mind! Please, do something! My sister is just nine years old." He told me not to worry.

Holding tightly onto the rusty handrail with two hands and testing each step of the stairway with my foot, I made my way up to the platform over the wastewater pool. My uncle and Nadir Amca, the fire chief, were standing in the middle of the platform. They were wearing masks as well, looking down at the muck in the pool that gleamed in the afternoon sun, bubbling and boiling and frothing, giving off such a stench that it seemed that all the shit in the world was down there. In front of the platform, about two yards down, I could see the moldy domed tops of huge metal vats in the pool. Nadir Amca glanced at the gauges on the front of a device that was sitting on top of a plastic stool. The device reminded me of an old gramophone. The round speakers on the device kept making a sound like *tsssss, tsssss* as it did whatever it was doing. I closed my eyes and listened to that sound, which was like the rhythmic snoring of a cruel monster.

My uncle looked at me and said, "Why don't you go sit down below?" but I didn't bother replying and he didn't insist. He turned to Nadir Amca and asked, "Nadir Ağbi, is something wrong?" Nadir Amca drew closer to the gauges and flicked the glass covers of two of them. Then he straightened up, held onto the handrail, and looked down into the vat. "No," he said. "Everything's normal." With a worried expression, my uncle looked at his watch, an old windup that used to belong to my grandpa. He said in a voice tinged with exasperation, "He's been down there an hour, why hasn't he come back up?"

One of the ass-kissers always trailing along behind my uncle, an older guy, pulled down his mask a little and said, "It's only been twenty minutes, Altan Bey. It takes a while."

My uncle turned to the guy and looked at him with such hatred that I thought he was going to grab him by his jacket and push him into the pool. Nadir Amca, sensing the tension in the air, said, "There's nothing to worry about. The gauges are normal."

"Nadir Ağbi, that's not what I'm mad about." My uncle loosened his tie and snapped, "That's not what I'm mad about! We keep having to deal with problems like this. If Çağlar hadn't called me, I wouldn't have even known anything was wrong here."

We all stared down into the pool as if the slightest bubbling, gurgling, splashing, and splishing were developments of the gravest importance. My uncle muttered something under his breath. Then the device, which had been so regularly sputtering, fell silent, and after a few squeals, it started making sounds like the white noise of radio waves. We were all staring at the device with expressions of horror. Nadir Amca leaned down and hit the side of the device a few times, but to no effect, and then wiped the sweat off his forehead with the back of his hand.

"Goddamn you!" my uncle yelled.

A cold chill ran down my spine, as if a secret power had grazed my back with its hand and vanished again. It was all too much. As panic took hold of me, I shouted, "What the fuck!"

My uncle shouted again, "Goddamn you!" He shouted so loud that some women hoeing in a field nearby turned and looked at us. One of the men that my uncle shouted at placed his hands on his chest and said, "Altan Bey, we were going to call an industrial diver. We've been in touch with the company. But then he came and said that there's a bit of welding that needs to be done on the main valve and that he'd do it. He said that he'd get the materials from the fire department and take care of it."

"Just because he said that he'd do it, does that mean you had to tell him to get started? There are some things that should be done and others that shouldn't. What does he know about diving? No one would want to get into that pool of shit."

"He said that it was just a small problem and that he'd take care of it. We've already gone over budget because of the part for the transformer so when he said it was just a little welding, we told him to go ahead and do it."

"Screw your budget! Goddamn it, that guy's my cousin! Do you get it? My cousin!"

My uncle ran to the staircase on the left side of the platform and went down a few steps, holding the handrail, and put his other hand to his mouth and started shouting, "Tufaaaan! Tufaaaan!" I ran after him and held onto his jacket because I was afraid that he'd fall into the pool in his panic.

"Be quiet!" Nadir Amca yelled from above. "Be quiet and listen."

His eyes wide with fear, my uncle looked at me, putting his finger to his lips. We listened in silence, and then the *tssss, tssss* sound started again. We walked back toward the device.

"The pressure in the tank is fine," Nadir Amca said. "I think there was a problem with the speakers."

"Nadir Ağbi, are you sure?"

"That's what I think, Altan, but this isn't our line of work. I told those guys up front that this isn't our line of work. If he dies down there, the blame is going to fall on me."

My uncle turned back to the ass-lickers and hissed, "Goddamn you!"

They looked at their feet. One of the younger men's faces was bright red. For a second, I pitied them, but I was glad that I wasn't in their shoes.

"How much did he ask for?" my uncle asked.

They didn't answer. My uncle poked the younger guy's shoulder. "How much did he ask for? Answer me, damn it!"

"Seven hundred and fifty lira."

"Seven hundred and fifty lira . . . You sent him down into that shit for seven hundred and fifty lira? If he dies down there, it's going to be for seven hundred and fifty lira?"

I stepped in and held my uncle's arm, saying, "It's okay, calm down."

My uncle took a pen out of his pocket and threw it at the guy. It bounced off his shoulder and fell into the pool below. "Seven hundred and fifty shitty lira!" he shouted. "Goddamn it, that's my cousin down there!"

I tugged at my uncle's arm, and he looked at me with the same expression of fury. "Calm down," I said.

The young guy's eyes were filling with tears. "It's not my fault," he muttered. "He insisted. He said not to worry. He told us that he had all the materials and that he'd handle it."

The guy next to him said, "Shh, enough."

"You animal!" my uncle yelled. "You goddamn animal! Just look at what the hell you've done! Seven hundred and fifty goddamn lira. Have I ever said no to you? Haven't I given you everything you asked for? I gave your goddamn brother a shop. You fucking animal, you told me that he had just gotten back from the military and was going to get married, so I gave him a goddamn shop in the middle of town!"

Until that point, the guy had been on the verge of tears, but now he turned to my uncle and said, "I told you about this last week. You told me that Tufan would solve it, and you said I shouldn't waste any money."

The older guy shut him up again.

I looked at my uncle and he turned his eyes away.

"Goddamn it, when I told you that Tufan would take care of it, that didn't mean I wanted him to dive into that pool of shit."

"Altan Bey, how was he going to weld that valve without getting into the pool? I told you everything from the very start."

Taking him by the arm, the older guy led him down the stairs of the platform. When they got to the bottom, the younger guy shouted up at my uncle, "Who the hell are you calling an animal?"

My uncle made a move for the stairs, but I held him back.

"Hold on a second, hold on," Nadir Amca said.

A knocking sound rose up from between the vats, and we all rushed to the handrail. There was a slight stirring at the surface of the muck, and then after a little while the head of a diver emerged.

"Thank God," Nadir Amca murmured.

Oaf Tufan Ağbi placed the strange-looking device used for underwater welding onto a platform suspended below. Holding his head above the water, he swam through the shit toward the ladder. Carefully, I watched as he swam the breaststroke, moving confidently and easily through the water. He climbed onto the platform and walked past us to the area down below. They hosed him off for a few minutes, and then he took off his diving helmet. My uncle walked up to him and hugged him like he was embracing a huge tree. Oaf Tufan Ağbi put his arm over my uncle's shoulder and said, "I took care of it." A bright smile spread over Oaf Tufan Ağbi's face, probably because he thought my uncle was hugging him out of joy for welding the main valve.

The year before, when a forest fire broke out in Teşvikiye, snakes started fleeing the fire, taking refuge under the roofs and in the basements of nearby houses. Oaf Tufan Ağbi was given the job of gathering them up with a pair of tongs, and one of the snakes bit him. My uncle and I visited him at the hospital. They said that he had smiled at the poisonous snake that bit him.

SEVENTEEN

I held one end of the sheet and Microbe held the other, and we pulled it tight and gave it a shake and then folded it over. Then we approached each other, and he took the top end and I took the bottom, and then we pulled the sheet tight again, folding it over, and then approached each other again for the final fold, and then we put it on the long steel shelf along with the other three hundred thousand sheets. That night, we had gone to our front desk management class at the training hotel. The main idea of the class was that we'd stand at the front desk, but I don't know if it was because our teacher, the office manager, thought that it wouldn't be appropriate for people like us to work the front desk, without considering the fact that he himself looked like the world's biggest wanker, or if there was some other problem, but he said to us, "Go help with room cleaning. They need some more people." He'd said that three months before, and apparently they still needed help. Every Monday, we folded sheets from four o'clock to eight o'clock, getting no salary or social security, with no incentive other than a passion for national education.

Microbe carried in a new bundle of sheets from the ironing room and said, "Actually, it could work."

"What could work?"

He put the sheets on the Formica table and said, "I talked to Çiğdem, boss. Her plan to go to Istanbul actually makes sense."

He grabbed the sheet on top of the pile, which was still warm, and as I took hold of the other end, I eyed him suspiciously, waiting for him to go on, but he didn't. "And?" I asked.

"The protesters are in control of Taksim Square. We could go with her. It wouldn't be dangerous."

I pulled the sheet tight. "They may be in control of the square, but people are still clashing with the police. Do you think that they're going to let them occupy Taksim forever, that the police won't go back?" I gave the sheet a good, hard shake and said, "My sister is just nine years old. I told you that she would calm down and give up on the idea, but you went off and talked to her about it!"

"No, boss. You've misunderstood me. I didn't talk to her about anything like that. I was just making a suggestion, that's all."

I pulled the sheet with all my strength, tugging it from his hands. Microbe stood there looking at the sheet with the surprise and sadness of a kid whose scoop of ice cream just plopped to the ground.

"Well then, think a little before making suggestions! Think just a little bit! Just look at what you're saying!"

I took the dark, gloomy stairs of the emergency exit up to the second floor of the hotel. I padded along silently on the thick green rug, trailing my fingers over the reproduction paintings hung on the cream-colored walls, the automatic lights going dark behind me as I proceeded farther down the long hall. Stepping out onto the fire escape, I started puffing on my electronic cigarette and watching the dump trucks rumble up and down Bağlaraltı Street. Then I took out my iPhone and updated Facebook, Twitter, Instagram, Tumblr, Foursquare, Yonja Netlog, and Badoo, all in the hope of finding answers to the question, "In the last forty-five minutes, what has happened in this old world we're stomping around on, what kind of life is this, where are we coming from, where are we going?" Microbe showed up a few minutes later and took out his electronic cigarette. He looked at me, head cocked to one side, his thumb on his belt buckle. There was a wild light in the depths of his brown eyes, and perhaps a bit of a sullen glow as well.

"Sorry, boss."

"You go on and apologize," I said. "You know that my sister is a sensitive issue for me."

Just then I saw my uncle's tweets. He'd been silent on social media in the previous days, which raised my suspicions because until then he'd sent thousands of tweets. I wasn't sure if he was scared, offering up a silent critique, or enshrouding himself in the silence of the wise. Two years earlier, I had created a Twitter account for him. For his profile picture, I put a photograph of him wearing sunglasses, and in the background were the trees he was having planted on the median of the town's main intersection. I wrote his first tweet—"I'm here together with you for a happier Kıyıdere"—and then gave him the password. In the beginning, things were going well, and he was posting tweets about various municipal services. But then, like all new users, he went overboard and he started posting drunken ramblings, and as people unfollowed him he slumped into depression and made jabs at people regardless of how well known they were. We all know how it goes, and he did it all. I sat him down and said, "Look, everything you post is tied to you politically. You're the mayor, and if you're going to chase after women, don't do it publicly. Just send direct messages." I was acting as his social media adviser for no salary and no social security benefits. I just pitied him.

On this day, he'd started with calls for calm and then moved on to the mode of "Who's paying you to do this?" and from there to conspiracy theories. I showed the tweets to Microbe. He shook his head with a blank expression that said, "I just don't know what to say."

We went back to the laundry room and folded a million more sheets. If you attend a vocational school for tourism, that's one thing they teach you: how to become a pro in the art of sheet folding. Don't think that it won't do you any good, just get out there and fold some sheets. Maybe you'll have a husband who is just as thoughtful as you. He'll see you folding sheets and fall in love with you. "Look," he'll say, "a woman who folds sheets. She's good at ironing, too. I'd better marry her. Laundry, dishes, free sex. If I get bored, I'll divorce her and get myself a girlfriend, a nice fresh young one."

At home later that night, I made some Nesquik for my sister and handed her this note:

Memo:
Sweetheart,

I promise you the following things. Issue 1: You will dance and achieve the fame that you deserve! Issue 2: You will live in Istanbul! Issue 3: But you must be a little more patient . . . If you dance in all that smoke and dust, no one will see you. There are crowds of people in front of the riot trucks cruising around Istanbul. People are throwing themselves in front of them. If you were to do the moonwalk in all that chaos, you might not get the attention that you deserve. Today I talked with Microbe Cengiz Ağbi, and after evaluating all the possibilities, we arrived at the following decision. In September, you'll take part in the dance program. This summer, we'll work with all our might to get ready for it. In any case, the police will put down these protests in a month or two, and calmer times will begin as things go back to normal. Sweetheart, I promise that you'll be the star of those times! When you dance, people will find the excitement they've been longing for.

*Your dear brother, who loves you more than any-
thing else,*

Çağlar İyice
June 3, 2013, Kıyıdere

My sister carefully read the memo, took a few sips of Nesquik, set
her cup aside, and tore out a page from her notebook. Holding her pen
straight up between her fingers, she started to write a reply. Five minutes
later, she held out the piece of paper. Even though I read it over and
over, all I could understand was the first sentence, which read, "I'm not
going anywhere in September." Normally, her writing is like strings of
pearls, but I think because of stress and sadness it had become illegible.
When she realized that I couldn't read what she'd written, she said, "I
don't trust that uncle of ours. He always says that he's taken care of
things, but he never does."

After looking around to make sure that there weren't any sharp
objects within reach, I quietly said, "Don't you worry about that. This
time, I'm going to personally look after everything, from the TV channel to the production company. I'm not going to put you in any risky
situations. If I see that there is the slightest risk, we'll try using social
media again and go from there. Don't distrust our uncle so much. He
loves you and he means well, but he's a bit inexperienced."

I heard the rattling of keys as someone opened the front door. It
was our uncle. He walked in and stood in the doorway of our bedroom,
putting his hands on either side of the doorjamb. He looked angry and
disgruntled. As he stood there glaring at me, I waited for him to say
something.

"What did you do?"

"What are you talking about?"

"I know what you did!"

"What?"

My uncle lunged toward me and grabbed me by the front of my shirt. I tried to break free of his grip. He pulled me into the hallway and shoved me against the wall. His face was pale, and he hadn't shaved for a few days. The fact that he looked tired and sleepless made him appear all the angrier. Raising her hand to her mouth, my sister looked at us, eyes wide with fear.

"What's going on here?" she shouted.

"All day long, he swore at me on Twitter," my uncle growled.

"I wasn't swearing at you! Just offering some harsh criticism."

"Do you realize what a disgrace it will be if people realize that you're the nephew of the mayor of Kıyıdere?"

"Well then, you should be more careful about your tweets."

My uncle slammed me against the wall a few more times, tearing a few buttons off my shirt in the process, and said, "I can't send any damn tweets! I'm going to kill you!"

"Uncle, stop it please," my sister said on the verge of tears.

He let go of me and closed his eyes, and then took a deep breath and rubbed his face. Then he turned to my sister and stammered, "He spammed me. I lost my twenty-three hundred followers, and I can't get into my account. I'm telling you, I'm about to lose it." He turned to me and said, "So tell me, are you part of that damn Masked Digital Hooligan group?"

"Sweetheart," I said to my sister, "go to your room for a little while. Uncle and I need to talk over some things."

"No, Çağlar, I'm not going to my room. Why do you always send me away? Why are you guys always fighting? Why does our family fight all the time? Why don't Mervenaz's and Ecem's parents ever fight?"

"They fight, too, but they just don't let anyone see it."

My uncle shook his fist in my face and said, "Unlock my damn account! Unlock it right now! Unlock my goddamn account!"

"Politically, you're better off not being on Twitter. One day, you'll thank me for this."

He grabbed me by the shirt again, practically foaming at the mouth, and pulled me toward the kitchen. His expression betrayed the bitter pain he was feeling. That was the concrete pain of having lost his 2,300 virtual followers. And that's why he was capable of any kind of madness at that moment.

"Be careful," I said. "My sister is watching you."

He let go of my shirt and wiped his nose, and then he leaned against the doorjamb, putting his forehead on his hand. "Çağlar, don't do this to me. I'm so tired."

"That's the exhaustion that comes from hiding lies."

"Unlock my damn account, Çağlar! Unlock it!"

"No. I'm the one who got you started on Twitter, and today I'm putting an end to it."

"Why, goddamn it?"

"Because instead of tweeting about municipal services, you started spreading lies and slander."

The chorus of pots and pans began. I looked at the clock at the end of the hall. It was nine o'clock, the time it always began. The anger on my uncle's face gave way to bewilderment. Gazing blankly at nothing in particular, he scratched his tuft of hair with his index finger. The sound of banging pots and pans was getting louder and louder.

"Are you on their side now?" he asked. "Were you tweeting those things about me just to piss me off, or have you really switched sides?"

"Uncle," I said, "I haven't gone anywhere. I'm right where I should be. What were you expecting? That I'd take your side? The other night in Liberation Square, the people took out all their anger on me. Anger for all the years that you've oppressed them. I had to take it all by myself. Even then, I didn't say anything."

"They're plotting a coup!"

"Who's plotting a coup? Aunt Ayla, banging a pot on her balcony? A fifteen-year-old kid who doesn't have any more minutes on his phone? Are those stylish women who go to the protests wearing high heels plotting a coup? What about my father, that peaceful pleasure-seeker who paid to do short-term military service when he was thirty-two years old after the earthquake? Is he plotting, too?"

"You're twisting things around. You just don't get it! You don't see that what's happening here is a big game."

"A big game? Okay, so tell me about it."

"All right," he said. "I'll tell you. I won't even shout, but you have to listen like a human being."

"I'm all ears."

"In the first days of the Gezi protests, like everyone else, I supported what was going on."

"Hmm."

"Don't cut me off! I supported them, I honestly did. For three years, I planted palm trees all over Kıyıdere. I planted acacia trees, lemon trees, pine trees. I think those kids were right to protest the cutting down of trees in Gezi Park. But then it went beyond the environment, and people started destroying public property."

I started laughing. I couldn't help it, and I doubled over in laughter.

"What are you laughing at? What the hell are you laughing at? What the hell is it? Go on, tell me! If you're laughing about the hotel project, I'll have you know that it's all legal. Papa Sadi Hoca threw a wrench in the works, but we got it sorted out. Goddamn it, stop pissing me off! What the hell are you laughing about? Go on, out with it! If you're laughing about the ferry in the square, just so you know I'm going to turn it into a museum. That investment can always be recycled."

I took a deep breath and tried to pull myself together. "Did I," I asked, "say anything about the hotel or the land or the ferry? You were the one going on about those things. What I'm wondering is how screwed you're going to be when they come in and audit the municipality."

"My books are all in order."

"Go on thinking like that, but when the tables are turned and Asshole Bey comes to take his due, you're going to be the one who pays the price."

"Nothing will happen. Everything I've done is legal! We're not vandals like those plotters. We provide services. We haven't burned any buses or gone around breaking windows. They attacked a woman wearing a headscarf, and when they did that, they attacked society's sensitivities. Our patience has its limits, and we're religious people."

"What the hell about you is religious, you damn worshipper of concrete!"

He came after me again, and I grabbed him by the front of his shirt, pulling with all my might on that crooked tie of his, and we slammed against the other wall. He tried to turn me around, but I held out with the last of my strength. I pushed away his hand and raised my guard. At that point, my sister ran up and hugged me, and then she started crying.

"You," my uncle said, "can go to hell!"

That bastard of an uncle of mine was never cut out to be a politician. He had an anger-management problem. If he had taken after my grandpa a little more, if he had held him up as a role model, maybe he would've had a chance. My late grandpa was a dignified man, a real gentleman who weighed every word he said, so much so that people who talked to him got the impression that they were talking to a set of scales.

"Who do you think you are?" I asked. "Would you have been elected if my grandpa hadn't been elected mayor five elections ago? Who cleaned up the crap-filled creek? Who built the first bridge in Kıyıdere? Who paved Fetih Street? Who expanded the development plan for the county? My grandpa! You went around telling everyone, 'I'm the son of Ragıp Baysal.' You used his name. They voted for you thinking that they were voting for my grandpa."

"That's got nothing to do with it. They voted for my projects."

He straightened his tie and tried to smooth his ruffled jacket. I could tell that he was feeling trapped. "My father may have paved Fetih Street, but I built the junction overpass. I built a covered parking lot that can hold fifteen hundred cars. I built the Ragıp Baysal Kıyıderespor Sports Complex. I didn't use his name—I put his name on it."

"That was just tactical. When you went out to the villages, didn't you always throw his name around so the old people would vote for you? Wasn't it my grandpa who had telephone lines installed in the villages? Didn't he renovate the waterworks and electrical lines? Didn't he build the roads out there? Whenever someone in the village got sick, wasn't he the one who called the head doctor and sent an ambulance to pick them up?"

"Okay, maybe he did do some work in the villages, but I won my right to be mayor here in the center of town. That's why the people here have loved me for all these years. I followed up on their jobs, I followed up on what was best for them. All without asking for anything in return."

"You can't even love without asking for something in return. You don't go after anything unless there's something in it for you. All you've done is trick people and lie! Until the day he died, my grandpa was a member of the Busy Bee Party. He was a Busy Bee before the party was even born, and second to his Alcatel phone that was the most important thing to him. It was only because he didn't switch over from the Busy Bees to the Horses that he lost the elections in ninety-four."

"What the hell would you know about the elections of ninety-four? You weren't even born yet!"

"Do you think grandpa didn't tell me about those days? Until his very last breath, I was his sole confidante, his black box. But what did you do? You switched over to the Giving Gramps Cancer Party to keep your position."

My uncle pulled back his jacket and put his hands on his waist, tilting his head to the side as he leered at me. "Am I hearing you right?

Aren't you ashamed of yourself? For years, didn't you hound me to leave the Spurned Horses Party and switch over to the Giving Gramps Cancer Party?"

"That's a lie!"

"Didn't you tear down the posters of the opposition before the vote on the constitutional referendum?"

"That's a lie!"

"Isn't that why you got into a fight with the kids from the youth branch of the You'll Vote for Us No Matter What Party?"

"That's a lie!"

"Weren't you the first person to congratulate me when I switched over to the Giving Gramps Cancer Party?"

"That's a lie!"

"Come on, if there had been room in the car, you were going to go with me to watch the badge-pinning ceremony. Look me in the eye."

"I was ignorant in those days. I didn't have an iPhone."

"Who bought you that iPhone for your birthday? Me!"

"Ha-ha! You bought it? You got it from Bahadır Electronics and sent the bill to the municipality. Did you think I wouldn't dig around and find out about that? Did you think you could buy my respect? You can't buy my respect with presents. You can't buy my respect with money. You can't buy my respect with praise. You can't buy my respect with junction overpasses. My respect is not up for sale! You're nothing but a corrupt thief!"

"Then give me back that damn phone."

"No. This telephone belongs to the people! It was bought with the municipality's money."

I pulled my electronic cigarette from my pocket and took a few deep puffs. With the back of my hand, I felt my forehead; I was feverish. My uncle's mocking expression was filled with secret, poisonous, scornful joy. He loved seeing an honest person having to wade through the same muck and mud in which he'd spent his whole life.

"So this is how it is when things suit you," he said. "Just you wait. I know exactly what I need to do."

"What are you going to do?"

"What am I going to do? Well, let me tell you. Who has always gotten your ass out of trouble? Me. You went off and crashed into a traffic light in Karamürsel. You were drunk; you didn't even have a license. You resisted the cop who pulled you over. They were going to beat you at the police station. Who came and rescued you? Wasn't it me and the district representative? What about the time, you shameless bastard, that you got drunk and went to Gözde Hoca's home and started pounding on her door. You were crying and shouting, 'I read a thousand-page book for you! I love you!' She was going to file a complaint, but the party president and I came and saved your ass."

I walked into the living room and sat on the couch. For a while I sat there, holding my cheeks. A lump rose in my throat. I had a desire to take that lump and smash it into my uncle's face, but I held myself back.

"Next time you get in trouble, don't call me."

"Don't worry, I'll never call you again."

"We'll see about that!"

I charged toward my uncle, but my sister got between us.

Knocking my fist against my head, I said, "There's something so vile about you, so deeply vile that it's gone beyond vileness and become arrogance, even beyond that. That's the one and only quality you have."

"What the hell are you talking about?"

"Enough already! That's what I'm saying. Say whatever you want about me. You're right, I might be a loser. Maybe I have lost control sometimes because of a certain lack of love. But what right do you have to spout off about my grandpa? What did he ever do to you? What's the deal with this hatred for your father? What's this Ivan Karamazov complex?"

"I don't hate my father."

"But you do! I know you do! You said that he may have done some things for the villages, but you won your right to be mayor in the town center. You go on about your mediocre projects trying to cast a shadow over all the big steps my grandpa made. He was a real man of service. For years, he tried to make everything more beautiful. Then you come along and start digging around everywhere, tearing down things, rebuilding them, and then tearing them down again! They applauded you. When they applauded you, you tore down more things and built more things. Can't you see what you've done to these people? Can't you see what you've done to our lives? Can't you see what you did to my childhood? Where's the old building of the Ministry of Agriculture? My dad would sit in the yard there with his friends, talking and drinking beer, and I would play in front of the small fountain. Now the place is a construction site. Where's the old Aydın Cinema? My grandpa and I would eat popcorn as we watched movies. Now it's a covered parking lot. Where's the old Ergun Wedding Hall? Sure, people weren't getting married there anymore because they started having their receptions at hotels, but those political parties that can't get past the voting threshold would hold panels there and talk about politics. Now it's a shopping center. Where's old Şefika Street? Those big loves and first kisses? Now it's an underpass. In four years, you managed to wear our lives down to nothing."

"Quite the opposite. I renovated everything, working day and night. I went sleepless, I was stressed, I got sick. I had nightmares that we wouldn't be ready in time for opening ceremonies. They were all big projects. We poured labor into them, we poured our sweat and tears into them, we made investments and did modern city planning. We saved you from getting hung up on the past. We drove you forward."

"We're not going forward. We're on a darkening path leading us downward. You don't even realize that you've gone blind trying so hard to outdo my grandpa. By trying to outdo him, you've lost your identity.

You lost an identity that you never even had. That's why you try to brush him aside as if he were nothing."

"I'm not brushing him aside. I'm just saying that I've worked, too. I just want you to see that. That's all I'm trying to say."

"You left my grandpa just as he was dying and ran off to count your votes. Is that how you were proving your existence? By killing my grandpa and starting a new era of municipal work? If that's the case, congratulations!"

"Çağlar, take that back!"

"No!"

"Take it back or I'll smash your face in!"

"Go right ahead. Do you think I'm afraid of you? If you were a real man, would my grandpa have said that with his dying breath?"

"Said what?"

Just then a slap came from out of nowhere, catching me on the cheek. I turned and saw my mother standing there. Her face was pale and her lips were drawn tight in pain. With that distant look in her eyes, she looked more like my grandma than my mom. I hadn't noticed that she'd come out of her bedroom.

"Enough!" she shouted. "Goddamn the both of you."

She grabbed my uncle by the jacket and shook him, saying, "Get your stuff and get the hell out of here. I don't want to ever see you here again."

"Abla," he said, trying to smile at her, "what's going on?"

"What's going on? I'm losing my mind because of you, that's what. You tricked me. You stole those four plots of land that belonged to the ministry. When we asked about it, you said it was too late and you couldn't do anything. You told me to be quiet. You threatened me. You threatened your own sister."

"Abla, don't talk such nonsense in front of the kids!"

"Nonsense? Didn't you tell me not to mention any of this business to anyone, or else things would get ugly? For two years, I've been waiting for the police to show up or for a state inspector to come along. I can't sleep, and my days and nights are all mixed up. I already had a ton of problems. The last thing I needed was all this corruption, and you pulled me into the middle of it all. Goddamn you! Get the hell out! Get out!"

My uncle opened the door and left.

My mom turned to me and said, "I've had it with you. Since the day you were born, you've brought me nothing but suffering."

Then she took my sister by the hand and led her to our room.

EIGHTEEN

I stepped outside and walked around where our old apartment used to be, trying to find my lost soul. Glancing around behind the apartment building, I looked at the leafless trees, which were like telephone poles, at the coal cellar with its steel door and ramp, and at the empty clothes-lines on the balconies. There was a furniture store on the ground floor of the building, and whenever we passed by we would peer through the window at the armchairs, dining sets, side tables, and floor lamps that glowed a soft yellow. That shop gave you a comforting feeling. But like so many other places, it had closed down, too. The window was now covered in yellowed newspapers. I read one of the headlines: "A Bad Year for Elephants and Rhinos: 30,000 Elephants and 950,000 Rhinos Poached." I cupped my hands around my eyes and peered through a gap in the newspapers, my nose pressed against the glass, but I couldn't see anything. Crossing the street, I leaned against an unlit streetlight and put my hands in my pockets. I looked up at the windows of our old third-floor apartment. The living room light was on, but the window of the back room was dark. Until that night, I had never wondered who might be living there now. What did it matter? Would it change anything? I stood there waiting, but I didn't know what I was waiting for. But I went on leaning there, as if I were waiting for someone. *We aren't a family,* I thought. *We're just a group of people who were brought together so we could make each other suffer.* There was no way out, my friend, no way out at all.

I walked down to the shore in the direction of the jetty. The rubble from the thousands of buildings that had collapsed in the earthquake had been dumped into the sea, and a park was built on top of the landfill, a dark, silent, calm park inhabited by the spirits of the dead.

When my grandpa got sick, they said to him, "We're going to take you to the Bursa Medical Faculty," but he didn't want to go.

"I didn't get sick so that students could practice on me," he snapped.

"Okay then, we'll take you to the state hospital."

"I don't trust the state," he said.

"Then we'll take you to a private hospital."

"I trust them even less. Take me to Dr. Sami."

In my grandpa's opinion, Dr. Sami was the only doctor who could help him. Years ago, when he came down with pneumonia in the Istranca Mountains, Dr. Sami had saved my grandpa's life.

"Dr. Sami doesn't practice medicine anymore," they said. "He's an alcoholic now."

"Dr. Sami," my grandpa said, "is the only person who can understand what's wrong with me."

My uncle and Oaf Tufan Ağbi went to Kırklareli to find Dr. Sami. They did find him, but he ran off at some point before they got to Kıyıdere.

I walked around the earthquake memorial for a while. My mind was filled with random thoughts, and I was so tired that I couldn't focus on a single one of them. The memorial consisted of stacked marble columns, and they had inscribed them with the names of all the people who had died in the earthquake. There were so many names that it would take an entire day to read all of them, and only if you read them with technical detachedness. If you started thinking about a name, wondering who that person might have been, you would never get through all the names. I doubt that anyone has ever read all of the names, or ever will. *What the hell kind of monument is this?* I thought and started walking along the seaside. I heard a boat puttering along behind me. Eventually, it passed me and continued along its way, a small fishing boat with a red light on top. It steered out toward the open sea, getting smaller and smaller until it was just a flickering red light in the distance.

A doctor sat down with my grandpa, and after a long talk finally convinced him to go to the hospital. In all his life, my grandpa hadn't even gone to an eye doctor. There was a guy who used to show up at the Friends Coffeehouse with a James Bond briefcase filled with eyeglasses of varying prescriptions. Trying them out one by one, my grandpa would eventually find the right pair. At the hospital, they diagnosed my grandpa with pancreatic cancer—the disease that killed Steve Jobs, the affliction of geniuses. That night, he showed up at home with a big bottle of rakı and drank by himself for a little while. I tiptoed up to the door of the living room and peered inside. A few teardrops glistened on his eyelashes. When he realized I was looking at him, he smiled and waved me over.

"Grandpa, don't be sad," I said, sitting down across from him. "Last year, when I had surgery for appendicitis people bought me all kinds of presents. We'll get you whatever you want. How about if I sell the house and buy you a Porsche?"

Smiling sadly, he stroked my head. "Çağlar, I'm dying. What would I do with a Porsche? I've got a better idea. Go to Migros and buy me some cheese."

He didn't see many people when he was sick. The people who did come around to see him immediately started smiling when they came in; that was the only way they could conceal their sadness at seeing him so drained and weak. He got worse each time someone came by to visit him. After a while, his hair and his eyebrows fell out, and when that happened he stopped seeing people altogether. At that point, he rarely talked to me.

One night, he said to me, "Çağlar, in the end even this has happened."

"What's happened, Grandpa?"

He didn't answer.

That morning, we were at the rec area of Kıyıdere Anatolian High School to tally the votes. Observers from the Giving Gramps Cancer Party had objected when they lost the election by twenty votes, and they were counting the votes for the second time. My mom called and said, "Your grandpa isn't doing very well. Come to the hospital." He was unconscious when we got there. Someone from my uncle's party showed up and said they were trying to strong-arm the ballot officer, claiming that some of the votes weren't valid. My uncle told me to stay at the hospital, and he went off to see what was going on. Two hours later, he called my mom and said, "We won by thirty-five votes. Those are the final results." At that moment, my grandpa opened his eyes and asked, "Ayfer, what happened?" My mom looked at him and said, "Altan won the election." That's when my grandpa uttered his last words. My mom and I were the only people in the room so no one else heard what he said, but I'm not going to tell you what he said. His entire body was covered in sores, and he looked completely helpless. Despair had overtaken him, and he was wracked by a physical and spiritual pain. In a situation like that, what does it matter what you say? I can't understand why people are so interested in last words. We're surrounded by the living dead, people who have been packaged up, labeled, and then cast aside and forgotten. When they are remembered, they are remembered with curses. Maybe that curiosity would actually make a little more sense if it were focused on the last words that people speak before they are relegated to a life of social death.

At the funeral, everyone had a photocopied picture of my grandpa pinned to their lapels. Mourners packed the courtyard of the central mosque, spilling out into the street, and the balconies of the apartments facing the courtyard were filled with people as well. Some people had even climbed nearby trees to get a better view. Everyone was looking at my grandpa's coffin. The white marble of the coffin bier gleamed in the sunlight. In my pocket, I had my grandpa's Alcatel, which I had set to vibrate, his favorite setting. Sometimes he would have people call him and he'd say, "Çağlar, this thing is a real miracle. Just look at it vibrate!" That day, the phone was constantly vibrating in my pocket because people kept calling when they found out that he'd died, as if he'd be able to answer from the other world. In the bottom drawer of the hutch in our living room there was a small flag of the Busy Bees Party. I had brought it with me to the funeral and put it on top of his coffin. The district president of the Spurned Horses Party walked up to me and said, "Çağlar, a lot of people from the Bees have joined our party, so I don't think it's right to have that flag there. I told your uncle, but he told me to ask you. Maybe it would be better if we put the flag of our party on his coffin?"

"Please shut up," I said. "Shut up and show some respect. This isn't the place for politics."

Before the funeral prayers, the muezzin gave a nice talk, speaking into a lapel mic clipped to his robe. I can't remember what he said right now, but I know that he didn't say anything that got on my nerves. There were so many people at the funeral that he knew better than to try and show off with a flashy speech. After the prayers, they carried my grandpa's coffin on their shoulders to the hearse, and my uncle and I sat up front with the muezzin. We set out for the cemetery, followed by a long convoy of cars. As we went down Fetih Street, the sidewalks and apartment balconies were filled with people, and then thunderous applause broke out as people paid their last respects to my grandpa. People waved, wept, and clapped in memory of the fact that my grandpa was the one who'd paved that street. They tossed flowers at the hearse in memory of the fact that my grandpa had worked hard to boost the flower business in Kıyıdere.

I walked to the end of the park, passing by the construction site at the old Directorate of Agriculture, and headed down the concrete walkway of the jetty. The scent of the sea filled my nostrils; the treatment plant had probably stopped pumping sewage into the water. Seagulls circled around overhead. When one of them started squawking, the others joined in, as if they'd been waiting for me. I shook my fist at them and shouted, "Old Mr. Hitchcock knew what bastards you are! Hitchcock knew! You're just waiting for the right day to attack us. I'll never trust you. I have no pity for you, and I never will. Get the hell out of here! Go to Istanbul and fly around the ferries, begging for crumbs of bread!"

I had been quite calm during my grandpa's funeral until they lowered his body in his death shroud into the grave. My calmness surprised even me. Oaf Tufan Ağbi and my uncle had gotten into the empty grave, my uncle holding the head end of the shroud and Oaf Tufan Ağbi at the feet, and following the orders of the muezzin they placed him so he was facing Mecca. My grandpa had lost a lot of weight in the final months of his life, and he was just skin and bones in the end. They leaned a concrete slab over his body to keep the dirt off him when they filled the grave. Then they started shoveling in the dirt. I was down on my knees beside the muezzin as he prayed, looking into the grave. The afternoon sun glinted on the shovels as they were passed from hand to hand. The weather was nice, not the kind of weather for death. Lying there in the ground was an honest man who loved me. As the grave was filled, I realized that I had lost the one person who supported me in life.

God, what difference would it have made? What difference would it have made if he'd lived for another fifty years? In this world that is millions and millions of years old, would that wonderful grandpa of mine have been such a problem for you if he'd lived another fifty years? Is fifty years so much? Okay then, twenty-five years. Is that too much, too? What a stingy God you are! If there's even just a little bit of justice left, you should have let my grandpa live just another fifteen years, if you want that grand compassion to hold sway over the world. Okay then, ten years! Five years! Is even that too much? God, I can't hear you. Ha! What did you say? I can't hear you. Not even just another year? Not even another month? A week? A day? A night? Just let him have another glass of rakı!

I still miss my grandpa. I watch the rain, missing him. I look at unused telephone booths, forgotten side roads, windup watches, old TVs, crappy antennas, the amplifiers of those crappy antennas, VHS tapes, eyeglasses sold on the street, the first cell phones that came out—whatever is left of the past, even the most ridiculous of things. I look at them and miss my grandpa. When I miss him, it's not just him I miss but who I was at the time. In fact, I miss that even more. I miss who I was when I was with my grandpa.

At the end of the jetty, I stood between the two lights that flash red and green. I listened to the sound of the dark waves splashing against the dark boulders. Then I gazed out toward Istanbul, toward the islands as they glittered in the distance. The sky was clear and there wasn't a cloud between us. Those lights looked so close that I could reach out and touch them. Whenever the lights of Istanbul gleam like that across the sea, something goes dark inside of me. "Brits," I shouted at the lights in the distance. "You're all Brits! Go live in Manchester!"

NINETEEN

With my hands in my pockets, I stood at the crosswalk waiting for the light to change. It had started sprinkling, and the raindrops gleamed in the headlights of the passing cars and washed the soot of car exhaust from the trees on the median. When the light turned green, I crossed the road to the steep two-lane ramp at the entrance of KIYPARK and opened the door of the white security booth, which stood just to the left of the entrance. When I opened the door, I saw that Süleyman, the guard, was busy sending a message on his phone, a sly smile on his face. When he looked up at me, that sly smile lingered on his lips.

"Çağlar Ağbi, how's it going?"

"I'm good. Can I have the keys?"

His face grew tense as he put his phone on a small table and crossed his arms, glancing out the window. "Ağbi, I can't give them to you."

"What do you mean you can't?"

"That's what they told me."

"Who told you that?"

"The boss."

"Forget about him and give me the keys."

"Ağbi, I can't."

"Who the hell do you think you are? Give me the keys."

I lunged for the drawer where the keys were kept, but he blocked my way so I put him in a headlock and we tumbled back over his chair. As I fell, I hit my head on the steel legs of the television stand in the right corner of the booth, but I still managed to get hold of Süleyman's collar and pull him toward me. After slamming his back against the door of the booth a few times, I shook my finger in his face and said, "Don't even think about trying to stop me!" I rubbed the back of my head and then looked at my hand; there wasn't any blood. I reached out, opened the drawer, and rummaged around trying to find the keys to the Honda. Part of me felt like a thief, and I was getting nervous because I couldn't find the keys.

"Ağbi, please," Süleyman said. "Your uncle left a note saying that we shouldn't give you the keys."

"Screw my uncle and his note! Who was the one who found the damn car on sahibinden.com in the first place?"

Finally, I found the keys and I leaned toward Süleyman as if I were going to hit him on the head with the keys. "Those shameless bastards!"

"Ağbi, you're putting me in a tight spot here."

"You in a tight spot? Ha! You! When the hell have you ever been in a tight spot? Look at me. Look into my eyes! Tell me who is in the tight spot! There used to be a little shop here. That's where my grandpa and I used to buy popcorn. A pretty girl worked behind the counter, and whenever the weather got cold, her little nose would turn red. When she saw us approaching, she would start filling a small tub of popcorn. 'Ragıp Amca, how are you?' she'd ask. 'Did you like the film? The second half was better.' And she'd smile at me. That pretty girl would look at me and smile. I always wanted to stroke that little nose of hers. You know, in a friendly way. We were happy here. For fuck's sake, we were happy! As if it weren't enough that you built a parking lot on top of our happy days, now you say you won't give me the damn keys to the car!"

I stormed out toward where the car was parked. I kicked a metal stool that was near the wall, sending it spinning into the air. It landed with a clatter and rolled over a few times. "Thieves," I shouted, my voice echoing through the dark parking lot. The Honda Civic was in its usual place on the second floor. I pressed the alarm button on the keychain, and the emergency lights winked at me. I opened the door and got in, breathing in the car's slightly sour smell. Leaning over, I opened the glove box and shuffled through the CDs and registration papers until I found the honeydew-scented bottle of air freshener. I opened the cap and took a sniff, but I was still undecided. In the end, I sprayed a few squirts in the direction of the backseat. I adjusted the seat and the mirrors, put on my seatbelt, and started the engine, pumping the gas a few times. All was in order. Backing out in a quick arc, I shifted into first and headed for the exit. I stopped next to the security booth and opened the passenger-side window. Süleyman stepped outside.

"Don't call anyone. I just have a few things to take care of. I'll be back in a few hours."

"Ağbi, please, I'll get into—"

"It'll be fine."

"Ağbi, the headlights."

I scratched my chin with my thumb and then flicked on the headlights.

Turning onto the street of the Alkaş Residences, I drove up to the entrance of the Migros depot and turned on the hazard lights. In the old days, they would set up a market there and you could buy stuff like pantyhose and bras for just a few lira.

"Look, old boy," I said to myself, "stop thinking about these things. You never even went to that market. You're tired. You're mentally tired. Because of those crooks, you've been beating your brains for a hundred and seventy years in the short seventeen years you've been alive. Don't tear yourself up so much. Let your engine idle for a bit."

The rain started coming down a little harder, and the drops were gathering on the windshield, but I didn't turn on the wipers. The world outside looked like a television screen with the cigarettes, beer, and other forbidden things blurred out by the censors. I pulled down the visor and looked in the mirror. There was a blackhead on the side of my nose. I squeezed it and scraped off the little ball of pus that emerged. With my other thumbnail, I squished it flat and then wiped off my hands with a tissue and ran my fingers through my hair.

The façade of the Alkaş Residences was sheathed in horizontal wooden planking that was illuminated from below by yellowish lights. The railings of the balconies were made of glass. They'd done a hell of a job. The place didn't look anything like our crappy apartment building. T. C. Sinem Uzun stepped out of the front door, and I ran the wipers a few times. She was wearing a green dress that zipped up the side and hung a few inches above her knees, and she wasn't wearing any stockings. A small black purse hung over her bare shoulder, and a black scarf was draped over her purse. She looked to the left and the right. I looked over my black denim shirt, at the cutoff sleeves and two missing buttons. Beneath it I was wearing a light-blue T-shirt that Microbe had bought for me as a birthday present from the İzmit Outlet Center. I took a look at my blue jeans, the cuffs of which were worn ragged. Lightly, I tapped the horn and T. C. Sinem Uzun looked at the Honda. Slowly, she made her way down the stairs in her pumps and started walking toward the car. She opened the door and got in, kissing me on the cheek. I breathed in the scent of her perfume. I don't know much about that kind of stuff, but it smelled really good.

"Why did you bring the car? We could've taken a taxi."

"There's nothing as safe as your own car."

Without being flashy about it, I pulled up to the streetlight, flicked on my right blinker, and turned onto Fetih Street. I flipped through the radio stations until I found some romantic foreign music. At the end of the street, I turned onto Samanlık Road. T. C. Sinem Uzun, in the meantime, was fiddling around on her widescreen Galaxy S4, writing something with her elegant fingers. Occasionally, she giggled, and when she did, her face glowed as if she were in possession of an important secret. She didn't even look like she was holding a phone; that Galaxy S4 was like a natural extension of her body, a helping hand of sorts. I turned onto the road to Çınarcık.

"I'm glad you wrote," she said. "I was bored out of my mind sitting at home."

Just when I had decided to turn to her and smile, she went back to her phone. Out of the corner of my eye, I glanced at her green dress. It was now a full hand's width above her knee. The seatbelt crossed between her breasts, the contours of which were quite clear. I could see the black strap of her bra beneath the loose collar of her dress. Just then, the right tires of the car slipped onto the shoulder of the road so I whipped the wheel to the left, but because of the slope of the road the car fishtailed a little, and I had to snap to the right to get back on the asphalt. T. C. Sinem Uzun turned to me and smiled. But I couldn't tell if her smile was sarcastic or sincere. I had a suspicion that she knew I'd been looking at her legs.

"We won't get pulled over, will we?"

"Don't worry," I said, pointing to the official sticker on the right side of the windshield.

She started paying closer attention to the road. Perhaps she thought I didn't have much experience driving. But the truth of the matter is that I started driving when I was nine years old. My grandpa taught me how to drive in his Broadway. For a moment, I considered telling her about that pleasant memory, but then I decided against it. It wouldn't be right to come on too strong. Thinking through all these things, unconsciously I had started to speed up. As we passed the sign for the Castle Club on the Koruköy turnoff, she looked up at it, and I took the opportunity to steal another glance at her knees. They were shapely and quite distracting. The year before, Batuhan, the son of Orhan the tailor, crashed into the back of a Sütaş truck at the corner of old Ali's Place because he was looking at T. C. Sinem Uzun's legs. Later, he blamed it on the municipality, saying that the road was slippery because of the sprinklers, but we all knew what had really happened.

As we drew closer to the Dostel Liquor Shop, I asked, "Do you want to have a drink on the beach before we go in?"

"That would be nice," she said. "The show just started. It would be kind of lame to go there so early."

I bought five cans of beer and some mint gum at the liquor store. The rain was lightening up. I saw that T. C. Sinem Uzun was looking at herself in the mirror on the visor. She wasn't freshening her makeup or anything. No, she was just checking to see if she was still herself. Maybe she was always pestered by fears about whether or not she was desirable.

I parked the car between two palm trees facing the pebbly beach just past the port. The tips of the palm fronds were dry and turning yellow. For a while, we sat in silence. She opened the door and got out, and I followed suit, grabbing two cans of Efes. I opened them and handed her one of the cans. We sat on the edge of the Honda's hood, which glowed in the moonlight like it had just been washed, and started drinking.

"What's bothering you?" she asked. "Did something happen?"

"Family stuff."

"Did you get into an argument with your uncle?"

"Who else?"

Putting her hand on my left shoulder, she said, "Forget about it. We'll have a good time tonight."

I turned to her. She had a slender neck, a fact that was all the more noticeable because her hair was pulled into a bun. The depths of her blue eyes were glimmering with the desire for a natural life. Somehow she looked more beautiful to me at that moment than she ever had before. There was no one else at the beach, and we were sitting so close to each other it felt like we were touching. She let her hand fall back to her side.

I took my electronic cigarette from my pocket and took a few puffs. The blue light at the tip started to flash, so I took the tube of e-liquid out of my pants pocket and set it on the hood. Then I unscrewed the cigarette in the middle and turned the reservoir right side up, filling it with the injector of the e-liquid. After I screwed the cigarette back together, I set it upside down on the hood so that the liquid would fill the chamber.

"So . . . How's it going with you?" I asked.

"You don't want to know. I spent all day dealing with Çisem. She's always getting into fights with Metehan and then she comes crying to me, wanting to talk about their relationship."

I tapped the tip of the cigarette on the hood a few times and then held it up at eye level with two fingers. A few drops of liquid had seeped out, so I wiped them off on the collar of my shirt. I took a puff and looked at the blue light. It wasn't flashing anymore.

"Yes," I said.

"It's her fault. These days, Metehan needs a little space, but Çisem doesn't understand that. She's always getting on his case. She texts him all day long. Every single hour, she calls him just to say, 'I miss you. I feel like I haven't seen you in years.' Who says that kind of thing?"

I turned toward her. The pout of her pink lips expressed how upset she was, as if Çisem's relationship problems actually bothered her. She opened her purse and took out a pack of cigarettes. I didn't notice the brand, but they were the long, slim kind. She took one out and lit it with a red lighter. After her first puff she held it out and tried to knock off the ash.

"It's the usual Çisem gibberish," she said. "But then again, you would know about that. You're her ex-boyfriend."

"Yes."

"I mean, Metehan told her a few times in a gentle way, 'You really should eat a little less, you know.' Between me and you, she's like a hundred and fifteen pounds. That's a lot for someone her height. So then she comes to me and starts crying, saying, 'Your arms are so slender, why are mine like sausages?' So I tell her, 'Look, you spend every night in front of the TV with a big tub of ice cream, with one eye on Facebook and the other on WhatsApp, pigging out. Anyway, I've chatted your ear off."

"Not at all. It's just—"

"The other night we were sitting at the old Bankers' Clubhouse, and she had a few beers and shots of Jägermeister and then got hung up on the idea of singing a song. Metehan said, 'Look, sweets, the place is packed. Let's wait for it to empty out a little, and then we'll ask Anıl Amca to play something you can sing along with when he finishes his set.' But Çisem goes, 'No, I want to sing now,' so she got up and sang this emotional song, 'Dark Night Train' or something, but it would've been better if she'd sung something a little more upbeat. At least then that raven's voice of hers would've been drowned out a little as people sang along. Her voice was so bad that people even started laughing. Thank God that Anıl cut the song short. She was making him look bad. She was making herself look bad, and us, too, for that matter."

"Actually, her voice isn't so, well, you know."

"It isn't so what?"

"I don't know, her voice has a certain air about it. It's one of a kind. You know, kind of husky. That's what I always thought."

Touching her little nose, she laughed and said, "Çağlar, you crack me up."

"Then again I haven't heard her sing in a long time."

"You see Çisem in a different way. From the very start, I told her not to break up with you. Now she's making Metehan unhappy, and she's making herself even unhappier. But she just didn't want to be with you. She said, 'I just don't see Çağlar that way.'"

"Did she ever tell you how she does see me?"

"No."

I went on drinking my beer. A light rain started falling, as light as dust, and I acted like nothing was wrong. My ear was drawn to the sound that the waves made as they washed over the pebbles, as if they were digging at something and carrying it away. I thought, *If I listen carefully to the sound of those waves, will they dig out and wash away my troubles?* I swirled around the last drops of beer in the bottom of the can and then drank it down. Crumpling the can, I got another beer from the car and then I sat down next to T. C. Sinem Uzun.

She put her hand on my shoulder and asked, "Çağlar, are you okay?"

I turned toward her. We were almost nose to nose. "How do I look to you?"

She didn't answer. I leaned in and kissed her. My lips stayed on hers for just a second. It was more like the deposit for a kiss than the real thing.

She pulled away and said, "You're crazy."

I looked at her legs. T. C. Sinem Uzun really did have beautiful legs, and you can believe me when I say that because I'm an expert in the field. I had a desire to run my hands over her legs, but I held back and took a long pull from my beer.

"Why did you do that?" she asked.

"No reason. I just did."

"I think you're still in love with Çisem."

"What gives you that idea?"

"I felt it. Just now, we were talking about things that friends always talk about, but you got all distracted."

I put my hand on the back of her neck and said, "Honey, give me a kiss and be quick about it."

"Çağlar, please be serious."

"I am being serious."

"Do you still love Çisem?"

My hand was still on the back of her neck, and I stroked the curve of the bone behind her ear. There are moments in life when you feel that you have no choice but to keep your word. That was one of those moments, but the thing was, I hadn't made any promises to anyone. It was just a feeling. I felt like I had to keep my word for a promise I'd never made.

"Yes," I said.

She put her hand on mine and then pulled it from her neck and let it go.

"If you still love Çisem, why do you want to kiss me?"

I heaved a deep sigh. After taking another drink from my beer, I swirled the can around. For some reason, I laughed. I knew I was about to slip into another one of my fits of laughter. When I told myself to stop, when I told myself that it would be rude to laugh at that particular moment, the fit just got worse.

"What are you laughing at? I'm trying to ask you something serious here."

"Oh, just fuck off," I said.

"What?"

"Fuck off, T. C. Sinem Uzun."

"What the hell are you saying? Who do you think you are? I asked you a serious question. First you laugh, and then you start cussing at me."

"What are you asking me? Hmm? What are you trying to ask? Go on, ask me again!"

"Fuck off, Çağlar!"

"Ask me again!"

"What's so weird about what I asked? All I wanted to know is why you want to kiss me when you're still in love with Çisem."

"Hmm, that's a tough question! An enormous question. With that question, you've got me completely cornered. You know what, T. C.

Sinem Uzun? I think that you're a true detective. A real cop. Yes, that's what you are. You're a real cop. What's your helmet number? Ha! What's your helmet number?" I grabbed her head, and she struggled to break free, but I held on, pulling her toward me, and when my mouth was near her ear I shouted, "I can't see it! I can't see your helmet number! Did you take it off? Did you take it off, just like all the cops on the streets these days?"

"Let me go!"

I yanked the collar of her green dress and the strap tore loose, revealing her black bra and jostling breasts.

She pulled up her dress to cover her bra and screamed, "You bastard! Get the hell away from me. Don't you dare touch me again!"

I got in her face and said, "I have absolutely no intention of touching you. I'm just trying to understand whether or not you know anything. T. C. Sinem Uzun, do you think that you know everything? Were you there when infinity was created? Is that why you think about everything down to the last detail? Then go on, make the best of it. Make the best of looking like you're smarter than Çağlar İyice right up until the point that he puts his brilliant moves into action!"

"What the hell are you saying, you moron?"

"I'm saying you're a whore. What right do you have to emotionally exploit my love for my ex-girlfriend? Have you ever thought about how your parents have sex when they don't even love each other? Have you ever thought about all those fake smiles that people throw around? Have you ever thought about the fights that people have in their bedrooms because they're ashamed of fighting in public? You cunt, T. C. Sinem Uzun, have you ever thought about this farce we call civilization?"

"That's enough, shut the hell up!"

"No! I won't shut up! Only the wise and the dead shut up, but thank God I'm ignorant and alive, and now I'm going to put you in your place, T. C. Sinem Uzun, you whore! Why? Because you wanted to pull me into a trap. You wanted me to say that I don't love my ex-girlfriend anymore, and in exchange for that you were going to give me a few kisses. Well, fuck you! Fuck that trap of falsehood you set for me. Çağlar İyice doesn't fall for shit like that. Do I look like someone who would fall for a trap like that? I wanted to kiss you for the simple reason that I wanted to kiss you. That was it. I just had the desire to kiss you. So fuck off! I don't feel like kissing you anymore. Society is full of sons of bitches who don't want your money, just your memories and your past. Well, damn it all! Isn't there a single innocent feeling or genuine desire left in this fucking world?"

I had more to say, but I fell silent. I'm not quite sure what it was that made me stop talking. Maybe it was a desire to just disappear. I kicked the tire of the car and started walking toward the sea. "You're pathetic," I shouted behind me, laughing.

I continued walking toward the sea, looking around on the ground for a good flat skipping stone.

"That's what Çisem thought about you. She thought you were pathetic."

I laughed some more. I found a medium-sized flat stone and weighed it in my hand. It was the kind that would skip well over the small waves.

"I can't tell you how many times she told me that she thought you were pathetic!"

A strange feeling of doubt started gnawing at my heart. I turned around and said, "Stop trying to piss me off. Çisem and I may have had a short relationship, but we always respected each other."

"What respect? She didn't even answer your texts."

I threw the stone and said, "Fuck off! Maybe she didn't answer them because she didn't want me to get even more hurt. Damn you! You're just doing this because last summer I wouldn't give you the time of day. Do you know why I wasn't interested in you? You don't have a goddamn soul. You're nothing but two legs, two tits, and an ass. You jealous cunt! You lying whore!"

"You ass! Shithead! Bastard! I'm the one who's lying? I'll show you."

She held up her dress with one hand and started scrolling through her Galaxy S4 with her other. Her hands were trembling so much that she was having a hard time hitting the buttons on the screen. For the first time, that phone actually looked like a phone in her hand. Tears were gathering on her cheeks, but she couldn't wipe them away because she was holding up her dress.

"What are you doing?"

She didn't answer. With the phone in one hand, she tucked the strap of her dress under her armpit and wiped away her tears. She was muttering something. For a few more minutes, she fiddled with her phone, and then I got five or six messages on my iPhone.

"What are you doing?" I asked.

Again, no answer. I couldn't decide if I should take out my phone or not.

"Look at them," she screamed. "Go on, look at them!"

I took out my phone. She had taken screenshots of some of her conversations with my ex-girlfriend and sent them to me. Because I've read them a million times, I memorized them, down to the last comma and period:

```
T. C. Sinem Uzun: Whats up slut?????

Çisem Trinity: Hahahahahaha . . . Not a
hell of a lot . . . That fckwit Çağlar
sentt me a bunch of dumb messages again
last night. I'm erasing them

T. C. Sinem Uzun: Çisemmm why are you
messing with that guy, he's not so bad

Çisem Trinity: If you think so he's all
```

```
yours biyatch he's pathetic I'm telling
you PATHETIC

T. C. Sinem Uzun: His damn uncle's the
mayor what's so pathetic about him????

Çisem Trinity: if his uncle were the
president he'd still be pa-the-tic

T. C. Sinem Uzun: Hahahahahahahahaha I
just fell off the damn couch . . .

Çisem Trinity: if his uncle were the
prime minister that stupid fucker would
get into a fight with his uncle and end up
working as a waiterr at the parliament
restaurant ☺

T. C. Sinem Uzun: HAHAHAHAHAHAHAHAHA . . .
don't make me laugh you damn twat I'm on
the floor kissing the rug already . . .
```

I put my phone in my back pocket. My jaws were clenched tight, and I was biting my lower lip, breathing heavily through my nose. Then a feeling of breathlessness swept over me, and I found myself breathing faster and faster. My heart was beating madly, and I was afraid that I would have a seizure brought on by some unknown disease. My hands were shaking, and I put them on the back of my neck to try to stop the trembling. When I realized I probably looked like a prisoner of war like that, I put my hands down and then struck my chest with the palms of my hands. When I realized I probably looked like a caveman when I did that, I hit my knees four or five times. But my fucking hands wouldn't stop shaking. When I tasted blood, I stopped biting my lip. The world around me was going blurry. All the dark emotions that I'd carried within me up until that day were thrown into a strange chaotic order and illuminated with a terrifying light. I felt like my life of just five minutes before was driven a hundred years into the past. I spit out the blood in my mouth. It felt good to see that blood, as if I'd gotten rid of some of the poison in my body.

"What did I ever do to you?" I asked, my voice as calm as ever. "Okay, I can accept that I might have been a little selfish, a little lonely, a little ridiculous. But was it worth it? Making fun of me for those things? Couldn't you find something else in the world to make fun of? Wasn't there anyone else except for Çağlar İyice to make fun of?"

"Read the rest of them."

"Are you getting some kind of pleasure out of this?"

"Were *you* when you called me a lying whore? When you called me a jealous cunt? When you called me T. C. T. C. T. C.? Don't you have any respect for me? So what if I put T. C. in front of my name. I'm patriotic, that's all, and I happen to like the abbreviation for my country. The damn government wants to take it off the names of state institutions, so I wanted to protest that. But does that mean you have to make fun of me? Aren't I a person, too? Are you that barbaric? Or are you some kind of reactionary? An enemy of the republic?"

"For the love of God, where did you get that? At the concert last year for the October twenty-ninth celebrations, who was it that climbed on stage between songs and grabbed the microphone from Mustafa Keçeli and shouted, 'Long live the republic'?"

"Everyone knows that you did that just to show off in front of Çisem! But when we clapped for you, she didn't even clap. I've always been nice to you. Tonight when you said, 'Sinem, I'm not feeling so hot tonight, do you want to go to Castle? There's going to be a DJ,' I said sure. I was being nice to you."

"Okay, great you came, thanks, I'm getting all teary eyed. But why did you laugh so hard that you fell off the couch over that business of me working as a waiter? What the hell was I supposed to do? Smuggle drugs? What would you do then, kiss the sky for joy? Is that what you call being nice? Is that what you call treating me like a person? If that's the case, then what the fuck does it mean to be a motherfucking person? What is it? If you take away someone's pride, then what's left? If you take away their dignity? What the hell will be left then?"

I put my shaking hands into my pockets, bit my lip some more, and spit out some more blood. That fit of rage wouldn't let go. What was it that was killing me? I couldn't purge myself of the poison coursing through me; it was rushing through my brain, the center of my chest, my stomach, my arms, my hands, even inside my eyes. At times, it acted like it wasn't there, hiding itself, but then at other times it made its presence felt throughout my entire body. There was no solution. I pulled out my phone again and read another one of the messages:

Çisem Trinity: He drove off the road today . . . and he sprayed some melon-scented air freshener in the car, the nitwit ☺ ☺:9

T. C. Sinem Uzun: engough already you're killing me ☺ Whattya think of Cengiz???????

Çisem Trinity: Why do you ask??????

T. C. Sinem Uzun: he was writng to me all nite on fb

Çisem Trinity: hey biyatch send me the caps rite noooow

T. C. Sinem Uzun: Hang on . . . tell me what do you think of him

Çisem Trinity: Cengiz???? He's not right . . . something went wrong during production

T. C. Sinem Uzun: yeah he's a bit lame, nothiing refined about him at all

Çisem Trinity: ☹ ☹ ☹ hes always following çagalar around . . . he's the reason why çağalr is so pathetic . . . for years they've been like glued together and çağlaer has even started to act like him . . . but he'd be good for you ☺

T. C. Sinem Uzun: why?????

Çisem Trinity: all the bums find you biyatch . . . baby its your fate . . .

T. C. Sinem Uzun: ashisdjgalsfdkhgald kfjgadflkjg

Çisem Trinity: theres sth I was going to tell you . . . metehan said to me today, that night you asked for my phone number even though there were lots of girls at the table ☺

T. C. Sinem Uzun: oooooh . . . a fast one, what did he say then?????

Çisem Trinity: look don't misunderstand me, he said, but did you have a reason . . . I was so embarrassed . . . I couldn't say anything . . .

T. C. Sinem Uzun: you should've said you're just a slut lol ☺

Çisem Trinity: hahahahahaha ☺

T. C. Sinem Uzun: is he the prize jewel you've been after????

Çisem Trinity: screw the jewel he's the hope fucking diamond <3 <3 <3

T. C. Sinem Uzun: nkasjdhfladjfhaseouirhg

Çisem Trinity: ohhh he's my prince charming <3 <3 <3 if it works out I'll be over the damn moon . . . that's the kind of guy you want on your relationship status on fb . . . he's worth all this time I've been waiting <3 <3 <3

T. C. Sinem Uzun: but you just kissed çağlrar not too long ago . . . wtf you weren't waiting ☺☺☺

Çisem Trinity: hahahahaha . . . it was just one time that dooesnnt count

T. C. Sinem Uzun: How was it ☺☺☺

Çisem Trinity: Like kissing my own damn hand . . .When he stopped to get a breath of air that was it. There was no second kiss. Tried it once and that was one time too many. ☺

T. C. Sinem Uzun: Aqdgahgaggaq lmao

Çisem Trinity: I was really drunk anyways . . . there was no tonguing that's for sure . . . I sobered up with the first taste of spit. ☺☺☺

T. C. Sinem Uzun: hahahahahaha lmao, that's all I have to say

TWENTY

At the edge of the roof, there was a short wall about a yard and a half high, and I was sitting there looking at the cars parked bumper to bumper all along the street. It was an old four-story apartment building, and the roof was more like a terrace. Turkcell had installed a cell site on the side of the building facing the street; the company paid five hundred lira a month to use the space, which worked out to sixty-seven and a half lira for each apartment, easy money. Because it was a quiet, calm space that had everything he needed, Microbe used it as a workplace and hangout. Three steps led down to it from a door to the right of the roof at the end of the hallway.

He grabbed a green plastic chair that was in front of the Formica-topped table and held it out to me. "You're drunk," he said. "Get off the wall and sit down."

I pushed him in the chest and said, "Mind your own business!"

"What's going on?"

Instead of answering, I raised my beer and took a long pull, drinking about a third of the can. The front of my shirt was open because of the missing buttons, and I held the cold can to my chest.

"You!" I said. "Damn you! Did you write to T. C. Sinem Uzun?"

He put his hands in his pockets and looked down. "Yes. But it was a long time ago."

"How long ago?"

"Six months."

"You call six months a long time? You've got a warped understanding of what a long time means."

"Did she tell you?"

"It doesn't matter."

"Did she send you the caps of our conversation?"

"What does it matter?"

He held his hands out and said, "Look, boss, I was drunk."

Raising my beer, I said, "Well, I'm drunk now. I'm drunk, Microbe! But do you see me running around hitting on girls, using the excuse that I'm drunk?"

He walked up to me and put his right hand on my back, pointing to the chair with his left hand. "Come have a seat. Please, sit down here."

Pushing his shoulder, I said, "Mind your own business!"

I looked down. There were some scrawny cherry trees in the garden that never bore fruit. As I looked at them, they started zooming in and out of focus. I steadied myself, holding onto the wall's weathered marble coping.

Microbe's father called from inside, "Cengiz! Get in here."

Not taking his eyes from me, Microbe said, "Coming!"

"Are you using that iPhone to write to T. C. Sinem Uzun?" I asked. "Is that all your iPhone is good for? Do you think we're the only people who have to deal with hard times? Whenever you see a pair of legs, do you just throw in the towel? Do you get all soft?"

Lunging forward he grabbed me by the front of my shirt and pulled me down from the wall and pushed me onto the chair. He held me there by the shoulders.

"You're going to fall!" he said. "Boss, you were going to fall off the wall! Please, sit there! Stay put, please! What's the problem?"

"What's the problem? Because of you, they think I'm pathetic! That's the problem!"

I threw my empty beer can at the cell antenna and then got up to grab another beer. "They think I'm a loser, and it's your fault," I said. "You made me become like you. They can smell us a mile off now. It follows us everywhere, that stink of losers. That stink follows us everywhere. Because of you!"

Microbe's father shouted again, "Cengiz! Cengiz, get in here, damn it!"

Microbe looked at the door but didn't answer, and then he turned to me and coldly said, "All right then, let's not hang out anymore."

He took his iPhone 4s out of his pocket and removed the SIM card from its slot. After putting the SIM card into the change pocket of his wallet, he held out the phone.

His dad shouted, "Cengiz! Get your ass in here!"

"What's this about?" I asked.

"Take it."

"Don't be ridiculous."

"Take it!"

"That's absurd, presents can't be given back."

"Cengiz, get in here right now!"

Microbe suddenly grabbed my shirt and tucked the phone in my hand, folding my fingers over it.

"Cengiz, get in here, damn it!"

He turned and stormed inside. He had this great belt he got from the İzmit Outlet Center, a Diesel belt, and he started taking it off as he walked. I followed him down the dark hallway, which was lit by a dim bulb. The walls were green with mildew. Microbe started running, and I ran after him. I turned into the small, smoke-filled living room of their apartment. Microbe was standing over his father, who was lying on the sofa, and then hit his father with the belt and screamed, "Why the hell are you shouting? Why are you shouting at me?"

"What the fuck are you doing?" I said, pulling Microbe back by the shoulders. Then I got between him and his father, spreading my arms out. Microbe pushed me aside and hit his father with the belt again. By this time, his father had started crying and was trying to cover his head with his arms. I grabbed Microbe around the waist and tried to pull the belt away, but he held on tight, so I grabbed the end of the belt that was dangling on the ground and pulled it toward me. With my free hand, I grabbed Microbe by the chin and looked into his eyes, but he wouldn't look at me. He was looking over my shoulder, still glaring at his father. I gave him a few light slaps and said, "Get a hold of yourself, man."

Microbe said, "What the hell are you shouting about?"

His father was hiding under a blanket on the couch. He poked his head out, wiped away the spittle on his lips, and said, "I'm afraid, Cengiz."

Microbe dropped the belt and asked, "What the hell are you afraid of?"

"Of being alone."

"I'm right upstairs!"

"It's all so overwhelming, Cengiz! You don't know what I'm going through."

He wiped away his tears with the back of his hand. His face was pale and thin, and his chin and cheekbones stood out. The skin on his forehead was stretched tight, his cheeks were sunken, and his sparse beard seemed to somehow float above his skin. If there hadn't been the slightest flicker of light in his sunken eyes, you might have thought he was a cadaver about to be dissected in an anatomy class.

Microbe snapped, "Do you expect me to watch over you night and day?"

"Ingrate! You filthy ingrate! For years I worked at Pirelli just so I could take care of you."

"Enough already, quit going on about Pirelli!"

"Why the hell shouldn't I talk about it? I say it with pride. I worked at Pirelli!"

"So, you worked at Pirelli! So what?"

There was a Pirelli calendar hanging from a nail on the wall. Microbe tore it down and flung it at his father. "Here, take it! These are the people working at Pirelli now. You're not riding Pirelli's cock anymore; these girls are."

Microbe's father threw the calendar back and said, "They're just for advertising. We were the ones who made Pirelli what it is! Us! The people at the Pirelli factory in İzmit!"

He started crying again, wildly punching the sofa. As he squirmed and writhed, it seemed like he was trying to get to his feet by punching the sofa.

"We were the ones who made Pirelli what it is! We were the world's biggest Pirelli factory!"

"Screw your factory!"

"Don't be so ungrateful! Damn ingrate!"

Microbe raised his fist as if he were going to hit his father and hissed, "What are you talking about? Ungrateful? It was Pirelli that brought you to this. Is Pirelli cleaning your damn ass when you shit yourself?"

Clamping my hand over Microbe's mouth, I said, "Enough, damn it! Enough!" I spun him around so he was facing the living room door. I shoved him with all my might toward the door. He tried to turn back but I snapped, "Move it! Get the fuck going." I pushed him toward the door of the apartment building. He grabbed his tennis shoes from a plastic shelf next to the door and, using a long steel shoehorn, put one of them on.

"Ingrate! You damn ingrate! Hitting your sick dad. Is that how I taught you to act? Is that how a man acts?"

Microbe put on his other shoe. I took the shoehorn from him.

"You've still got food on the table because of Pirelli. Ingrate! Get moving!"

Microbe took a step out the door and then turned around and shouted, "You're going to be buried under those fucking tires you made. They're not even paying your severance. Even if you had a lawyer working for years on it, they'd never pay you. But you're still going on about Pirelli. Screw you, you brainless fuck!"

I said, "You really are an ingrate! Shitting on the bread you eat!"

Microbe leaned against the dirty wall next to the door, looking down with his hands cupped around his nose.

"Damn ingrate! Who the hell raised you? It was Pirelli, too," his father said.

"Ha!"

"You always looked forward to the New Year holiday! You used to say, 'Dad, is Pirelli going to give you a bonus this year, too? What are you going to get me?' When you started primary school, you said, 'I'm not ever going to take off this hat.' When you went out to play at recess, you wore that damn hat. It was your fault that the principal chewed out your mom. It was you who upset your poor dead mom."

"Fuck off, you son of a bitch! You goddamn motherfucker!"

Microbe made a move for the hallway, and I threw one arm around his neck and the other over his shoulder. He dragged me like that to the middle of the hallway, and then he shrugged me off. I fell, hitting my head on a wall mirror on the way down, cracking the glass in two. Taking a deep breath, I pushed myself up and ran back into the living room. Microbe was swinging at his father with both fists, and when I tried to grab him from behind, one of his elbows caught me in the nose, sending a jolt of pain through my head, and I pressed my hand against my forehead. Then I managed to get in a kick that sent him sprawling, and I lunged between him and the sofa, shouting, "Microbe, stop it, damn it—stop it!" He grabbed me by the throat with his left hand and kept swinging at his father with his right. There wasn't a sound coming from beneath the blanket, and it occurred to me that Microbe's father might be dead. The thought of it filled me with horror. I grabbed Microbe from behind, latching onto his arms, and I yelled toward the window, "Eyüp Ağbiiiii! Eyüp Ağbiiiii!" Microbe was trying to break free, kicking out wildly at his father, and with each kick he inched closer to the sofa. Eventually, he got close enough to start kicking the blanket with his right foot.

From beneath the blanket came a single cry of "Aaaaaaaaaaaaaaaaaah!" I latched onto Microbe's right leg with both arms, and he tumbled onto the blanket. With one hand he was pressing down on the blanket, and with his other he was throwing punches. I tried to pull him off, but he held on tight.

Eyüp Ağbi, who lived in the basement apartment, came running into the living room. He shouted, "Cengiiiizzz!" and locked his massive hands on Microbe's shoulders, but that didn't work. By grabbing Microbe around the neck and bracing his legs against the sofa, he managed to pull him off and the blanket came away as well, still in Microbe's grip. His father was curled up in a fetal position on the sofa, not moving or making a sound.

Eyüp Ağbi pinned Microbe on his back and held down his wrists. "Cengiz, look at me! Cengiz! Look at me! What the hell are you doing? Cengiz! Look at me! Cengiz!"

But Microbe wasn't looking at him. Maybe he hadn't even noticed him yet. He thrashed around for another minute or so, and then fell still.

I approached Microbe's father. I wanted to check his pulse, but I was afraid. He had shit himself, and a foul stench rose from the sofa. I pressed two fingers to his neck, but I didn't feel a pulse. Slowly, I rolled him onto his back, and his eyes snapped open. He smiled at me, and there were only three or four yellow teeth left in his bloodied mouth. Out of fear, I backed away, and my knees started to buckle. I stumbled toward the wall, flexing my legs in an attempt to get rid of the trembling in my knees, but it didn't help. I sat down and leaned against the wall.

"Cengiz," Eyüp Ağbi said. "Cengiz, what the hell are you doing? What are you doing? Look at me! Cengiz!"

There was no anger in Eyüp Ağbi's voice, just shock. He was a brawny man in his early thirties and a pleasant person to be around, and he and I got along well. He worked on the assembly line at an auto body factory, Yaşar Bodyworks on the Bursa highway—trailers, dump trucks, flatbeds, cabs. If you ever have time, you should go and see him for yourself, he's probably still working there. Eyüp Ağbi took Microbe by the arm and led him out of the living room. The old lady living across the hall had come out by this point. Sometimes she recognized me and sometimes she didn't. "You run along," she said and then went into Microbe's father's apartment. We started going down the stairs. All of the neighbors were standing at their doors, looking at us with a mixture of fear and concern.

When Eyüp Ağbi and Microbe reached the front of the apartment building, Eyüp Ağbi let go of his arm. He looked at Microbe as if he wanted to say something, but Microbe clearly wasn't interested. After straightening the collar of his T-shirt and running his hands through his hair, Microbe started walking toward the street. I followed after him. He silently walked along with his usual calm, measured steps.

"Microbe," I said, but he ignored me and kept on walking as if I wasn't there. We went into the Migros under the Alkaş Residences, and the bright white lights were dazzling as we walked down the aisles. Microbe stopped in front of the SuperFresh refrigerator and looked at the sandwiches behind the glass door for a while. He opened the door and grabbed a tuna sandwich, holding the triangular package with two hands as he read the expiration date. Then he walked to the beverages aisle and, opening the sliding glass door, grabbed a bottle of cola and headed for the checkout counter. Across from the checkout counter, there were shelves of sweets, and he grabbed a package of wafer cookies, a bar of chocolate, and a package of gummy bears. Just in front of the checkout counter, there was another display, and he grabbed a pack of gum and a small box of fruit candies. After the girl working at the counter scanned the bar codes of his items, he opened his Velcro wallet, paid, and got his change. He didn't take the receipt she held out to him or bother to put everything in a bag. We walked out of Migros, and he started heading toward the shore. There were a lot of people on the seaside. He walked until he found an empty bench facing the sea and sat down. I sat down beside him. He opened the tuna sandwich and threw the package into the garbage can beside the bench. A flood of people were moving up and down the sidewalk in front of us.

"Microbe," I said.

"Don't call me Microbe in front of other people."

"Why the hell not?"

"No one else calls me Microbe."

"What are you talking about? When we were in eighth grade—"

"That just lasted a few months, and then everyone forgot about it. Aside from you, no one calls me that. If you're going to, only do it when it's just the two of us."

"Look, don't get the wrong idea. It's just out of respect for the past. Don't be ridiculous, man—it's a sign of how close we are."

"All right, boss, don't drag it out."

He started eating his sandwich, chewing each bite slowly and methodically. For a moment, I felt something, a feeling the name of which I'd rather not remember now. I didn't know what to say. I mean, it was complicated, because I really loved the guy.

"Cengiz," I said. "Cengiz, I . . ."

"You're drunk. We'll talk tomorrow."

"My biggest fear came true. In this fucked-up crock of a world, I brought myself to disgrace by running after women. I'm a disgrace. Forgive me."

"Leave, boss. You're drunk."

I got up and walked a few steps away, and then I turned back. "At least take the phone back." He just sat there, eating his sandwich in silence. "If you take it, I'll feel a little better at least."

He finished the sandwich and took the package of wafer cookies out of his pocket. Slowly, he opened the package, pulled out a cookie, and oh, what were they? Nestle, or Choconut, I can't remember now what fucking brand it was; they were wafer cookies, damn it! And then, he took a bite.

"If you're mad at me, then don't think of the phone as a present I gave you. I had the bill sent to the municipality anyway. So think of it as a present from the people of Kıyıdere."

He turned toward me and took another bite of the wafer. He continued chewing as he looked at the phone I was holding out to him, a smile on my face.

"Fuck you," he said. "Just fuck off!"

So I fucked off. Holding my bag of beer, I walked down a shadowy street, unsure of where the shadows ended and where the actual street began. The shadows looked like you could reach out and touch them, and the objects along the street looked like shadows. The ground was muddy, and at one point my shoe sank deep into the mud, and when I tried to pull it out, my foot came out of my shoe. I lost my balance and stepped into the mud with my sock. Blue tarps fluttered on each side of the road, undulating in the wind like ghosts. I walked until there was nothing but darkness in front of me. Placing my hand over my eyes, I peered into the pitch dark. It was as if darkness had swallowed up the street.

I turned on my iPhone flashlight app and kept walking. At one point, I heard a faint sound, a rustling of some kind. I couldn't tell where it was coming from. Then the sound got louder and louder, and I shined my light in that direction and saw some rats. Big rats. They ran away when I shined the light at them, except for one. I walked up to it. The reason it hadn't run away was that it was dead. There was a deep gash in its neck, and its eyes had popped out of their sockets. I guessed that it had probably gotten stuck in the mud, thrashing in pain until it died all alone. There was nothing to be done. Rats don't get funerals. We can be afraid of them, we can feel sorry for them, but there are no funerals for rats. I decided that the best course of action was to observe a moment of silence. Why not? "You lived and you died," I said. "I don't know what kind of rat you were when you were alive. Maybe you led a lonely and simple life as you calmly went your way. If I'd known you, I would've respected you. Then again, if you had suddenly appeared in front of me in the darkness, I might have been afraid of you. But seeing you now, stuck in the mud like this, makes me feel sorry for you, because I'm a person. That's what we do, we feel sad about things. But don't you be afraid, little rat. Dying isn't the end, it's just the transition from the world of events to the world of memory. Now you will live on in the memories of other rats. You will live on until you vanish from the minds of rats. You will live on until you vanish from the mind of the cat that clawed you. It's a good thing that you met me because I won't ever forget you. How could I? Look at those eyes filled with such pain. Who could forget you? Anyone who saw you like this just once would never ever forget you."

I heard the faint roar of an approaching rainstorm. Shining my light ahead, I made my way forward. I saw a yellow bulldozer. I tried the door, but it was locked. Using the stairs on the side of the dozer, I climbed up to the roof. I set my black plastic bag on the roof and opened a can of beer. It opened with a pop and foamed up, and I held the can away from my shirt and sucked the foam off the top of the can with my lips.

My mind was filled with thoughts, but I don't want to write about them now. If this had happened, then that would've happened; if that had happened, then this would've happened. What's the point?

I decided to call my ex-girlfriend. I said to myself, "Now look, son, one way or another, you're going to make that call. You can either get smashed and call once you've become a complete monkey, or you can drink eight or nine beers and call her like a gentleman. The choice is yours. In any case, she won't answer." I decided to call and let it ring five times and then hang up the phone forever, waiting to see what would happen in the coming days, each and every one of those days as long as a year. But things didn't turn out as I expected—she picked up on the second ring. I couldn't say anything because that was the last thing I expected.

"Çağlar."

"Yes?"

"Why aren't you saying anything? Is something wrong?"

"No, not at all."

"Where are you?"

"On a bulldozer."

"What? I can't believe it! I just saw it on TV! I thought it looked like you, but then I said, no that's impossible. He wouldn't do that. He and his dad aren't getting along. He wouldn't go there. He would never do that! I can't believe you, Çağlar! Please be careful!"

"I don't understand."

"Aren't you in Beşiktaş?"

"No. What happened?"

"They stole a bulldozer and are chasing the riot control trucks toward the office of the prime minister. It was just on live TV. One of the guys looked like you. Just like you. Çağlar, I could swear it was you. Tell me the truth."

"I'm not there. I'm on a bulldozer on old Şefika Street."

Silence. For a while, I sat and listened to my ex-girlfriend's regret for having answered the phone.

"Then why did you call?"

"I don't know. I forgot everything that I was going to say. Never mind. These are difficult days. Big days. It was just a little thing, just a really small thing. Never mind."

I waited for a while and then hung up. *If I were to take a walk with the aim of gathering my thoughts,* I thought, *I would have to walk around the entire world.* I opened another beer. I had three beers, my electronic cigarette in my shirt pocket, a bottle of e-liquid in my pants pocket. I had just lost my best friend because I'm a disgrace—I had lost just about everything in the world. There was a roaring in the distance. The roaring of rain. It was speeding up. I went on sitting there, listening to it speeding up and slowing down. When the rain stopped, I listened to the silence. Then I looked up at the darkness above me. I kissed my hand. I closed my eyes. I kissed it again.

TWENTY-ONE

Clouds with edges like shorn wool hung in the darkening blue sky. In the distance, I could see the top floors of a tall building and a red light flashing on its roof. About fifty steps ahead, there was a cluster of trees, and under the streetlights their leaves took on the yellows of autumn. On the curved roof of a bus stop, the glass walls of which were busted out, there were two young men sitting with their arms draped over each other's shoulders. They swung their legs as they looked around, weary but mischievous smiles on their faces. A street vendor passed by me, his cart loaded with slices of watermelon. He was wearing a rather odd tall hat with a wavy brim, not unlike the kind a magician would wear. A gray apron was tied around his waist, the fabric wrinkled and damp. He pushed his cart forward, making his way through the throng of people, eventually disappearing into the crowd. There were flashes of light here and there, probably from cameras. I stood listening to the deep roar that filled the air, reminiscent of a high-ceilinged school cafeteria. That mysterious hum got louder, quieter, and then louder again, never fading away. My shadow stretched out ahead of me, zigzagging across a broad flight of stairs. At the top of the stairs, there were flags affixed to long plastic poles fluttering in the breeze. Taking a deep breath, I pulled my

Guy Fawkes mask over my face. It was Sunday, June 9, 2013, and I was in Taksim's Gezi Park.

Let me ask you a question: Has your best friend ever kidnapped your sister to take her to a protest, using the Renault Broadway that used to belong to your grandfather? Just imagine, you find the Broadway abandoned in a parking lot in the neighborhood of Tepebaşı. Then you go from police station to police station trying to get help, and they just brush you off. Do you think they are silently hinting at the fact that for days the police haven't had any control for miles around Taksim? When you tell them that, as an honest tax-paying citizen, you have no intention of backing down, will they sneer and say, "Why haven't you kept an eye on her yourself?" Wouldn't your mother lose what little sanity she has left? Would she paint herself from head to toe during an oil painting class at the community center and then throw herself naked into the streets, shouting, "Take me, but give me back my daughter!" No, that's not what would happen. If that were the case, it would mean that you didn't yet know anything about life. But don't be upset. Soon enough, Çağlar İyice will explain it all to you. Taking you by the hand as he divulges a secret that has been kept for years, he will explain it all word for word, whispering at times and shouting at others, but never deviating from the truth. You see, he's no manipulator who goes out of his way to dramatize what's already dramatic. He's just the last representative of the experiences of real life, the last distributor of technologies that have gone out of fashion. He speaks to you now in the name of everything that has succumbed to defeat, speaking in the name of feelings that have been rent asunder by callous thoughts. He lays waste to himself in the dark of night. Why? Because, my friend, one day it may be useful to you.

When you have to take matters into your own hands, you will search high and low for someone you love, as if rushing headlong toward a fire. Step by step, I began ascending the stairs. Before reaching the top, I stopped and looked around to see if anyone was going to ask for my identity card or search my backpack. Two lovers walking hand in hand passed by me, and I followed behind them, slowly approaching the park. As I passed by an overturned police car, a powerfully built man wearing a red plaid shirt called out to me, "Hey! Can you come over here for a second?" I stopped in my tracks. There was something rough about him, and his thin lips made me think of knives. He was probably in his twenties, and he had a scruffy beard. He took me by the arm, and I thought he was going to say, "What the hell are you doing here?" and then send me packing. I cleared my throat so my voice wouldn't tremble, and said, "Hi there," but the words came out as an embarrassing squeak. Trying to sound gruffer, I added, "So, what can I do?"

He handed me his phone and asked, "Can you take our picture?"

"Sure," I said, and he walked over to his friend who was waiting in front of the police car.

They smiled, standing there with crossed arms, and I was sure that just five minutes earlier they had turned over that car, smashing the windows and setting it on fire, and then spray-painted it and hung a socialist flag on the fender. Just to be safe, I took a second picture and checked it. They were solid-looking characters, the kind that would be happy to destroy another dozen police cars if they had the chance. I handed back the phone, and he thanked me. "Not at all," I said. Pulling my mask back down, I took a deep breath and continued on my way.

I passed under the banners that had been strung up between the trunks of trees at the front of the park. I turned back and read them, but there was nothing about my sister. Then I came across what appeared to have once been a police van, and I walked around it a few times. The van was brightly painted, and flags and balloons hung all over it. I stood by the door, watching as people emerged from the van, their faces lit up with childlike glee.

Along the sidewalk that led into the park, open-air tents had been set up, one after the other. On tables in front of them there were brochures, leaflets, and small speakers blaring music. Seated on stools and bundles of magazines, people were enjoying cups of tea, but in my eyes, there was something sinister about them. The tents were covered with political statements; there were so many that it would take a million years to read them all. Some were taped to the tents and some were clipped to strings that ran between them. The trunks of the trees were covered in leaflets and posters, and between the trees there were wires from which hung warm yellow lights. Clothespinned to the wires were more declarations written on brightly colored paper. The park was like a massive, shapeless book, the first page of which you would never be able to find. Everything except the air was covered in writing, and I'm sure that if the technology existed, they would've written on that as well.

I continued walking along, passing by a play area for children and lean-tos strung up along a wall, and entered a space filled with colorful tents. Among the tents were groups of people sitting on the ground. I approached five people sitting in their socks on a blanket spread over the grass. They were talking quickly, flicking the ashes of their cigarettes into paper cups and nodding to one another. I leaned against a tree, placing my hand on one of the announcements that had been stapled to the trunk. It was printed on brown packaging paper and started with a poem; toward the middle, it invited the reader to a soup potluck, and at the end I saw the words "Taksim Commune." I squinted, acting like I was reading the announcement with communist seriousness as I tried to follow their conversation. But it was impossible. When one of them stopped talking, another would start. To really understand what they were saying, I would've had to rewind the conversation three years back. The first person in the group who noticed that I'd been standing there was a blond girl sitting with her back to me. She was wearing a pink T-shirt with a large collar, and her hair was loosely tied with a red hair band. When she turned and looked at me, the others looked up as well. I thought about asking if they'd seen my sister but changed my mind because maybe they were talking about something important and didn't want to be disturbed. I had no idea what might set them off; a single spark could do it, and then I would've really been in a bind. The police were totally absent. It was no laughing matter. Slowly, I began to back away. When I realized that they were watching me, I quickened my steps. They knew that I'd been secretly listening to them. Who knows, maybe they thought I was a spy or something. After I was a safe distance away, I turned around to see if I was being followed. They were all still sitting there looking at me, and when they saw that I was looking back at them, they laughed. When the people in the neighboring tent asked why they were laughing, they pointed to me and said something.

I rushed headlong into a crowd of people. Turning left and right, I tried to find a way out, but I was surrounded. Everyone was hopping, shouting, "Hop! Hop! Hop!" and there I was, stuck in the middle of that ruckus. Someone hopping next to me grabbed my shirt, trying to pull me up and down, and I knew that if I didn't hop, I'd look like I was a member of the Giving Gramps Cancer Party, and damn it all, that hospital smell came to mind again so I started hopping. As I hopped, I noticed that we were near the rear of an open space in the middle of the park, and up toward the front there was a high stage flanked by speakers mounted on poles. A group took to the stage—they must have been popular because everyone was applauding—and the singer grabbed the microphone with two hands, pulling it toward him as if he were going to bite it, and in a nasal but resonant voice he made a wonderful speech, which I can't remember because I was busy trying to find a way out of the crowd. Slipping past the hoppers, I found a spot for myself on a wall overlooking the stage.

The people swarming like ants on the narrow pathways through the park began surging toward the stage. When the group started playing, people raised their phones into the air. It looked like a sea of light, and I guessed that they were afraid that if they didn't record the song, it would be gone from their lives forever. I tried to scan the faces of the people at the front of the stage, but it was impossible; there was no way I'd find my sister in that heaving mass of bodies. I wished I could freeze everyone in place so I could walk among them and look for her. Raising my mask, I took a few pictures, because that's what you do. When the band reached the chorus of the song, the crowd began cheering and clapping. Not wanting to draw attention to myself, I clapped as well, trying to look like I, too, had come to listen to enjoyable songs under the warm yellow light.

But I had no time to spare so I slipped out of the crowd and continued walking. Among the trees near the boulevard, I saw a cluster of dim lights, and I headed toward them. The setting looked romantic. When I got there, I was transported from the raucousness of the concert to an entirely spiritual realm. Pieces of wood in the shapes of letters were staked to the ground, upon which small round candles flickered in the wind. To the left was a star, and next to that the word "TAKSIM," and below that "IS OURS." Some of the candles had gone out, and the candles of the upper triangle of the star were completely out. I looked around. Hadn't anyone noticed this negligence? I thought about getting some candles and lighting them, all in the name of humanity, but then changed my mind. A red-and-white strip of plastic had been wound around the words, and I could imagine someone accusing me of trying to enter a forbidden zone. It occurred to me that the protesters in Taksim were quite different from those in Kıyıdere. I spotted a man sitting on a curb who looked like a figure of authority. He had long hair and a beard, and his elbows were on his knees as he looked at his phone. I tried but failed to get his attention. I could tell from his face that something serious was happening on his phone. Stretching out his legs, at last he put the phone in his pocket. Gazing at nothing in particular, he sighed, and a strange expression settled over his face. Whatever he'd seen on his phone, it had really done something to him. I took a step closer, and cleared my throat, but he didn't look up. He was in another world. Even if he had seen my sister, he'd surely forgotten about her.

I knew that I'd never find her just by looking around. I came up with a plan, but it would take some time. Starting at the uppermost edge of the park, I would make my way down, checking every single tent along the way. They'd taken my grandpa's camping equipment with them, so I knew that I'd recognize our two-person tent. The park was quieter up near the top, and it was easier to see the people coming and going. After checking the tents there, I walked down the stone-paved walkway, stopping every few steps like I was checking a message on my phone, looking at the tents around me. Soon enough, I saw our green tent up near the left wall of the park on a patch of grass.

I scanned the area. They'd marked off the group of tents with a rope, and had even given it a name: We Are What You Call Us. I supposed it was a proclamation of their independence. There were two people sitting on a concrete outcropping at the camp's entrance. The man had his hand in the woman's lap and was whispering something into her ear, making her giggle. Many of the inhabitants of the camp had spread tarps on the ground, and just like people do at their summer homes, they were playing rummy. I walked down the narrow path toward our tent. Small placards were placed at the entrance of each tent, and they indicated who was staying there or what was on their minds. Some people had gone so far as to spray-paint their messages on their tents. I stopped and read each of them; they were like the names written next to doorbells at apartment buildings.

Nothing was written at our tent. There was no light on inside, and there didn't seem to be any movement. I guessed that they were tired from the journey and had gone to sleep, and hadn't found the time yet to make a sign. Slowly, I opened the zipper and stuck my head inside. It was dark, and I couldn't see a thing, so I whispered, "Cengiz," trying not to wake up my sister. Someone grabbed my arm, and I leaped back. The occupant was a curly-haired woman in her twenties.

"What do you think you're doing!" she shouted.

A few people walked up and asked, "Who are you?" They took the mask from my face and held my arms.

"Just a second," I said, hoping to explain myself. "That's our tent."

They tightened their grip on my arms.

The woman screeched. "What are you talking about? That's my tent!"

Someone asked, "Is he a thief?"

"What the hell do you mean, thief?" I shouted.

The crowd gathering around stared at me with hatred in their eyes. Someone else murmured, "Is he really a thief?" and the word "thief" drifted through the crowd like a radio wave bouncing from place to place until it was transformed into "He's a thief!" and began spreading through the park.

The curly-haired woman said, "Hold onto him and don't let him go. I'm going to tell the We Came for Trees and Almost Had a Revolution Solidarity Platform. Let them come and take care of this."

Someone trotted up and said, "Forget about the platform. I complained to Hazard Assistance. That's the best way to deal with this sort of thing."

"Please, just a second," I said. "There's been a big misunderstanding here."

Someone shouted, "Here they come!"

The Hazard Assistance crew was coming down the pathway. The crowd around me relaxed as they drew near, and some people even took pictures of them and cheered. Brushing aside the attention they were getting, they quickened their pace when they set their sights on me. When I saw that they were wearing the black-and-white jerseys of the Çarşı soccer fan club, I knew that this was neither a mere tasteless joke nor the imaginary realm of social media. This was real life. My blood ran cold. The fear rising up from my stomach spread out, squeezing my chest and vanquishing what was left of my courage, and the air was sucked from my lungs. I was so scared that it didn't occur to me to try to defend myself. My sole desire was to flee to the ends of the earth, perhaps to the jungles of India, where I could hide among the elephants. Driven by the instinct to survive, I began to struggle, but I couldn't break free of their grip. I was trapped, and what was left of my energy drained away. A chill ran down my spine, my knees buckled, and my lips trembled. I started crying.

The person I assumed to be the chief of Hazard Assistance grabbed my chin and, looking straight in my eyes, asked, "What did you steal?" The question was like a whip across my face, and I started crying harder. "Stop your bawling," he snapped. "Tell me, what did you steal? Why are you stealing stuff?"

He grabbed my shirt. My eyes were blurry, but I saw that his scarf was wrapped around his neck up to his chin, and between his eyebrows there was a deep furrow.

"I didn't steal anything," I said, addressing the furrow between his eyes.

He let me go and said to the group, "What did he steal?"

"We don't know."

"What the hell do you mean, you don't know? You said there was a thief so we came. He says he didn't steal anything, and you don't know what was stolen."

Another member of the Hazard Assistance crew said, "That guy's not a thief. He's just a punk."

The owner of the tent said, "So what was he doing in my tent?"

Everyone started laughing. But as the victims of a misunderstanding, she and I were the only ones standing there in silence.

"We have the same tent," I said sheepishly. "We bought it at KIPA for seventy-eight lira and ninety kuruş. We were planning on going camping this summer. We had some other plans, too."

Someone suggested, "Check his backpack."

"Open your bag," the chief said.

I unzipped my backpack, saying, "I'm not a thief! I'm just looking for my sister. It was your protest that stole her from *me*. Who's the thief now?"

I pulled the leaflets from my backpack and showed them around. At the top was a picture of Microbe and my sister. Below that, I'd added my phone number and written, "If you see my sister, Çiğdem İyice, and my best friend, Cengiz Altınel, in the name of humanity call me." The chief examined the leaflet carefully and then passed it to another member of the crew. My fate was in his hands, but he was confused, unable to hand down a decision.

He asked, "So which soccer team do you support?"

"Kıyıderespor," I said, unable to keep a shade of embarrassment out of my voice. "But don't get the wrong idea, I'm not one of those Kıylums."

"What's a Kıylum?"

"That's what they call our more avid fans. It comes from Kıyıdere Hoodlums."

The chief turned around and asked, "What's he talking about?"

"No idea."

"Their biggest issue is with Gölcükspor, actually," I said. "We've never even played your team."

At that moment, a man came running up in a panic, thumping his fist into his palm, shouting, "Chiefchiefchiefchiefchiefchief!"

The chief took him by the shoulders and shook him, saying, "Mali, what the hell's happened?"

"Chief, they stabbed our Hoca!"

Grabbing him by the shirt as if he were about to punch him, the chief shouted, "Who? How did you let them get away with this?"

"Chief, I swear it's not our fault, we didn't even see it happen. You know those guys with the beer carts? We were kicking them out of the park. Just when we were tossing one guy out, another one snuck up and stabbed our Hoca in the back."

The Hazard Assistance crew rushed off, and people started drifting away. The only ones left were those from the camp.

"Your sister is missing?" they asked.

"Yes," I said. "Well, not exactly missing. It would be better to say that we've lost each other."

Their expressions softened, but still I couldn't stop crying. Those tense days had taken their toll on me, and on top of that, I'd been humiliated and accused of being a thief. But I was the only one who knew everything that I'd been through since May 31. Ten long days that shook Çağlar İyice to his core. I felt something warm in my pants. I reached down and realized that I'd wet myself. My ears started to burn, and then my cheeks, nose, eyes, and forehead were burning. Someone brought me a stool. They all pretended not to notice that I'd peed my pants. Someone brought me a cup of water, which cooled the burning in my throat. The young woman who had been at the entrance of the camp listening to the coos of her lover took my hand in hers and said, "Don't worry. We'll find your sister. The Solidarity Platform has a tent nearby. Let's go there and explain the situation."

I blew my nose and wiped my cheeks. It made me a little uncomfortable, and even irritated me, that their anger had turned so quickly into compassion. "No," I said, "I'll find her myself. I don't need anyone's solidarity." After passing out leaflets to everyone there, I walked off in silence.

"You forgot your mask," someone shouted, but I pretended that I didn't hear. One of them ran after me and handed me my mask, which I took without even looking up. I put on the mask and walked off, avoiding people as best as I could, steering clear of their collective prejudices and organized exclusion, walking toward the darkness of the park, the darkness that is brethren to more darkness, the darkness so sorely needed by people who have suffered shame.

I walked until I reached two steel shipping containers facing the boulevard. Between them was an upside-down wooden crate, and I sat down. I didn't want anyone to see me like this. Someone started playing the *saz*, and the sound of the plucked strings echoed across the park. Four or five people sat in the grass with the saz player, drinking beer and singing along. Because there were no open grassy areas left, they had set up their tent on the dirt, and there was another tent set up away from the others. A young man was lying with his feet in the tent; he had folded up his blanket and was using it as a pillow. In the greenish light of a park lamp, he was reading a book that he held with one hand. His other hand was pressed to his forehead, as if the book had given him a fever.

I waited like that. I waited a long, long time. My mind was empty. Utterly empty, not even a trace of a thought. I was surprised to find that I had started crying again. I curled my hands into fists, pressing them against my head.

"Çağlar," I said to myself. "My dear, dear Çağlar."

Twenty-Two

There comes a point in your life when you have no choice but to continue down the dark path you're on because you're too tired to turn around and you're too torn apart to stay where you are. Most of the time, that's what we need most in life: to gather up the remaining parts of ourselves that are still intact and continue along in the blind darkness. "At last, old boy," I said to myself, "while you're sitting here between these containers crying, it's time to address the real issue: people. That grand suffering. For example, now that the conditions are all equal, I wonder who is the saddest person in this city. Me? Why not, it's possible. In that case, what's the point of being sad and further stoking those feelings of self-pity tonight? What's the point of calling out everything that's going wrong in your life and demoralizing yourself even more?" I hit myself in the head, trying to pull myself together, the history of philosophy in a single punch. "Come on," I said, "put your mind to work, put your heart to work, put your tongue to work, and, if necessary, put your hands to work. Do whatever you have to do, but make sure you find your sister. You have to find her. You have to find Microbe, your best friend. What'll be left in your life if you lose them? The depths of a loveless hell and piss-stained pants. Let them make fun of you as much as they want, let them say, 'Pew, nasty, he stinks,' let them call you a thief, a punk, whatever they want. Haven't you lost everything anyway, including your dignity? You're smack in the middle of one of those magical moments when you realize that you've lost everything. You're slipping into the void, and nothingness is dripping from the cuffs of your pants. So what does it matter? Ha! Old boy, you've got to just keep right on going your own unique way. Set off down that path wherever it may lead you, and don't give up."

I got up and walked through the dark space between the containers until I reached the boulevard, and then I started descending into the construction pit with firm, controlled steps. At the bottom of the pit, at that blind spot filled with the entirety of night, I took off my pants and tossed them aside, and then I took my sweatpants out of my backpack and put them on. When I put on those light-blue sweatpants, which I had bought at the İzmit Outlet Center, I felt like a brand-new person, as if I'd just rolled off the production line. That's how I am. When it's time to get emotional, I don't hold back, and when it's time to pull myself together, I'm an expert in that as well. Frankly speaking, in the art of gathering oneself from your ashes, I'm a true master. I marched out of the pit and started walking around the park, whistling as I went, and within fifteen minutes I discovered one of the fundamental laws of atomic physics. If you're trying to find your sister in a place that is swarming with people, then you should stand still at the most active spot. That's known as the İyice Law. It's been recognized by the Scientific and Technological Research Council of Turkey, and NASA's recognition will be bestowed soon.

I made that discovery when I was passing by the From Right to Left Market. The place was as busy as a beehive, and people were always coming and going. It was surrounded by a low steel fence that I guessed had once been a police barrier. The line out front was long but moving quickly. I walked a little closer and saw that there was a lot of activity going on under the blue tarp, and people were rapidly sorting out items on rectangular tables. When I saw the variety of products that were being offered, my hopes of finding my sister soared. The boxes on the tables were filled with wafer cookies, chocolate bars, crackers, and just about every kind of snack you can imagine. It was all being given away for free: pastries served on plastic plates, freshly brewed tea, Nescafe, paper cups of Fanta, slices of watermelon. They had just about anything you could possibly want, and all you had to do was wait in line. I was sure that my sister wouldn't pass up such an opportunity. The previous year, the Kıyıdere Charity Association—KIYCA—held a charity sale, and my sister made their greatest contribution to supporting people in need by eating more than anyone else. She just loved such acts of solidarity. If we set aside the fact that she wanted to become the symbol of the resistance by doing the moonwalk in front of a riot control truck, her presence itself would lend support to the struggle.

I got in line with the others in need, looking over the people working inside. My goal was to find someone who was easygoing, an individual who didn't place much stock in appearances, who had been cleansed of society's prejudices, and who understood what it meant to be engulfed by sorrow. In short, someone I could approach easily. I set my sights on a young woman wearing a bandana. She had a tattoo of a butterfly on her wrist, and she helped every single person who asked her questions. As if she were singing on the inside, she focused on the solving of problems. I guess that she was indebted to the problems she heard about, problems filled with the cruel energy of life. Her hair was light brown, and she had prominent cheekbones, and when she smiled, dimples appeared in her cheeks. She was slightly bucktoothed and had blue eyes, and her warm glances had the effect of a kiss. She was just what I was looking for. The line moved along, and I found myself standing in front of her.

"Hi there," I said. "Everything is free, right?"

"Yes."

"If I ate a hundred wafer cookies, they would be free?"

She held out her hands and said, "If you can eat them all, they're free."

"Actually, it's my sister who would eat them," I said. "Have you seen a girl who looks about twelve or thirteen years old but is really just nine? She's wearing a Michael Jackson outfit."

"No, I haven't. But there's a Children's Art Corner over there; the kids are all painting pictures. You might check and see if she's there."

"I looked, but she wasn't there. Plus, my sister's not the doodling type. She's got other goals," I said, handing her one of my flyers.

Holding it with her slender fingers, she looked it over and then raised her eyes to me. "Is she your sister?"

"Yes. Have you seen her?"

"Of course."

"Really? Where?"

"On Twitter. But as far as I know, she was found earlier this evening."

"No, the rumor that my sister was found is just one more instance of false information spreading quickly on social media. That was another kid, another Çiğdem who was lost for ten minutes during the protest."

"Well, as far as I know the Solidarity Team had been looking everywhere for her since yesterday. Have you talked to them?"

"I'm not interested in talking with them."

"Why?"

"Politically, they're quite shallow people."

She tossed back a few strands of hair that had fallen over her forehead and narrowed her eyes. There was a slight smile on her lips. When I realized that she had tensed up and was waiting silently for me to offer an explanation, I said, "Above all, they're quite rude. Some of them broke their families apart and abandoned them, and as if that weren't enough, they went off trying to bring down the government. They've got no respect for people's feelings. Anyway, there's no need to dwell on such things. There's something else I want to ask you. Do you need any more volunteers? Can I work here?"

She squinted and looked me up and down, taking stock of my height, weight, style, general state of mind, minor perversities, and degree of trustworthiness. With a faint expression of approval, she nodded and said, "Come on back," and pointed to the entrance on the right.

I left the line and walked in an arc through the crowd, and we met at the entrance. She unhooked a strap that ran between two tall police barricades and pushed out a shopping cart.

"Take this," she said, "and go to the park entrance. Across from the Toilet Phone-Charger Tear-Gas-Escape Hotel, you'll see someone with a red armband. His name is Metin Ali. Get some more supplies from him and bring them here."

"But I want to work behind the counter," I said. "Isn't it possible for me to work behind the table with the chocolates and wafer cookies?"

"First bring the stock and we'll see."

"All right. Where's this hotel?"

Her eyes widened and she pouted her lips, and for a little while she stood there experiencing the horror of being in the presence of the world's most ignorant person. Slowly, she pulled herself together and took me by the elbow, walked around me, put her hands on my shoulders, pressed her firm breasts against my back—I'm pretty sure she wasn't wearing a bra because I felt her nipples through my shirt—and breathing warmly in my ear, she pointed in the direction of the hotel. Everything about her demeanor said, "These kinds of people always find me. No matter where I go, they find me. What have I done to deserve this?"

I pushed the empty shopping cart in the direction she'd indicated, the cart rattling and bouncing along on the walkway's cobblestones. I felt that things were starting to look up a little. That's the most common sentiment felt in the world. Because life is generally crappy, the human heart gets calloused and numb. But when things start looking up a little, it starts to go pitter-patter, as if there were shit worth getting excited about.

As I was going down the sloping dirt path to the street, I lost control of the cart and came flying out of the park, lurching left and right. When I reached the sidewalk below, I regained my balance, but I found myself in a sea of thick smoke. With its unique minty aroma, at first I thought it was tear gas, that indispensable element of protests, and I got quite excited. Soon enough, however, I realized that it was just the smoke of a street vendor's grill. There were other guys around with shopping carts selling beer, and they eyed me as I passed by. Maybe I gave them the impression that I'd sold all my beer and was heading off to restock. Passing silently among them, I made my way down to the main street. Across from the hotel, there was a guy wearing a red armband, and when he saw me, he shouted, "Where have you been?" He was about my age but gave the impression that he had more experience than me in the business of protests.

"I just got here, but I've been following what's been going on since the very first day."

"Where are the others?"

"What others?"

"They only sent you?"

"That's how it looks."

"Well, come on then," he said and quickly walked off to the right with me in hot pursuit. We passed through a narrow gap in a medium-sized street barricade that had been constructed entirely from materials bought with innocent taxpayers' money. The other side of the barricade faced a taxi stand, and there were a lot of people coming and going. We stopped next to a delivery van, and he opened the rear door and hopped inside. The back of the van was filled to the top with twenty-four-pack boxes of water. He tossed one of the boxes down to me. I wasn't expecting it, but thanks to my quick reflexes I didn't drop it.

"Hang on a second," I said. "They sent me to pick up some supplies, not water."

"These are the supplies."

I had imagined medical supplies or something along those lines. That way, it would look like I was going back into the park to tend to wounds. That would've been better, but what can you do? You have to make do with what you have. In fact, that's the very basis of life. And so Çağlar hauled water. We filled the cart to the brim with boxes of water, and I headed back to the free market. I stopped at the foot of the path leading up to the park. I eyed the slope and the cart, thinking that the cart didn't look like it had much of a chance of making it up there, but still I pushed with all my might and had made it about two yards when some of the boxes on top came tumbling down. I decided to carry the boxes up and then push the empty cart up to the top, where I'd reload it. It was hard pushing even the empty cart up the slope, but in the end I managed. My first trip was almost complete.

As I pushed the cart along, I looked left and right, hoping to catch a glimpse of my sister. When I was carrying the second load of boxes up the slope, I came eye to eye with a guy who was sitting with some others in front of a tent playing cards. "What are you carrying around?" he said, but I didn't reply. As I was heading out for the third trip, the people sitting in front of the tent applauded as I passed by with my empty cart. One of the girls in the group was sitting there in her socks doing something on an iPad, but when the others started clapping, she lightly kicked one of them on the back of the neck and said, "Instead of clapping, why don't you give him a hand." When I came back with the cart, the people sitting around the tent had formed a line up the slope and were passing the boxes up to the top. They dropped one of the boxes and it burst, sending bottles of water rolling everywhere, and they had an extraordinarily fun time with that. The moron who dropped the box was laughing particularly loudly. I was irritated to no end, but I didn't show it. As I said, when I was down at the bottom of the construction pit, I had charged myself up with so much energy that no one could get me riled up. In a way, I had broken free of the world and established my own spiritual kingdom. But still, you have to be a little thoughtful, and you shouldn't go around carelessly using up people's stocks of tolerance. Take me, for example: I had just started working at the From Right to Left Market, and I had no salary or social security benefits, and I did it all in the hope that my sister would come and eat some wafer cookies and we'd be reunited. But then you come along, you freak of nature, busting one of the boxes so you laugh your head off about it. Living like you just don't give a flying fuck gives rise to characteristics like that. In all of the critical twists and turns of life, people are ready to sell you out in a heartbeat. Our generation isn't so bad, but the generation before, especially people born before '91, are mostly irresponsible deadbeats. In fact, there are so many of them that if we said that all of them are irresponsible, not many people would have the right to get upset. February 28, 1991, is the cutoff date, the end of the First Gulf War, and before that date, not a single profoundly sensitive person was born in this country.

For a full hour, I traipsed back and forth between the delivery van and the park, and with the help of the irresponsible deadbeats who lined up on the path, I delivered the entire vanload of water to the market, probably more than a ton of water. After unloading the last load in the depot area, I plopped down on the ground and leaned against the boxes of water, catching my breath. As I sat there crunching some dry leaves that had fallen unseasonably early, my employer came back and tousled my hair as a token of congratulations. In that way, I experienced the joy of knowing that my efforts hadn't been in vain. I took a few puffs on my electronic cigarette and then asked if she wanted to take a puff, too. She twirled it between her fingers for a little while, looking at it as if it had just fallen from space, and then she took a drag. Her gaze shifted from my blue sweatpants to my electronic cigarette to my face as she tried to make a connection between the three. When someone called out, "Orsa," she hurried off. I watched her, wondering how she could have gotten such an odd name; probably the first thing her father did when she was born was set about trying to come up with something strange, like one of the articles of the code of civil law that was never written down, and then he hit upon that name and went to the registry office, but the registry officer looked at him with confusion in his eyes, and the father said, "What do you mean, you don't understand?" But in the end, he walked out with a birth certificate, and for years we've been struggling with her name, but her father doesn't care. He's quite happy, everyone loves his daughter, and he thinks it's because of her name.

I watched the front of the market as the line grew longer and longer. I got up and looked at the tables of wafer cookies and chocolate bars. Our stock was running low so I asked, "Do we have any more?" and they said, "Look in the back of the fridge." So I went over and checked, and at the bottom of the fridge there were enough snacks to feed a family of four for a century. I opened up three or four boxes and restocked the table after a preliminary evaluation to determine the best color harmony and symmetry. Drawing on all of my artistic sensibilities, I tried to breathe some spirit into the snack table and make it as festive as possible, and all the while I studied every single person who came into the market.

An older guy came up and planted himself across from the line of people and started complaining about his bills, trying to stir up trouble. His jeans were pulled up over his belly and his light-green button-up sweater was open in front, revealing a purple shirt beneath. He was wearing glasses with colored lenses, the name of which slips my mind at the moment, and a white hat with an upturned brim, and he was holding a medium-sized Turkish flag, gripping the plastic pole as if it were a handrail on a lurching bus. "We're afraid to turn up the heat from one to two!" he shouted and was met with waves of applause, which stirred him to enthusiastically wave his flag. He was seventy-three years old, a retired civil servant, and public enemy number one of the gas company. His daughter and two grandchildren lived in Austria, and the year before his wife had died of stomach cancer. He lived in the Burak Apartment Complex in Koşuyolu and had fought with the management and all of his neighbors about the monthly maintenance fee. *Goddamn,* I thought, *this old guy is fucking lonely!* When his wife was sick, they got a gas bill for 350 lira, and because they couldn't pay it, their gas was turned off. His daughter blamed him for her death, saying that it was his stinginess that killed her, and she didn't let him see his grandkids anymore. He called his son-in-law and told him that he'd paid for all of her medicine and hadn't been stingy at all, but his son-in-law told him that he couldn't get involved and that he'd have to sort it out with his daughter, but that summer they weren't going to come out for a visit. "What did I do wrong?" he asked. "What am I going to do now?" He had come all the way from the other side of the city to vent. He said that the previous month he had gone to a protest held by the Bird Lovers' Association because plans were underway to cut down some trees in a wooded part of the city.

"Amca, which woods?" I asked.

He looked left and right, trying to figure out who had asked the question, and I raised my hand. At first, the people within earshot were lightly poking fun at the old guy, but then they started listening more seriously as he spoke. I suppose it's because I asked such a pertinent question and people glanced at me as if to say, "Who's that sensitive person?" I felt good.

The old man said, "Which woods? The woods across from our apartment building. The newspapers wrote all about it. That's where they filmed *The Chaos Class*. We went there during the filming and got the signatures of Adile Naşit and Münir Özkul. Those were wonderful times, but they're all gone now. What are we going to do now? What are we going to do?"

No one answered, and he didn't press the issue. He lowered his flag onto his shoulder. They offered him tea, but he refused. They offered him a stool, but he didn't sit down. Slowly, people started going back to their original conversations. As he glanced around sadly, I felt close to him. At first, I thought that maybe he'd dedicated himself to political opposition because he was just bored of the monotony of retired life, but I was wrong. As usual, I was wrong. I couldn't bring myself to look away from him because I thought that maybe he had something else he wanted to say. The hollows under his eyes were like craters, and it looked like his face had been pelted by meteorites. All the pain he'd ever suffered manifested in a face full of wrinkles, creases, and spots. He looked at me and nodded his head side to side as if to say, "Never mind," and he started to shuffle toward the entrance of the park with timid, crestfallen steps.

As the night wore on, the line in front of the market got shorter, and fewer and fewer people were walking by. In the end, the last lovers held hands and left the park. Those who remained started heading toward their tents. My sister hadn't come around, which was odd because she always had a snack before going to bed, or at the least a glass of warm milk. Where was she? What was she doing? Without her, I was on the verge of madness, and I constantly had to calm myself down. That in itself was tiring. Not once had I ever thought about the idea of life without my sister.

Then people started emerging with blue plastic bags as they set out on a hunt for garbage. They were wearing white gloves and dust masks. For an entire hour, they swept up every nook and cranny of the park, down to the very last cigarette butts. Then they stood in a line and passed the bags of trash out of the park. An earringed guy wearing capri pants persisted in walking around with an empty bag, looking for garbage like a treasure hunter. Eventually, he found a plastic bottle, which he tossed into his bag, and his face glowed with joy. But his happiness was meaningless. That plastic bottle was going to live five hundred years, and it was going to bury even our grandchildren's grandchildren's grandchildren. In the end, it would say, "You picked me up at the foot of a tree and threw me away, and then I buried your entire family. The next generation is next!"

I sensed that there was some tension in the cooking area so I walked over there. Orsa—we'd taken our closeness a step further by that time—was sitting in a chair holding her head in her hands, silently having a nervous breakdown.

In the end, she couldn't restrain herself, and she shouted at no one in particular, "Sure, we'll paint over the curses people write on the walls. And then soup has to be made for breakfast, so we'll do that, too!" She raised her fingers to her nose and said, "My hands reek of garlic. Do we always have to fight on two fronts?"

I sat down across from her and said, "Orsa, calm down. As someone who's fought on two fronts, even three, all his life, I understand what you're feeling. Please, let me make the soup."

At first, she glared at me, but then her expression softened a little and a laugh escaped her lips. You don't come across people like that very often, people who are always ready to laugh. The kind of people who, after arguing for twenty-three hours, can just pick up from where they left off and go on having fun—such people never nurture grievances in the depths of their hearts or hold grudges. They're simply incapable of it. It's like a joke, a cartoon.

"In your entire life," she asked, "have you ever made soup?"

For half an hour, I had sat there watching her work away at the counter. She was trying to make *ezogelin* soup, but from the get-go she'd made three fundamental mistakes. First of all, you can't make it just using tomato paste. You have to add a reasonable amount of red pepper paste as well. Second, if you add a cup of rice, you have to add more than half a cup of bulgur because that's what gives ezogelin its unique consistency. Third, and this was the gravest problem, she didn't know that spices and tomato and pepper paste are the roux of the soup.

I would even go so far as to say that she didn't even know that the essential element in the making of soup is called roux. You can't put the roux of ezogelin straight into the pot. You have to roast it in a separate pot and make sure that it doesn't get lumpy; your best friend Microbe has to add a little bit of water once in a while.

Without trying to look like a know-it-all, and without breaking her heart, I explained this all to her, and then I said, "Give me your hands." I picked up a stainless-steel knife from the counter and said, "Please, just give me your hands." As she looked at me with surprise in her eyes, I took her hands and started stroking them with the knife, slowly, as if I were caressing them. "If you want to get the smell of garlic off your hands, you have to rub them with a stainless-steel knife and hold them under running water."

As she went to rinse her hands, I put on her apron and started working on the soup.

"Where did you learn all this?" she asked.

"Have you ever heard of the Kıyıdere Training Hotel?" I asked. "There's a head cook there who happens to be a complete psycho. He trains the best chefs in the Marmara region. That's where."

Hoping to change the fate of the soup, I started working away at another pot. Orsa sat down back to back with one of her friends, knees bent, moving her feet from side to side like windshield wipers. She watched me and tiredly smoked a cigarette. Things were working out nicely between us. She was born on February 28, 1991, had studied journalism with a minor in sociology, was addicted to tear gas, didn't have a job, and was the vice president of the Beyoğlu branch of the We Don't Have to Do Anything That People with Weenies Say Collective, and in her spare time she liked to watch men make soup. She thought it was sexy. I said to myself, "Goddamn, this girl is hot." I turned to her and winked. She scowled. Using two hands, I traced the shape of a heart on the front of my apron and she melted, smiling so wide she showed all her teeth. What else could she do? I know what makes women tick.

TWENTY-THREE

When the first rays of dawn broke over the park, they were few and far between, but they slowly increased in number as they reflected off the trunks of the tall trees; at first they were tranquil, but little by little they came alive and then burst into color, setting the tarps aflame with orange and painting the leaves above green as the light filtered down. All the people, those in tents and hammocks, those under blankets spread out on tarps, and those on benches with iron armrests, were dozing side by side, back to back, shoulder to shoulder, face to face, and some of them were alone. But as the light spread over the park, they started to stir. An ant was crawling on my arm, and, trying to minimize the amount of harm I might cause, I picked it up between my fingers and placed it on the ground close to its nest. After relocating the ant, I walked over to the steaming pot of soup, yawned, and banged the lid of the pot a few times with the ladle.

"You make the announcement," I said to Meti. "I'm too shy."

Meti was the guy who had tossed the boxes of water to me from the van like a machine gun. He shouted, "Soup's ready!" four or five times. His way of shouting was polite but suggested that, if necessary, he was ready to take on anyone. Sleepy faces started appearing as people lined up along the barrier. Using a towel, I lifted the hot lid off the pot and steam billowed up. I observed the impatient expressions of the people waiting in line as the scent of the soup started filling the air. I felt useful. I hadn't felt that way when I was making the soup, but at that moment, when I saw those hungry, sleepy faces, I did. It had been a long time since I'd felt that way.

I had put up my flyers where everyone lining up for soup would see them. People started saying things like, "She hasn't been found yet? What do you mean, of course she was found. They found her at the protest yesterday. I saw her, I know she was found." Trying to make eye contact with each and every person, I said, "No, she hasn't," and explained the situation. I managed to convince everyone in line that she hadn't been found yet, but that was just the tip of the iceberg. Passing the ladle to Meti, I got on Twitter: "MY SISTER STILL HASN'T BEEN FOUND! THE GIRL WHO WAS FOUND AT THE PROTEST YESTERDAY JUST HAS THE SAME NAME! SHE'S NOT THE SAME ÇİĞDEM!!! PLS RT FORTHOSEWHODON'TKNOW." Of course, what happened next? People tweeted things like "You're lying, she's been found." Others accused me of emotional exploitation. Some made pointless arguments like "What business do kids have being there?" Still others said, "Who's that guy in the pictures he shared, that guy Cengiz who he says is his best friend?" And some people styled themselves as detectives, saying, "This was all planned out before." So I tweeted: "WE IMMEDIATELY FALL FOR LIES BUT BELIEVING TAKES MORE TIME." Some people got even more riled up: "Friends, that swindler T. C. İyice isn't the girl's brother. This ASS is just trying to get more followers." Then came the worst of all: "Friends SPAM THIS LIAR -------> @geceninsabirlisesi #spamtheliars #spamtobefree."

I considered deleting my account, even though I wasn't worried about being spammed because I knew my sensitive followers wouldn't do that, but then I changed my mind. In any case, what would it change? If I did delete my account, they would question that as well, saying things like, "He deleted his account, so he must've been lying." So there you have it, the daily evils of people are always ready to gush forth, above ideologies, deep and indelible. Those daily evils hang over you, waiting to strike you in the head like a judge's gavel every hour of every day, never asking for overtime pay, never giving up. "God!" I said to myself. "Hey, God! Did you create people just so they could rain their daily evils on us like a shower of atoms? If so, you should have created Twitter at the same time you created people. You should have created man from tweets, not from clay. Since we were spiritually ready for it, since we were morally inclined that way, why did we have to wait thousands of years for this technology? I don't want to appeal to the Constitutional Court or the European Court of Human Rights. I'm appealing to you, God, in all your mystery. I hope you're aware that I'm calling out to you for the first time since my grandpa died. I hope you know that it's been such a long time. Long ago, you forgot the deep wounds you inflicted on me. Maybe you've even completely forgotten who I am. But that's okay, I can let that go. But please, let's not sever all ties. We can put the past behind us. Dear God, let's make peace! I'm sorry, I've always called you God because I'm agnostic. Maybe that upset you? Maybe that's why you did a U-turn on me? If that's the case, I'm very sorry. Please forgive me, Allah. Oh, great Allah, grant me your forgiveness. Please answer me. What's the deal with all this cruelty being dealt out to a guy who's just looking for his little sister? What powers are behind these calls for spam, this lynching on social media? Don't you think it's about time to step in and intervene? If millions of people are at each other's throats on their time lines, if they're ranting and raving without listening to each other, if they're clamoring and crying out, then surely you can hear them, right? You can hear every single whisper. Do you have any ideas for a solution? Are you saying that Armageddon is drawing near? My sweet Allah, we have no need for Armageddon! We have so little left after having been shaken to our foundations, and now what else are you going to bring down upon us? At least do a little for us, I mean in terms of Turkey. Let's narrow down the framework a bit and focus on this country of impoverished souls. Will the Armageddon you have in store for us be the same one you unleashed on Denmark? As you raze Switzerland, are you going to tear down our country, too? As you pummel France and Germany, are you going to batter us as well? Is that your divine justice? Let them have their morality and technology; in any case, isn't that how they got powerful? At least give us a little spiritual reinforcement. Send us the spirit of Dostoyevsky, and a translator as well. If you unleash Armageddon before you send us his spirit, a great injustice will be committed in terms of international conjecture. Please, answer me! My dear Allah, answer me! Okay, okay. I get it. Thanks anyway. Pay close attention to these years: 2024, 2032, 2114."

After signing out of Twitter, I put my iPhone in my back pocket. I fixed my eyes on a light-blue banner that was strung up between a tree and a lamppost. It filled like a sail in the morning breeze, and I sat there staring at it until I had completely lost myself. Given my situation, the banner couldn't have been more appropriate. It read "Enough Is Enough!" Within five minutes, I felt much calmer. Just then, the last person standing in line caught my eye. He was wearing a Guy Fawkes mask and nervously fidgeting. What plunged me into suspicion was his hair, which was parted on the side. I put on my mask and went toward the end of the barrier and started fiddling around with a box of sandwiches wrapped in plastic, first lining them up and then scattering them in the box. Eventually, he moved through the line until we were next to each other.

"Good morning," I said, as if just shooting the breeze. "I hope you're enjoying the protests. Did you buy your mask at the entrance of the metro?"

He simply nodded instead of answering, which merely increased my suspicions. My sister is just mad about morning soup, and she can smell it miles away. If she was hiding somewhere in the park, I had no doubt that she would run the risk of being found for a bowl of soup. But still, I wasn't sure. I thought of looking at his hands, but they were in his pockets.

"That's where I bought mine, too," I said. "They were selling them on İstiklal Street, but they said they were ten lira, so I didn't get one. What's the point of spending five extra lira in this fucking place just because the beard's a little blacker and it looks a little more like Guy Fawkes?"

Suddenly, he turned to me, and I saw that wild light in his eyes, the light of pain suffered too early, the light of a childhood that had been shit upon. That light will never change, and it will give you away your entire life. It was Microbe. The day his mother died, that light settled into his eyes. He stepped out of line and started walking away. "Microbe!" I shouted, and he tossed aside the soup bowl and started running in the direction of the hotel. I leaped over the barrier and took off after him.

He was running at top speed toward the Don't Step There Cooperative. I called out to some people who were hoeing in the coop-erative's garden, "Catch him, catch him!" but by the time they realized what was going on, he'd already sped past them like an arrow. He turned left and entered an area paved in marble, which under the light of the sun looked like it had been polished for centuries on end. There was a group of about thirty or forty people there, and they had laid mats on the ground in the shade of the trees. At first, they were lying on their backs with their hands by their sides holding their asses in the air, and then they lowered their asses down and spread their legs into a V, and, using their arms to support themselves on the ground, raised their legs at a ninety-degree angle. As we ran past them, I was just about to catch hold of Microbe's T-shirt, but he jumped over a guy who couldn't quite do the move and got away. Near the stairs, he looked back to see if I was still chasing him and ran into a guy with a white beard who was teaching math to a group of nerds, and I knocked over their table. Shouts of anger ensued, and some of them went after me instead of Microbe, but I dashed off, still in pursuit. He ran down the stairs and turned onto the walkway, and ran the length of the sidewalk, which at that hour was in shadows. Just as I was about to catch hold of him, he jumped into a city bus that the protesters had turned into a photo gallery. As he ran past the rows of empty seats, I tried to grab him, but he dashed out the front door of the bus. I was running with all my might, but it felt like my lungs were about to explode. I didn't even bother calling out to him. There was so much I wanted to tell him: that he was still my best friend, that he didn't need to be afraid, that I was sincerely impressed by his determination to help my sister make her dreams come true when I myself had given up. He was almost within reach. I thought that once I caught him we would finally get to talk everything over. There was no other choice. I made a final lunge and took him down in front of the Banner Culture Center.

We wrestled around on the ground, but I managed to get on top of him and pin down his wrists. When I pulled off his mask, he said, "Ağbi, please don't hit me. I swear, I'm just hungry! I just wanted to get a second one for me, I swear."

I looked at the mask in my hand and then at its owner. It was as if the face I'd been pursuing vanished between the two of them. Some people ran over and grabbed my arms, pulling me off him. He got up and looked at me and the crowd gathering around us.

"I swear," he said, "I'm just hungry. It was for me."

No one understood what he was talking about. An older guy with a beard decided to intervene. He must have been someone important because when he spoke up, everyone fell into respectful silence. He put one hand on the other guy's shoulder and one on mine. "Boys," he said in a loud but gentle voice, "tell me what's going on here. Why are you fighting?"

Tears in his eyes, the kid said, "I hitchhiked here from Antalya. One of my friends is here. He told me that it was nice here and that everything is free. I just got here today. We're living on the streets. I'm hungry and the soup was really good. I didn't think that they'd let me have another bowl so I put on a mask and got back in line. This guy here caught me. I'm sorry!"

The bearded guy turned to me and grabbed me by the shoulders. His beard was so bushy that I couldn't see the expression on his face. His eyes were wide, but I couldn't tell if it was surprise or anger or both, and he started shaking me. Hoarsely he roared, "Get a hold of yourself, young man! Get a hold of yourself! If these kids can't have more than one bowl of soup, then why did we set up this commune in the first place?"

"I don't know this guy. I thought he was someone else."

But he didn't hear me, and he started shaking me even more violently, repeating, "Get a hold of yourself, young man!"

"I assure you, I have a firm grip on myself."

But no, he wouldn't let go, as if he'd sworn an oath to make me get a hold of myself. "No," he said, "you don't!" He turned to the crowd that had gathered around us and said, "You don't! You still don't understand the spirit of our struggle! Get a hold of yourselves! Get a hold of yourselves!"

Two guys stepped in and patted his back, and said, "Calm down, ağbi." Slowly, they pulled me from his grip. I tried to shake off the unease I was feeling. They led the old guy a few steps away, and I looked at him as they tried to get him settled down. He was shaking his fists, shouting, "Why did we start this commune? Why did we start this commune if a kid can't have a second bowl of soup?"

I thought about trying to explain things but decided against it. He was obsessed with that imaginary bowl of soup, which for him was the last straw. When he looked at me, he saw that withheld bowl of soup, as if it were the denial of a human right. Smiling sadly and shaking my head, I turned and started to walk away.

Someone new joined the crowd and asked, "What's going on?"

"I don't know. I think they wouldn't give any soup to some street kids or something."

When I heard that, I turned around and walked back. The old guy had put his hand on the kid's shoulder and was listening to him as if he were worried that he might have some other troubles. At first, they didn't notice that I'd come back. I had a burning desire to say something, but I just couldn't pull together my thoughts. It was like that feeling you get when you sit down to take a test and realize that you've forgotten everything you've studied. I felt that if I didn't express myself with the right words, I would never be able to express myself again. Unable to conceal the irritation in my voice and not knowing what I was going to say next, I said to the old guy, "Hang on a second, there's something I'd like to say." He and the others looked at me, but I couldn't tell from their expressions if they were exasperated or angry. "Why won't you listen to me? I didn't refuse to give anyone soup. I thought he was someone else; that's why I chased after him. He can come and have as much soup as he wants. I spent all night making that soup so that people would come and have some. It's real soup! Not some imaginary soup that you think I refused to give someone. Really real soup. There's still half a pot."

"Don't take it so personally," the old guy said. "It's got nothing to do with you. A lot of mistakes have been made since we got started. I was talking about a principle."

"Goddamn," I yelled, grabbing the front of his shirt. "There aren't any principles here, Çağlar İyice is here. If it's got nothing to do with me, then why were you yelling at me in front of everyone? You need to get a hold of yourself! Then we'll see who needs to get a hold of themselves!"

A few guys jumped in and pulled me off the old guy, leading me a few steps away. Some guy who I assumed was friends with the bearer of imaginary soup pulled me aside and gave me a summary of the old guy's political life and his experiences in prison. I didn't pay much attention. It was just another story that started nicely and ended badly. There's disdain and torture, there's exile and tears, and people that suffered the former suffered the latter, and in the end our lives are turned into dust.

My phone started vibrating in my pocket, and I looked to see who was calling. It was my uncle. I walked a few steps away and answered. "What the hell do you want?"

"Where are you?"

"Where else would I be? I'm in Taksim, looking for my sister."

"I'm in Taksim, too. Let's talk."

"Where are you in Taksim?"

"In Gezi Park."

"Where in the park?"

"Let's see . . . There are some young people sitting under the trees. I'm in front of them."

"What the hell kind of description is that?"

"Then you tell me where the hell you are! This place is confusing. You tell me a place, and we'll meet there."

"Meet me at the entrance facing the square. The Association of Muslims Who Make People Scorn Money have a stand there. There are some long, narrow flags at the stand. They're red and black. Do you see them? Good. Wait there. I'm on my way, as if I believe that you're actually here. I'm on my way, so wait there as if you haven't committed the gravest sin in life, you bastard."

TWENTY-FOUR

My uncle was looking at the ground, running his hands through his hair. His face was pale and his voice was hoarse. Coughing into his hand, he said, "The president of the Istanbul provincial office of our party got to work last night and made some calls. They've put together a special four-man homeland search team to find Çiğdem."

"Where in the homeland? I haven't seen any special teams looking for my sister."

Nervously, he eyed the people walking by. "At the Homeland Police headquarters," he whispered, motioning for me to lean in. "There are some in the park, too."

"Some what in the park?"

"Undercover police. They're coordinating with headquarters. But they told me it's hard to keep track of a place that has two million people going in and out every day."

We were sitting across from each other on white stools in the dappled light shining through the leaves. Oaf Tufan Ağbi was standing over us like another tree. He had refused to sit down when I handed him a stool, and he stood there, slowly eating ezogelin soup and looking around, taking in every last detail. My uncle took a pack of Marlboro

Reds out of his shirt pocket and stuck a cigarette in the corner of his mouth. He lit it and eyed me suspiciously.

"Where's your dad?"

"I don't know."

"Haven't you seen him?"

"Forget about him," I said. "What else did the police tell you?"

He looked at his shoes and took a few drags on his cigarette, the filter of which he'd squeezed nearly flat. "They said that something bad might have happened."

"Like what?"

"If only we could talk to your dad, too."

"Forget about him! What might have happened?"

"I called three times, but he was on the phone with someone else. You haven't seen him at all?"

"Fuck this shit about me seeing my dad! I don't have anything to talk about with him. Tell me what the police said!"

"They said that maybe she was kidnapped."

"Who would want to kidnap my sister?"

"Organizations."

"What organizations?"

"Terrorist organizations."

"Why would they want to kidnap her?"

He didn't reply. Oaf Tufan Ağbi put his soup bowl on the empty stool and tapped my shoulder with his index finger. "Çağlar," he said.

"Just a second, Oaf Tufan Ağbi, hang on a second! Why would they want to kidnap my sister?"

My uncle flicked ash on the ground and said, "For propaganda. They kidnap kids and hurt them, and then blame the government to stir up unrest. That's what they told me. They think that's the only way they can bring down the government."

Oaf Tufan Ağbi tapped me on the shoulder again. "Çağlar," he said.

A jolt of irritation ran through me. "What?!" I said, looking up at him.

Eyes wide with wonder, he pointed at a man who was standing about ten steps away. The man was wearing tight black pants with red suspenders over a white button-up shirt. Taking hold of the handrails on each side, he proceeded to ascend a flight of stairs, carefully testing each step. When he reached the top, he picked up a rope and started proceeding down a hallway. He came to a door and put his ear to the door, and someone called out. The door was locked, but he found a key under the doormat. Opening the door, he stepped inside.

"Oaf Tufan Ağbi, he's a mime. He does pantomime."

"What's that?"

"Think of it as theater, a kind of art."

"Does he need help?"

"No. It's a one-man act."

The mime was surprised to find that there wasn't anyone in the room, and he was trying to figure out what was going on. The room was quite small, and he started feeling the walls with the palms of his hands. I turned to my uncle. "Cengiz is with her," I said, turning to my uncle. "An organization like that couldn't kidnap her. Cengiz would never let it happen."

My uncle grabbed my arm and started shaking it. I could tell that he wanted to shout, but he held back. "Don't get me started with that damn Cengiz!" he hissed. "What the hell are you talking about it? He already kidnapped your sister. How well do you know him, huh? How well do you know him?"

Pulling away my arm, I said, "As well as I know myself."

"Is he a member of an organization?"

"What kind of organization?"

"Tell me the truth. Because he's a member of the Armed Organization That Hasn't Fired a Shot in Thirty Years."

"What the hell kind of organization is that?"

"How the hell should I know? That's what they told me at police headquarters. He's a member of a legal branch of the organization. So are you. Both of you are sympathizers."

"You are a fucking moron," I said, rubbing my face. "Just because we saw one of their protests in Kıyıdere, does that mean we're sympathizers, you idiot? That's a hell of a special team you're putting together."

"What's wrong with the team? They know about everything. It all checked out at the police station. Someone named Eyüp is the regional leader. You've been letting them use municipal resources. What the hell have you gotten yourself into? Because of you, I'm a suspect, too. Who's Eyüp?"

"You mean Eyüp Ağbi?"

"How should I know?"

"He's Cengiz's downstairs neighbor," I said, thinking for a moment before continuing. "I see what's going on. Okay then, I'll explain it all to you, step by step. Listen close, you goddamn enemy of the people. Pirelli didn't pay compensation to Cengiz's dad, so Eyüp Ağbi went to İzmit and hired a lawyer. The lawyer worked on the case for a year and settled things, and didn't even ask to be paid. So I said, 'Eyüp Ağbi, that's not how it works. Let's do something through the municipality in return; we've got the means.' And he said, 'The guys went to protest at the auto body factory, and they've taken over the plant. They have the same lawyer, so let's do them a favor.' So I told Communist Numan Amca—you know him, the jerk who works at the housing authority but never signs off on a damn thing—'Let's go,' I said, and he was as happy as a clam. So we got the truck we use to pass out tea and soup at public concerts and went to the factory to cater the protest."

"Why didn't I know about this?"

"Don't you remember? I told you that we needed the truck because we were going on a picnic."

"You goddamn liar! Why the hell would you take a municipal truck to a protest?"

"What's it to you? It's not your damn factory!"

"But it's my truck!"

"The hell it is! It belongs to the municipality. We said, 'For once, let's use the municipality's money to do something good,' and now look where it landed us."

I unzipped the side pocket of my blue sweatpants and took out my iPhone.

"Who are you calling?" my uncle asked.

"Constable Hakkı. Doesn't the Kıyıdere Police Department have anything better to do than look into my social responsibility projects? Are they tracking everything we do?"

"Constable Hakkı didn't have anything to do with it. I talked to him already. He said, 'If I had heard anything about it, I would've told Çağlar without even bothering to look into it. It was the İzmit police.'" My uncle tossed his cigarette on the ground and stepped on it. Cupping his cheeks, he said, "What have you gotten yourself into? And at your age? That organization has taken out Cengiz and kidnapped your sister. What the hell are we going to do now? All the security cameras in Taksim have been smashed, and the police can't see what's going on. What the hell are we going to do?"

A wave of nausea washed over me when he said that all the security cameras were broken. We were talking about a terrorist organization. It was no laughing matter. Terrorist organizations were nothing like the protesters in Taksim. They would blow up the cameras and do so much more. There was no telling what they might do. Thinking about it was bad enough. I gazed blankly at the ground, lost in thought.

After a while, my uncle said, "Tufan? Tufan? Where the hell are you?"

Just as he said that, we heard some shouting and screaming. I looked up and saw Oaf Tufan Ağbi standing there with the mime over his shoulder, shaking his fist menacingly. He wouldn't let anyone get near him. We ran over and said to the crowd, "Everyone, please calm down," and then we shouted to Oaf Tufan Ağbi, "What the hell are you doing? Stop it!" When Oaf Tufan Ağbi saw us, he lowered his fist. The mime was pounding on his back, trying to wriggle free. My uncle raised his hand as if he were about to slap Oaf Tufan Ağbi and said, "Tufan, put him down." The poor guy's face was white with fear, and he ran off when Oaf Tufan Ağbi set him on his feet.

"What the hell were you doing?" I asked.

"Çağlar, he got stuck between the walls. He couldn't get out."

"Those are imaginary walls. It's a performance. It's art."

"No, Çağlar, he really was stuck! He was trapped in there and he was crying."

People were staring at us, reproach in their eyes, and we apologized a thousand times before sitting back down. "Tufan, sit down," my uncle said and then lit a cigarette. After taking a drag, he punched Oaf Tufan Ağbi in the shoulder, and then he punched me in the shoulder as well. "What am I supposed to do now?" he asked. "Try to deal with your mom, try to deal with Tufan, or try to deal with you? Or should I try to find your sister? Doesn't anyone in this family have their head on their shoulders? Where's your dad?"

I took out my electronic cigarette and puffed on it for a bit.

"When I was in Tirana," Oaf Tufan Ağbi said, "my dad said to me, 'Your mother is twenty-eight percent Bosnian. That's why you're so messed up. I wish I hadn't married your mother. You could've been one hundred percent Albanian.'"

"Tufan, enough of that crap. Çağlar, where's your dad?"

I pointed: "In that big tent over there."

"Which one?"

"Ask for We Came for the Trees Group."

My uncle got up, smoothed out his pants, and rushed off.

"I'm telling you, Çağlar, that guy really was stuck."

"Okay," I said. "He's been rescued now, so you can stop thinking about it."

Oaf Tufan Ağbi scratched his cheek and smiled. A group of people wearing colorful outfits passed in front of us. Some of them were playing trumpets and others were announcing a protest that was going to be held on İstiklal Street. I couldn't understand what the protest was supposed to be about, and in any case there were protests upon protests going on, and I couldn't keep track of them all. Oaf Tufan Ağbi got to his feet. I grabbed his elbow, knowing that if I didn't hold him back, he would follow the group of trumpet players.

"Oaf Tufan Ağbi, sit down. Please. Just have a seat."

He sat down and looked at me.

"What happened to Cengiz's dad?" he asked.

"I carried him."

"Where to?"

"Downstairs."

"And then where?"

"I don't know. They took him away."

"Who did?"

"An ambulance."

"Did they take him to the hospital?"

"Yes. They couldn't get the stretcher up the stairs."

With sluggish steps, my uncle came back. He sat on a stool and started crying. I didn't say anything. My mind was filled with thoughts about what could have happened to my sister. Things the names of which I'd rather not remember now. After a long silence, I asked, "What happened?"

"He wasn't there."

"Where is he?"

"He went to the Grumpy Union Confederation in Şişli. They said he'd come back tonight."

"He's on the Anatolian side of the city?"

"What the hell are you talking about? Şişli is just up the road."

"Then why are you crying?"

He put his arms around my neck and rested his forehead on my shoulder. "I'm tired, Çağlar," he said. "I'm so tired. My nerves are shot. I don't think I can take this anymore."

We sat there for a while. The girl who'd held my hand the night before when I was crying walked by. I smiled at her.

She stopped and mouthed, "Who's that?"

"My uncle. This is what we do as a family. Start communes and start crying."

Getting to his feet, my uncle pulled himself together and they left, saying that they'd come back in the evening. I went into the cooking area of the kitchen, and the kid who I'd thought was Microbe walked up to the barrier.

"Çağlar Ağbi, can I have another club sandwich?"

"Sure," I said. After putting some salad and fries on the plate with the sandwich, I handed it to him. "Enjoy."

"Thanks, Çağlar Ağbi."

"Want a cola?"

"Sure, that would be great."

He took a big bite out of the sandwich, and as he chewed, he took a long look at the flyer I'd put up. "Ağbi, I've seen this girl."

"Where?"

Pointing to the entrance of the park, he said, "Over there."

"Where over there?"

"Come on, I'll show you."

We left the market and headed in the direction he pointed. After a little while, he stopped, pointed again, and said, "In that tent at the entrance."

I looked at the tent. Kurdish flags were fluttering in the wind in front of it.

"What the hell are you talking about?" I said. "What would my sister be doing there?"

"I'm telling you I saw her there. She was playing behind the table."

"What do you mean she was playing?"

"She was running around."

"Like she was dancing?"

"Yes."

My chest felt tight, and I seemed to be slipping into a sort of melancholy tinged with joy.

"Go back to the market and drink your cola. I'll be back in a bit."

Slowly, I made my way to the tent. As I passed by, I looked inside, but I didn't see my sister. I walked around behind the tent for a while, but she was nowhere to be seen. After checking the neighboring stands and kiosks, I leaned against a tree facing the tent and started observing it. Some rather unsavory characters were sitting behind the table at the front of the tent, and I looked at all the people going in and out and the others loitering around the entrance. But my sister wasn't there.

I raced back to the market. Taking the kid by the shoulders and giving him a shake, I said, "Tell me the truth. Did you really see my sister in that tent? Tell me the truth. Don't get me all worked up for nothing."

He realized I was quite serious and said, "Çağlar Ağbi, I'm not sure. I saw a girl, and she looked like your sister. But maybe it wasn't her."

"What were you doing there?"

"I go to all of the tents to see if they're passing anything out for free."

I went back and took up my post across from the tent, eyeing all the people coming and going. The music they were playing wasn't my sister's style. I decided that the kid must've been confused and went back to the kitchen. As I mixed together some flour and water, adding just a little bit of salt, I brushed the incident from my thoughts, reproaching myself for letting such a random comment get to me. I kneaded the dough until it was soft and smooth and then let it rest. I decided to rest as well, so I went to the depot and sat with my back against the boxes of water, my legs stretched out in front of me. At some point, I dozed off. Probably because of the noise around me, I had a rather ridiculous dream. I dreamed that my grandpa and I were trying to hijack a plane. Well, not so much hijack a plane but get it to change its route. My grandpa kept saying, "Çağlar, we have to go to Ankara. We have to go to the capital! That's how the Reçkos took down the Albanian government. They went to Tirana." In our Broadway, we drove to a place that looked like a runway. There was a bus with tinted windows, and somehow I knew that inside there were officials or police, whoever it was we were trying to avoid. "Don't be afraid," my grandpa said. "They can't see us, but we can see them." We ended up at a fueling station. At that point, my grandpa disappeared from the dream. The fuel trucks were floating in the air, and it was my job to fill them up. But I didn't know how to do it. There was a panel with a bunch of buttons on it, and I guessed that if I pushed them, the pump would start running. The buttons seemed quite familiar, and I realized that they were the same as the ones on the air pumps at gas stations. I pressed the button for flat tires, but nothing happened.

Then I woke up. At first, I thought that I'd only slept for five minutes or so, but when I looked around I saw that the sun had set and someone had put a blanket over me, my mind still half-shrouded in the darkness of sleep. I softened the overrested dough with plenty of oil and rolled it out, cutting it into five sections. Then I sprinkled some feta cheese over the spinach-and-onion filling and spread it on the dough, which I rolled into long coils in a shallow pan.

"There's Bosnian pastry in the oven," I said to Orsa. "I have some business to take care of. I'll be back in a bit."

She said something as I walked out, but I didn't hear her. I went to the side of the park facing the hotel and found one of the street kids who had eaten a pound of crackers at the market the night before.

"Can we talk?" I asked him. "I want to ask you about something."

"Go right ahead."

"Last night, you and a few of your friends were in front of the market. You were saying that we should beat up the supporters of the We

Call Everything Something Else Party and kick them out of the park. Why did you say that?"

"Because they call everything something else. They call the town of Uludere Roboski. They call Diyarbakır Amed. They say Mehmet instead of Ahmet. Enough already!"

"What's the big deal? All my life, I've called everything something else."

"That may be true. Everyone has the right to call everything something else. But they are doing even worse things."

"Like what?"

"They put up a poster of their leader in their tent."

Dark looks fell over our faces. You see, they were talking about a poster of their leader. But I thought of Lieutenant Necati Karapınar, our town's martyr. He'd been killed by those terrorists and was buried in the Kıyıdere Martyr's Cemetery. He was the son of Şenol Hoca, the Turkish teacher we had in seventh grade. When I was little, Necati helped me once when I was lost. I liked the guy. We went way back.

"I understand your sensitivities," I said. "But my situation is different. I came to this park to find my little sister, not to talk about politics."

"Then why are you asking me these things?"

I bit my lower lip, unsure of how to proceed. In the end, I said, "Do you think they might have kidnapped my sister?"

Punching his palm, he said, "Of course. You know, I actually thought of that, too."

"Why would they kidnap my sister?"

"To get house arrest for their leader instead of prison. That was their last demand."

"That's ridiculous!"

"Wait here. I'll be right back," he said. He came back with a guy who was maybe four or five years older than himself. We explained the situation to him.

He nodded knowingly and then put his hand on my shoulder and said, "Follow me."

We found an empty space at the corner of the park facing the hotel and sat down. He offered me a cigarette, which I declined, and then he started talking. His voice was like smoke. The words he spoke seemed to hang in the air, but I might have thought that because of my drowsiness, my exhaustion, my stress, my worries.

"In Turkey," he said, "there's just one organization that would pull off such a sensational act. It must've been them."

"Okay, but why?" I said, looking at the ground.

"Because those guys are world renowned when it comes to terror. They're capable of anything. Baby killers. That's what they are. They're baby killers; just imagine what they'd do to your sister."

"Goddamn it!" I said. "Aren't we in the middle of trying to make peace with those guys?"

Giving my shoulder a hard squeeze, he said, "Calm down. Think about it. We may be in the middle of a peace process, but does America want peace? Just look at the Middle East. It's a mess. Aren't kids getting pushed to the front lines every day? Aren't kids getting killed every day? But still, you have to keep your cool. Wait for news from us. Don't even think about doing anything on your own. This is no laughing matter."

He got up and walked away. I got up, and just as I was about to go into the market, I flew into a rage. What the hell was that supposed to mean, "Wait for news from us"? What if they had my sister? I walked to the tent at the entrance of the park. Without looking at anyone, I walked straight in and put my hands on the table at the front of the tent. I stared into the eyes of the guy sitting there. He started to smile, but I remained as serious as ever.

"I'm not looking for any trouble here," I said.

"In that case, welcome!"

"I would like to meet the so-called regional leader of your armed organization."

His expression changed. I could feel the icy stares of the people around me.

"What's wrong?" I asked. "Did it bother you that I said 'so-called'? Wherever he is, tell that leader of yours to come out and talk to me."

A youngish guy charged up to me and said, "Get the hell out of here."

A woman got between us, and as everyone was calling everything something else she pulled me outside.

"Where the hell are you hiding my sister?" I shouted. I slammed my fists on the stand, and brochures and flags fluttered to the ground. A group of about ten guys rushed out of the tent. The youngish guy got up on the stand and jumped toward me. Some women got between us, and they held him in midleap, but he was still trying to get at me. Another guy clambered up there and jumped, but they caught him in midleap as well. Applauding them, I said, "Oh, I'm really scared. *Kurdish Airlines, Globally Yours.* Get all the frequent flyer miles you want trying to get to me! I'm not going anywhere until I get my sister back!"

Just then, a guy appeared at my side and caught me with a kick. I turned to deal with him, but someone else punched me in the jaw. A group of about ten guys rushed into the melee when they saw me getting knocked around and started swinging away with the poles of their flags. Then a bunch of park leaders rushed in from every direction and tried to break up the fight, and I took a few steps back to pull myself together, but a group of about four or five guys charged up, throwing punches and kicking me. My eyes went dark, and I couldn't even see the people who were hitting me. It always happens like this. Every revolution devours its children, and in Taksim Çağlar İyice was being devoured.

A voice cried out, "Leave him alone!"

Whoever it was pushed the guys off me and grabbed my wrists, pulling me to my feet. Holding me in both arms, he pulled me out of the crowd. We stopped when we were a little ways off. My mouth and nose were bleeding, and I couldn't see anything.

"Are you all right?" he asked.

"Fuck you," I said, walking away.

He started following me, and I turned around.

"Are you okay? Let's go to the medical tent."

"Fuck off," I said.

Because I'm the sensitive kind of person who doesn't like to draw out problems, I left the park and started heading down into the construction pit. He was still following me. He came all the way down into the heart of the pit and stood there looking at me. I squeezed my hands into fists. He was wearing dark canvas pants and a shirt with black stripes. He went on looking at me with his cold grayish eyes.

"Why were you fighting with those guys?"

I didn't answer.

"I asked you a question. Why were you fighting?"

"What, am I supposed to get your permission if I want to get in a fight?"

Two young guys appeared at the top of the pit. One of them shouted, "Sabahattin Ağbi, is everything okay?"

"Screw your Sabahattin Ağbi," I shouted from the depths of the pit.

"You guys go on, I'll catch up," he said and then turned to me. "Have you been staying in the park?"

I didn't answer.

"Your uncle called me. He said that you stayed in the park last night. Why didn't you tell me?"

"Why should I tell you? The park doesn't belong to you. Did they sign it over to you just because you gave two press releases? What the hell? Now you think you're all big and mighty because you started a commune in Taksim."

I swung at him, but he grabbed my wrist.

"Where the hell is my sister?"

He pulled down my arm and held it there tightly, and then let go. I rubbed my wrist.

"So you started a commune in Taksim, now what? There's no government, no police, no sheriffs. Who's going to find my sister? Nongovernmental organizations that kick me out? Where the hell is my sister?"

"All of our constituents are working on it."

"Fuck your constituents! My sister is only nine years old."

"Don't you dare talk to me that way!"

"Fuck off! Some damn organization has kidnapped my sister."

"It's not like that at all! Your uncle has a screw loose. Last night, they stayed at the union clubhouse."

"Really?"

"Yes."

"Then where is she now? Bring her to me."

"We'll find her in a few hours."

"What the hell do you mean you'll find her in a few hours? Where is she? If she wasn't kidnapped, where is she now?"

"The police misled your uncle. Why would an organization kidnap your sister? What an idiot. Why do you believe the stuff he tells you?"

"Why the hell shouldn't I believe him? What right do you have to talk bad about my uncle? What's the deal with your animosity for our family, for your kids? Why do you go around acting like Fyodor Pavlovich Karamazov? What would I have done without my uncle? When you weren't around, who took me to Çınarcık and Esenköy? Who bought me ice cream? Who blew up my raft? Who made a newspaper hat for me when I lost my cap? Do you think you're a better person than my uncle because you're a political know-it-all? What did you do for me except send me tree-planting certificates on my birthday? You're the reason my sister ran away. Why didn't you have her come to Istanbul? What would be the big deal if she saw some of the clashes on the streets?"

"You're saying I should have brought her to the clashes?"

"Yes! Do you think it's better like this? While you were here choking on tear gas, we were in Kıyıdere choking on your freedom! You didn't share that freedom with us. That's why my sister ran away. What would've been the big deal if you'd brought my sister to Istanbul? She would've looked around a little at the barricades. If you'd taken some precautions, she could have done the moonwalk in front of a riot control truck. In the first days of the protests, if she'd done the moonwalk like that, then at least wouldn't a few important people on the Cabinet Council have resigned? Think about it! Just think about what's become of my sister. Don't think about me, saying that I know a bit more because I'm older, but for years my sister hasn't known what it means to have a dad. For her, when you say 'dad,' it's like *four zero four not found.*"

"I've always been there for your sister."

"Where were you for a whole month?"

"You know the answer to that."

"No, I don't. I don't know anything. Do you know what a month means for a nine-year-old kid? It's like what three years is for us. Not three years, thirty years. Goddamn you! She has a picture of you, but you aren't even looking into the camera. You're not even looking at her."

"She told me not to look at the camera when she took the picture."

"You could've secretly looked. She's your daughter, and daughters are always attached to their dads. Every night, she looks at that picture by her bedside and sighs. For the love of God, haven't you ever read Freud? What kind of shallow Marxism is this? What stonehearted materialism! What godless atheism! I'm sorry, but what you're doing here is no innocent environmental protest, and this isn't the work of marginal groups—it's a sheer disgrace!"

He started laughing, and I grabbed him by the front of his shirt.

"Why the hell are you grinning? I'm trying to tell you something serious here! Do you think that you're the only person who knows how to get up and talk? Are you the only person who gets to say important things? Does life just consist of your press statements? What the hell are you still laughing about? Do you think that Çağlar İyice is just a joke? I am the personification of reality! I'm a joke that's more real than reality! I'm a joke that's got you collared. I'm the joke that will bring about your ruin. At night, I gather up all the words I want to say to you and all by myself argue with you until dawn. But you're going to hear them here in this pit. I came here so that you wouldn't be humiliated in front of your friends, so that maybe you would see what a sensitive person I am."

He took a pack of Camels out of his shirt pocket and lit one.

"Let me have one of those."

"You started smoking?"

"Yes."

I put the cigarette in my mouth, and when he lit it, we looked at each other in the glow of the lighter. I took a long drag on the cigarette, pulling the smoke deep into my lungs, and exhaled like a sigh, blowing the smoke up into the sky.

"Why didn't you RT any of my tweets?" I said.

"Which tweets?"

"I've posted a bunch of tweets about my sister. Everyone RT'd them, but not you. Why?"

"I didn't see them."

"Why haven't you added me on Facebook?"

"Because I haven't used it for years."

"But you still have an account. Do you remember the day that you forgot about me? You were in the yard of the old Ministry of Agriculture building drinking beer with your friends. You drove off without me."

"That's true. But I came right back for you, didn't I?"

I laughed.

"Didn't I come back five minutes later?"

"No, it was half an hour. And you laughed about it, as if forgetting about me were the funniest thing in the world. You had another beer when you came back. The old head of agriculture was there with his wife. Do you remember that?"

"Yes."

"Why didn't you take me to Istanbul?"

"I'm always telling you to come."

"Not now. When you and Mom got divorced."

"You were young. Your mom didn't want you to go with me."

"Did you ask me if I wanted to go?"

"How could I? Your mom had custody."

"Goddamn it!" I snapped. "The only person who has custody of Çağlar İyice is Çağlar İyice! That's how it is now, and that's how it's always been. Court decisions mean nothing to me."

He looked at his cigarette.

"It's your fault that I slid to the right during the most rebellious period of my life. I became a Bee when the Bees didn't even exist. I took up an approach to politics that focused on votes. I didn't even oppose the new constitution because of you. If I had lived in Istanbul, would I have been like this? No, I would've become a completely different person. I would've been a protester like everyone else. I wouldn't have come to the park with this municipal mentality."

"I've told you again and again to come live in Istanbul."

"I don't want to. You should have said that seven years ago. Who else was at the table?"

"Which table?"

"The day that you forgot about me, the table at the old agriculture building. You said that you remembered that day. Who else was at the table?"

He looked away.

"Okay, then I'll tell you. Nermin Hanım, the librarian who I later discovered is a big fan of Marquez, was there. Şenol Hoca, who would later be my Turkish teacher, was there as well, as was his daughter, Asuman Karapınar, who would get into the law department at Marmara

University and become a lawyer. Necati Ağbi was there. At the time, he was studying at the military high school, and later he would die as Lieutenant Necati Karapınar. Çisem Trinity, the daughter of the director of the agriculture office, was there. We were the same age, and much later she would become my girlfriend. How the hell could you forget about your own kid? What kind of person are you? What was so funny about that? Why did you laugh like that in front of everyone, as if forgetting about me were so damn funny? Do you remember what you said? Do you?"

I scrutinized his face to see if he would remember. He couldn't. He wouldn't.

"What did I say?"

Despair washed over me, and the argument we were having started to seem quite pointless. "Forget about it," I said. "What you said doesn't matter anymore. You look at those days through a telescope, but I've been looking at them through a microscope. I'll never forget the things you can't remember. So what's the point of talking about all this, what good will it do? It won't do anything but make the pain worse. That's it, nothing more."

He reached out to touch my arm, but I brushed his hand aside and walked away, leaving him standing there. When I reached the top, I looked down into the pit. Spreading my arms, I shouted, "Fuck the school where you studied architecture! You ruined our lives!"

I went back to the park and walked toward the market. When I got there, they wouldn't let me in. Some guy I didn't recognize was behind the barrier. "Don't ever come back here again," he said.

"Don't be ridiculous," I said. "I've got pastries in the oven."

"Wait there," he said.

A few minutes later, he emerged with Orsa.

"Were you part of the fight that broke out?" she asked.

"No."

"Tell me the truth."

"I was just walking by."

A guy wearing coveralls said, "That's the guy. He wasn't part of the fight, he's the one who started it. He went over and started banging on the table. That's when the fight broke out."

"Okay, that part's true. But I was told that they'd kidnapped my sister."

"Çağlar, how could you do that?"

"Orsa, I'm sorry. I'm really very sorry. Let me apologize, to all of you. Later, I'll go to their tent and apologize to them, too. Can I come in now?"

"No."

"But I have to be here."

"No, Çağlar. Last night, you were talking with those kids, saying 'We'll beat them up' and garbage like that. What did I tell you guys? Didn't I tell you to calm down and not to do anything like that? Didn't I explain it all to you at length and tell you that talking that way is hate speech?"

"It's not just that," a woman in the market said. "He's sexist, too!"

I cupped my hands around my mouth and shouted, "What? For the love of God, what about me is sexist? I've never had an ounce of sexism in me. Orsa, you tell her. We were quite close. Did I ever say anything that was sexist?"

"It's not like that. Since yesterday, you've been using sexist swear-words and making homophobic comments."

"Look, I'll never swear again. If you want, I won't even talk. But I need to be here."

"I'm sorry, Çağlar. We can't let you in. It would go against our principles."

I started punching the barriers. Five or six guys wearing coveralls came running up, and they held my arms and legs and covered my mouth, and then they dragged me to the side exit of the park and down the stairs. One of them threw my backpack at my chest and said, "We don't ever want to see you in this park again." I tried to get back in, but one of the guys menacingly shook a broom at me. I waited there for a while. Some people who saw the altercation walked up and said, "What's going on here? What did this guy do? Why are you kicking him out of the park?"

One by one, they listed off the crimes I'd been accused of a few minutes before. The small crowd that had gathered started looking at me as if I should die of shame on the spot. When I saw those glances I wilted inside. It was as embarrassing as going to someone's house as a guest and realizing as you're sitting on the living room couch that there's a big hole in your sock and your big toe is poking out. That shame made me want to explode. I wanted pieces of me to scatter to the four winds. I shuffled off like a dog with a can tied to its tail. I went into a shop off İstiklal Street and bought four cans of beer, a packet of roasted chickpeas, a packet of Haribo gummy bears, some bandages, and a pack of moist towelettes. First, I cleaned my face and put a Band-Aid on the cut on my eyebrow.

I went back to the square and then went up onto the roof of the Banner Culture Center. For a long time, I'd been thinking of going up there to take in the view. I sat down at the farthest end and started watching Taksim Square. That roof really is a great place; if you ever have the time, you should go up there and check it out. The guys at the door said, "It could cave in so don't hang around up there too long," but it seemed to me that everything in my life had caved in so what did I have to lose? I opened a beer and said, "Çağlar, old boy, is there a single family member, NGO, political party, or splinter group that you *haven't* fought with? You're on bad terms with everyone and everything." A cat walked past me, probably the resident cat of the roof, and I said, "Here kitty kitty," but it just glared at me and walked on. That's what you call high-level loneliness. "That's all right," I said. "It's okay. If I'm alone and all the governments in the world and all the people who voted for them are against me, and if all the people in the world rising up against their governments are against me, too, along with their support-ers, if the nearly seven billion people in the world are opposed to my existence along with all the elephants in the forests in India, it would be enough for me if my sister said that I'm in the right. If Çiğdem İyice, who is only nine years old and goes to Evliya Çelebi Primary School, class 3-A, the world's best moonwalker, were by the side of Çağlar İyice, that would console me, that would be enough for me. My pain would subside. But where is she now? Where is she, my sweet baby girl, where is she, the light of my life, where is she, my sweetheart who looks up at the stars with me as we chat?" I couldn't bear it any longer and I got up, spreading my arms wide, and shouted toward the square: "My love, where are you? Where are you, my love?"

"I'm right here, my love!"

I looked down, trying to figure out who had replied. Was it my sister? Had she been found? Had she been following me around as a kind of joke?

"My love, where are you?" I shouted again.

"I'm right here, my love!"

I saw a group of eight or ten people down below, men and women. They were looking up at me and clapping.

"Excuse me," I said. "Are you really applauding me?"

"Yes."

"Why? Which organization do you belong to?"

It turned out that they were from the Man to Man, Woman to Woman, and All Other Forms of Kissing Rights Group. They blew me a kiss, and I kissed my hand and sent them one back.

"My love, come down. Let's sit in the park. What are you doing up there?"

"They kicked me out of the park."

"Why?"

"Sexism, homophobia and, above all, hate speech. Of course, at the root of it all is a screwed-up childhood, and a severe lack of love. You know how it goes."

TWENTY-FIVE

I left the bathroom and walked through the gentle glow of the hotel's lobby. I collapsed on one of the long velvet sofas and started watching the line in front of the women's bathroom. It hadn't occurred to me that I might be able to find my sister there. With every passing moment, more and more women were standing in the line that snaked through the lobby. Five people wearing yellow hard hats rushed past me and went out the side door of the hotel. When they left, an air of tension filled the lobby and people clustered into groups and started murmuring. Some of the women waiting in line started walking toward the lobby doors, and I heard someone ask on the phone, "Are the riot police coming?" I looked out one of the lobby's oval windows, but I didn't see any police so I approached a group of people up near reception and leaned against the desk, crossing my arms. As I eavesdropped on their conversation, I kept an eye on the door of the women's bathroom. Eventually, they realized I was listening and they stopped talking and turned to look at me. Ignoring them, I took the packet of gummy bears out of my pocket and started eating them, one by one, until I finished off the packet.

One of their friends came running up and asked in a panic, "What's going on?"

"Riot trucks are coming."

"People said the same thing last night, but nothing happened."

"No. I just talked to one of my friends. Twenty-one trucks are heading this way from Beşiktaş."

My heart sank because Beşiktaş was just down the hill. I went and unplugged the chargers for my phone and electronic cigarette. Near the wall outlet, a foreign woman was lying on her stomach on the thick rug, propped up on her elbows, writing what appeared to be a news piece on her laptop. I decided to test out my English. "Tell your news agency, please, that twenty-one TOMAs coming to Taksim."

"What?"

As I was stepping out the door leading to the hotel garden, she said something to me, but I didn't understand a single word of it. I spread my arms and said, "I am doing you favor, honey. Certainly info."

I passed through the revolving doors and stopped under the glasswork on the ceiling, which ran the length of the entrance and consisted of cubes and curves. It made me think of dolphins undulating in the sea as they surfaced and dove, and warm yellow light shone through the glass, illuminating the garden. *Those guys really pulled out all the stops,* I thought. I leaned against one of the round columns and started puffing on my electronic cigarette. A group of people sitting at a cafe on the left of the garden had gotten to their feet and started arguing beneath the large cloth umbrella of their table, their hands and arms waving in the soft light. From where I was standing, I could hear people whispering, "TOMAs are coming, TOMAs are coming!" I was actually quite pleased to hear that the riot control trucks were on their way because it meant that my sister would come around. I approached a security guard wearing a black suit and said, "Ağbi, people are saying that some TOMAs are on the way. Have they gotten here yet? Have you heard anything?"

"I don't know," he said. "If they are coming, they've probably reached the street barricades by now."

The people in the garden had put on all the gear they had: full-face gas masks, dust masks, hard hats, bicycle helmets, swimming goggles, snow goggles—whatever they had. When I saw them fully decked out like that, I felt quite naked. As naked as if I were naked in the face of infinity. I unzipped the front pocket of my backpack and took out the mask that my sister had bought. I put it on and then took it off out of embarrassment; that technology had gone out of style long ago. I went out and walked to the stairs of the side entrance of the park and waited there for a little while. Guys wearing coveralls were walking around at the top of the stairs, and I wasn't sure if I should try to get into the park. I decided to call Meti.

"Meti," I said, "can you bring me a gas mask and hard hat?"

"What are you going to do?"

"I don't know. Everyone else around here is all fully equipped. You're at the market, aren't you? There were a bunch of gas masks and hard hats in the depot with the green tarp."

"No, I'm in Gümüşsuyu."

"What are you doing there?"

"I'm at the barricade."

"Really? Are there any TOMAs around?"

"No."

"Do you think they're going to come?"

"I don't know. We're waiting."

"Okay, maybe I should come down, too."

"Come."

"Which barricade are you at?"

"The one at the bottom of the hill. The first one."

Just then, a group of people passed behind me, shouting, "What are you guys waiting for? Come on! To the barricades! To the barricades!" I followed behind them. We crossed the square and started walking down the winding road that led to the sea, our long shadows intertwining on the asphalt. We passed eleven barricades and arrived at the twelfth, which had a view of the sea. I saw Meti sitting on a large paving stone on top of the barricade, looking down as if he were lost in thought.

I stepped up onto the paving stones that served as the foundation of the barricade, jumped up onto a dumpster that was lying on its side, and from there clambered up onto the side of a fiberglass booth and picked my way along the ISTANPARK signs at the top of the barricade. I sat down beside Meti and asked, "How's it going?" But he didn't answer. He was holding a paving stone, on top of which a smiley face had been drawn.

"Why aren't you at the park?"

"We had an argument. I left."

"Why?"

"It seems that I'm a classic leftist."

"Classic?"

"Orthodox Marxist."

"Are you Armenian?"

"No, nothing like that. In the sectarian sense."

"Sectarian?"

"Extremist."

There was no end to it all.

"Meti," I said, "for the love of God, you're none of those things."

He put the stone down by his feet. "I made a mistake," he said. "I never should have come here. It's a different world. They won't let us in."

I looked at the old İnönü Stadium and thought for a little while. I do that a lot. I look at the old İnönü Stadium and think, *What's the point? What's the purpose of it all? What's our destination? How far is it, and how will we get there? Why are we so confused?*

"Meti, what makes you think that they won't let you in? They let everyone in. Hell, they even let me in. There are certain things that set them off, but if you don't do those things, then there's no problem."

"They want to exclude us."

"Why?"

"I don't know. These days, excluding us is all the rage."

"Meti, I want to ask you something, but please don't misunderstand me, okay? Which group do you belong to?"

"The Armed Group That Occasionally Carries Out Attacks."

I was shocked. I looked around at the other people around us and quietly said, "Wow, you're one of them? I thought they were all older guys. Do you have a gun with you?"

Apparently, he didn't; he was a member of the legal branch.

"Çağlar, the real shame is what happened to you. Especially after you carried all those boxes of water."

"What does it matter how many boxes of water I carried? I'm the grandson of Ragıp Baysal."

"Who's that?"

"The old mayor of Kıyıdere. Have you heard of the Gökçe Dam? In those years, we had a capacity of thirty-seven cubic kilometers. For years, we piped that water to Istanbul. We didn't drink it ourselves; we just piped it out so there wouldn't be a water crisis here in the summer. In the last days of his life, my grandpa started thinking that his doctor was the head of the Istanbul Waterworks."

He put his hand on my back and smiled. "Forget about it." That was the first time I ever saw him smile.

I said, "That's how it goes, man."

He leaned forward and shook the iron bars at the front of the barricade to make sure they were secure. "My first impression of you," he said, "was that you thought highly of yourself. But you're not like that. You're really not like that at all."

Meti was a good judge of character. I thought nothing of myself. I mean, to the extent that it's possible for someone to not like themselves without going overboard. I looked down the street. It was completely desolate, nothing was stirring. It was like a movie put on pause. The galvanized street signs at the top of the barricade glowed in the light cast by barrels burning on the sidewalk. I put my hand on Meti's shoulder. My heart sank; I wished that I'd met Meti before. Sometimes friendships that develop so quickly merely remind us of just how lonely we really are.

At that moment, the lights down the street went out. The buses full of riot police that were parked in front of the mosque on the seaside were enveloped in darkness. We couldn't see anything. "They're getting ready to attack," someone behind the barricade said. "They're going to come in the dark." Yet again, I felt that fear rising up from my stomach. "Calm down," I said to myself. "If the police come and your knees shake and you start crying, you'll be a disgrace. You came here to find your sister. Don't ever forget that." I looked at the guy behind the barricade. He was probably around thirty-five years old, and although he looked like he was experienced in this kind of thing, he had started pacing back and forth, saying, "What are we going to do? Just what are we going to do?" The others said to him, "Ağbi, keep your cool," but he went on pacing and muttering, setting everyone on edge. His swimming goggles were on his forehead, and I noticed that his disheveled hair was receding. My guess was that he was a child of the coup years, born in 1975 or thereabouts. Every morning, he would get up and look out the window at the street corner and say, "What the hell, are those soldiers?" If you wanted to calm him down, you had to shout, "At ease!" He was at the barricade to share his wisdom and experience with the younger generation. But he had no experience except for the jitters, and he was making the younger generation nervous.

"Really, what the hell are we going to do?" I asked Meti nervously.

Meti didn't reply. He turned to the guy pacing back and forth behind us and snapped, "Ağbi, shut up!" He was crushed, completely crushed, without even knowing why. He regretted that he'd come out of his shell. They didn't understand. They couldn't understand. But understand what? How should I know! He had nothing to do with me!

An hour passed and nothing happened. I was feeling a little bit calmer. The crowd of people behind the barricade started trailing away, and I decided to check the other barricades up the hill to see if my sister was there. Meti came with me. We looked at the groups standing guard behind the other eleven barricades, but I didn't see my sister or Microbe.

Meti took a can of spray paint out of his vest pocket and shook it. "There's a little bit left," he said. "Here, write something."

"What should I write?" I asked, holding the can out to him. "I don't know anything about trendy slogans."

But he wouldn't take the can back. "Write something that is rich in wordplay and strong in content."

After putting a little more thought into it, I painted on the asphalt: "We're going to call you to account for all the hearts that have been broken." Then I sat down next to my masterpiece, and Meti took my picture. I posted it on Twitter and got eighteen favorites. We went back to the barricade at the bottom of the hill. The guys from the legal branch of the organization had painted goal markers on the street and were playing soccer. To the left of the barricade, there was a curving flight of stairs, and we sat down there, leaning against the wall. We sat there for half an hour, but nothing happened. Then we heard the sound of the riot trucks. Everyone leaped up, and we shouted toward the barricades up the hill, "The TOMAs are coming! The TOMAs are coming!" A group of about ten guys ran out in front of the riot trucks and held out their arms. I held Meti by the arm, but he told me to let go and ran out to join them. I looked at the group of people in the street, but I didn't see my sister. The riot trucks were racing up the road. I climbed up to the top of the stairs. The first TOMA had tracks, and it started smashing down the street signs on top of the barricade, leveling everything in its path. The tracks creaked and groaned, sounding like a hoarse cry in the night, and the green and red lights of the riot truck flashed.

Then I woke up. The sound of the tracks in my dream was actually the screeching of seagulls circling overhead. *Of course,* I thought,

TOMAs don't have tracks. From where I was sitting, I shook my fist and shouted at the seagulls, "Damn you! What the hell are you doing here? Leave me the hell alone! There's no end to the suffering you've brought me." But they went on screeching. "Fine, go on and squawk." I wasn't mad at them anymore; I was angry with Swiss scientists! What kind of shit were they up to in Switzerland anyways? They should be busy making seagulls that don't squawk. They should be making seagulls that respect people's feelings, seagulls that are perfectly compatible with human beings. Meti woke up when I shouted. He had fallen asleep with his legs resting on my knees, and he leaped to his feet.

"What's going on?"

"Nothing," I said. "A personal matter."

Then we heard the first hoots and whistles. Some people were running up the road, and one guy ran up to the top of the first barricade and flashed a victory sign. Others started running down the hill from the other barricades, picking up stones along the way. I saw the first riot truck approaching. It was a magnificent machine, sparkling, plain, and perfect. When it wasn't on the attack, it was as calm as a mountain lake. I started clapping.

Someone behind me shouted, "What the hell are you clapping for?"

I didn't reply. The thing is, I was seeing a real TOMA for the first time in my life. But of course, I couldn't say that. I was so excited that a chill ran down my spine. He had no idea what I was feeling. Along with everyone else, I started booing that beautiful TOMA as it got closer. It stopped when it was about thirty or forty yards away and just sat there. Over the speakers of the TOMA, an announcement was made:

"Listen up! Please move away from the barricades. We have no intention of going into the park. I repeat: we will not go into the park. All we want to do is secure the culture center and the square. We're here for your safety. Please do not throw stones, and please move away from the barricades. We're not going to enter the park."

Three more riot trucks showed up. Behind them were backhoes and dump trucks, and behind those were around four or five million riot police. A small group of guys in their thirties ran to the front of the barricade and turned to face us. "Don't throw rocks! Don't throw rocks!" they said. "We're going back to the park. Passive resistance, no violence."

That was perfectly fine with me. I had been putting up active resistance every single day of my life, so on Tuesday, June 11, 2013, I decided to resist passively, and I started following the others back up the hill. I stopped and looked around for Meti. He had grabbed one of the guys in front of the barricade by the shirt and seemed to be having a nervous breakdown. I ran up to him and pulled him away. "Meti, come on," I said. "Calm the hell down." His hands were shaking. His entire body was shaking. A backhoe started tearing down the barricade, going forward and backward, and then a TOMA moved past the first barricade, its wheels crunching over the street signs on the ground. Meti started bawling.

"Why the hell are you crying? They said that they're not going to go into the park."

"Yes, they are. They're going to kick everyone out."

"Please, don't be so childish," I said. "Grow up a little. Would the police lie? Let's say they are lying. Were those guys lying, too? They're not going to go into the park."

"If they don't go in today, they'll go in tomorrow. If these barricades fall, the park falls."

I took him firmly by the shoulders and said, "Stop being ridiculous. There are all those people in Taksim. The whole world is watching what's happening here. They wouldn't dare do something like that. Trust me, for years I've been actively involved in politics, and I know how to keep my finger on the pulse of the people and politicians." I took him by the arm and started leading him up the hill. "What's more," I said, "we have new constitutional rights. I have the cell number of the

Kıyıdere chief of police. As a last resort, there's Oaf Tufan Ağbi. So try to smile a little."

We stood waiting in front of the towering light pole in the square. The sun had risen, but it was concealed by clouds. We saw the headlights of a TOMA as it cleared the last barricade, and it was followed by the others. They stopped in front of the culture center. People started shouting, "Down with fascism, we stand united!" I didn't want to draw attention to myself by not being part of the social harmony so I started shouting as well, but not too loudly.

Another announcement began: "Please evacuate the square. We have no intention of going into the park. We're here to restore security and order. I repeat: we are not going to raid the park. We're here for your security. Please do not throw stones. We're here for your own security. Please evacuate the square. We're not going to enter the park."

"If you're not going to go into the park, wait there!" someone shouted. But they didn't wait. Those four or five million riot police started moving into the square, tearing down posters, knocking over stands, and kicking over stools and stacks of books. One cop knocked down a tent in front of us and stomped its frame to pieces, and then he tried to pick it up but wasn't able to so he started stomping on it again. Clearly, he had a grudge against that particular tent.

A riot cop charged toward us shouting, "Get the hell out of here!"

"Should I get out of here, too?" I asked.

He lunged toward me, holding his nightstick like a baseball bat, and growled, "Get the fuck out of here!" so I hightailed it toward the monument. Meti and three of his friends were holding up a street sign as a shield and crouching behind it. I joined them. The police were getting closer and closer.

"Meti, what the hell are we going to do?"

"Calm down. Just wait."

"How do you expect me to calm down? I'm so scared I'm about to shit my pants right now."

People had started forming a human chain around the park, and they were shouting, "Everyone into the park! Everyone into the park!"

"Meti, let's go to the park."

"You go."

"Come on, let's go! Come with me. Come on!"

One of the other guys behind the sign said, "Would you shut the hell up! Enough already. If you're going to go, then go! It's bad enough already, and then you came along."

I ran toward the park. People were still shouting "Into the park!" and I asked one of them, "Can I come into the park, too?"

"Sure, come on!"

"But you kicked me out of the park."

"Just get into the damn park, you little twit!"

Ducking under their arms, I walked up the stairs of the park. The police had started shooting tear gas at the people who were still in the square. I climbed up onto the balustrade at the front of the park and looked at Meti and his friends as they crouched behind their shield. The police were shooting tear gas canisters at their shield and sparks were flying everywhere, and eventually the shield started to buckle. A few protesters near them fired off a few shots with slingshots, but they all missed. The riot police started heading toward the monument, and I saw two cops emerge from the smoke as they dragged Meti away.

"Goddamn you," I yelled. "What the hell are you doing? Do you think this is England?"

I had met a lawyer at the market, and he had given me his card so I called him. "Good morning, ağbi," I said. "This is Çağlar."

"Which Çağlar?"

"You know, ezogelin soup, Bosnian pastries, club sandwiches."

"Ah, Çağlar, how are you?"

"Not so hot, not so hot at all. The cops just hauled off one of my friends."

"Who?"

"Meti from the Armed Group That Occasionally Carries Out Attacks."

"You shouldn't say things like that on the phone."

"Goddamn, how should I talk then? I only had one friend left in the world, and the police just hauled him off. Do you think you can arrange things so that he can be set free in the most perfect way possible? It would also be okay if he were released on bail."

"Don't worry, Çağlar. We're following up on everyone who's been arrested."

After the police chased the people in the square down İstiklal Street, they came back and started firing tear gas at the human chain around the park. The chain scattered in thirty-six places, but then they regrouped in the middle and fled into the park. When the police started proceeding up the park stairs, people built a barricade and started throwing rocks. The police held up their shields one over the other, and the rocks rained down upon them, making a sound like the pitter-patter of hail. I picked up a medium-sized stone and looked around for a sensitive riot cop who might want to throw it, one who was fed up with his job because his captain was always on his ass, someone who had the self-confidence to not take social conflicts personally, a cop who would be able to understand the spirit of the commune in all its depths, someone I could talk to. But I couldn't find one so I dropped the stone. In any case, throwing stones, which was all the rage in those times, wasn't my thing. I'm the kind of guy who fights fist to fist. Anyway, after the police gassed the entire park, they withdrew.

I went to the tribune on the left side of the park to watch the clashes that were happening on the boulevard, but it was so crowded that I couldn't find a place to sit so I climbed on top of a shipping container and sat on the edge, letting my feet hang down. Then I put on my Guy Fawkes mask and crossed my arms. The battle was going on in the middle of the boulevard. The side streets across the way changed hands a few times. The tear gas team had some good shooters, but they were having trouble hitting the hardliners because it was a construction zone and there were shields aplenty. When a hardliner threw a tear gas canister back at the cops, he could easily find somewhere to hide, such as in a pit or behind a backhoe, barrier, or sign. Also, because of the construction, the riot trucks weren't able to get very close. The cops brought out a paintball team, and they shot at least twenty protesters. I checked Twitter, and according to information provided by a medical team, three protesters had suffered head trauma, two had their noses broken, and one lost an eye. The resistance was taking some heavy blows. In a timely move, three slingshot squads launched volleys at the cops from the park, a side street, and the main road. The cops responded with tear gas and backed away, not wanting to give up their wounded. The protesters pulled a piece of construction equipment that was next to the park into the boulevard and set it on fire. In the meantime, Hazard Assistance showed up in a pickup truck, and they lit that on fire, too. The black smoke pouring from the burning construction equipment and the white smoke of the tear gas, combined with the smoke from smaller fires burning here and there, were making it impossible to see. The cops withdrew to the square, and a time-out was called.

I was getting hungry so I decided to find something to snack on. Food and drink carts had been set up in front of all the large tents, and I managed to find a tuna sandwich and a bottle of Niğde Gazoz. In the tumult of the morning, the brick public library had been razed, and I enlisted as a volunteer to help put the twelve shelves back in order. A know-it-all walked up to me and scowled. "That's not what I told you to do. You've mixed up all the books."

"On the contrary," I said. "It's quite simple actually. I divided the library into two. The great writers are on one side and the rest are on the other."

"Who are you to say who the great writers are? Who do you think you are?"

There was no getting around our disagreement so I went back to my place on the shipping container, but there weren't any more clashes before evening fell. I guess that the two sides were resting so they could gather their strength. Groups of about ten people or so started walking around making announcements with megaphones: "Everyone is going to meet in the square, and a press statement is going to be made at seven." I decided to see what was going on, but I hung back around the stairs just in case anything went wrong. When the press statement was just about to get started, I noticed that there was a group of people playing drums in front of the riot trucks, and there were some people dancing. Thinking that my sister might be there, I headed over to take a look. The police started making an announcement when I was about halfway there. I can't remember now what they said, but before the announcement was even over, tear gas canisters started flying. Everyone turned around and started running to the park, and I couldn't make my way through the stampeding crowd. When they finally all passed by, I found myself in a cloud of tear gas. It is my hope that God will thoroughly damn whoever it was who first started the trend of arming the police with tear gas! That's why people are dying, you bastard of a bastard, whoever you are, you insensitive piece of shit! I was choking, my vision was fading, I couldn't see a damn thing around me, and it felt like there wasn't an ounce of oxygen left in the air. That gas smelled worse than the moss on boulders, worse than the shit pools at the purification plant, and worse than our dreams that have been fucked over and tossed aside to rot, and the more you breathed it in, the more it burned. I heard a woman cry out, "Help, help!" Then she shouted again, "Someone help me!" At first, I couldn't see where she was, but I stumbled in the direction of her voice. I found her lying on the ground, unable to get up. I started pulling her toward the park, but when I reached the stairs, I collapsed. Some people came over and held us under our arms and helped us up the stairs. They washed our faces with a mixture of Talcid and water, squirting it with a plastic bottle with a hole in the cap.

"Trumpet," I shouted between coughs. "Trumpet!"

"What are you talking about? What trumpet?"

"There were some drummers and a trumpet player. Where are they?"

I found them sprawled out next to the stage. One by one, I showed them a picture of my sister, but none of them had seen her.

The police were in control of the square, and they were heading down İstiklal Street and up the boulevard. It was clear that the second half was going to be even rougher than the first. I headed back to my place on top of the container, but someone was already sitting there so I moved two containers down and found a place to sit.

For a long time, the police didn't let people gather on the boulevard. If anyone so much as poked their heads out of the park or from a side street, the cops started firing plastic bullets and tear gas. I saw one cop take a look at me, and I backed away from the edge of the container. An hour later, people started gathering behind small barricades and took control of the boulevard up to a certain point. Foot by foot, they started making their way toward the square.

That's when a supercop came onto the field of play. Tear gas launcher on his shoulder, he took a few confident steps forward and fired off two rounds. The sparks that flew from the muzzle of his launcher illuminated the dark boulevard. Taking a step back, he flicked open his launcher and dumped out the empty shells as he watched the capsules sail through the air. Then he pulled fresh cartridges from his vest and reloaded. The protesters managed to throw one of them back. He ran up to it and, stepping forward with his left foot, swung his right foot in an arc, catching the canister with his toe, sending it flying back to where he'd first shot it. Then he shot another round, hitting the leg of the guy who'd thrown the canister back, and then another, hitting the arm of the guy who was carrying the guy who'd just been hit in the leg. From all sides, the protesters went after his eyes with green lasers, but to no avail, and he went on firing off round after round. I thought of taking down his helmet number so that later I could track him down and hire him as a bodyguard when my sister got famous. The number on his helmet was 10. Obviously, he'd removed the other numbers. But that was his right because he was player number 10 on his team, the lead attacker, and he did complete justice to that uniform of his. He deserved every last cent of his salary, paid with the taxes of innocent citizens. No one could mess with him. Although the captain of the riot police, who had a walkie-talkie on his shoulder placed over his stars of rank, shouted and shook his finger in the faces of the other cops, he would fall silent in the presence of number 10; he had talent, big talent, and you can't raise your voice with people like him; you can't give them orders. The world press broadcast his policing live, all the way to Alabama. In half an hour, he fired off 38 rounds and scored 4 head traumas, 2 lost eyes, 8 blunt trauma wounds, and 186 minor injuries brought on by breathing difficulties. The medical tents were at full capacity thanks to that cop. Stocks of Talcid and Batticon were depleted, all the oxygen tanks were empty, there were no painkillers or bandages to be found, and the volunteer doctors were having nervous breakdowns as they saw all the wounded being brought in. But this cop didn't care. He was merciless; single-handedly, he was keeping the government on its feet in Taksim with his tear gas launcher as he moved through the darkness. He raised his hand and, without turning around, motioned for the others to move forward. With their shields raised, they fired off more rounds of tear gas, taking control of the boulevard all the way to Harbiye. On June 11, 2013, they maintained their rule over the street until 11:40 p.m.

Then two green-gloved brothers appeared out of the smoke rising from canisters hissing on the street. They picked up two canisters and ran forward, and after twenty steps, they stopped at the same moment, raising their left arms into the air as they coiled their bodies for the throw, and then they hurled the canisters back in the direction of the riot police. The canisters traced an arc through the air, leaving contrails of smoke, and landed right in the midst of the cops with their shields. They threw a second round of canisters the same way. This was a new sport: synchronized gas-canister throwing. They threw whatever they could get their hands on. According to my calculations, they threw twenty canisters back at the cops. "My God," I said to myself, "these guys are the best on the team, the stuff of nightmares for security forces, even if they were late to the game. If there were two more brothers like them, tear gas would be outlawed."

Number 10 was quick to spot them, though, and with surefooted steps he moved toward them, pointing at the brothers, and he fired off a round. The canister whizzed past the head of one of the brothers, and then they faked right and whipped around to the left, taking cover behind an excavator's tire. When the smoke dissipated, a team of ten stone throwers emerged, but the supercop wasn't interested in them. He fired a low shot that skipped over the ground, coming to a stop in the middle of the group of stone throwers, and they scattered. They didn't mean anything to him; he was after the green-gloved brothers. He fired a round at the wheel of the excavator, and it bounced off to the other side of the street. The police and the brothers yelled some things to each other, but I couldn't hear what they were saying because of all the noise. I think that they knew each other, which shouldn't come as a surprise since all great talents know one another. When they got closer, I heard the cop shout, "Come out where I can see you!"

"Come on over, we're waiting for you," they replied.

A slingshot squad emerged next in an attempt to drive back the cops, who then called in the paintball team. With sure steps, they inched closer to the excavator. The larger of the two brothers took a bottle of water out of his backpack and took a drink, and then offered the bottle to his smaller partner. Calmly, they stood there waiting. "Goddamn," I said to myself, "what the hell are they doing? Great talents always have eccentric sides. But aren't they taking this a little far? Or do they think they'll be heroes by being shot in the head with a canister from ten yards away? Aren't they putting this new wave of resistance into jeopardy?" The smaller of the two unzipped his backpack, and then they stepped out from behind the tire, each of them holding a small rectangular box.

When number 10 saw those boxes, he took off running toward the row of cops with shields, the back of his feet slapping his ass as he ran. I had no idea what was going on. Then fireworks began exploding left and right. The show had just begun! Two exploded in the middle of the wall of shields, and one of the shields flew into the air, and then there was another explosion in the same place and three more shields went flying. The cops started running toward the riot trucks parked in the square. The brothers advanced up the middle of the boulevard, dancing with those boxes in their hands, and the fireworks exploded one after the other. The resistance had been transformed into a visual feast. There was a burst of applause from the rear, and hundreds of people rushed forward when they saw the police running away, throwing whatever they could get their hands on and gathering up materials so they could barricade the road. The police stayed in the square for quite a while.

There were nine wounded cops, two riot trucks that needed servicing, twenty broken shields, one lost gun, six lost nightsticks, four lost helmets, two lost gas masks, a suspension at the police department, a dip in the Istanbul Stock Exchange, two ministers who would get their asses chewed out along with one governor, one provincial police commissioner, two assistant provincial police commissioners, one chief of security, one chief of the riot police, and countless chiefs of cabinet. On top of all that, there was a phone bill for 2,800 lira and one captain of the riot police who was about to start crying as he hid behind a riot truck. His phone was ringing, but he didn't want to answer it. The assistant chief of the riot police was calling, which meant that it was his turn to get his ass chewed out. But the green-gloved brothers didn't care; they went on shooting off fireworks. They weren't joking around, and the resistance was back on its feet. It didn't take more than two boxes of roman candles, which they'd bought for 150 lira; if we include the cost of the fireproof gloves they bought, the total cost comes to 170 lira—that's how much it cost them to make the national economy stagger. They had shaken the government with those green gloves that appeared and disappeared in the clouds of tear gas. The people sitting at the edge of the park watching the green-gloved brothers were applauding them madly, and I was, too. We were living in a country that promised hope, and we had athletes, young and old alike.

The captain of the riot police hung up his phone, and then he went ballistic when he saw the people sitting on the stairs applauding. He pointed toward the park and the tear gas started flying. I saw them coming, but I just sat there like a deer caught in headlights. I was planning on hopping down on the side of the park, but there were crowds of people running past, and if I fell, I worried that I might hurt someone so I made a strategic decision and got down on the side facing the front of the park and joined the others who were running away. At one point, I tripped and tumbled into a pit, but I managed to grab onto a water pipe at the edge to keep myself from rolling in deeper. In the process, however, I'd gotten muddy from head to toe. I clambered out and saw that the park was full of tear gas. The area in front of the park was clear, however, so I headed there and sat on a stone to catch my breath.

A minute or two later, a blond girl approached me. She was the most beautiful girl I'd seen in the last two days. I don't have the time right now to describe her face or body, but suffice it to say that she was wearing a white apron.

"Are you hurt?" she asked.

"No."

She placed her thumb on my chin and put her other hand on my head and asked, "What happened to your forehead?"

I raised my fingers to my forehead and found that it was bleeding.

"Don't touch it," she said. "What happened?"

"I tripped when I was running away. I don't know."

A few more people wearing white aprons showed up and started shouting, "We've got a wounded one here!"

They had me lie down and put a blanket over me. One of the more senior looking of them held up four fingers and asked me how many fingers I saw.

"What does that have to do with anything?" I asked.

They started shouting, "He's losing consciousness! Hurry up, he's losing consciousness!"

They put me on a wheeled stretcher, and as I was being pushed along, someone stood at the front of the stretcher with a megaphone that was set to siren mode and had flashing lights as well. People moved aside as we made our way through the crowd. We went back into the park on the side facing the hotel, and I saw that there was a human chain on each side of the path leading to the medical tent. I heard people shouting, "What happened, what happened?" "He was hit in the head with a tear gas canister. Emergency, clear the way!" People clapped as my stretcher was pushed along.

I flashed a victory sign, which elicited even more applause, and shouted, "Taksim belongs to the people!"

I was transferred to another stretcher in the medical tent. A white-haired doctor, who I assumed was the head doctor, approached me. He started examining the wound on my forehead. "How did this happen?" he asked.

I gestured for him to lean in closer. "I fell down when the police started chasing us," I whispered. "Let's keep this between you and me."

After cleaning the wound and examining it a little more, he pressed the back of his hand against my cheek. Then he took my temperature with an ear thermometer. "Are you sick?" he asked.

"No."

"Your temperature is a hundred and two."

"Normally it's ninety-eight, but of course it might be a little high now because of all the excitement."

They moved me into the area for people with minor injuries, and some medical students got to work on me. First, they bandaged my wound and then hooked me up to an IV, per the doctor's instructions. I started waiting. The police had started throwing sound grenades and were advancing up the street. The closer they got, the more the medical tent began to resemble a scene from the Day of Judgment.

A woman sat down next to me, holding a black file on her lap. She took down all the information she needed for the official records. According to the Turkish Medical Association data, during the protests that took place in the summer of 2013, a total of 8,163 civilians were wounded, one of whom was Çağlar İyice, seventeen years of age, a specialist in public relations, injured near the barricade in Harbiye as he was looking for his sister. He's an honest tax-paying citizen with no connections to any organizations whatsoever, a completely innocent civilian. His e-mail address is geceninsabirlisesi@gmail.com.

After the woman left, I saw him, my tormenter, and I turned my back to him. I said to the head doctor, who was stitching up someone's wound on the stretcher beside me, "Hoca, could you please have that man removed? He's not wounded, and he's taking up space in the medical tent."

The head doctor looked up and smiled. "Sabahattin, how's it going? Is this your son?"

I said, "Goddamn it, I've got nothing to do with this guy. I'm here in the capacity of a protester."

I pushed my father in the shoulder. "You can't come in here! I'm the one who's wounded. The medical tent is for wounded people, for people in pain. You think you can just walk in here, too? Get out. You're a blot on our family! I curse the day that we let you in. My mother's side of the family brought down the government of Albania, but you can't even hold two barricades. You said that nothing would happen if we let them take down the barricades, but look what happened. The cops went into the park. The show is over, Mr. İyice! The show is over!"

As he was standing there beside my stretcher, he lifted up the IV bag a little. "We found your sister," he said.

"Really? Where?"

"In Ankara."

"Ankara? Why did they go to Ankara?"

"I don't know. Probably so no one would find them. But they're here now, waiting for you."

I hugged my father. And when I did, a feeling of warmth spread across my chest, and a lump rose in my throat; tears welled in my eyes, and I started coughing like crazy because a tear gas canister flew into the tent followed by another, and then fires broke out where they landed and people scattered in panic as pieces of burning tent started falling down. But there really was nothing to be afraid of. The tent was made of plastic, that's all.

TWENTY-SIX

My sister is proud, stubborn, and a dreamer. She's fearless, free from any and all restrictions, inclined toward extremities, and uncompromising. That's why I didn't find it strange when I found out that she had gone to Ankara with Microbe because she wanted to moonwalk in the garden of the parliament building in an attempt to shake up the government.

But now, just as when she'd been waiting to perform for those television morons, she kept fidgeting as she waited off to the side of the portable stage set up in the park, so I massaged her shoulders. A large group of people had gathered in the stone square in the center of the park, and finally the day of forums and discussions was over. They'd decided to stay in the park, and now it was time for music; it was time for some dance and spirit. That night, my sister was going to be the last performer, even after the We Call Everything Something Else Party. The group on stage had really nailed down their sound and were playing a great song, but because I was nervous I didn't really notice.

My sister grabbed my hand as I massaged her shoulders and turned toward me. "Çağlar," she said, "should I close my eyes or keep them open before I start dancing?"

"Do whatever you like, sweetie, whatever makes you feel better. This is your night."

"Thanks, Çağlar."

Finally, the pandemonium on the stage was over, and the guy working the mixing board turned to us and said, "You're up." Microbe had shimmied up the flagpole next to the stage, and he gave me the okay sign when he started recording with his iPhone. Before she went on stage, my sister and I did our special greeting, and then she turned around and did it with our dad, too. It's a Freudian weakness, you see.

She stepped onto the stage flashing a victory sign with either hand, waving them like windshield wipers. Hundreds of phones were raised in the air in a flood of light, and then thunderous applause broke out. The way that she took to the stage was so magnificent that it could make you forget about that German guy who'd played the piano in the square during the protests. Even with her first steps, she gave the impression that she was going to secure a permanent place for herself in the memories of the resistance.

"They Don't Care about Us" started to play over the speakers, and without a moment of hesitation, she raised the brim of her hat and smiled at the crowd. Then she held out her arms and spun around, and then, pointing her toes outward, she shimmied forward and backward. With one hand on the back of her neck and the other on her belt buckle, she thrust her hips out twice. Swinging her knees left and right, she moved toward the front of the stage as if she were biting imaginary monsters that rose up in front of her. She had come up with an improvisation that suited the spirit of the resistance. The audience went wild, clapping with mad abandon. The musicians started playing along with their cymbals, drums, and trumpets. My sister suddenly stopped at the front of the stage, spun around one more time, and then threw her hat into the crowd. I watched as my grandpa's hat spun through the air. When we wander aimlessly like idle souls tormented by worries and hesitation and we try to attach meanings to the meaningless trials we endure, everything seems to be conspiring against us and the days are tedious and filled with the blackest darkness. But you see, that is the moment when we suddenly find hope, and that moment can't ever be turned back. At first, the human mind has trouble accepting such things, and it wants to think that the extraordinary moments in life are just moments and nothing more. But those moments shatter time, and the nerve endings of time come into being; everything shifts in that direction, the past and the present, everything that has or hasn't been experienced, everything that will and won't be experienced, they all pass through those points.

Next came the moonwalk, but after her first moonwalk routine an uneasy silence fell over the crowd and whistles rose up in the night air. At first, I didn't understand what was happening. Just a minute before, people had been clapping madly. Had they gotten bored? Then the music was shut off, and I grabbed the guy operating the mixing board. "What the hell are you doing? What are you doing?" He looked at me blankly, and in the distance I heard the crackling sound of an announcement being made over a megaphone.

"The police are attacking the park," he said. He made a few adjustments on the mixing board and handed the microphone to a woman. Even though the music had been cut off, my sister kept right on going with her routine and was still doing the moonwalk. The woman walked to the stage and said, "Stay calm, everyone, stay calm! When they start shooting tear gas, we're going to pull back in an orderly way and then return to where we were. We're not going to leave the park! We're not going to leave the stage! We're never going to leave Gezi Park! Stay calm! This is only just the start! Fight, fight, fight!"

Everyone started shouting together: "This is only just the start! Fight, fight, fight!" I saw some people running down the road behind the park followed by two tear gas canisters flying through the air. My father and I ran up to the stage, and Microbe took a full-face gas mask and hard hat out of his backpack and put them on my sister. We started heading toward the entrance of the park that faces the hotel. I saw that a tree had caught on fire and some people were trying to put it out with a fire extinguisher.

At one point, I turned around and looked back. The police were tearing down the tents as they moved forward, kicking down everything in their path. Plastic bullets pelted the trunks of the trees around us, and hand-thrown tear gas canisters skidded over the cobblestone path, spinning and hissing with evil intent.

We went down the path to the front of the park, and I grabbed my father's arm, shouting, "The police weren't supposed to raid the park tonight! That's what you said. Did you talk to the people from the government about this? The police weren't supposed to raid the park tonight!"

My father told two of his friends to look after us. "Take your sister and go," he said.

"Where are you going?"

"To our office up the hill. Now go!"

"Come with us."

"I'll join you later."

Squeezing his arm, I said, "Come with us."

"Go, now," he said, pulling away and heading back into the park.

We walked for a little ways. I looked back and saw that there was a fine, barely discernable mist in the air on the side of the park near the hotel, like a sheer curtain. The police, wearing gas masks and with tear gas launchers resting on their shoulders, had advanced all the way to the park entrance. The people standing on the street started whistling, clapping, and shouting when they saw the cops at the edge of the park. Some of them were crying as well, but not because of the tear gas. We looked at the park, but there was nothing we could do. That's how, on June 15, 2013, at 8:50 p.m., near the entrance of the park facing the hotel, I understood that just as some things are filled with both melancholy and hope, most people become miserable when the chance to be happy appears on the horizon. I looked at the trees forking up as they rose through the smoke, branching off at the top. The park was an airy place where you could find every kind of tree: willow, acacia, chestnut, walnut. If you ever have the time, you should go there one day and see for yourself; the trees are probably still there.

My mom called. "Çağlar," she said, "are you guys okay? I heard that the police went into the park. Are you guys okay?"

"Please, Mom, calm down. The police haven't gone into the park. That's just a rumor that the pro-government media is spreading. We're fine and we're having a good time."

"Where's your dad? Where is he? Put him on the phone."

I looked up and saw that the police were shoving my dad and a group of about ten people with their shields, driving them out of the park.

"Dad says hi. I'll call you back later."

Just then, the police went after my dad with pepper spray and pushed him to the ground with their shields. Once he was down, they started kicking him.

I said to Microbe, "Take my sister and go to the hotel. I'm going back for my dad."

Pushing my way past the cops, I leaped on top of my father and started shouting, "Goddamn it, stop, stop, stop it, goddamn it!" They stopped kicking after a little while, and when they saw someone shouting at their captain they rushed toward him. The last thing I heard the guy yell was "I'm a member of parliament!" A punch to the nose silenced him. I pulled my father up by his wrists, and we headed toward the hotel. We walked through the spinning doors and sat down with Microbe and my sister. My father still couldn't see because of the pepper spray.

"Why were you messing with those cops?" I asked. "Just look at you. A grown man, and I'm still saving your ass from the riot police. Those assholes are probably going to raid the hotel next, so let's go wherever it is we're going, to your office or secret hideout or whatever it is."

"All right," he said.

Baring my teeth, I shook my fist in his face. "You irresponsible bastard," I said. "If my sister hadn't had a full-face gas mask, what would we have done?"

My father's phone rang. He peered at the screen but couldn't see who was calling so I grabbed his phone. It was the Channel That Breaks Viewing Records by Airing the Protests. They wanted him to go live on air.

"He's lightly wounded at the moment," I said. "If you want, you can put me on the air. I can tell you everything that happened."

"What's your connection with Sabahattin Bey?"

"I'm his neighbor from Kıyıdere, from where he used to live."

"Okay, we'll call back later."

We left the hotel and went to his secret hideout office on a street in an area known as Elmadağ. The office was filled with people rushing around, and the telephone wouldn't stop ringing. I sat my sister down on an empty table. She just sat there, hands folded, looking at the ground. We uploaded the video that Microbe shot to YouTube with the title "Nine-Year-Old Girl Does Amazing Moonwalk at Gezi Park and More," but no one watched it. We removed the video and then uploaded it again with the title "Nine-Year-Old Girl Doing Moonwalk as the Police Raid Gezi Park." Within a minute, five hundred people watched it. My sister raised her head and read the comments. Eighty people had written, "There aren't any damn police in this video," along with some unsavory swearing. That night, no one wanted to see anyone doing the moonwalk; they were only interested in what happened when the police stormed the park. So we deleted the video and sat there watching the people rushing around the office in a flurry of shouting and talking. We sat there waiting, not knowing what we were waiting for. My sister went back to staring at the floor, large teardrops dripping onto her wrist as she silently cried with a calmness I'd never seen before.

I kneeled down in front of her and pinched her cheek. "Don't you worry about a thing, sweetie. Soon enough everything will be set right."

"How?"

"Cengiz Ağbi and I are going to take back the park tonight. Tomorrow night, you'll go onstage again. You'll be the star of the new resistance."

"But that's craziness."

"Don't worry, my love. If it's craziness, we've been driven crazy enough to pull it off."

My sister said, "Okay, but come over here with me for a second." She pulled me to a corner and wiped away her tears with the back of her hand. "Watch out for Cengiz," she said.

I looked at her, my eyes full of questions.

"I'm in love with him. One day, I'm going to marry him. He's the only person aside from you who ever loved me."

I was so shocked I couldn't say anything. I tousled her hair and nodded. We walked out into the corridor. My father was talking on the phone, and when he saw that we were leaving, he rushed over. "Hang on a second," he said into the phone and grabbed my arm. "Where do you think you're going?"

"Out."

"No, you're not!"

I pulled my arm away. "Leave me alone."

He hung up the phone. "Son," he said, "please don't go. Just wait a minute. Okay, I made a mistake. I've done a lot of things wrong when it comes to you. Let's sit down and talk them over. Let's just get through this night, and tomorrow we'll talk about it all. We'll go have some tea and talk it over."

"I'm not going to drink any damn tea with you."

"Son, listen to me. The police are attacking people left and right. Who knows what they'll do next. Who knows how far they'll go. You'll get killed or locked up. If you won't think of me, then think of your sister. Think of your mom."

"I think about my mom and sister every day. Not just when I'm in trouble, like you."

We walked out and started going down the spiral staircase. Microbe pulled two full-face gas masks from his backpack and handed one of them to me.

"What's the deal with this unending supply of gas masks?" I asked.

"Erkut sent them to me from Wisconsin."

"Who the hell is Erkut?"

"Do you remember that whiz kid from seventh grade who made electricity from lemons? He took part in a competition put together by the Scientific and Technological Research Council of Turkey, and they sent the genius to the States."

"Right. That twit who couldn't eat watermelon. He was with us when we went on a field trip to İznik Lake."

"Yep, that sucker. In the first days of the protest, he wrote to me on Twitter and asked if I needed anything. I told him to send me some full-face gas masks if he had any. He sent me ten. They came the other day."

"Good on him. The guy still thinks of us."

We put on our masks and started heading up the dark street. Soon, we could hardly see anything because the smoke was so thick. We turned onto a side street, but it didn't look like it would lead anywhere. In the middle of the street, we stopped and looked at each other, and then we heard the sound of people chanting slogans. We headed in the direction of the voices. It was becoming clear to us how this business was handled at night. My phone started vibrating in my pocket, and I pulled it out, holding it up close to my mask, which had started to fog up. It was my mom. I put the phone back in my pocket, and we kept on walking. We turned onto another street and came upon a group of about thirty people. Up ahead at the corner of the main road, there were two or three people waving their arms. "Run, run, run!" they shouted, and we all started running.

People were setting up a barricade on the main road, grabbing whatever they could and piling it up on the street. Microbe and I started yanking on the pole of an ISTANPARK sign, but at first it didn't seem like we'd get it out of the sidewalk. We kicked, pulled, and twisted the pole, and finally it started loosening up and we got it out, and then we tossed it onto the barricade. Some people were pulling a dumpster from a side street so we headed down there as well, thinking that we might find one, too, but we didn't. About fifty yards farther up the road, the ground had been dug up, and we went over to investigate. We saw a large spool of cable stamped with the insignia of the state electrical company so we wheeled it out onto the main road. When the others saw us, they helped us roll it over to the barricade, shouting, "Out of the way, out of the way!" and then we tipped it on its side in the middle of the barricade. Two riot trucks appeared up the road, and everyone grabbed sticks and started banging on the barricade and the iron railing along the median. The rhythmic pounding echoed the pounding of my heart. A large fire was blazing in front of the barricade. Sound grenades exploded and the riot trucks approached. I tried to clamber up onto the top of the barricade, but someone held me back. "Don't go out there," he said.

"Let go of my arm. I know what I'm doing."

Microbe followed me up to the top. The headlights of the riot truck were shining through the flames of the fire. I handed Microbe my iPhone, and then I pointed at the riot control truck, shouting, "You stopped the king's return! So tonight Çağlar İyice is going to take to the stage. Deal with that!"

I jumped down in front of the barricade. The water cannon took aim, and I saw the blast coming right at me. I turned to the side to keep from falling down when it hit me, and I managed to stay on my feet.

I turned to the riot trucks and yelled, "Do you have a drying service, too?" I pointed to the ground, tracing a circle around the area where I was going to dance, and shouted, "Squirt a little water here, too." When the blast of water came, I stepped back, and then I tore the front of my shirt like MJ does in a lot of his videos. I spread my arms and then ran forward and slid on my knees on the wet asphalt. As soon as I got up, I started doing the moonwalk. A burst of applause rose from behind me and they started banging the barricade to the beat of my moonwalk. Two tear gas canisters went whizzing by to my left and right.

"Don't waste your time," I said. "You can't hit Michael Jackson with tear gas!" I started doing a sideways moonwalk, but the water cannon got me in the shoulder, knocking me to the ground. I looked up to Microbe, who was on top of the barricade, and shouted, "Are you recording?"

"Keep going. We've got the psychological advantage."

I pulled myself up and started doing the moonwalk on my knees. I don't know how many people in Turkey can do that, and I know that even in India they have a tough time pulling it off. One of the riot trucks was approaching me so I got up and started running for the barricade. The riot truck tried to break through the middle of the barricade but couldn't get through so it backed up for another try. Microbe grabbed my arm, and we ran after the others. They had started prying up paving stones from a side street, and we joined them as they passed them from person to person, building another barricade at the head of the street. When the barricade was about knee high, we walked off a ways and stopped to catch our breath, leaning against a Telecom utility box.

"Microbe, show me the video. How did it turn out?"

He started scrolling through my phone, but he couldn't find it, and he hung his head and said, "It's not here."

"What do you mean?"

"I guess I forgot to switch it to video mode."

He handed me the phone. I looked at the blurry picture and then stuck the phone in my back pocket. I grabbed Microbe by the front of his shirt and dragged him to the entryway of an apartment building and slammed him against the door.

"What the hell did you do to my sister? What did you do to her?"

"Don't be absurd, boss. What could I possibly do to Çiğdem?"

"Then why didn't you shoot the video?"

"I panicked when they went after you with the water cannon. I forgot to switch it to video mode." He pushed away my hands. "Enough man, enough. That's Çiğdem's gig, not yours. And I'm in love with her. Is that what you want to hear? Are you happy now?"

I knocked him hard in the chin and he stumbled, but then he lunged at me and got me in a stranglehold. Then he tried to knee me and I grabbed his leg, pulling him down to the sidewalk. Pinning down his arms, I said, "Goddamn you! You sick pervert! I'm going to kill you! My sister's only nine years old! What the hell did you do to her? What the hell did you do?"

"Nothing! I swear, I didn't do anything! I just love her!"

"She's only nine fucking years old!"

"So what! She's got spirit."

"Goddamn you! Fucking pervert! I'm going to kill you!"

I looked around for a paving stone to hit him in the head with, but we'd pried them all up and carried them off.

"I'm not a pervert," he said. "Boss, I've been thinking about this. Just listen to me. I've thought about this a lot. Look at the people around us. Who has spirit in today's world? Who is so fearless, so daring? Who feels such joy when it's time to feel joy, and who feels so sad when it's time to feel sad? Who is willing to go through with something to the very end when they set their mind on something? Look, I've got nothing. No one else loves me, and no one ever will. But not now, not now. Ten years from now. What's wrong with that? I love her."

"What the hell do you mean, ten years from now? You're a god-damn pervert! I'm going to kill you! Microbe, you deserve it! You deserve to die!"

"You're in love with your sister, too! That's why you're reacting like this!"

I let go of his wrists. He got up, and I kicked him in the thigh.

"What the hell are you saying? That I'm in love with her? That I'm in love with my sister?"

Microbe got me in a headlock and shoved me to the ground, pin-ning me down. "You are! You're in love with her! After your grandpa died, who else did you have left? Why did you give your room to your uncle without even putting up a fight? Why did you go on sleeping in your sister's room even after he moved out? Don't make me say these things. Don't do it! You're screwed in the head, and you don't even realize what the fuck you've gotten yourself into. You always think that everything is something else. You go around making fun of shit, but then you think that the things you've made up are real. You're living in your own imaginary world. If you had spent more time looking at reality rather than what you've made up, do you think you'd be in this situation now?"

He let go of my arms. Lying there on my back, I looked at the crooked streetlight on the corner. There was a red light on the top of the pole that was flashing through the combination of dust and smoke that hung in the air. I couldn't pull my eyes from that red light. All the feelings that had remained silently buried in the depths of my soul until that moment were breaking apart in a roar of crackling and crunching. There comes a time when you want to be someone else, when you really, truly want to be someone else. The guys who were up at the head of the street came running toward us when a few tear gas canisters thudded against the wall. Pressing my palms against the asphalt, I pushed myself up to my feet and pulled off my gas mask. I threw it hard against the gray wall of the apartment building behind us.

"Come on," he said, taking me by the arm.

"Let me go," I said.

The cops climbed on top of the barricade at the head of the street, brandishing their tear gas launchers. There was a plainclothes cop with them, probably their captain. He took off his hat and pulled his gas mask up to his forehead. "Get the hell out of here," he shouted. "Get out of here!"

I sat down in the middle of the street and spread out my arms. "Do you think you're the FBI just because you cleared some protesters off two streets around Taksim? Ten thousand people are on their way here from Gazi. So let's have them come here and shove those tear gas launchers and canisters up your ass." An expression of stunned fury came over his face, and he started running toward me. I spread my legs apart and tilted my head to the right. "Bring it on," I said. When he charged up, I drove my fist into his stomach, and he doubled over and staggered, but then he swung around and slammed me in the ear with his open hand. Next came a left uppercut that caught me in the nose, sending a jolt of pain all the way to the back of my brain. Microbe tried to pull us apart, but the other cops came running up and laid into him, pulling the mask from his face. The plainclothes cop caught me with a right jab to the eye followed by a left to the jaw and a knee to my stomach, and there we were living in a world with such deep sadness, spiritual chaos, closed windows, vibrating phones in our pockets, and the hoarse screeching of seagulls. He wouldn't stop, and I was in so much pain I could hardly breathe. We'd spent our lives rebounding from the mistakes we made, but we still saw life as something that could move forward because we were human and we had achieved moronic victories that were useless, and suffered shrewd defeats that tied us closer together with desperation and sorrow. Within ourselves, we had taken on silent, terrifying struggles. We were all veterans of our own internal civil wars, and we were defeated by ourselves. We accepted ourselves and bowed down to ourselves, but now we would no longer bow down to anyone else!

I pushed myself up into a sitting position and spit bloody shards of teeth in the cop's face. "If I don't bring you and your whole damn family to account for my sister's tears, then my name isn't Çağlar İyice, Çağlar of Taksim Square, and may I be forgotten forever! From this day on, may no one ever raise their glass to me!"

He grabbed a metal street sign, and as he started bashing me in the head with it, I tried to raise my guard. My vision was going blurry, but at one point I saw a woman in the apartment building behind us open a window. She started shouting hysterically, "Enough, enough, enough! Stop beating up those kids! What are you doing? Stop it!" Other people leaned out of their windows and started shouting, "Stop beating those kids! Murderers! Get the hell out of here!"

A guy came up to the cop on top of me and pushed him in the shoulder. "Get your ass moving," he said. "Move it!" Then he went up to the cops kicking Microbe and started shoving them away. "Get moving! Go on!" He had stars on his shoulders, which made me think that he must've been the chief of police. Another guy came up and pulled me to my feet and then dragged me toward Microbe and pulled him up, too. Nodding to the police chief, he asked, "What about these guys? Should we take them in?"

"There's nothing left of them to take in. They've been fucked up enough already. I don't want to be stuck with them! Now move! Don't stop until you get to Kurtuluş."

We sat up on the curb, and when the cop with the stars on his shoulder walked past, I said, "Chief! Hey, chief! Yeah, I'm fucking talking to you. Hang on a second."

He turned to me with an expression of utter shock on his face.

"How do I get to Kurtuluş from here?"

He stepped up and booted me in the face, and I tumbled onto my back into the sand where the paving stones used to be. "Fuck off!" he said. "Get the fuck out of here before I kill you!"

A few of the cops with him started charging toward me, but he grabbed them by the shoulder and pushed them back. "Get moving, I said!" They started walking off down the street. A feeling of despair welled up within me because I didn't know where Kurtuluş was. I stretched out and looked up at the sky. Some drunk asshole had made off with all the stars.

Microbe pulled me up, and we started weaving down the street, bumping into each other and coughing. I was coughing so hard that my ears ached. My chest felt tight, and it felt like some of my ribs were broken. As we stumbled along, I noticed that the door of an apartment building had been propped open with a broomstick. We pushed open the door and collapsed on the floor in a tangled heap of coughing. A profound silence had descended over the street.

The tenants of the building had put a spray bottle of Talcid mixed with water beside the door, and we used it to wash our hands and faces. We heard a sound grenade go off and then a cloud of tear gas rose up, eventually filling the whole street. I heard a hoarse cry coming from outside, but I couldn't tell what it was. I peered out through the window of the door and saw a seagull on the other side of the street desperately flapping its wings as it tried to take to the air. Eventually, it managed to fly up about two stories, and then it flew into the iron railing of a balcony and fell to the ground. Stunned, it glanced around and took a few steps and then took off again and disappeared from sight. A few seconds later, it landed with a thud on a telephone utility box. It got to its feet and took a few steps and then toppled down. I dashed out the door and grabbed the seagull and brought it into the entryway, setting it on the floor.

The seagull sat there looking at me and Microbe, fear in its eyes. I ran my hand over its neck and chest. I could feel the weak, irregular beating of its heart. The air was heavy with suffocating smoke, and it was even seeping into the building's entryway.

The seagull kept shaking its head from side to side as if it wanted to escape its own thoughts, and then it started pecking at the floor tiles with its orange beak. I sprayed some Talcid onto my hand and slowly rubbed it around its eyes. "Calm down, little seagull," I said. "Please just calm down. Everything's going to be fine. Think about the deep blue of the sky, think about the infinity of the universe. Don't think about these narrow smoke-filled streets that we're stuck in. Everything's going to be okay."

The seagull looked me in the eye and went on flapping its wings against the floor. Microbe tried to put his arm in mine, but I pushed him away. I sprayed some more Talcid on my hand, but the seagull kept trying to get away. Tightly, I held its wings and rubbed some more of the solution onto its beak and around its eyes. For a moment, it calmed down and then it started flapping its wings again. *Why did it have to be my lot to give first aid to a seagull?* I thought. *What kind of country is this? Can't anyone see those seagulls writhing in pain, completely alone? Are people's stocks of compassion depleted? Is there no compassion left in the world?*

Slowly, I stroked the seagull's long neck. "Little seagull," I said, "what you need more than anything else right now is a sad person who can understand you. So look at me, look at me one last time. Don't worry, I'm not going to try to sell you a bunch of regrets that won't bring anything back, or words that won't soothe your pain. And don't think about us, forget about all that. This isn't such a dark day for us. Maybe we're a little lonely and a little bitter, and maybe our dreams have been taken from us, but that's okay. It's all okay. We're hanging in there, little seagull, we're getting used to it. We're getting used to this world. Days will come when we'll run barefoot in the rain and sing happy songs in the sunshine. At some point, you just stop caring. But if people still talk about their problems, it means they still have hope. So go on, little seagull. Talk to me."

It wasn't flapping its wings so much anymore, and it was having trouble even holding them out. Little by little, its eyes were glazing over, pulling further away from us and the world. As its song came to an end, the seagull took one or two more steps with its small webbed feet. Its eyes went still, filled with an expression that seemed to say that it would never be able to get over that pain, and its body stiffened. All that was left of the seagull in the night were two wings and two glimmers of light. I thought about trying to do CPR, but how do you do CPR on a seagull?

Microbe put his arms under mine and pulled with all his might. "Let go of the bird, boss. Let it go. It's dead. The seagull is dead!"

I tried to get away from him, but he held on tightly. After a while, I started calming down. I put my arms around him and said, "I'm sorry, man. I'm so sorry. I'm sorry for everything."

He patted my back and said, "It's okay, boss. It's all okay."

"I accused you of trying to hook up with Sinem. I'm sorry for that, too."

"It's okay, boss. Stop thinking about those things. Let's just forget about it all. We're friends."

We sat down on the stairs. I looked at the blank eyes of the seagull, at its feathers turned gray by the tear gas and its rigid wings. In its carefree days in the past, could it ever have known that one day, in an uncertain moment of an uncertain future, at that very moment, it would perish like that, vanishing into infinity? I sat there for a long while, hands cupped over my cheeks, looking at the seagull. What business did it have being on that narrow street choked with tear gas when there was life out there over the broad streets of the city, over the vastness of the sea, in the infinity of the sky and the roads that led to its home?

The greatest love is coming to an end, I thought. *A plastic bottle lives for five hundred years. So tell me, little seagull, why did you die? When the electricity comes back on, who's going to blow out the candles? When morning comes, who's going to unplug the electronic mosquito repellant? Who's going to close those yawning chasms in our soul? Who's going to take away the pain of our stung pride? When will the time come for happiness, for goodness, and for justice?*

I looked at our reflection in the window of the door. It was as if the darkness we carried within had swallowed us up and vomited out completely different people. That's how it always happens, every single time; as the sun goes down, the windows that have been set aflame go out one by one as they are filled with shadows, and they give way to darkness. And two friends are left there in the night, along with one dead seagull; a soul is left, and there they are, together, holding each other in the emptiness left behind by the others who have left. But that's okay. It's all okay. So be it that as the curtain is drawn shut, there aren't any happy people on this stage. May everything be plunged into darkness when all the bare truths are revealed. In the end, reality will be the most deserving of that. In the night closing over us, it will belong to those who travel the farthest.

But that's okay. So be it. When my grandpa was sick, every part of his body ached, but there was always one part that ached even more. I thought, *That's how my memories should be from now on. The blank eyes of that seagull should bring on the most pain. Old boy, people only learn the things that they are forced to learn. We only remember the things we learn from pain. It doesn't matter when it happens, but the pain that you feel in the deepest depths of your heart, that purest of pain, that unadulterated, distilled pain that flows into you, is the pain of all times.*

I took my electronic cigarette out of my pocket. I had wrapped it in a plastic bag, and I sat there puffing away as I looked at the seagull. I said, "I wish we'd known each other when you were alive." It's a shame. It's such a shame. That seagull and I could've really had something together. I wish that seagull and I could've been friends. That seagull and I should have flown together, following along behind the ferries, soaring to the left and to the right like we were dancing; even though we were full, we'd eat the pieces of bread rings that people tossed into the air just to make them happy. That seagull and I should have perched on roofs, and when day was breaking we would raise hell with our shrill cries. That seagull and I should have swooped down in the silent blue of the sky like the hand of a metronome and then soared back up. That seagull and I should have circled around lighthouses. That seagull and I should have flown over the frothing waves of the sea, carefree as can be. That seagull and I should have perched on the breakwater in the evening, and there I would think about the passing days. That seagull and I should have watched the rain together, missing the people who've silently come and gone through our lives. My friend, let me tell you: I wish I could've kissed that seagull, I really wish I could've kissed that seagull.

June 24, 2013–May 24, 2014, Beşiktaş—Yalova

ABOUT THE AUTHOR

Emrah Serbes was born in Yalova, Turkey. He graduated from the theater department of Ankara University, and he currently writes for newspapers, magazines, and television. His short story collection, *Erken Kaybedenler* (*Predestined Losers*), was published in 2009. Serbes's novels include *Her Temas İz Bırakır* (*Every Touch Leaves a Trace*) and *Son Hafriyat* (*The Last Excavation*), both noir mysteries set in Ankara and later developed into the hit television series *Behzat Ç.*, followed by the film *Behzat Ç.: Seni Kalbime Gömdüm* (*Behzat Ç.: I Buried My Heart*). His newest novel, *The King of Taksim Square*, is his English debut.

ABOUT THE AUTHOR

ABOUT THE TRANSLATOR

Photo © 2015 Senem Caralan

Mark David Wyers completed his BA in literature at the University of Tampa and his MA in Turkish studies at the University of Arizona. He has translated the novels *Boundless Solitude* by Selim İleri and *As the Red Carnation Fades* by Feyza Hepçilingirler from Turkish into English, and he is the author of a historical study titled *Wicked Istanbul: The Regulation of Prostitution in the Early Turkish Republic*. His translations of Turkish short stories have been published in anthologies such as *Istanbul in Women's Short Stories* and *Europe in Women's Short Stories*, as well as *Aeolian Visions/Versions: Modern Classic and New Writing from Turkey*.